The Englishman

Nina Lewis

OMNIFIC PUBLISHING
DALLAS

Omnific Publishing
10000 North Central Expressway, Dallas, TX 75231
www.omnificpublishing.com

First Omnific eBook edition, May 2013
First Omnific trade paperback edition, May 2013

The characters and events in this book are fictitious.
Any similarity to real persons, living or dead,
is coincidental and not intended by the author.

Library of Congress Cataloguing-in-Publication Data

Lewis, Nina.
  The Englishman / Nina Lewis – 1st ed.
  ISBN: 978-1-623420-12-3
  1. Love — Fiction. 2. Romance — Fiction.
  3. Academia — Fiction. 4. Contemporary Romance — Fiction. I. Title

10 9 8 7 6 5 4 3 2 1

Cover Design by Micha Stone and Amy Brokaw
Interior Book Design by Coreen Montagna

Printed in the United States of America

For G.
*It was not the passion that was new to her,
it was the yearning adoration.*

D. H. Lawrence, *Lady Chatterley's Lover*

Chapter 1

I knew from studying the map that at some point after turning off I-95 I would catch a glimpse of it across a long bend of the river. So I was expecting this view, and after all, I have been here once before. But I have never seen it from the road, never from this angle, and it takes my breath away. The place looks like the film set for a pastiche of *Dracula* and *Sleeping Beauty*. Spine-chilling and romantic at the same time.

Ardrossan University, familiarly known as "The Folly," is architecturally disadvantaged in that it cannot present itself to the world in the form of the stern elegance to which venerable academic institutions aspire. Its multi-colored brickwork sparkles and shimmers red, black, blue, and green in the glaring sun of the June afternoon, as if a giant baby had turned over its box of Lego bricks and built a castle. Its gables are over-long, its pinnacles and turrets and cornices too ornate, its arches too pointy, its glazed bricks too shiny — a hideously neo-gothic extravaganza of such silliness that it has its very own and unique grandeur.

This is where I am going to work.

But not yet. Today my destination lies due east of the campus, past the halls, the dormitories, the library, and the sprawling four-story building that houses the English department and where, come August, one little office will be mine. Today my cue is a big wooden board on the roadside, advertising *Calderbrook Farm: Organic Fruit Orchard.*

I turn left into a lane bordered with woods on the right and on the left, seemingly endless rows of dark green bushes, about chest-high, hung with bright green billiard balls. The farm at the end of the lane is unmistakably the one that Mr. Larsen, the Shaftsboro Realtor, described to me on the phone. Apart from several low-roofed steel barns, garages, and a canopied farm stand, there are two white clapboard farmhouses, connected by a sort of one-story conservatory. I am just pulling up next to the silver-metallic BMW convertible in front of the gate when my phone rings.

"Are we there yet?"

"Listen, Irene, I got here literally this second, and I'm late as it is! I'll call you afterward."

"*You* listen! Are you homesick yet? Are you regretting it yet? It's not too late to come back home! We'll slaughter a bottle of *Moët & Chandon* for the prodigal, um, friend!"

"Be quiet! Some friend you are. You're supposed to support me in this, not undermine me!"

"I am totally your friend when I say that moving to the South is a huge mistake, Anna." Her voice is serious now; she means every word she says.

Casting a hurried look at the dashboard clock, I sit back in my seat. "Look, we've been through this, like, twenty-seven times. An assistant professorship at Ardrossan University is a once-in-a-lifetime opportunity. I can't turn it down, and I don't want to turn it down!"

"But it's in the boonies!" she wails.

"Don't be ridiculous. Shaftsboro is practically on the outskirts of D.C."

"Ha!"

An ambitious junior associate in the reputable Manhattan legal firm of Barton, Scherer and Nussbaum, she should be the first to urge me to go where my career takes me. But for Irene, a career worthy of the name can only happen north of the Mason-Dixon line. Virginia, to her, is the deepest South, beyond the pale of civilization.

"Look, I am moving down here, and I am late for my appointment with a tomato farmer who I hope will be my new landlord. I'll talk to you when I'm done, okay?"

"Oh, says she who's only ever lived in New York and London! You have no idea what you're letting yourself in for! You should live somewhere where you feel at home!"

"Then just be glad I didn't stay in London. Reenie, I gotta go. Further bulletins as events warrant."

I leave the phone on the passenger seat, check my hair in the rearview mirror, and get out of the car. Wary of letting any free-roaming animals escape, I carefully latch the gate behind me, turn toward the main house, and freeze. Something that looks like the Hound of the Baskervilles comes tearing toward me, skids to a halt about two yards away, and challenges me at the top of its lungs.

"Dude! If I move here, we gotta work on our relationship!"

My words make no impression at all, but the sharp whistle from the direction of the house does. The shaggy black beast briefly weighs up the pros and cons of obedience versus vigilance and trots off. Three people have appeared from the newer of the two houses: a man in beige pants and a yellow polo-neck shirt, a woman in a light summer dress, and an older man in baggy jeans, a checkered shirt and a baseball cap. He seems to be in charge of the dog, because it bounds up to him and he pets it and tells it to sit by the house.

While the men loiter by the door, the woman comes forward, and for a crazy moment I feel like a European explorer making contact with a delegation of natives.

"Sorry 'bout that!" she shouts. And when she is in speaking distance she adds, "She's only seven months old. We're still training her."

"That's okay. No harm done. Hi, I'm Anna Lieberman."

Up close she is a little older than I first guessed, in her mid-thirties and very lean, almost wiry. The flowery dress looks completely wrong on her. Why is she wearing clothes that suit her so little? Social convention? A concession to the prospective tenant? She introduces herself as Karen Walsh and takes me across the yard to meet the men.

Mr. Larsen, the Shaftsboro Realtor, has a muddy, paw-shaped smudge on his linen thigh and appears uncomfortable and out of place on a working farm. Howard Walsh, Sr., whose paunch is as substantial as Mr. Larsen's but who looks strong as an ox, takes hardly any notice of me from under his cap but cannot very well avoid shaking my hand. I make a point of this, gripping his big, calloused hand for a fraction longer than he wants, and he briefly glances at me and actually takes off his cap. He has Paul Newman eyes and a handsome weather-beaten face.

"Well, ma'am, you better not get your hopes up too high," he says. "Reckon our cabin ain't what you're looking for."

"I'm very much looking forward to seeing it, sir."

Seeing as I drove down from New York City today with that specific purpose.

"Go on in for a drink," Karen Walsh says, and the men immediately turn and go back into the house.

Right. Drink and interview first. We sit around the massive kitchen table and Karen Walsh pours a dark golden-brown liquid from a big glass pitcher for all of us. It is so cold that the walls of my glass mist up, and a cautious sip reveals it to be extremely sweet black tea. Of course. Silly me. Welcome to the South. Unsure of protocol, I sip my tea, which is delicious in this hot weather, and answer the ritual questions about my trip down, the traffic around Washington, and whether I have ever visited these parts before. If this is an exam, I fail at least the last of these questions.

"Dr. Lieberman, if you'd like a cookie or a muffin?" Karen Walsh piles jugs and plates onto the table and finally sits down.

"Anna, please, if—if that's okay."

"What kind of a doctor are you, ma'am, if you don't mind me asking?" The Paul Newman eyes look straight at me.

"Dr. Lieberman works at the Folly, Pop. Didn't you hear Mr. Larsen say? These are blueberry and whole grain and these are chocolate chip."

"Beats me why they wanna call their own business foolish," Mr. Walsh observes deliberately. "I wouldn't."

"Thank you, they look delicious." I smile up at Karen. "Actually, it's a reference to an architectural—never mind. I'm in English literature."

"So you're a doctor in English literature from New York City, and now you want to live on a Piedmont tomato farm." Mr. Walsh leans back in his chair and crosses his arms.

"Y-Yes, sir, that about sums it up."

He is much too reserved to ask *why*—let alone, as my big-city friends and relations did, *why the hell?*—I want to live on a tomato farm.

Why do I? I can't really say, except that I knew right away that I am not interested in the Shaftsboro riverside lofts ("real popular with folk from your part of the country") that Mr. Larsen made me look at on his website.

"And how long would you be planning on staying in the South, ma'am?"

I lean back in my chair and nerve myself to brave his subtle antagonism. "Three years at least, maybe six, maybe longer, if I get tenure."

"What's that thing my old father used to say?" Mr. Larsen turns to Mr. Walsh as if for information. "'Yankees is like hemorrhoids—a pain when they come down and a relief when they go back up again.'"

"Dr. Lieberman!" Karen jumps up, and so does the dog under the table, yelping. "Would you like to see the cabin now?"

I half hope that it will turn out to be a derelict pile, but it's a city girl's dream in light-blue clapboard, with white window frames and a white porch. Situated almost a hundred yards away from the main house, it stands on its own in splendid isolation on the edge of the woods, and I have an unnerving vision of myself as Connie Chatterley, engaged in amorous trysts with my illicit lover in our quiet, leafy retreat.

"You don't need me for this, right?" Mr. Larsen fingers the cigarettes in his breast pocket. Mr. Walsh wanders off into the direction of the garage. Showing people round is evidently woman's work again.

We enter an L-shaped living room with kitchen; a bedroom is tucked into the inner right angle of the L and looks out toward the woods. All the rooms have dark hardwood floorboards, even the bathroom and the tiny utility room.

Karen Walsh breaks the silence. "My husband's grandfather used to have pickers sleep in here during the summer, but—well, it's much too small now."

"How many people do you employ?" I ask, making conversation to cover my delight at what I'm seeing.

"Up to forty once picking starts. It's mostly students from schools and colleges around here. And backpackers, from Europe and Australia. They have a camp site over there." She cocks her head toward the forest.

"And who lived in here before? I mean, before now?"

She tucks her short, light brown hair behind her ears in a nervous little gesture. "Our previous tenants—they moved out three months ago—well, it was a very unsuccessful arrangement. They kept complaining about everything—the dogs, the dirt, the dial-up Internet access, of course, and in the end they left one weekend when we were all away on a family visit, without ever paying the rent that was due."

She gazes at me as if she was going to say more, but then she decides against it. With her long, sinewy arm she reaches up the banister. "Will you come and see upstairs?"

The upstairs bedroom is larger than the downstairs one, and it has two dormer windows that look away from the farmhouse toward the woods. It's the perfect place for a study. I have to bite my lips not to burst out laughing.

"It would be very different from what you're used to," Karen Walsh says tactfully.

"But I don't want what I'm used to! I want to get away from what I'm used to! I want a change, a real change! May I?"

My vehemence seems to take her aback a little but she nods, and I open the bedroom window.

"Smell that?"

"N-No —"

"That's what I mean. This would feel like a vacation in the country, not like work at all!"

We laugh together, and she lays a quick hand on my arm. "Leave it to me."

When we come back into the living room, Mr. Walsh is fiddling with one of the doorknobs.

"Pop? Dr. Lieberman says it's exactly what she is looking for."

"You reckon?"

I try to look resolute but keep my mouth shut.

"We don't rent out for longer than a year at a time." He straightens up, his fists propped against his hips.

"That's fine with me, sir."

I'm not sure why I want this place at all, given that my prospective landlord seems convinced that I will be a pain in his neck. The only answer I can come up with is that I am in love with the idea of living on a farm, and that I have fallen in love at first sight with the blue cabin.

Mr. Walsh gives his daughter-in-law the curtest of nods and leaves the house.

"So you don't wanna look at the lofts in town?" Mr. Larsen throws away his cigarette and squints into the late afternoon sun.

The Paul Newman eyes and mine meet in similar stupefaction on their way from the cigarette butt on the porch back to the Realtor's face. I half expect Mr. Walsh to take Mr. Larsen by the scruff of his polo shirt and shake him till he picks up the offending piece of garbage, but he just walks off toward the main house.

"No, thank you," I say.

The signing of the lease goes without a hitch. I thank Karen Walsh for her hospitality, feeling that we have established a tentative kind of rapport. When I offer to shake Mr. Walsh's hand, he indicates by an abrupt little jerk of his head that he intends to accompany the Realtor and me to our cars.

"That your'n?" He points his thumb at my battered ol' Subaru.

I shrug. "Sorry that I'm not driving my VW Beetle Cabrio today. Or some other fancy European car — you know, a Peugeot or an Audi — like all the other snooty Yankee women."

The verbal slap does not even make him flinch.

"No, ma'am," he says slowly and scrapes something off the hood with his fingernail. "I was hoping you came in a Mini Cooper."

At home in Queens, my report about house-hunting in Virginia produces mixed reactions.

Mom and Nathan stare at me as if I had announced I was going to live under a bridge. Dad gives an incredulous little snort, but Jessica, Nat's wife, beams at me.

"I *love* that! A cottage! Cottage, or cabin? Is it in the mountains, this place?"

"No, not quite. Shaftsboro is sort of halfway between the coast and the mountains. But it's on the river. The college, that is. Not the farm."

"Like Brandeis," Mom informs nobody in particular.

I shouldn't have told my mother that I withdrew from the shortlist for a job that would have been half as far away as Ardrossan.

"What do they farm?" Nat wants to know. "Tobacco? Pigs? Chickens? I thought you were a vegetarian!"

"No, not like Brandeis. It's directly on the river. There's a sort of… promenade, esplanade, a riverside walk, and the campus is right next to it. It's beautiful. Come and visit!"

"So you fork out eight hundred bucks a month to share a cramped little apartment in Manhattan because the 'burbs make you heave," Nathan scoffs, "but move away four hundred miles, and the suburbs are, like, the green belt of heaven?"

"Listen, bub, I'm not moving to the suburbs, I'm moving into the country, and the farmer grows tomatoes and all sorts of berries. Totally vegetarian."

I know why Nat is giving me a hard time, though. With me out of reach, Mom will turn her maternal searchlight onto Nat and his family, and he hates that.

"Six months, and you'll be a Bible-thumping Republican," he predicts with brotherly brutality.

"Have you been talking to Irene, or what? Anyway, on the farm I'll have lots of space, a forest to walk in, and peace and quiet to do my writing. And that's all I want, Mom."

My mother turns to the lunchbox she is packing for me and does that thing where she raises her eyebrows and purses her lips. An allegory of doubt, with a bit of don't-say-I-didn't-tell-you-so-when-this-goes-wrong thrown in.

"You may not like living on your own," she tells my sandwich. "You think you will, because Sheena has been getting on your nerves, but you may find you don't actually like it."

"Only one way to find out." I shrug.

"I'm just worried you will turn into a recluse if you live at the back of beyond all alone in a cabin!"

"Mom, what you're really worried about is that I might find that I *do* like living at the back of beyond all alone in a cabin."

"You should be worried, too. How will you ever find a man down there?"

"Not my problem right now. I want a job, not a man."

"I don't see why you can't have both!"

"I'm a one-trick pony, Mom. One trick is all this horse can do."

Chapter 2

My first two weeks in the South are the first holiday I have had in three years, and I am determined not to open a book to do with teaching or research, nor to write anything at all except a few emails. Instead, and to my deep satisfaction, I have acquired new kitchenware, a faux-suede three-seater sofa and an armchair for my living-room, a rocking chair for my porch (because I want to do this in style), and six wooden bookcases in a chestnut finish. I have been scrubbing, wiping, dusting, unpacking, and sorting, going to work on my new nest.

Here's a house-warming resolution: I will lug books and paper into my nest but no new man. Men leave me in a mess. The kitchen windows and the living-room windows change from grubby to invisible while I revel in the determination that I will not allow anything or anyone to distract my attention from the project ahead, and that is to press on toward my first tenure review in three years' time. "Publish or perish!" is the war cry. I intend to publish.

I get a soda from the fridge, sit down in the shade of the porch, and watch the harvest activities on the farm while behind me Bruce Springsteen is singing of the simple life and the ordinary tragedies of heartland America. This is the busiest time of the year for the Walshes. Pop, Karen, and her husband, Howie, seem to be out and about from the crack of dawn till sundown, while Mrs. Walsh — Grandma Shirley — shoulders the household chores and looks after the twin girls when they come home from school.

It would be lonely out here, all on my own. I'm glad I have neighbors, particularly as I zoom out of the picture of me on my porch: the cottage…the main house…the barns…the garages…the fields…the woods. So much of this region is still wooded, and the river winds like a snake away from the Blue Ridge Mountains through the woods toward the sea. No, not like a snake, more like a lizard, one with short legs and small toes. I imagine the lizard trying to make its way toward… someplace…dashing from rock to rock, from cover to cover, because there is an unnamed danger overhead. Gathering strength in the shelter of the stone, panting, then—with only a vague sense of opportunity to guide it—it dashes out and runs as fast as its little legs and tiny toes can carry it to the next shelter. Why can the lizard not stay where it is, and where is it rushing so frantically when there is danger overhead—

"Hey."

"W-Wha—hey." I fell asleep again. Must get that under control.

A slim teenager in torn army pants and a purple tank top has materialized, apparently out of nowhere, and she has the same expression of curiosity mingled with suspicion as the raccoon I came across yesterday morning when I went for a stroll in the woods. Her dark hair is cut short, but neither the boy hair nor the camouflage pants can disguise the fact that there is something waifish about her, something vulnerable and stubborn. She looks vaguely familiar, but I can't put my finger on it, and since she doesn't seem inclined to speak, I suppose I must.

"Are you one of the tomato pickers?"

Her eyebrows slam together and she shifts on her feet.

"I'm Jules. They didn't tell you about me, did they? Karen's daughter."

She is right; they didn't tell me about her. And I don't blame myself for not having caught the resemblance, because if Karen is her mother, her father must be black.

"Hi, Jules, Karen's daughter. I'm Anna. But I guess you knew that."

She rolls her eyes, but it is in embarrassment about her own awkwardness.

"Yeah, I knew that. Doctor Anna Lieberman. You're from New York. Yeah, I knew that too. Man, what wouldn't I give—" She shifts her weight again and sighs.

"D'you want to come up for a moment? Let me get you a soda." Yielding to the air of hopefulness that surrounds her like a cloud of smoke, I indicate the rickety bench on my porch. She grins and skips up the steps, and I mentally subtract a couple of years from her estimated age.

She is sitting on the bench with her feet pulled up to her chest, and it strikes me who else she reminds me of: myself when I was her age. I cut off my hair, too, shortly after my *Bat Mitzvah*. I would have cut it off before, but my Grandma got wind of the plan and was so horrified that I waited out my performance at the synagogue before I, as my mother put it, "mutilated" myself. Studying my *haftarah* got me hooked on biblical Hebrew and began a phase of deep immersion in Jewish history and Torah studies, much to the bewilderment—and sometimes irritation—of my almost completely secular parents. Nathan took to calling me "Anshel," the male alter ego of Isaac Bashevis Singer's Yentl, the girl who wanted to be a yeshiva student; and although I knew he meant to taunt me, I was proud of his acknowledgement of my commitment and academic prowess.

Whoa! Hold the projection, Lieberman.

"I guess you're really bummed you had to come and live out here." She considers her drink but doesn't unlock her arms around her knees.

"Do you mean 'out here in Ardrossan' or 'out here on the farm'? Neither, actually. I wanted to. But then I'm not your age. Fifteen?"

"Sixteen in December. Mistake, though. This place sucks. It's all rednecks and girls who wear purity rings and give blowjobs to the All Stars behind the gym. Do girls do that in New York?"

She glares at me almost accusingly, and I realize that I have become a canvas of projection for her, too. My estimate of her age was supposed to flatter her; I'm surprised that she is almost sixteen. Mental note: mustn't let her air of an orphaned street-urchin fool me.

"Do you mean the purity rings, or the blowjobs, or the hypocrisy?" I grin. "I'm sure there's hypocrisy everywhere. But in a big city in the Northeast it's less likely to be evangelical."

She seems delighted with me for calling a spade a spade, and her rigid posture relaxes a little.

"I still don't understand why you wanted to leave New York City. Why would anyone?"

There are a few things I could say in answer to this question, but since she clearly doesn't know what she is talking about, I let it go.

"Well, I'm guessing that *you* can't wait to leave home, either, right? So what's not to understand?" I give her a meaningful look that has more to do with my mother and Irene than with this belligerent teenager.

"You ran away from home?" Her skin is like creamy caramel, smooth and flawless.

"I think so. But I call it 'building a career.' Sounds so much better, doesn't it?"

The corners of her mouth twitch, but for some reason she is reluctant to laugh with me.

"Well, I won't go to college."

"Mmm. Why not?"

"I'm not exactly an A student."

"You don't have to be an A student to go to college."

More sneering. "To get into the Folly?"

"Yeah, okay, to get into Ardrossan you need good grades. But Ardrossan is only one kind of college, and not necessarily the best one, depending on what you want to do with your life."

"You're a doctor." She changes the subject from herself to me.

"Not a medical doctor."

"Of…English?" She reproduces what she must have picked up at home, complete with doubtful frown.

"English literature is my subject, but I'm a Doctor of Philosophy, really. 'Philosophy' is Greek, it means 'love of wisdom.' And wisdom is preserved in books, because books live longer than people."

She watches me closely during this little lecture.

"But you're…pretty." She can blush, too, and again she looks younger than she claims to be.

"Thanks. But you don't actually have to be homely to like studying. That's what people say who mistrust books and studying. It's a slur, nothing more. Besides, if you—hang on, that's my phone. I gotta take that, it may be the college."

It is the college. They are looking forward to seeing me again, and one little office is waiting to have a nameplate attached to it that reads *Anna Lieberman*. Or, better still, *Straunger, thou art now enteringe the realme of Anna Lieberman, she who hath prevailed!* Taking possession of my new home and being lionized by the Cinderella of Calderbrook Farm are amusing pastimes, but they pall next to the unprecedented privilege that awaits me at college. Yup, after years of sharing tiny windowless holes with half a dozen other teaching assistants or adjuncts, having my own office is definitely a big deal to me.

"Jules, I'm sorry, I have to run in and see my——"

But the bench is empty. So is the bottle of cola. It is lying, empty, on the steps up to my porch, in a bubbling pool of sticky brown fluid.

Oh, for God's sake!

I pour a kettleful of hot water down the steps of the porch, take a cold shower to clear my head, scrub my hands and fingernails, put on both my best summer college dress and my best behavior, and drive in to meet Elizabeth Mayfield, Professor of Renaissance Literature and parting Chair of English. According to the meter in my car it is only three miles from the farm to the edge of the campus, three and a half to the English department, and I am toying with the idea of adding a bicycle to the list of my new acquisitions. This is absurdly like a second date, or like finding yourself engaged to be married to someone you've only met once. We met, fancied each other, and made a commitment for a six-year try-out period. I'm the pretty young fortune-seeker; the college is the rich old guy setting up a detailed pre-nup to make sure it is I who will end up poor and homeless, if our relationship goes down the drain.

Chapter 3

The English department is housed in the old Observatory, a huge red-and-black building dominated by an octagonal tower with a decrepit-looking dome. The observatory for which the building was named was housed up there, but nobody goes up there now, I was informed on my campus tour. The tower contains the elevator and, snaking round the elevator shaft, the main staircase, a grand stone-tiled construction that gives access to administration and offices on the eastern side, classrooms on the western side, and the department library, an auditorium, and a cafeteria to the south. Fantastically different from University Place, New York City. Prettier, of course, no competition, but I hope it isn't going to make me feel claustrophobic.

Lorraine Forster, the department's administrative assistant, asks whether I'd like a glass of tea and points out firmly that she is "Mrs." not "Ms." Forster. They make a remarkable pair, Mrs. Forster and Professor Mayfield. Both are, in their different ways, well-coiffed, well-preserved brunettes, but while Lorraine seems to live on carrots and coffee, Elizabeth Mayfield is an imposing woman in layered silk with the bosom and the girth of an opera singer. The voice, too.

"Anna — good to see you again. Welcome to Ardrossan."

If I have half this woman's poise and authority by the time I turn fifty, I will consider myself extremely lucky.

"Hello, Professor Mayfield. Thanks — I'm still a little stunned. This place is so beautiful it's unreal!"

She smiles like someone who hears this all the time about her workplace, but I know it's still expected that I say it.

"Yes, we are fortunate. Now, I'm guessing you're impatient to see your new office—" My beaming smile elicits a chuckle of mild amusement. "Well, I'll have to keep you a little with some administrative business. I'm handing over the chair at the end of the month, but because I chaired your search committee, I agreed to oversee your initiation at Ardrossan."

"No hot radiators or bottles of Jack Daniel's, I hope."

"I beg your pardon?" She looks up from my file, as if she thought she had misheard me.

"Nothing, sorry. Who will take over from you?"

"Nick Hornberger." She focuses her attention back on my file, and I wonder whether her terseness is significant. Hornberger was on my search committee, too, and he baffled me. With his close-cropped hair and the physique of an aging linebacker, he looks nothing like a paper-shuffling administrator, let alone the reconstructed male I had assumed him to be after surveying his list of publications. His most recent book is called *Rakes, Rogues and Renegades,* an unpardonable title for anything but a paperback with two pairs of nipples and swathes of red silk on the cover. In fact, it purports to be a study of masculinity—or, as the subtitle puts it more correctly, *masculinities*—in the Old South.

Perhaps it is his understanding of antebellum gentlemanliness that made him touch my arm or my back every time we passed through a door on my campus tour. I don't think there is any harm in Hornberger; he is just a middle-aged macho who needs to flirt with younger women. But I am thankful that it is Elizabeth Mayfield who seems to be taking me under her wing.

"I think Giles Cleveland would be the right person to take you under his wing," she says in her placid alto voice.

"Oh—uh—that's—great."

"Do you know Giles?"

"N-No. Well, I know of him, of course, and I heard him at a conference once, but I haven't *met* him."

Giles Cleveland, associate professor of Renaissance Literature and director of the Early Modern Studies program, has, in the last few years, turned into a force to be reckoned with among scholars of the English Renaissance. A good choice as a mentor, as regards his scholarship. But he is also a bit of an oddball. An Englishman born and raised, he came to Harvard as a postdoc and never went back home. I heard a rumor that he would go to Stanford, but apparently he is still here. Now in his early forties, he is reputed to be charming but difficult, an interesting and entertaining speaker at conferences, but I have heard people say about him that he is an embodiment of English arrogance, bringing civilization to the colonials. He is definitely not popular with everyone. Elizabeth seems to think she is doing me a favor. I jolly well hope she is right.

"We had most of the little offices on the fourth floor painted during the vacations." She looks up and smiles. "But your humble abode might benefit from a quick sweep and wipe. You could ask the cleaning staff to put you on their list, but frankly, I wouldn't advise it. Everyone is coming back right now and finding that their offices need cleaning, and—well, you know what it's like. They'd probably make it up there in December."

The next day I put my home improvement on hold, chuck rubber gloves, dustpan, liquid soap, and rags into a plastic bucket, put on jeans and t-shirt again, and go on another nesting mission. Appropriate to their insignificance in the larger scheme of things, assistant professors are located on the top floor, like a mixture between children and servants in the upper-class Victorian household. I am comfortable with that. I reckon it will be much cozier up here, with the other assistant profs, the adjuncts and the graduate assistants, than downstairs with the—um—grown-up folk.

My office is small—a third the size of the study at the cottage—but it has a proper desk, a filing cabinet, and floor-to-ceiling shelves that need scrubbing, and—oh, glory!—leaded windows. The only flaw in the set-up is that the whole room is clogged up with dozens of plastic bags, boxes, folders, hardcover volumes of journals I've never heard of, stacks of what seem to be old student essays—*Katie Clough, 1/8/1985,* I read on one—and piles of overhead transparencies.

"You must be joking. This?" I ask the janitor who unlocks the room for me and is making me sign for the key.

He checks the small print on the sheet.

"'Fraid so. Lieberman, E-four-twenty-nine. This is it, ma'am. You can phone for garbage disposal, extension thirty-three twenty-two. But they won't go on and empty the room for you, they'll just leave a big trash can." He shrugs and leaves me to my own devices.

I blow the dust off the grubby phone on the desk and call admin. "Mrs. Forster? Anna Lieberman here. Oh, you're the intern…Katie, right. Not Katie Clough, by any chance? No, of course not. Sorry. The thing is, Katie, I'm upstairs in my office, but it's full of books and paper, and some of it seems to be old essays. I need to know what to do with them."

Katie promises to ask Mrs. Forster to call me back, which she does forty minutes later.

"Your office is full of paper, dear? But that can't be — oh. You're in four twenty-nine? That's — wait a moment — " She covers the mouthpiece with her hand and goes on speaking; then she is back, a little rushed. "Actually, Dr. Lieberman, Professor Mayfield was wondering whether you could spare her a few minutes."

"Now? I'm in the middle of cleaning out my office, only I don't know what to do with — "

"Anna." Professor Mayfield takes over the phone. "I saw you drive in earlier. I don't mean to inconvenience you, but if you have a moment, this would be a good time to meet Giles."

Oy gevalt!

"Gosh! Thanks, Elizabeth." I was given to understand that I might address Professor Mayfield by her first name but to play it by ear with the other senior professors. "That's very kind of you, but I just came in to bring some books and clean the place. I'm not — dressed."

But Elizabeth has no time for time-wasters. When I arrive at her office two minutes later, a short, sharp double-take indicates that I have committed my first *faux pas*. I bite on an impulse to protest — after all, she told me to scrub my office, and now she slaps me for not doing it in silk and cashmere? Vowing never again to assume that I am off-duty when I am on campus, I slink along the hall in Elizabeth's wake.

Giles Cleveland, of all people. I had planned to be introduced to Giles Cleveland when I was at my most professionally professorial, cool and well-groomed. I would have my contacts in and *not* have my hair in an untidy ponytail and most probably dirt under my fingernails, wearing jeans, a little t-shirt, and Birkenstock sandals. But unless I want to risk alienating Elizabeth Mayfield, I cannot dive into an unlocked office or the ladies' restroom and pretend I was swept up by Martians. It takes us about three minutes to reach the garden end of the hallway where Cleveland has his office.

God give I don't have sweat marks under my armpits.

"Giles would have been on your search committee, of course, but he's just back from a sabbatical."

Oh, great. The man is probably peeved as hell that he didn't get to select the newbie in his subfield!

"Actually, Elizabeth, before we go in—I have a question about my off—"

"You know he's English, don't you?" she says before she knocks once on the half-open door and pushes me in.

Now what the hell is *that* supposed to mean?

I wonder whether in a decade or two my sparsely-furnished little office will also look more like a living room than a workplace. Cleveland has a shabby but comfortable-looking leather sofa in his, a big rug on the floor and lots of picture frames on the walls. I am too nervous to take them in properly, but there is a beautiful set of medieval illuminations. And nature—water, mountains, trees. Perhaps Scotland, or Canada.

"Giles, I've brought our new assistant professor to meet you. Anna Lieberman."

"Professor Cleveland…"

In a split second I debate with myself whether to extend my hand or not, and decide on a gut feeling that I will not. Reserve seems a better strategy here than familiarity. He sits at his desk—not a particularly tidy desk—and looks reluctant even to rise from his chair, let alone to shake my hand. Eventually he does get up, and my heart beats faster, nervousness becoming tinged with alarm. Tall I knew him to be, but up close his six-foot-something towers above my five-foot-four like Gandalf over a Hobbit. A Celt, with light eyes and dark hair gone prematurely gray. There is nothing remarkable about his appearance, except that a tall man, halfway between gangly and gaunt, will always look good in light brown cotton pants and a blue shirt, open at the neck and rolled up at the sleeves. Next to him I look like a complete klutz. I am furious that I have allowed Elizabeth Mayfield to put me at such a disadvantage.

I nerve myself to smile up into his face. His features are lean and regular but not wildly handsome, and there is nothing charming about him at all when he looks down at me—*on* me, too—with that particularly English brand of polite dislike and says, "Dr. Lieberman. How do you do. I was…told of your appointment."

The sound of that well-educated, faintly nasal English voice hits me in the middle of my body and contracts the muscles of my womb in a spasm of response.

I feel a spate of explanations and justifications rushing to my tongue. I want him to know that although I have been foisted on him I am sure that we will get along well, that I will do my best to honor the confidence the college has shown in me. But I say none of these things. Could not, because my tongue is in knots, and do not want to, either, suddenly, because he is so pompous and unwelcoming to a junior colleague who really cannot help the situation at all.

"How do you do, sir."

He blinks, as if taken aback. "I assume you've been well looked after?"

"Yes, sir, thank you."

"Right. Well, then…" *Get the hell outta here, bitch.* He does not say it out loud, but I can see the words forming behind his forehead. Evidently Cleveland hasn't been told yet that he is to play Mother Goose to this gosling.

"Can you spare a few minutes, Giles? The least we can do is make sure Anna has a smooth start, and I was hoping you'd show her the ropes." There is an edge in Elizabeth's voice now, a note of admonishment, which he hears and, to my surprise, heeds. He comes down from his high horse and suddenly looks very much younger. He looks at a loss, almost vulnerable, with his soft gray hair curling in wisps behind his ears, and his broad, lean, boyish shoulders.

"By all means. Dr. Lieberman, won't you sit down?"

It is all I can do not to clutch Elizabeth's skirt to beg her not to leave me alone with him, but she closes the door behind herself and we are alone. In very non-companionable silence. He points toward the sofa, which has clearly been chosen to make people feel small. Its seat is very deep, so I can either perch on the edge, looking nervous, or sit back, in which case my feet will hardly touch the floor and I will look like a five-year-old. I choose a mid-position, put my bunch of keys on the low table in front of me and hope Cleveland will not see my hairy little Hobbit-feet.

He stands over me, reluctant, a very remote fortress, like Isengard.

"Would you care for a cup of tea? Hot tea, I should say."

Actually, I want to get this over with as quickly as possible. But you only have one chance to make a first impression, and when a senior colleague offers you a drink, you accept. Besides, I have to acknowledge the gesture of an Englishman making an effort.

The water in the kettle on the sideboard apparently just boiled, so he is busy about the cups and teabags for no more than half a minute. Half a minute during which I can surreptitiously observe him. His hands and feet — his feet naked in leather boat shoes — are a fraction too large for his body. He must have been one of those loosely-knit youths who are a little embarrassed about shooting up to their full height. Middle age has tightened his frame, but I can still see the awkward boy in his hands and shoulders.

"Do you take sugar? I don't have any artificial sweetener, I'm afraid." He still has his back turned to me, but I am sure that this is a jab.

"No, just milk, thank you. I suppose you've got milk?"

At this, he casts me a quick, suspicious glance, and I can't suppress a smile and a shrug. Can't live in England for years without picking up some habits.

"Sure, I've got milk," he says and surprises me by answering my smile. It is a smile of extraordinary attractiveness — bright, young and full of humor.

Just as well, perhaps, that it doesn't last.

He sets down our two mugs — I get a fine bone china one, with a William Morris motif and a chipped rim — and swivels his chair by a hundred and eighty degrees so that he faces away from his desk and toward the sofa.

"Are they making you go to those torturous New Faculty Orientation events?"

One ankle on the opposite thigh, he balances his mug somewhat precariously on the inside of his knee.

"Yes, that's next week, spread over two days." "Torturous" is probably the correct word, but it wouldn't do for me to agree with him on this.

"Well, if there's anything of that nature—where to find things and how to work things—ask the other people on tenure track, or the TAs."

And don't come bothering me!

"I hear ya."

"Do come to me," he goes on, glaring at me with those light eyes, "if you ever run into trouble with senior colleagues or admin."

"Well, sir, funny you should mention th—"

"You have settled your teaching, haven't you? Be an unfortunate omission if not, seeing as term starts in a week's time."

"I was asked to teach the first-year course on English Comedy this semester, and—"

"Have you made any changes to the syllabus?"

No idea whether yes or no would be the right answer, so I answer truthfully.

"Just a few."

"Such as?"

"Well, I prefer *The Rivals* to *The School for Scandal*, but—"

"What about *She Stoops to Conquer*?"

"I'd rather not." Too late I notice my blunder.

"Oh, I think stooping is all right," he says dryly. "As long as you don't bend over backward."

The shock of hearing him play on my inadvertent reply sends a hot flash through my body; it might have been a joke, even an inept attempt at flirting. But his voice is cold with hostility, and the image so violent; he isn't inviting me to laugh with him at all. In one fell swoop he has put his sharp pencil right on the sore spot of every young, tolerably attractive female academic—in fact, every young, tolerably attractive female professional: the implication that we achieve success by way of the casting couch. And the really devious thing about it is that it is usually no more than an insinuation, which you can't defend yourself against without coming across like a defensive, neurotic cow.

So I keep my mouth shut and try to weather the insult like a flower weathers a storm: hunch up and wait till it's over. And then a really strange thing happens: While I am pretending that I am merely an uninvolved bystander, my eyes stray over the objects cluttering the table in front of me: a pile of unopened letters, a pile of new books (probably review copies sent to him by hapless postdocs), my bunch of keys with its Royal Shakespeare Company dangly, my half-empty mug, his mug, with his hand…with his fingers…with his long, hard fingers wrapped round it. He grips it more tightly and the bones ripple across the back of his hand, the muscles in it flex, and so do the muscles deep in my belly, the muscles that sooner or later atrophy in any academic environment. I stare at his hand, and my body seems to anticipate its touch, and to anticipate it with keen impatience. Like a bolt of lightning that hits me in the solar plexus, I suddenly feel those hands on my skin, clasping my waist much more tightly than the tea mug, bending me over backward on this shabby leather sofa…

I am reeling under the sudden conviction that all this talk — all these words between Professor Cleveland and myself, cagey and aloof on both sides — is completely beside the point, because what we really should be doing is — unthinkable. Except I *am* thinking it.

I look up quietly, my mind in a whirl, and I say nothing. I don't know what to say, and Cleveland almost apologizes. His eyes flicker and the groove between his eyes deepens — the pained look of a man about to apologize.

Of course he doesn't.

"What's — " He clears his throat. "What's your take on Renaissance drama, Dr. Lieberman? I suppose you are a feminist new historicist?"

"Of course I am. Isn't everybody, these days?" I can be blasé, too, if sufficiently provoked.

He is still staring at me, and I could swear that there is a grin lurking in the light eyes, and my chest expands in anticipation. But then he hides his face behind his mug, and I feel as if he had pushed me away.

"Only I'd like to coordinate my course requirements with my colleagues, particularly with Tim Blundell, who will be teaching English Comedy II next semester. I've no mind to become the Nasty Newbie by making them read or write more than they have to in other first-year classes, or — "

"Didn't Hornberger take it upon himself to instruct you in this matter?"

"No, why—" *I am saying the wrong thing here, aren't I?* "—why should he?"

"Well, you would naturally turn to him, seeing as he's our new chair."

"No, sir, I didn't."

"Christ, woman, will you stop calling me sir!"

Driven by my particular demon, I grin manically and do my Marcie-and-Peppermint-Patty impersonation.

"Yes, sir."

He stares at me, still caught up in his irritation, and inwardly I quail at my audacity. *Play with me! I'm nice! Come out of there and play with me!*

His gaze begins to waver and that impossibly attractive smile flits across his face.

"All right. What are you going to do in the other one?"

"Third- and fourth-year concentration, *Paradise Lost*." My voice is squeaky, for a number of reasons.

He is scribbling away on a clipboard that he rests against his hunched-up knee. I don't even know whether his notes have anything to do with me, or whether this interview is conducted on the side of more important matters.

"No, I think not…"

"But I've taught Milton before, I'm perfectly capable of—"

"Dr. Lieberman, I don't doubt that you are…perfectly capable." He is still scribbling, unaware that I am becoming increasingly capable of hitting him where it really hurts. "Save it, you can do Milton next year. Don't you have something a little more sweet 'n' fun? Something you can pull out of your hat?"

I push my hands under my thighs in a gesture that must seem childish to him, but I desperately need to steady myself. "Parody and satire? I taught that last winter at NYU."

"We won't hold that against you. And?"

"I—I concentrated on the motifs and discourses of courtly love and how they were subverted in the sixteenth and seventeenth centuries. In carnival, for instance, or in the sonnet. The process of a genre's exhaustion, and how parody can infuse new life into it."

"*Subversion, no end of subversion, but not for us,*" he quotes. And that is not a smile. That is a sneer.

I can feel a damp patch forming between my shoulder blades.

"The subversive thrust of parody may be out of our reach, I agree, but we can analyze the *inversion*, and the…well, as Bakhtin says, the processes by which high and noble ideas were degraded to the level of the body, to the digestive and reproductive systems."

"Food and sex, you mean." He is looking straight at me for a change, but I can't tell whether he is deliberately provoking me or merely impatient with my display of theory.

"Food and sex…yes, that—yes."

"Do one on parody, then, and *Paradise Lost* next year. What is your…thing on?"

I am so bewildered by his interruptions and his oscillations between humor and hauteur that it takes me a couple of seconds to latch on.

"My what? Oh, my dissertation! Early modern civic culture. Urban processions, drama, ritual…that sort of thing."

"See that you finish it within the next couple of years."

"I have finished it. The 'thing.' If that's what you mean."

"No, that's not what I mean! Even Hornberger wouldn't hire someone who hadn't finished her dissertation! I meant publish it."

"I *have* published it. As good as. It's been with the readers at Cambridge University Press for about a month, and of course I don't know how long their list of queries will be, but for now it's out of my hands."

The feeling of being unjustly treated gives me the courage to look him straight in the eyes. They aren't blue at all but green, like seawater, with a thin scar running from the corner of the left eye across his temple to his ear. He seems even more Celtic to me, with those light eyes gleaming like the holy wells on Avalon. He has a mercurial energy, a kind of quicksilvery passion that makes him very attractive—exciting, even—but boy, do I see where he gets his reputation for being difficult!

Satisfied, I want to lean back but remember just in time that if I recline on this sofa, I will be practically horizontal. So I smirk sitting up and wait for him to come back.

"Why?"

"Why what?"

"Why the rush?"

Funny. That is what my grandmother, my darling *bubbe*, also asked when I told her that I was planning to hand in my book within the next six months. She was dying then, and one of her most urgent concerns was to leave knowing that my life was working out. "Will that make you happy?" she asked, anxiously. And I laughed and said, "Yes, of course it will! It's what I want!"

It *is* what I want.

"I don't see anything rushed about wanting to have a book publication to my name by the time I turn thirty! How else was I to stand a chance in the scramble for a tenure-track position? I'm relatively old as it is!" I have to attack him, or the wet film on my eyes will not go away.

"Two book publications." Well, whaddayaknow. He has looked at my CV. "You're a workaholic!"

Words fail me. Given that I have spent half my life working toward a job at a good university at a time of economic recession and in a discipline that is notoriously overrun, this is a ludicrous observation.

"Well…*duh!*" is all I can manage by way of a response.

"So instead of using this summer to recharge your batteries in order to be fit for a new job, you slaved away at your desk to get a book out that could easily have waited another year or two. I don't see the sense in that." He shifts in his chair, his long legs twitch, but it isn't embarrassment at his own audacity to judge what is really no concern of his at all, it is anger. Impossible. He can't be angry with me.

"I just…wanted it out of the way," I stutter. "It's a load off. And I think that'll make it easier for me, here. Start a new phase."

"But don't you see, you—" He cuts himself off in exasperation. "You were sittin' pretty without this stunt! You have to learn to pace yourself, or you'll be burnt out by the time you're thirty!"

Something is very wrong here. This is the second time Cleveland is about to make me cry. And this apart from the fact that he is making me want to climb onto his lap and—do something. I don't exactly know what. Touch him?

"I'll be thirty in three months. Thanks for the warning, but I think I'll be okay. Sir."

"You should get David Bergeron to have a look at your book." Scribbling on his sheet of paper again.

"David has offered to review it for the *Shakespeare Quarterly.*"

"Has he." Same tone of voice. Scribbling. "And what does David think of it?"

"He thinks it's crap." The word and my frosty voice make him look up again, startled. The blood rushes to my head, but I am in a panic of self-defense, too upset to care. "Yeah, he's going to waste four hundred words panning the book of a total nobody. As one does. You know."

The seawater eyes, deep-set under their grizzled brows, are glistening with icy resentment.

"Does one? Well, Professor Lieberman, I think we've settled the most pressing matters—don't let me keep you. I'm sure you must be very…busy."

Well, fine. Not only will there be a snake in the grass in my new-found academic Eden, it has already reared its ugly head. Except—not all that ugly. Squatting on the floor of my li'l office a few minutes later, I wait as the muscles in my body unclench, slowly. I can't remember when I last received such a pasting. My job interviews, by comparison, were walks in the park. But then if a search committee turns out to be a bunch of jerks, you shrug and delete that place from your list of desirable prospects. This is different; I really wanted Giles Cleveland to like me. I still do, except it is all a lot more confusing than it was an hour ago.

When I reach for the bottle of water in my rucksack, my fingers are trembling. Okay, so Cleveland won't be a friend; that is a pity but no big deal. It would have been nice to network with him, but it is not as if I need him to get tenure.

Keep your head down, smile, publish, and everything will be all right.

"What are you doing here?"

I am getting ready to leave when my open door is darkened by an elderly man in a baggy suit and a purple bow-tie. His face is an unhealthy shade of purple, too.

"Pardon me?"

"Up here it's offices only!" He stares at me with pale blue eyes from under a pair of very impressive bushy eyebrows; in fact, all of his hair seems bushy, including that protruding from his nostrils. I jump up from the floor and wipe my hands on the seat of my jeans, but as I advance toward him to shake hands, he backs off into the hallway.

"All this—" he waves his arms toward the right "—is English literature, and all this—" he turns round and waves into the opposite direction "—is Modern Languages! Classrooms are in the other wing!"

"Um…thank you, sir, I know that. I work here."

"You do?" The bushy eyebrows wriggle like distressed caterpillars. "You are not cleaning staff—you're not wearing a uniform!"

"No, sir, that's right—I'm faculty."

"Faculty? Nonsense! Which professor do you work for?"

"Professor Lieberman." Well, it's worth a try. The sound of that little phrase still makes my heart skip. I wish they would screw that name tag to my office door.

The caterpillars, too, perform a little skip 'n' dance routine.

"Lieberman? You must be on the wrong floor. Or the wrong building. This is English, up to here—" he actually scrapes his shoe across the floor tiles "—and over there it's Modern Languages!"

At this point it dawns on me that I am dealing with something more disturbing than professorial eccentricity. A bunch of keys is dangling from the door to the office next to mine; his demonstration of inter-departmental boundaries shows that his office is the last English Lit post on the frontier. There is a big black bag on its threshold, and three open boxes with books and papers are stacked up next to it.

"Yes, sir, I know." I smile in a way that I hope will calm him down. "We haven't been introduced. Anna Lieberman. This is my first semester here. Assistant Professor, British Literature."

He comes forward to shake my hand, but then changes his mind and withdraws toward his office door like a flustered, angry old dog.

"You're a professor? You don't look like a professor!"

"Um…"

"Lieberman?"

"Yes."

"You're Jewish!"

"That is correct."

"I knew nothing of this!"

"I'm sorry that I'm coming as a surprise to you, Professor —?"

"No, no — this is wrong! Nick has not spoken to me about you!"

"Well, sir, if you care to mention my name to Professor Hornberger, I am sure he will be happy to verify my appointment. Now if you'll excuse me, I'm actually rather — uh — busy."

Chapter 4

When I reach the cottage after my encounters with Giles Cleveland and the crazy old man in the next-door office, I feel tense enough to scream. I was determined not to go back to writing again until I had my house in some sort of order, but Cleveland's interrogation has pushed me over the brink into a state of acute withdrawal. I must work. Work, write, publish — the only thing to calm me down. There are the essays of the collection that I'm co-editing and its introduction; there are two conference paper proposals and one review to be written; there is an essay on Ralph Glasser and the Whitechapel Boys to revise for submission to a journal; there is the paper to be presented in November at Notre Dame University. Oh, and there is the class on parody and satire to prep, foisted on me at the eleventh hour by my mentor, who doesn't think I'm up to teaching Milton. Cleveland is such a *jerk!*

My early morning walks are during the only cool hours of the day. Now the air is full of the sweet, sticky smells and the insects of a hot summer evening. It's still a relief to escape across the brook, on the four stepping stones that must have been put there by a Walsh last year or thirty years ago, and into the green world. The characters in Shakespeare's comedies escape from civilization into the green world of the Athenian forest, or the Forest of Arden, or the Welsh mountains. The forest is a place for metamorphoses, for playing out the impulses of the subconscious. If I could metamorphose, what would I choose to be?

I float on my blanket next to the big patch of blue-violet flowers I have discovered for this purpose (*must pick one and ask a Walsh what they are*) and squint up against the glistening emerald ceiling overhead.

I am a squirrel. Dashing around with inexhaustible energy, gathering a fat hoard of publications. Books like brazil nuts, articles like hazelnuts, reviews like sunflower seeds. A nice, nourishing portfolio to keep me alive.

Or maybe I should be a bird. One that builds its nest out of the twigs and grass it collects all day long. I'm trying to build my nest, aren't I?

A bed of moss. Dark green, heavy moss. Soft, for something warm and furry to lie on. Rest on. Sleep.

A plot of land. Just…a measure of earth. Heavy. Just heavy and still. And little gray-furred creatures would burrow into me and I would hold them safe, and we would sleep.

I should go to bed without checking my email again, but of course I can't. There is an email from Debbie Crocker, my friend and co-editor in England, and because I feel guilty, I decide to call her. Debbie's day is structured by the feat of combining a full-time job in the English department at Bristol University, marriage and motherhood, and since it is now late afternoon in England, she is probably at home.

This is the second English voice I have heard today. Familiar, of course, this one, with its hard Mancunian consonants, and something in my chest tightens. I do miss my friends, but I can't afford to miss them.

"Hey — hello! Dave!" she shouts up the stairs. "It's Scarlett O'Hara!"

"I thought I'd let you shout at me for slacking on the collection. I'm sorry, Deb, but right now —"

"Well, yes, I certainly hope you are sorry — new job, new town, new house, that's no reason to stop working on Our Book ten hours a day, now, is it?"

"Thanks," I breathe, grinning. "I'll get back on it as soon as I have an afternoon, okay?"

"I've told them to expect the manuscript by April."

"April? We can easily manage sooner than that!"

"Fine, then we'll finish it sooner. But if we don't, we don't. You have more important things on your plate now."

"Debbie—"

She cuts me short. "So, Ardrossan…what's it like? Private, eh? Plummy and posh?"

"Private, yes. I know you disapprove of that, but that's how it works over here."

"Does that mean you get all the snooty youngsters with a sense of entitlement as big as mummy's hair and daddy's bank account?"

"Entitlement is always a problem. But it isn't just rich kids. If you're poor and bright, you're more likely to get a good deal at a top private place; if you're a poor kid who can hit a ball really well, you're more likely to get it at a top public place." I simplify the matter to make it comprehensible to a foreigner.

"And the colleagues? Friendly?"

"Well, I…I can't really say yet."

"But you still think it was the right decision."

I know what she's driving at, so I get a beer from the fridge, sit down on the back porch in the rays of the setting sun, and watch the light and the wind play with the leaves of the poplars.

"To be honest, today was a little rough. That doesn't mean it wasn't the right decision, though."

"Do you want to tell me what happened?"

"No, it's—my office is next to this weird old fogey's. One of those unhinged people you walk past quickly in the street, or try not to sit next to on the subway. Not just unhinged, but aggressive. And of course I can't really ask anyone, 'Hey, who's the crazy loon in the office next to mine'? What if he's the revered emeritus who has been allowed to keep an office in recognition of his services to the department? I'm trying not to step into more cow pats than absolutely necessary."

"Yes, by all means stay out of the cow pats. But the fogey isn't important, is he?"

"Nah, shouldn't think so. Just aggravating."

"Oh, Anna…" She sighs.

"Oh, Anna what?"

"Only, the American tenure system sounds so brutal to us, that's all. If you'd stayed and accepted the job at Portsmouth, you'd be happily publishing away now, free to apply elsewhere if you wanted to, or not if you didn't want to. And you could be dating Rafie Molina. Don't shout."

I don't shout, but I rumble.

"Rafie and I didn't click. Ask him. And I couldn't stay because if I'd stayed in your funny little country any longer, I'd pretty much have had to stay there forever! Have you heard about that job at Leicester?"

"The permanent, full-time position you should have applied for and didn't? Oliver Hobart-Kelly got it."

"Okay. He's done heaps of stuff. And he's got a double-barreled name. I couldn't compete with that."

"Whatever lets you sleep, dear. Right, let's see—" I hear her typing into her computer keyboard. "Ardrossan. University. English. Staff."

"Faculty. But, Debbie, don't—please—"

"Right, faculty. Let's see whether I know any of the lucky sods who are going to work with you…"

I hold my breath.

"Hm…Joseph J. Banks—I know the name, he edited *The Cambridge Guide to African-American Poetry*. Nancy Benning, Timothy R. Blundell, Erin Gallagher, Mary-Kay Chang, no, I don't know any of these people. Giles Cleveland—hang on, isn't that—yes, Giles Cleveland. He wrote that biography of Raleigh, didn't he? Dave read it during the holidays. Dave?" she shouts upstairs. "Dave, remember you were reading that biography of Sir Walter Raleigh when we were in Devon—the author is one of Anna's new colleagues!"

"He is?" The line crackles. "Hello, Anna, you're on speaker! Well done on the job!"

"Thanks, Dave!"

"Wanna phone!" a muffled young voice cries in the background.

"Jonah, Daddy will be on the phone for five minutes—see if you can build that tower all the way up to the doorknob, all right? Listen, this Cleveland fellow is really good! Tracy Evans told me he's been shortlisted for the James Tait Black Memorial prize for this one, the biography on Raleigh; the prize-giving ceremony in Edinburgh is at the end of the month. Have you read the book?"

"No."

"You should. He's probably a git, though. These people always are. Have you met him yet?"

"Don't prejudice her against her new colleagues, darling!"

"I met him today. Um…"

"What's that sigh, Anna? He *is* a git, am I right?"

"Yes, actually—he is! He made me feel like an utter incompetent!" Talking to friends about my day is almost counter-productive, because I suddenly realize how shaken I still am.

"See?" Dave is triumphant. "He's brilliant but a bastard. Brilliant people in the Arts and Humanities invariably are. Brilliant people in the Sciences are invariably very nice. Sense of humor, good-looking—"

"Modest," Debbie cuts in wryly. "Go away. I want to talk to Anna woman to woman about this."

"Bye, Anna, all the best! *Yes*, Jonah, I'm *coming!*"

Another click in the line, and Debbie settles into her interrogation.

"So tell me again. Cleveland was horrid to you? Why? He could be useful."

"Thanks, Debbie, I know! Dave is probably right and he's just an arrogant ass. Maybe he expected me to gush about his wonderful book and was peeved because I didn't."

"Attractive, though. Judging by the photo. Anna?"

"Yes, I'm here. Oh, well, all right, he's not unattractive. But soooo… English."

"Since when has that been a problem for you?"

"*Frightfully* English, don't you know, in *that* way. Oxbridge. *Lethally* polite! I hate that smooth English politeness! If he thinks that's going to camouflage the fact that he's an arrogant, stiff-necked, condescending git, he has another think coming!"

"It's early days yet. Perhaps he just had a headache, or a quarrel with his wife."

"Well, I hope whatever it was, she won't sleep with him for a month!"

"Talking of sleeping—are you?"

"Sleeping with anyone? Now look here, young Deborah…"

"Sleeping!" she protests. "Sleeping, eating!"

"I'm going to hang up if you don't stop that."

"All right—give me a number out of ten on your scale of well-being, and I'll stop. Promise."

Something started today. My office is a mess, and I hope Elizabeth Mayfield won't decide I'm some sort of *shlub* who should never have been hired, and I'm worried about how I'll get on with my students and my colleagues. But there is something else, something instinctive, feral — something primeval to do with the roots of the trees among which I lay earlier. Those roots, thick as a man's arms, intertwined with the earth in which they rest.

"A wobbly seven and a half."

"Seven and a half is good. I'll stop worrying about you for a bit, if you're a seven and a half."

"Just stop it. I'm fine."

Chapter 5

As far as my senior colleagues at Ardrossan are concerned, England has prepared me well. Take your time, have patience, and trust in yourself. Sooner or later you will connect with people. Tenured folk have no reason to notice untenured folk, unless a) they are bullies looking for victims, b) they are politicians looking for allies— *"a" and "b" often go together*—or, c) they want to bed them. The rule of thumb is simple: be suspicious of anyone who goes out of his or her way to compliment you. Academics are busy, competitive, and neurotic. That doesn't mean they can't be nice. But it does mean that if they show more than common courtesy to a newbie, they probably have ulterior motives.

The only colleague who goes out of his way to notice me is Tim Blundell.

"So, how are the old nerves?" he asks when he runs into me in the great hall on the day before classes start. Tim was on my search committee, and we instantly clicked when I came down for my interview last February.

"Is it a good idea to ask me that?"

"Probably not." He grins and propels me into a quiet corner of the cafeteria. "It's just that I haven't forgotten what it was like. Mind you, if you think this is stressful, wait till you have your tenure review coming up."

"It can't be worse than this."

"It can—if only because you're five years older than you are now, and you know that all your dear friends from grad school will be laughing like hyenas when they hear that you're teaching at a community college in Wyoming."

"How you cheer me, Professor Blundell."

He seems delighted, and a little surprised, that I am taking his snarks in good humor. Tim has the look of an intellectual baby, with a high, very convex forehead, round blue eyes and a pug nose, and it gives him an utterly deceptive air of innocence. In fact, his caustic treatment is doing a great deal to steady the old nerves.

"A word of advice," he goes on, his manner changing abruptly from camp to astringently professional, "but we never had this conversation, and I would swear on the Bible that we didn't!"

"Understood."

"You hate New York and couldn't wait to move to the South. That includes hating NYU and looking forward to teaching at a much smaller college. Remember: *We. Are. Faaa-mi-ly!*"

"Got ya."

"You are aware of the fact that a British Ph.D, lacking the coursework and the teaching requirements of an American Ph.D, is by definition inferior—"

"That depends on—"

"—which is why you completed optional graduate courses in Britain and took on teaching jobs to be able to compete with your American contemporaries."

"Well, I did!"

"I know you did!" He rolls his eyes in ostentatious despair. "But you have to remind them of that, like, every ten minutes. And third: you didn't just come here to kill time till you get offered a place at an Ivy."

"I don't even want a job at an Ivy!" I blurt out, conscious the next second of the fact that I have been manipulated into exposing myself.

"You're not all that New Yorkerish," Tim observes unemotionally. "That's good. Sweet, modest, and polite; that's what they like in a woman around here." He checks the size of my breasts underneath the tailored jacket and blouse I am wearing. "Pretty, in a *gamine* sort of way. Seems conservative. Young-looking, but very professional in manner and attire. Should fit in just fine."

I glower at him, open-mouthed, suddenly uncertain how to take him, and my evil angel overpowers me.

"You gotta be fuckin' kiddin' me with that speech, mister!"

This convulses him in cackling laughter so infectious that it smoothes my ruffled feathers.

"Correction: *Can* be New Yorkerish if provoked! — Hey, Erin!" he calls out to a woman standing in line for coffee. "Look who I found!"

Erin Gallagher, who was very attentive toward me during my day on campus in February, comes to sit with us and tells me, without any sign of bashfulness, that she went out and got pregnant with her first and only child a week after she received the letter announcing that she had been given tenure. Her little girl is now two years old and has been in college daycare since she was able to sit up. Everything about Erin, from her serviceable chestnut-colored bob to her sensible slacks and shirt to her no-nonsense flats, suggests a woman who has no time to waste.

"You are going to waste *so* much time waiting for people to get things done for you," she predicts. "Be prepared for that, and get yourself into a *zen* place. Do you have a PC yet? An *office?*"

"I have both, but no phone, and my office is full of stuff. Maintenance brought me a huge trash cart, but Mrs. Forster hasn't been able to tell me whether I can chuck everything away. Some of it is old essays." Since Tim and Erin are both dumbly staring at me, I add, "I'm in E-four-twenty-nine, next to this…elderly gentleman. Bushy white hair, a little — um — mad?"

"They put her into Corvin's cabinet?" Erin casts an incredulous glance at Tim, who rolls his eyes.

"You've met the department ghost, Anna. Andrew Corvin. He turned seventy shortly after I came here, but he refuses to let go, and they haven't the heart to take official action against him. We thought he would retreat licking his wounds when Elizabeth Mayfield made him give up his office on the first floor and relegated him to the fourth. No such luck. He sits there like an ancient crone on a treasure and won't budge."

"So it is Corvin's hoard, in my office? He was really upset when he found me trying to straighten up in it."

"He has keys to doors even maintenance doesn't have keys to. He's been here longer than anyone else. That's why they defer to him."

"Plus, Hornberger is holding his wing over him," Erin adds. "Did you speak to Elizabeth about him?"

"I tried, but that day she wanted to introduce me to Giles Cleveland, so we never got around to Corvin."

"Ah, you've met Giles!" Tim's face lights up like that of an infant shown its favorite rattle. "It's a good thing he's back. Is Giles going to mentor you?"

"I believe so."

"You can come to me, too, any time, Anna," Erin says quickly. "You really must ask for help if you run up against a problem. I can tell you're the type who wants to do everything by herself, be independent. That's cool, but there comes a point at which it is less than efficient. I only realized that when I had Deidre. Some things you just can't do on your own."

I love it when women tell me they only really discovered what's what in life after they had children. Very helpful, that.

Most of the people I meet these days I meet through Tim Blundell. All of them are in that familiar pre-semester scramble, but everyone welcomes me with a word of advice about the library services, the uncooperative Xerox machine, or the cafeteria food (I'm told to call the Observatory cafeteria "The Eatery" to avoid looking like a greenhorn).

The rings around Tim's eyes, however, are due not only to the start of the semester. He has handed in his tenure file to be assessed, aye or nay, for tenure and promotion. After years of hard work and strenuously-maintained conformity, he has taken the dive off the ten-meter platform, performed his twists and somersaults, tried not to make too much of a splash upon entering the water, and is now waiting for the jury to decide whether he will be placed or not. It is a nerve-wracking time, and I attribute some of his bitchiness to it.

New Faculty Orientation, as Giles Cleveland predicted, is tortuous. New assistant professors and adjuncts clutch their notebooks and diligently follow the endless series of presentations on equity, diversity, honor codes, benefits, the campus topography, and "How to Write a Syllabus."

"I *know* how to write a syllabus," groans the woman next to me behind the curtain of her long braids. "I wouldn't have gotten this job if I didn't, would I?"

"I wish they'd just give us a six-inch folder with info to take home," I murmur back. "I won't remember a quarter of this by tomorrow."

She looks up and smiles, evidently relieved that we "chime."

"Everyone else is so *keen*," she sighs over a muffin and coffee later on. "I mean, I know this stuff is important, but I just want to get on with it. Meet the students. Teach."

"What do you teach?"

"Black Atlantic Cultural Studies, mainly. Identity theory, race and gender. You?"

"Where—which department? Sociology? Politics?"

"No, English. Why—are you?"

We hail each other as long-lost friends and bond over the confession that Elizabeth Mayfield makes us shake in our shoes. Her name is Yvonne Roberts; she is ten years older than me, divorced with two kids, and has more energy than just about anyone I have ever met.

"Do you think students here will be very different than the ones you're used to?" she asks. "Bound to be, aren't they?"

"You think? Top American colleges are peopled by middle-class American nineteen-year-olds—how different from each other can they be?"

"You gotta keep 'em on their toes." Yvonne grins, while the next speaker is clearing her throat. "Surprise 'em. Stun 'em. Not like—" She discreetly cocks her head into the direction of the panel.

"—veland. I'm the Associate Vice President of Finance and Administration, and I'm going to talk briefly about the services offered by our department. First, you'll need us in all matters concerning—"

"Sorry," I hiss at my left-hand neighbor. "Who's that?"

"Amanda Cleveland, Finance and Ad—"

"Thanks!"

Well, shave my legs and call me smoothie!

"What?" Yvonne mouths, startled by how startled I am.

She must be. The name is not that common.

Capable.

That is first word that forms in my mind as I stare, slack-jawed with curiosity, at the slim blonde in a white blouse and raspberry-colored pencil skirt taking us through the slides of her PowerPoint presentation.

Southern belle turned business woman.

Professor Cleveland is married to a woman who is everything I am not. Her whole manner has that seemingly effortless self-confidence that I associate with a certain kind of sorority girl, or girls from the Upper East Side. Yvonne and I made sure we sit at the back of the room among the slackers, so now I'm not close enough to decide how old she might be (mid-thirties?) and whether she's a natural blonde (probably not). Cleveland likes blondes with big knockers and lots of poise. That's settled, then.

"Good speaking voice," Yvonne acknowledges while Amanda Cleveland sips at her water. "You know her?"

"I think she's Giles Cleveland's wife. He's my mentor."

"I've not met him yet. Is *he* like that?"

I think I know what she means by "that": the air of privilege that wafts around the tall, elegant figure.

"A little, yeah, but he's English, so he's…different. He's less…"

Amanda resumes her talk, and I try to work out what Giles Cleveland is less than his wife. I wanted to say, *less put together.* I could also say that he is more passionate. It strikes me, particularly now in contrast to his wife, how passionate Cleveland seemed to be. Very English, very cautious. Reserved. And then not cautious at all, but quick and brusque. *Why the rush? You'll be burned out by the time you're thirty!* He doesn't know that I almost burned out when I was twenty-six.

Not that it matters.

Before lunch I rush up to the Conservatory to get on with mucking out my office. Tomorrow I will bring my cleaning kit and maybe blow off the last orientation session to scrub shelves and floor. The walls need a coat of paint, but I'm not going to wait for a miracle. Empty and clean and freshly painted would be a miracle. Empty will do me.

What *is* empty as I rush along it, is the corridor. A dark figure in the shade between the dormer windows opposite my office melts into the wall, and I have a sickening premonition. The Dumpster is empty, too. I unlock my office and feel I've been catapulted into *Groundhog Day.* All semblance of order that the room might have had when I first saw it has been sacrificed to necessity. It looks as if someone had stood by the garbage cart and flung its contents back into the room through the open door. The defective lamps now lie on the floor in sprinkles of shattered glass, and stacks of paperbacks are in dog-eared piles or leaning crookedly against each other like drunken domino pieces.

My heart is racing in my chest, and I can't tell whether it's fury or fear. Afraid of the fear, I act on the fury and hammer my fist against Professor Corvin's door, calling out his name, but there is only silence and the giggle of two students loitering by the water cooler down the hall.

Calm.

Making a fuss would make me look like an idiot and the department admin like assclowns. But I can't help telling Yvonne as we are walking back to the Observatory at the end of the day.

"But if he has a key to your office, can you leave personal stuff in there? Purse, laptop, flash drive? It's not safe, is it?"

"No, I guess it isn't. There is a lockable drawer in the desk, but he may have a key to that, too. He hasn't *taken* anything, so far, or destroyed anything that belongs to me. He just wants me out, I think."

"I have no idea what I would do if I were in your shoes, Anna, I'm not going to lie. D'you think—no."

"All suggestions welcome, Yvonne—I'm floundering here!"

"No, I was wondering whether—have you met Dolph Bergstrom yet?"

"Who is Dolph Bergstrom?"

"Oh, my word!" Yvonne bites her lip. "You don't know? He's a postdoc in your field, early modern studies, and—well, don't tell anyone I told you, but you and he were neck and neck for this position—the one that you got? He's Matthew Dancey's protégé, so apparently there was a lot of wheelin' and dealin' goin' on before you got the offer. I'm wondering whether he is behind this, or Dancey—allocating an office to you that isn't habitable. That's how mobbing starts, Anna!"

"How do you know this?"

"Sam Ruffin, my mentor, told me over coffee after I'd signed my contract."

"I feel sick." It is as if a large fist had knocked all the air—and all the joy—out of me.

"I shouldn't have told you!"

"Yes, you should. It's better that I know. If he—"

"Dr. Lieberman!"

I wish I didn't immediately recognize the voice that stops me on the way to the main staircase. Giles Cleveland is striding toward us from the direction of the entrance portal, a leather satchel over his shoulder and a bag of books in each hand.

"Are you—"

"Sir, I believe you haven't—"

"—rushing off somewhere? No, I haven't, sorry. Giles Cleveland. Welcome to Ardrossan."

"—met Yvonne Roberts."

"Professor Cleveland." Yvonne clasps the two fingers that he awkwardly lifts to greet her without putting down the bag he is holding, and I have to stop myself from staring at her fingers around his hand. She is touching his hand. *Jealous!*

Yvonne looks at him, then at me, and something registers in her face.

"Catch you later, Anna!" She gives me a quick hug and rushes off. I wish I could do the same. Run away. Cleveland looks confusingly sexy in jeans and a blue-and-white rugby shirt, with that graying hair and a grizzled five-o'clock shadow, and I can only assume that he won't be coming to school in this outfit once teaching starts. This guy must be fighting them off with a stick. With a cricket bat.

I wonder how Amanda Cleveland deals with her husband's no doubt extensive fan club. I also wonder whether Cleveland strays from the pen of his marriage into the greener fields of grad school to avail himself of the opportunities that no doubt offer themselves to him there. But mostly I wonder that I have any thought at all to spare for the Clevelands' marriage, in view of the bombshell Yvonne just dropped. What with the bombshell—*Dolph Bergstrom?*—and the little hollow between Cleveland's collarbones, that warm, fragrant little hollow and the tan skin below, I am finding it hard to focus.

"This is a little sudden, but—" He glances over my shoulder at the glass-fronted cafeteria, and I think he is about to ask me to sit down for a coffee. "Here's the thing. We've just heard that Bob Morgan will be on sick leave for most of the semester, possibly for all of it. He's—" He shakes his head and moves his shoulders as if he was in pain. "Anyway, this means we are short-staffed in the graduate program, and I was wondering whether you'd be willing to upgrade your class on parody and satire."

He knows I can't say no, and he knows that I know that he knows I can't say no.

"What would that entail? The same syllabus, just tighten the screws a little?"

This earns me half a smile, but Cleveland doesn't want to be nice to me, so he stifles it. He also doesn't want to have coffee with me.

"That's right. The only thing is, you have to decide, well, *now*, really, because there's a bit of a flap on." Now he is looking down at me closely, warily, as if he expects me to lash out at him. And he is mocking me. There is a tension around his mouth as if he wanted to grin but will not, because that would give the game away. I avoid his eyes, playing for time, groping for an excuse to go away and think about it.

But the man is in a hurry.

"Good. Well, in that case, can I also ask you to muscle in on the graduate advisement? Since you'll be teaching them, it would make sense to also have you involved in their supervision, plus I expect there are a couple of people eager to pick your brain about your experiences on the job market."

Does the chair know about this? Should I tell Hornberger that Cleveland has recruited me for grad advisement? Should I make a deal with Cleveland, I'll teach your grad section if you'll get rid of Corvin's junk for me? On the other hand, teaching graduates is considered less arduous than teaching undergraduates, and I will have to demonstrate substantial activities in the area of graduate advisement when I'm reviewed. Perhaps he thinks he is doing me a favor. Perhaps he *is* doing me a favor.

"Sure." I shrug. "Besides, I wouldn't want to have time to twiddle my thumbs during my first semester here."

"No, that wouldn't do at all. Thumb twiddling is frowned on at all times."

It isn't that he doesn't hear my sarcasm, it's just that he chooses to deflect it with a deadpan irony that I would relish if he gave me any indication that he wants me to share it.

"May I ask to you send me an email about this? Where and when, and so forth?" This way, if anyone else tries to lumber me with more service or advisement, I can document that Cleveland got to me first.

"No problem."

He is enjoying my claims to independence, my pretense that we are negotiating, when in fact we both know that I am receiving orders. And then he bolts. I am struggling to muster the courage to tell him about Corvin when he gives me a quick nod and strides off toward the hallway behind the staircase. Doesn't even say good-bye, let alone thank you, or how are you getting on. Runs off, a gangly athlete, lurching a little because he hasn't fully realized he isn't an overgrown, diffident sixteen-year-old anymore.

"Hey, Anna. What's wrong?"

Tim overtakes me as I sleepwalk toward the elevator, his head cocked to one side, searching my face for clues.

"Nothing. Only that—no, nothing. Listen, do you have a couple of minutes to come up to my office? Could you show me the way around the online blackboards? I'm finally logged in, but the template still defeats me!"

He checks his phone. "I haven't got long, though. We should get together one evening and have a good natter about the place."

We reach the elevator, and he falls back a step to let me enter first.

"Thank you." I smile.

"*Manners Maketh Man,*" he murmurs, waiting till I've stepped out into the fourth-floor hallway, which is crowded with adjuncts and teaching assistants running into and out of their own and each other's offices.

"Are you…an Old Wykehamist?" I ask, curious about his background.

"W-What?"

"Sorry, just—a wild stab in the dark."

"But you're a clueless colonial! You're not meant to understand these things! Because I quoted—go, go!" Exasperated, he pushes me toward my office. "Nauseating anglophile!"

"You quoted the school motto, yeah. Winchester College. You said you grew up in England and went to a posh boarding school, so—what? Were you really at Winchester? Gosh, we *are* posh, aren't we?"

"Shut up and get on with it."

"Hey!" I protest. "You're lucky I allow all my gay friends to boss me around, or I'd slap you for that! Stop pushing me!"

"*Shshshut up!*" he hisses under his breath, his manner switching from petulant diva to alarmed professional.

Equally alarmed about the flash of anger in his baby-blues, I rummage in my bag for the key. There was never any doubt in my mind that Tim is gay, and I was convinced that he let me know as much when we first met. Leaves only one explanation.

"You don't mean to tell me there's a closet in this place, do you?"

"Of course there is." He flicks his finger at the Post-it that is standing in for the nameplate I still don't have.

"I'm sorry." I inhale deeply. "I—I had no idea. I'm so sorry."

"Can't blame you for not expecting that. We'll talk about it some other time, if you want. If you must."

"Don't be mad at me, Tim."

"Oh, stop being such a girl!" he snaps, back for a moment in bitch-mode. "*Jesus F. Christ!*"

"Welcome to Corvin's other office."

"Yes, but—this—" He slowly rotates around his own axis, which is about the only movement possible. "You can't work like this!"

"I know. The guy who came to set up my computer was laughing his head off. And most of this was in the Dumpster when I left the place on Friday evening. Today it's back in here. Mrs. Forster only says she'll put me on Hornberger's list—big joke, as if a department chair had nothing better to do at the beginning of the semester than to sort out piles of junk. I've written to Hornberger's personal email account, too, but—nothing."

"You must be furious." Gingerly he touches a couple of bags with the tip of his Kenneth Cole loafers. One of the bags falls open and reveals another bunch of photocopied articles.

"What's the point? I'm tenure-track. I'll shut the fuck up and wait till one of the higher-ups deigns to favor me with his attention. I tried to speak with Corvin, but when I met him this morning, he glared at me and ducked into his office like a toad into a hole. C'mon, huddle up—" I pull up the second chair and switch on my PC.

"You have to tell Giles."

"You say that as if Giles Cleveland were God. Or Darth Vader. Do you think he's going to choke Corvin? Using the Force?"

"For sure." Tim grins. "*Your lack of faith is disturbing!*"

"See, here. I get to this page, but when I try to select my courses—"

"Giles is your mentor," he insists. "It's his job to sort out problems like this!"

"I won't go running to Daddy the moment things don't go smoothly!"

"Don't you like Giles?" The baby blues are round as saucers.

"He calls me *doctor*."

Tim stares at me with glassy incomprehension.

"Who calls you what?"

"Cleveland. He calls me Dr. Lieberman! Not in front of the students. To my face."

"Seriously?"

"Tim! Cleveland can't stand me!" I say, as if he were the dumb boy who gets it last.

"I don't believe that. Maybe he's teasing you. He only does that when he likes someone. He's flirting with you!"

"I know how Englishmen flirt. He isn't flirting with me. He hasn't suggested I call him Giles, either, though he expressly told me not to call him sir."

"You called him sir?"

"Considering my options, sir seemed very restrained!"

"Ouch, he did rub you the wrong way!" Tim can't resist milking my indignation, but he clearly has no explanation for Cleveland's behavior. It would have been a relief to hear that he—Cleveland—was notorious throughout the department for his rudeness, but apparently not so. On the contrary, Tim seems to hero-worship him, which I find absolutely laughable.

"Whatever. I won't ask Cleveland for help, that's all."

I'm tempted to ask Tim about Dolph Bergstrom and the search committee, but something stops me. Tim is such a gossip; if he hasn't told me yet, there is a reason. Perhaps I should keep this tidbit under my cap for a little. The more I hear about Dolph beforehand, the more awkward I will feel when I meet him. At the end of the day all we can do is try and be grown-up about it. I got the job, and Dolph will just have to suck it up. Now I want my office.

Chapter 6

After about a trillion sessions of new faculty orientation, and cocktails with the Provost, and lunchtime finger food and jazz with the Dean and her staff—none of which addressed *my* most pressing problem, of course—we assemble for the first faculty meeting at the English department. I still have no idea what to do about Crazy Corvin and the mountain of his trash in my office, but I do know that my part as the new kid on the block is to be seen, not heard. I would get off to a very bad start indeed with my new colleagues if the first thing they heard from me was a complaint. My best course of action is to be as quiet as a mouse: watch, listen, and learn.

Our venue is the conference room at the Observatory. It is dominated by a table that is at once decorative and emblematic, an almost round oval at one end, it narrows down at the other end and connects, with a couple of tapering pieces in-between, with as many rectangular tables as are needed.

"What's with the tear-shaped table?" I whisper to Tim as we enter the room.

"Tear? We call it the Sperm Room, for all the whacking off that goes on in here."

"Okay, you sit at the window, I sit here. Go, reprobate. Shoo."

The full professors and highest-ranking associates sit at the head of the table, while the rest of us huddle round the, um, tail. Andrew Corvin, in the same suit he wore before, comes in and obliges half a dozen people to move down because he insists on sitting next to

Matthew Dancey. I'm a somewhere-in-the-middle-of-the-tail assistant professor, and I think—although I can't be sure because I don't want to be caught looking at him—that when Giles Cleveland enters, he scans the room, sees me among the infantry and checks that box. I was right; he doesn't wear jeans and rugby shirts when he is on duty. But even in a light gray summer suit and a white dress shirt there is a disheveled look about him, as if he had shrugged into his jacket in a hurry—top shirt buttons undone, cuff buttons undone, the sleeves peeking out from under the sleeves of the jacket. As if someone had been in the process of undressing him when he remembered the faculty meeting and dashed off.

Now *there's* a tantalizing thought.

Two young men take the seats further down from me, and I am glad I can turn to them.

"Hi, we haven't met. I'm Anna Lieberman."

"Mm." While my neighbor—a beefy blond with a goatee—is finishing an email, his friend tips his chair backward.

"Hey. I'm Steve Howell. Settling in all right?" He is weedier than the blond, but good-looking in a nineteen fifties kind of way.

"Yes, thanks, I'm—"

"You're in next to Corvin, aren't you?" He pulls up one corner of his mouth in a smile that could be sympathetic or malicious. "That's too bad."

The hunk's shoulders twitch.

I turn my body toward them to signal my readiness for confrontation, although my smile is sweet and harmless.

"You seem to know all about that. How come?"

"Well, we...saw you in there, that's all."

"The weakest link," the hunk says, straightening up from his notebook. "Someone has to be in next to Corvin, and that'll be the new hires who have no powerful friends in the place. Fuzzy end of the lollipop."

"So it goes." I shrug, pretending to be cool. "And you are—?" As if I didn't know.

"Dolph Bergstrom." He still can't get himself to look straight at me.

I have never met anyone actually called that. Why would parents *do* such a thing to their child? A blond, blue-eyed boy, yet! *Adolph.* Seriously?

"Oh, man—hi! I thought we'd meet here today—look, what can I say? Bad luck, that's all. I know you probably wish I'd go away and boil my head, and—well, I won't, but maybe we can have lunch soon? I have a ton of questions I'd love to ask you!"

Dolph stares at me as if his pet rabbit had suddenly spoken to him. In Swahili.

"I don't even know what you're talking about," he says.

For five mortifying seconds I am convinced I got it all wrong, but his rejection impulse is so strong he even inches his chair away from me with a nervous jolt.

"Head boiling seems a little excessive," Steve jokes, but I notice that he quickly checks Dolph's profile.

"Aren't you worried you're out of your depth here, with no experience of the American grad school system?" Dolph is irritated with me, as if I were the puny kid that wants to play on his team.

"Yeah, I'm sure that having been out of the country is going to be *such* a disadvantage."

"Good idea, going abroad," Steve murmurs, trying to sound like Tony Soprano.

"Around," Dolph adds.

"What goes around…"

"…comes around," Dolph completes Steve's sentence. "You did your MA and your Ph.D in England?"

Shut the fuck up, Anna. Do yourself a favor.

"Yeah, England University. Big place."

This makes him flinch, but he comes back straightaway.

"You won't last long," he tells me. "England can't cut it, compared with a graduate degree from a top American university."

"Actually, bub, neither of us has a graduate degree from a top American university."

Part of me is mature enough to understand that he needs a mantra to deal with the shitty situation he finds himself in, but another part of me wants to go for his jugular. I don't want to look at Cleveland, really, I don't, but my eyes sort of brush past him all of their own accord, and he is looking over. Our eyes meet, and he shakes his head. Just a fraction, just barely enough for me to notice. Did he just tell me to back off? Does Cleveland think Dolph could harm me?

I am following the proceedings with one ear only, so I only half catch something about the Graduate Careers Fair which takes place at the beginning of each fall semester. But I am all eyes and ears when Cleveland mentions by the way that "Tim and Tessa" will be going it alone from the English Lit side of the Early Modern Studies program.

"But you have to be there," Hornberger says tersely. "You're program director."

"Laurie Jacobs has agreed to stand in for me."

"Laurie Jacobs has a sabbatical this semester. She's in Florence, up to her elbows in headless torsos."

Even Cleveland has to grin at the image conjured up by Hornberger.

"I know, but when we last spoke, she said she was leaving mid-September. I'll be away over the weekend and back for my first class on Wednesday but not much before. Sorry."

"Giles cleared that with the Dean a while ago, Nick," Elizabeth steps in.

"If Giles thinks it is wise, we shouldn't interfere," Matthew Dancey addresses his colleagues, doing precisely that. "All other graduate programs are represented by their directors; if he thinks that an assistant professor and a graduate student will do justice to our contribution to Medieval and Renaissance Studies—fine. The phasing out of Medieval Studies will have an inevitable effect on Early Modern Studies anyway."

A low groan indicates that I am not alone in being taken aback by this bitch-slapping behavior.

"You're getting a little ahead of yourself, I think, Matthew," Elizabeth Mayfield says with awe-inspiring coolness, but Dancey ignores her.

"Maybe we shouldn't stray from the agenda. I'm sure we all have things left to prepare for next week." Hornberger doesn't look at Elizabeth either, and she doesn't pursue the issue, but Cleveland, for the first time since the meeting started, had an arrested look on his face when Dancey dropped that little bomb. I know that the ailing Robert Morgan is a medievalist, but one sick professor is hardly a reason to shut down a whole subfield.

On an unrelated note, I wonder why Cleveland does not come clean and announce that he has to be in Edinburgh, Scotland, for an award ceremony in which he might win a very prestigious prize. He is provoking Nick Hornberger for no other reason than that he can.

I look up and catch Tim looking at me. The question mark on his face is unmistakable, and it dawns on me that he wants to recruit me. I give him a mouth-shrug and a tiny nod.

"We could take Anna." Tim interrupts the awkward silence as if he was talking about a trip to the mall.

"Which one is Anna?" Professor Westley, an aging hippy in a crocheted beanie, puts on his red-rimmed glasses and leans forward to scan the lower end of the room. He came late and missed our introduction, and since neither Hornberger nor any of the others can be bothered to fill him in, I half-raise one hand and wave at him, which makes Steve Howell and Dolph Bergstrom double up over their notebooks.

Spotlight on Anna.

"Hi, Anna!" Westley grins and winks at me. "I thought you were a new grad student!"

"No offense, Anna — Dr. Lieberman — but she knows nothing yet about the program, how could she represent it?" This is a token objection; Hornberger himself is not convinced by it, so to clinch the matter I ignore my thumping heart and speak up.

"I could do my *shtick* on why Renaissance Studies is a great subject. That's the main point of the exercise, isn't it? And I do know a little about job-hunting in English Lit."

I haven't looked at Cleveland at all during this little intermezzo, and I won't.

Hornberger, looming handsomely but uncomfortably at the head of the table, makes a bid for control as a low hubbub wells up in the room. "Dr. Lieberman — Anna — would show a great deal of collegiality if she agreed to take over a composition section. I know it's short notice, but we're in a tight corner, so — "

"Nick, why are we in a tight corner?" Elizabeth interrupts him. "The teaching schedules were drawn up last spring. We had everything sorted out."

Hornberger pokes his keyboard as if it was a pile of dog poop. "One of the comp sections is without an instructor," he declares almost triumphantly, reading from his screen.

Dancey launches a smooth attack on me. "Anna, we'd be eternally grateful to you if you would help us out of this predicament."

I hadn't expected the policy of shut-the-fuck-up to become so hard to stick to so early in the game. Teaching composition is the equivalent of army boot camp, except you're both the drill sergeant and the recruit. It is a crazy amount of work—I know this from experience, and I really, really do not have time to repeat it.

The problem is, I really, really have no choice.

"Well, sir, I was hop—"

"I've asked Dr. Lieberman to make up for Bob's class in the graduate program. She has kindly agreed to do so, and I think you'll find, Matthew, that the change has already been entered in the course schedule. Asking her to agree to yet another change would really be playing fast and loose with a rookie, and I don't think we ought do that. Wouldn't be ethical."

Not a single glance at me during this little *pièce de résistance*. I hate that Cleveland makes me feel like a high-school freshman who needs protecting from the bullies. The miserable truth, however, is that I am, and I do.

"When did you arrange that?" Dancey snaps at him.

"Friday afternoon." Cleveland folds his arms again and scoots down in his chair so that only the protuberance of his tailbone is stopping his descent.

"On whose authority?" Hornberger apparently feels he has to assert himself as chair. "If we all went round changing the teaching arrangements, this place would descend into chaos! We're not a co-op, you know!"

This evokes subdued chuckles from some, and twisted grins from others. Cleveland is gazing at Hornberger with an odd, private little smile on his face, as if he was pleased that Hornberger had said something stupid.

"Communism, I thought, Nick. What's mine is yours…and so forth."

"This will have to be corrected," Dancey decides, still white around the mouth. "How can Anna take over Bob's class? She's not a medievalist."

"Matthew, who among our many medievalists were you going to suggest might take over Bob's classes?" Cleveland sits up and leans forward on his elbows as if he were interested in the answer. He doesn't get one, because the round table is now arguing among themselves in increasingly loud voices.

There is more to this than meets the eye—has to be, because the issue itself is so minor—but I take very great care not to seem overly curious. I keep my head down and draw a lacy border on my sheet of notepaper, and when Dolph Bergstrom murmurs, "Well, that's all going very nicely, isn't it?" I stupidly think at first that he is referring to my doodling.

"Oh, come on!" I groan when I realize what he means. "Could you please not be quite so blatantly hostile?"

I had been given conflicting advice on how to deal with Dolph. Irene advocated flattery, while Debbie felt I should give him some time to lick his wounds. Neither of them had recommended a cat fight.

"I would take on another comp section, sir," pipes a female voice lower down the table from me, below the salt, where the graduate assistants and the exploited adjuncts have to sit.

"Danielle! Would you? That's fantastic!" Hornberger leaps at her offer like a trout leaps at a mosquito. "Right, then, moving along to Family Weekend, and the black lining on that cloud, Homecoming. Any suggestions? Bright ideas?"

It is half past seven when we finally pile out of the stuffy room into the hallway, grateful for our escape. It is an eternal mystery why, if everybody hates them, faculty meetings are so endless. Ordinarily, I would dash back to my office, grab my stuff and head home, but these people are my new colleagues, and if there is any socializing to follow, I must not miss it.

"There." Tim comes over to me and whispers next to my ear. "Your baptism of fire is over. Let's see your burns."

"Anna!" Rich Westley appears from the direction of the men's room. "So great to see you back on campus! Sorry about earlier—that was meant to be a joke, about you being a new grad student. Not so funny, I know." He takes off his eyeglasses and peers at me.

"Thank you, sir—"

"Rich."

"Rich, it's wonderful to be back."

"Found your way to the Astrolabe yet? That's our watering-hole. Across the parking lot, and so considered to be off campus. We always adjourn there to moisten our throats after meetings. I'll take you, if you like."

"Sorry, Rich—Anna wanted me to show her my first editions." Tim tugs at my elbow. "We'll come later."

"Show her your—what?" Westley grins. "I've never heard it called *that* before!"

"Associating with you will soil my reputation," I say darkly when Tim's office door has closed behind us.

"Nonsense. I want to bitch to you about Dancey and Hornberger."

Tim's office is as functional as his suits and ties, very neat and tidy, no personal touch at all, except for a model of the Louvre glass pyramid on his desk and a steel-framed print of Jackson Pollock's *Convergence* on the wall. There is a knock on the door, and he narrows his baby blues in a grimace of ultimate vexation.

"Come in!"

"Listen, Tim, can you make sure that—oh. Sorry." Cleveland looks up from the sheaf of paper in his hand, sees me, and a deep crease appears between his eyebrows.

"I was just about to give Anna a few glosses on the meeting." Tim waves him in, but Cleveland remains rooted to the threshold.

"Right, I'll get back to you later. You should go and drink with the others." This is Giles Cleveland doing some mentoring. *Go and drink with the others.*

"Cleve, wait—is that the latest version of the application files? I want those."

Cleveland takes one step further into the room but doesn't even close the door behind him. While he and Tim are scanning the printouts, I debate whether I should thank him for saving me from a fate worse than death, or slap him upside the head for making me the center of a faculty quarrel. He turns over the pages and pins a second folder behind the first, lifting his arm so that his jacket hitches up and his shirt tautens across his left flank and lower ribcage.

"So," he suddenly addresses me, "you're all right." That's a statement, not a question, and since I was lost in very inappropriate thought and no response seems required, I am tempted to shrug and say nothing. But I don't want to seem peevish, so I rally for an enthusiastic reply and force myself to look up into his eyes. The second I do so, he looks away.

"Yes, I am, thank you. I was grateful for your intervention."

"Well, it's closed season yet for rookie-hunting."

"I wish you'd told me about Adolph, though."

"I thought you knew. It's in all the history books."

"*This* Adolph! The guy whose job I got, and who is still here as an adjunct! How awkward is *that!*"

Cleveland hesitates, and I know that I am destroying all the benefits of having shut up so valiantly during the meeting.

"I didn't think you should worry…" He either falters, or he makes an ironic show of faltering. I don't know him well enough yet to tell the difference. "You shouldn't worry your—"

Pretty little head about that? Say it, Cleveland, and I'll bite your balls off!

"—yourself about Dolph. Ignore him, is my advice. Well, then—" He inhales and straightens his shoulders. "I'll see y'all next week, bright-eyed and bushy-tailed!"

"I hope you'll be an also-ran!" I fling at him.

He understands at once what I am referring to, but either I've stumped him or I'm not worthy of a riposte.

"What do you mean 'also ran'? Cleve, where're you off to, anyway?" Tim, at first vaguely interested, notices our silent glaring and becomes attentive. "Oh, secrets," he says archly.

"Evidently not." The light in Cleveland's face dies down, and he rushes off in one of his abrupt exits.

"What's with you?" Tim splutters into the silence after the door snaps shut. "*Sweet and polite*, I said! Not *snide and pissy!*"

I throw myself into one of the steel-and-leather armchairs, feeling like a petulant teenager. "He started it."

"*He* has tenure! And he saved your ass in there! You'd be drowning in essays this semester if it wasn't for Giles!"

"I said I was grateful!"

A knock on the door saves me, but as the electricity tingles in my nerve endings, I have to confess to myself that I'm hoping Cleveland is back. I pissed him off, and I can't wait to see him again. Something's wrong there.

"Aren't you coming to the Astrolabe?" Erin Gallagher has her bag under one arm and a box of diapers under the other; above her shoulder Eugenia Russell's avid face appears. "We saw you dive in here, so we thought something was up."

"Follow-up meeting for Anna."

"Gosh, yes, you almost got Dancey's blade right between the third and fourth ribs there, Anna!" Eugenia leans against the sideboard, making the wood creak and Tim cringe, but he keeps his mouth shut.

"Giles bailed her out."

"Well, he didn't want to let Dancey and Hornberger get away with their little scheme. How did he know, though?"

"You don't exactly have to be clairvoyant to know that Dancey would get Nick to play gofer for him," Tim said. "And if you ask me, we ain't seen nothin' yet."

Erin contemplates me from the depth of the second armchair. "What you don't know, Anna, is that Dolph Bergstrom should have gotten your job."

"Erin! Don't tell her that!" Eugenia frowns at her. "What's she to do with that? Don't worry about it, Anna. Department politics, keep out of them."

"Well, I'd like to," I say.

"No, Ginny, Anna needs to know, because I what I think is that Dancey and Hornberger have it in for her," Erin insists. "Doofus doesn't have to teach comp, so why should you? Because teaching comp means one fewer article on your list of publications at the end of the semester, that's why!"

"Doofus?"

"Dolph. He's an Ardrossan seedling, bedded by—"

"Hush, now!" Tim flutters his eyelids in the manner of a scandalized aunt.

"—bedded by William DeGroot, our erstwhile Commonwealth Foundation professor, and currently cultivated by Matthew Dancey. So you may be sure that the burden of teaching comp was going to be lifted from his tender shoulders at the first opportunity."

"Dancey got Dolph shortlisted for your job," Tim says, taking over, "although there are unwritten rules against having in-house candidates for tenure-track positions. The third candidate was another woman from up north. Dartmouth, or Cornell, I forget. But we didn't like her, did we? Brusque, harsh."

"Jessica-Ann Wright," I say, because I don't want to appear like a totally lame dweeb. Tim, Erin and Eugenia beam at me like teachers at the dumb kid who unexpectedly produces a nugget of knowledge.

"I would have preferred her to Doofus, though, if she had been the only alternative. Luckily, as it turned out—" Erin stretches out her arms toward me like a compere to an award winner.

When the four of us enter the Astrolabe—Erin still with her thirty-six-pack of diapers, which adds a bizarre touch to the pseudo-*fin-de-siècle* décor of the bar—the first thing I see is Nick Hornberger handing drinks to a gaggle of female students. This is his comfort zone. Chairing a college department is a thankless task, but if the whip is passed to you, you must use it. I'm guessing that Nick Hornberger is neither willing nor equipped to rule as master and commander of this *navis academicum*, to ration bread and water if need be, and perhaps even subject slackers to the cat o' nine tails. He wants to be popular, and that is a dangerous motivation.

"Ah, Anna! Welcome to our haunt! What're you having?"

"I'm driving, thanks—soda, please, sir."

"None of that formal sir! Call me Nick! Or have you spent so long among the English that you've adopted their stick-in-the-mud arrogance?"

My field of vision is completely filled by a big chest in a golf shirt as he puts one arm around my shoulders and draws me against himself. A receding hairline is the fate of many a younger man, but the sagging jowls and the tell-tale thickness around the waist and chest must give him a pang when he looks in the mirror.

"Ted? Ted?" he calls over to the barkeeper. "Ted, this is Anna, and she will have—" He scans my face as if the answer lay there. "A white wine spritzer. You can drive after a wine spritzer!"

"Well, sir—Nick—if it's all the same to you, I'd rather—"

"To celebrate your appointment, Anna!" Hornberger insists as if he were a Sherpa tribesman obliged by custom to force food and drink onto a guest protesting his fullness.

The only person standing near Hornberger who comes up to his earlobe is a stunning brunette in a white pants suit and a figure-hugging top who has been watching our exchange very narrowly.

"Hello, Professor Lieberman! Welcome to Ardrossan!" She beams down at me with all the self-confidence of the spoiled and beautiful. "We're all so curious to meet you—may we introduce ourselves? We're all in offices next to yours. Only not so far down the hallway."

Bite me, Versace Girl.

My advice to a graduate student at a top-tier research university would always be to strive to be remembered for her work, not for her looks, but Irene calls this the German Protestant infiltration of my cultural heritage.

I hope and trust the Almighty is not among the aging males dazzled by visions of female fabulousness, but Nick Hornberger evidently is. There is a subtle but distinct difference in the way Hornberger bear-hugged me and the way he reaches past America's Next Top Model to take some glasses from Ted the barman. Not sure if I can put my finger on it. Familiarity coupled with a sense of reverence.

"This is Tessa Shephard," Versace Girl says, inviting a copiously freckled girl with dark red locks into our small circle. "Tessa's in her third year of grad school, so —"

"So if there's anything you need, ma'am, don't hesitate to ask," says Tessa, not visibly galled by her colleague's patronizing manner. She gives me a broad smile. "I'm in your class on parody, and Professor Cleveland said you'll be coming to the Early Modern Studies graduate seminar, so we'll meet there, too."

"And this is my friend Selena O'Neal." Versace Girl steps aside and pushes a third girl toward me. Selena is tall and very well-endowed, too, but two thick mouse-colored braids hang on either side of her pale face down to her waist, her face has a pasty sheen, and she manages to look almost dowdy in a pleated skirt and a white blouse. If it was Hornberger who recommended these girls as graduate assistants to the Academic Affairs Office, he is only partially guilty of selecting them with his loins. Maybe he makes deals with the AAO: one stunner for one nerd.

"Hello, Dr. Lieberman." Selena has a soft, strained voice, and I have to read her lips to hear her above the music. "I was sorry to see that your class on *Paradise Lost* was canceled. I was…I was looking forward to that."

"Oh, thanks! How nice of you to say that, Selena. Yes, I was sorry, too, but curriculum requirements made the change necessary. Maybe next semester!"

She smiles and bobs her head in a manner reminiscent of the late Princess Diana.

"That would be wonderful, because I'm actually working on —"

"Yeah, leave that for the grad sem, Selena," her frenemy butts in. "I'm Natalie Greco, Professor Lieberman. I'm in my first year of grad school and it's my first year as a grad assistant, so you can imagine how excited I am! Welcome to Ardrossan University, again, ma'am, and to The Old Dominion!"

I'm the new girl in class, and the popular girls are noticing me. That is definitely a new experience, only it comes fifteen years too late to be anything but awkward.

"Tessa, Selena and Natalie—thanks for coming to say hello." I give them my best teacher's smile. "I guess we'll be seeing a lot of each other, if we're…on the same floor."

In the same dorm, I almost said. Knee-jerk reflex.

Hornberger hands me my wine, and my eyes focus on the glittering drops of water that are running down the outside of the glass, gather at the bottom, fall onto his wrist and run down the underside of his arm. This is what stimulus overload does to me; I latch on to a tiny detail and close in on it. Then the still life of the drops of water on Nick Hornberger's hairy footballer's arm turns dramatic. Natalie Greco reaches out, and with the backs of her four fingers, slightly bent, she brushes the drops away. She is talking to him about something college-related—I catch the words "scanning" and "PDF"—but her eyes find the detail that mine had also found, and she lifts her hand and brushes the water away. Neither of them comments on her action or stops the conversation, and it is this that tells me that they are sleeping together.

I look up and around to see whether anyone else has seen what I just saw, and I catch Yvonne Roberts's pleading stare, urging me over to join her and Elizabeth Mayfield. It turns out that Elizabeth will not, after her stint as chair, go back to full-time teaching but proceed up the administrative ladder to the position of Dean of Studies. She graciously accepts our congratulations and encourages us to approach her, notwithstanding her principal duties, should we need her help or advice. There is not a single glance over at Hornberger and his circle of giggling admirers to indicate that she does, in fact, doubt the new chair's ability or willingness to look after us.

I decide to take Elizabeth at her word. She seems genuinely upset when she hears about the mess in my office; apparently it was reported clean and empty months ago. Neither of us mentions Andrew Corvin's name, and I am as certain as I can be that she appreciates my discretion. Relief at her promise to look into it gives me a second wind of sociability, and when Dancey beckons me over, I bound up to him like a trusting puppy.

Matthew Dancey, I decide after five minutes in which he scolds me with paternal sternness for volunteering to do service that isn't expected of me and stresses that cooperativeness is of course the first virtue of a valued team member, is a politician. Physically, he is nondescript: below medium height, nearly bald, very thin, a little ill-looking. The only attractive thing about him is his smooth, sonorous voice, but as he speaks I sink into an aural hallucination of this voice as it affably dissects a poor junior professor's failings and informs her that her three-year tenure review was unsuccessful. This man surely *can smile and smile and be a villain.* I am too exhausted and too pleased with the prospect of an uncluttered office to worry about the mixed messages that he is sending me. He is very upfront about the awkwardness of Dolph and me working together in the same subfield and suggests we might consider a project that would benefit us both. I can see that Dolphie, standing next to Dancey like a bodyguard with his biceps stretching the short sleeves of his shirt, hates the idea as much as I do, but with the non-tenured obsequiousness that unites us, we both nod and assure Dancey that this is a great idea.

"Anna, you have heard about the new jewel in our crown, haven't you?" Dancey continues. "The new Institute for Cognitive Science, Linguistics and Psychology? Nick Hornberger was instrumental in acquiring the necessary funds — well, he and the task force delegated to undertake this project. It would make an excellent impression if the English department were among the first to convene a conference there — perhaps about Renaissance art and neuroesthetics? That's Dolph's field, of course, but you have worked on iconography, too, so you wouldn't find yourself too much out of your depth!"

I just want to get out of this overheated bar and head back to my quiet little haven on the tomato farm, but I have to be polite. "You wrote your dissertation about neuroesthetics?"

"Visual art and visual images in Shakespeare, yes," Dolph speaks up for the first time. "That's how I cover the early modern requirement and bring cutting-edge theory to the table. I guess you see why it irks me that I lost out to two MILFs who sailed in here on a diversity ticket."

I can only stare at him, the last sip of wine unswallowed in my mouth.

"All search committees have to balance academic excellence and fit with political considerations." Dancey nods as if he hadn't heard. "These days, white, middle-class men sometimes get rough deals. That's only fair, of course, seen in a historical perspective. And Anna, you'd not be doing yourself a favor at all if you allowed this to reflect on your standing at Ardrossan. We are very happy to have you!"

"He said *what* to you?" Irene screeches into the phone.

"I know." Generally, I enjoy entertaining Irene with *Tidbits from Academia*, but I'm not enjoying this.

"He called you a MILF?"

"Not directly, but—yeah, he did. And if you love me, don't—!"

"Don't what?"

"Don't say, *I told you so!*"

"Well…"

"Reenie, I don't know how to play this." On my back porch, with another glass of wine, I don't feel as low as I did when I drove home, but I'm still depressed enough to send a little *cri de coeur* to Manhattan. "They're nice to me, don't get me wrong. But boy—these small departments are cans of slithery, scholarly worms!"

"So what's new?"

"That I'm in the thick of it. Well, not the thick of it, I'm not that important, but…involved. I didn't used to be. That's what was so great about England. I used to be just the li'l Yank and no one paid any attention to me. I preferred that."

"But, Anna, Anna Banana, you can't always be the promising grad student. Now it's time to be the badass prof. You gotta toughen up! What were you wearing?"

"Polka-dotted hammer pants and flip-flops. There is nothing badass about these petty power games and these malicious Machiavellian machinations!"

"Come on, Anna, you know that this is what college is like! What's the big surprise?"

I pull my knees close to my chest in a gesture that reminds me of Jules Walsh.

"I want to be Anshel, the Yeshiva boy."

"Like there ain't no power play at a shul!"

"But I hate it so! I want to concentrate on my work, not on playing games!"

"Power games are part of your work. That's the crucial thing you don't understand. Start shmoozing, girl! You still believe that all you have to do is work hard and be nice and you'll get the job, but eighty percent of it is connections!"

"I got this job."

"Yes, and why? Because you shmoozed that guy Schermerhorn. Matterhorn. Horny Horn."

"Hornberger."

"Hornberger!" Irene squeals. "Dude! Work him — you said he liked you, and you need allies."

"I do need allies, but he isn't one of them. Two reasons: a) I think Horny Horn is having an affair with one of the teaching assistants, and b) the people I like here don't like him. On the other hand, he is chair at the moment. And he's the golden boy because he nabbed a huge sponsorship deal."

"Your chair is a dirty old man who fucks grad students?" Once again, even pragmatic Irene is shocked.

"Oh, no, no, no, you have the wrong idea. He's not young anymore, maybe fifty, but big, and he looks good, or looked, if you like that sort of thing. Bronzed, brawny, but evidently with some brains, or he wouldn't be here. The worst I can say about Hornberger is that I think he'll be inefficient. No, it's that he's under Dancey's thumb."

"Not that he has sex with students?"

"As long as that doesn't make him corrupt, I couldn't care less. Nobody cared that Clinton was having sex with his intern, did they? Until she blabbed and he committed perjury. But if I have Dancey against me, who is one of the most influential people in the place, *and* his buddy, the department chair — maybe I should start polishing my CV right away."

"Don't panic. Create your own alliances. Bert Scherer can't stand me, but because I have the other senior partners on my side, I'm safe. Oh, I haven't told you. They're going to ask me to take over the Whettering case when Louise has her baby. Ed Barton told me yesterday."

"Whoa — hey! Props to Irene! Congratulations!"

"It would be a nice feather in my cap if I brought that one home. And I will." The tone of her voice leaves no doubt that she will. Irene usually gets what she wants.

"What does Jacques say? *On boit du champagne?*"

"He says if I win that one, he'll take me to *Per Se* for dinner."

Perhaps this is where Irene and I most differ. I would prefer a boyfriend who takes me to a romantic restaurant when I get the case, not if I win it. There is a reason why Jacques and I never warmed to each other, even though he has been a fixture since he and Irene met in law school.

"So, who do you like?" she asks. "Among your colleagues. Who could be an ally?"

"Dunno."

"C'mon, Anna, you gotta do better than that!"

"Tim Blundell — he does Brit Lit, too, he's half English and —"

"English, huh? Does that set your little heart a-flutter?"

"Well, no, in view of the fact that he is as gay as Christmas, it doesn't."

"He is? Down there? Yikes. Won't he get, like, fifty lashes and two years of hard labor if he's caught *in flagrante?*"

"Don't be stupid." I decide not to mention Tim's closet. "Anyway, I like Tim, and he introduces me to people I like, on the whole. But he does shoot his mouth off about our colleagues, and although he makes me laugh, I'm worried that I'm getting in with the worst set of the school."

"You want to be careful with that," Irene agrees. "Stay out of trouble, find a powerful prof who'll protect you, and a few people to hang out with. That's all you need right now. Are you getting enough exercise?"

"Mm…"

"Well, do, Anna! Because the only thing I'm worried about is that you'll work too hard and worry too much, panic, like you do, and then start an affair with, I dunno, a student, or the prez, or someone else totally inappropriate. *Like you do!*"

"You make me sound like a Pavlovian bitch."

"Just sayin', babycakes. Take that bitch out for long runs, and she won't show that stress-induced random mating behavior!"

"Irene, I wish you were here. So I could slap you!"

Chapter 7

"Don't let her bother you. She's never been easy. Well, it's not been easy for her, and that's my fault, of course."

All I said was that Jules came round to introduce herself to me. That was all it took for Karen Walsh to launch into a flood of apologies for her eldest daughter. It is Sunday afternoon, and Pop, Howie, and Grandma Shirley have driven off to see Shirley's brother and his wife in the next big town beyond Shaftsboro, leaving Karen and the girls to hold the fort. I've done all my prep for next week, and I am too nervous to concentrate on any of my other projects. Anyway, why did I move into the country if I'm not going to befriend my neighbors?

Karen seemed happy to see me and offered to set aside the huge box of peas she is shelling, but I reassured her I didn't mind at all and offered to help. She declined my offer as politely as it was given, and so I have a glass of cold tea in front of me and watch with considerable fascination how she twists the peas out of their pods with two flicks of her wrist.

"She didn't bother me at all," I reply diplomatically. "It's just that I hadn't…I hadn't expected her."

"No…she's away a lot. Out." Karen can probably shell peas in her sleep with one hand tied behind her back, but now she has her eyes trained on the green bowl in front of her. "She earns her monthly allowance picking, so she hangs out a lot with the students and the backpackers, and…well, I don't like it, but there isn't much I can do about it. I hope that when she's old enough to drive, she'll get a job in town, but of course my husband and my father-in-law want her to help on the farm."

"She mentioned that she'd been to stay with her Dad."

Karen glances up at me, and at first I take it to be a warning to back off, but it is in fact an expression of relief.

"Yes. I was married before, briefly. I was too young, and—well, she was an accident."

I try to picture this wiry, self-effacing woman, with her lean, capable hands, when she was eighteen or nineteen. Pregnant, under pressure to marry, or maybe not even under pressure, maybe happy, and eager to have a family and a home.

Light-years away from my own experience.

"Why are you worried about her?"

The busy fingers stop and sink onto the wax tablecloth.

"Well—" But what she means is not, *Well, let me think*, but *Well, how long have you got?*

"I mean, she's a teenager," I rush on. "She *has* to give you attitude."

She smiles, but it is an unconvincing effort.

"I was a student at the College of Agriculture and Life Sciences," she says. "I wanted to go into landscape contracting. Julianne's father and I met as interns working at the state zoo. I was pregnant six weeks after we met, married two months later, and divorced after less than two years. Didn't finish my degree, broke with my parents. I was working at the food market in town when Howie and I met. You can imagine that his parents were not pleased when he brought me home."

"I don't know. Degree or no degree, you must know a lot more about farming than other women Howie might have dated." I'm still busy assimilating this new and unexpected information.

"Oh, yes, my father-in-law couldn't hear enough about those fancy new ideas that people taught at college." I didn't think Karen Walsh capable of such withering sarcasm. But then I clearly underestimated her all round. "You're right, she's at a difficult age," she agrees, changing the subject, "and nobody knows what she would be like if she wasn't—you know. The odd one out. Don't let her adopt you."

"Adopt me?" I laugh, secretly relieved that Karen has identified what I suspect might become a problem.

"She has this thing about New York City. Of course she's never been to a place larger than Shaftsboro, except once on a school trip to D.C. It's all windmills. But if she makes a nuisance of herself, just tell me—oh, that's the car. Listen, you're welcome to stay for dinner, Anna."

We look at each other for a moment and, I think, understand each other tolerably well. So I return to my desk for an hour, then change into a clean blouse and join a very polite Walsh family at the long wooden table in the garden, between the apple trees that are hanging heavy with fruit. There is fried chicken, which I have to decline, rosemary potatoes, pea mash, buttermilk biscuits, tomato and bean salad, and warm blueberry pie. I have more carbohydrates on my plate than Irene eats in a week.

"Are you happy with that, ma'am?" Pop Walsh nods skeptically at my food.

"I am, sir, thank you." I'm not sure whether he is mocking me with the courtesy title, but I'm not taking any chances. Karen calls me Anna now, and so does Jules, who turns up late, and whose air of defiance I decode as worry that I may have squealed on her. I haven't, but I'm still annoyed about the sticky puddle of cola on my porch, so I don't reassure her with the smile she clearly hopes to catch from me. Instead, I stroke the dogs, of which there are two, Olive Oyl, the black giant schnauzer I met when I first came, and a chocolate-colored pointer called Jeanie, who is only moderately interested in me. Olive is still very much the exuberant puppy, with her paws on my thigh to see what I am about. I would indulge her, but the moment Pop spots her, he firmly orders her away from me.

"I don't mind," I assure him.

"But I do. We don't spoil our dogs."

I change tack, turning to Howie. "So tell me what I'm eating."

He looks at me with that mixture of alarm and lack of comprehension typical of people addressed in a foreign language. He resembles his soft-featured mother more than his handsome father, but he is not an unattractive man. He is, however, a very quiet man. So far, I have exchanged precisely one word with him ("Hello." "Hello…"), and I figure if I can't get him to talk about tomatoes, I can't get him to talk, period.

"Black cherries," he says, poking at the contents of his bowl. "And Aunt Ruby's, the green ones. Aunt Ruby's German Greens. They're both heirlooms."

"Heirlooms? Sounds as if you should wear them round your neck. You know, like hippy beads."

The twins stare at me, open-mouthed, and Jules gives me an appreciative grin.

"Far out," she says. "For Goths. Black tomato necklace. You'd have juice dripping out, like blood…gory!"

"Julianne!" her mother reproves her, but without much emphasis. She is more concerned to rescue her husband. "'Heirloom' means it's an old variety, a sort people used to grow in the old days, or that grew in the wild and were later cultivated. Not the sort produced by industrial farming."

"So you produce both industrial and…um, heirloom vegetables? Is that why there's an 'organic' sign at the top of the road?"

"It's my hobby," Karen says a little hastily, as if she was already taking up too much time talking about herself.

"Fruit," Pop Walsh says. "Tomatoes are fruit." He says it kindly, like an expert explains the basics of his discipline to a freshman, while he opens a bottle of beer and pours it for his son.

"It's something to do with the seeds, isn't it? If it has seeds, it's a fruit?" I sound a little too eager to demonstrate my knowledge.

Pop looks straight down at the bottle opener in his hand, and I could swear he is amused, but his face hasn't changed at all. "I never asked you whether you'd like a beer, ma'am," he says. "It's made locally in a small brewery."

Is that another dig? Yankee tourist exploring the indigenous culture.

"Is it nice?" I ask, a little too politely.

He shrugs and reaches for my empty water glass and pours it half full, as if I am a child that is not yet allowed an adult-size portion. It almost makes me laugh. I wouldn't want to be in Howie's shoes for the world, or in Grandma Shirley's, for that matter. On the other hand, I bet Shirley had a good time in bed with him. Maybe still has.

"It is nice," I report after two sips. "Tangy."

He gives Jules a quick nod and she trots off, meekly enough, to bring another bottle from the kitchen.

"Karen, will you share?" I ask her. "I'm worried if I have a whole bottle, I'll be pleasantly plastered tonight, but useless in the morning."

"Oh, I—" She exchanges an uneasy glance with Howie, who looks down at his plate. "No, thanks, I better not."

Grandma Shirley looks up from her piece of chicken with a sudden alertness that clashes with her usual, quiet demeanor, and even Pop sits up in his chair as if he had heard the sound of the cavalry in the distance.

"I might as well tell you, too, Anna—I'm…expecting. It's early days yet, so…I have to be careful. No alcohol, no coffee. No coffee is worse, to tell you the truth." She giggles a little, but to me it sounds nervous rather than delighted. Not everyone is cheered by the good news. The twins seem oblivious, but Jules is chewing her food as if it had been sitting on the counter for a week and begun to smell. I am very careful not to catch her eye, precisely because my instinct is to side with her.

Pop lifts his glass.

"God is good. If he wills it—here's to Howard Walsh III!"

My smile is as broad as anyone's, and I drink before I realize that this was not a joke. Pop Walsh is casting Karen's undeveloped fetus as the—apparently long-awaited—Calderbrook tomato princeling. In an urgent undertone Shirley asks Karen for details, while Pop and Howie sort out some farm business; I suspect that both the women and the men are channeling the same anxieties. I feel so much like an outsider that I take refuge in starting a conversation with Jules about her driving instruction. It is as if my affinity with the teenage girl struggling to leave home was stronger than my affinity with the adults who have made theirs. I have no home yet, nor am I sure how I would know if I had.

Home is where the heart is.

Well, in that case my home is my desk.

One of the twins—I can't tell them apart at all; they are both fair and pudgy—kept a beady eye on me while her grandfather was saying grace, and when the hubbub about the new baby has calmed down, she looks over.

"Doctor…will you come to church with us next Sunday?"

She is old enough to know that this is a charged question, but it is not a rhetorical one.

"I'm afraid not, no."

She gets a nudge from her sister, whose face is a study in curiosity and mischief.

"Do you go to another church? Are you a Catholic?"

"Dolly…" Karen makes a half-hearted attempt.

Since deflection fails, I go for the full frontal.

"No, I'm not a Christian at all. I'm Jewish."

This information shuts them up for about half a minute.

"What, like—in the Bible, like the Jews who—" Dolly blushes up to the roots of her wheaten hair at what she doesn't have the courage to say.

"The Lord Jesus was a Jew." Pop Walsh speaks, and no prophet addressing the Children of Israel ever had as *shtum* an audience. "And so were his mother Mary, and Joseph, and all the disciples."

"But—"

A glance from those steely eyes quells Dolly as effectively as it would have quelled me, but Grandma Shirley seems to rate the twins' spiritual enlightenment higher than the adults' embarrassment.

"Howard, if they have questions about the Bible, I think they should be allowed to ask."

He considers his wife's mild but firm intervention.

"Well—what's your question, Dolly?"

The twins have been feverishly exchanging views under their breaths and Dolly rises to the occasion.

"If Jesus and Joseph and Mary were Jews, why are we Christians?"

Go on, Solomon, I think grimly. *Do your shtick.*

"You should know the answer to that one," he replies without hesitation. "You know that your Grandma's father brought his family to this part of the world from the west of Germany?"

They nod.

"My great-grandfather came from County Antrim in Ireland. So why are we Americans, even though our families used to be German, in Grandma's case, and Irish and Scottish, in my case?"

While the girls are trying to negotiate this masterly bluff, I wait to see whether the blue eyes will glance over at me. They do, and I have to grin. *Well done, Pop.*

"Lieberman is a German name?" Grandma Shirley makes her statement sound like a question.

"Well, sort of. My father's family came from Warsaw, about a century ago."

"Ah, so that was…before…"

"Yes, in nineteen oh-six. But my grandmother's family escaped from Hamburg in thirty-five."

"Why did she have to escape?" Jenny has picked up the shift in the atmosphere and it makes her uncomfortable. Her question releases a chorus of sighs in the room, and Jules roughly elbows her in the ribs.

"Dumbass!" she hisses under her breath. "*Hitler!*"

"Oww! Who is Hettler? Dad, Jules hit me!"

In a concerted effort, Karen and Shirley start planning their trip to Georgia, where they are going to spend Thanksgiving week with Howie's sister and her family. The girls quietly spoon their blueberry pie and occasionally glance up with a mixture of speculation and rancor that has, I think, much to do with my withholding the story of my adventurous grandmother, who made a dare-devil escape from Germany pursued by a villain called Hettler.

"I hope you didn't hate it!" Karen whispers urgently when she sees me off an hour later amidst a flood of apologies. Of course I didn't. What's to hate? The food was delicious, the Walshes were civil, if not exactly friendly to me, and I found them fascinating to watch. My heart is at peace as I walk from the main house toward my cottage, which is a dark shape against the gray backdrop of the forest.

Oddly enough, I, too, am dealing with pregnancy. Academically. Not like Karen, who is breeding a child in her belly and will have to endure, for the next seven or eight months, her family's fervent hope it may be a boy. What if it's another girl? Here she is, her first daughter a beautiful teenager of mixed race, clearly even more confused about her identity than other fifteen-year-olds, and those blonde, rather unattractive twins. It would be better for all concerned if her next child was a boy.

I have never been pregnant, except possibly once for about eight hours, when Ciaran was too stoned to use the condom properly and I rushed off for a morning-after pill. I still feel about pregnancy and motherhood the way I felt about them when I was fourteen: I assume they will one day happen to me, but they would be unthinkable right now. While my mother went from dread that her daughter might get knocked up in college to the explicit appeal Not To Leave It Too Late, my own feelings on the subject have not changed at all. Have not *matured* at all, Mom would say if I gave her half a chance. Maybe she is right.

"Hey!"

A breathless form materializes in the dusk just as I'm about to step up to my porch.

"Jules! You startled me!"

"Sorry, sorry!" She is quietly panting. "I just wanted to say sorry about the other day. About the soda."

"That's okay. No harm done." I feel sorry for her, but the last thing I want is to encourage her to make me her Agony Aunt. I briefly touch her shoulder to make up for the neutral tone of my voice, and her face clears.

"So we're okay?"

"Yes, Jules, we're okay. Don't worry. Good night!" I leave her standing in the dusk and firmly shut the door behind me.

For the first time since I fanned them out in a corner of the study, I go to squat over the medical textbook illustrations that I will talk about at a conference on Medieval and Early Modern Iconography at Notre Dame University in November.

My subject is drawings included in sixteenth- and seventeenth-century works on anatomy; the first verisimilar images of dissected human bodies ever to be made in Western Christian culture. Nearly everyone who first sees them goes "Ewww!" because these are no naïve, symmetrically schematic drawings. These are the walking dead who display the functions of their bodies with a lack of self-consciousness that is both grotesque and graceful: a muscleman who—the better to show off the play of his limbs—has flayed himself and is holding the knife in one hand and his own skin in the other; a skeleton that leans nonchalantly against a pedestal, its ankles crossed and elbows bent to allow the viewer to see its joints. Naked females, depicted in the pastoral or urban settings of classical antiquity, their legs lasciviously spread and their abdominal walls peeled away like negligées, who display their reproductive organs complete with little mannikins huddling in their wombs.

These dissected pregnant ladies—and the web of iconographic codes and biblical symbols in which they are embedded—are my main focus of research at this moment. I have a feeling that Pop Walsh, if I tried to explain my fascination, would laugh me out of town, and Karen would smile politely and count the weeks and days of her own term. We do live in very different worlds, but that does not mean we cannot share a tomato salad and a beer occasionally.

It is still warm, and I go to bed with the window open to the forest's sounds of silence.

Chapter 8

"Dead woman walking!" Tim cries under his breath as he guides me along the hall into the classroom wing.

I'm too jittery to be distracted by his ribbing. It took me half an hour to get dressed this morning, only to end up with the same clothes I had put on first: a silk-and-cotton A-line skirt in a dark reddish-brown, a floral print blouse with three-quarter sleeves, and—the secret's in the shoes—red leather strap sandals with heels. In New York, I would have made sure to wear at least one black item of clothing, not because black is the New York uniform but because black exudes authority and makes you look older. But for some reason this morning I felt that black wouldn't be the right choice for my Ardrossan students. Now I wish I was dressed in the armor of Edward, the Black Prince of Wales.

"Hang on, this is me." Tim compares the number on the classroom door with the note in his folder. "Good luck! Oh, and Anna? You have to be gentler with our freshpeeps than with the scholarship kids from Brooklyn."

"Oh, c'mon, Tim! Give me a little credit here."

Walking into my classroom is like walking into an oven. The room has big south-facing windows that we will be glad of during the winter months but today, the thermometer by the main entrance of the Observatory already showed eighty-one degrees Farenheit when I arrived two hours ago. It is one of Murphy's laws that central A/C invariably breaks down in the first teaching week of the semester.

Thirty-three young people are lounging in their chairs, some openly curious, whispering with their neighbors as I arrange my pen, books, lists, and hand-outs on the desk, others pretending to ignore me. After the comforting routine of taking attendance I explain that I will hand out and discuss the syllabus at the end of the session.

"First I'm going to be boringly predictable for a moment. I'll try to be excitingly wild and erratic later on." This earns me my first titters of amusement. "Can someone define the term 'comedy' for us?"

One finger shoots up; it belongs to a ginger-haired boy in the last row.

"Yes — Logan, isn't it?"

"That's me, ma'am. Could we open the door, ma'am, to — " He waves his hand around to signify circulation. There are a few giggles, but they are nervous giggles. I have been challenged, and it takes me a second to overcome an instinctive reluctance to teach my first class for anyone to hear who walks along the hallway.

"Sure, be my guest." In subtle retaliation I remain where I am and smile my permission at him to stand up and walk over to the door himself.

Several of my prospective English majors are of the eager beaver variety, girls who always do their homework and don't let the teacher down. The eager beavers may not produce flights of fancy but they do keep a class afloat. We sort out that the everyday use of the term "comedy" has to be distinguished from its scholarly use and that a comedy is not necessarily belly-laugh funny.

"Isn't the difference that at the end of a tragedy everyone is dead, and at the end of a comedy everyone is married?" says a girl wearing a bandana to keep her bright blond curls out of her face.

"That's a little simplistic, but yes, let's work with this definition. How would you categorize, say, *Titanic*? The event was, we all agree, tragic. The hubris of one man leads to the death of hundreds. But how would we categorize the genre of the movie? Kate Winslet doesn't get to marry Leo di Caprio; that seems to rule out comedy. But do you remember the narrative frame of the movie?"

A low murmur arises as they begin to get involved in the debate, and I inwardly sigh with relief. I think I've got them. I make eye contact for a quick second with bandana girl and grin at her; she grins back.

"Now. If at the center of drama is the conflict between Life and Death, except that in comedy Life prevails while in tragedy Death prevails—" the class hurriedly starts scribbling notes "—then comedy and tragedy are basically about the same issues, but in different… flavors. Different *modes*. Now, I'd like to turn two more corners with you, and then we'll probably just have time to look at a very short text. Can we think about the origins of drama for a moment? Because I believe that an anthropological perspective will allow us to see even more clearly how comedy and tragedy are flip sides of the same coin."

This is either slightly over their heads, or not interesting enough after Leonardo di Caprio.

"Well, what cultural practices did people engage in that would, over time, develop into theatre?"

"Reality TV." Logan, his long hair flopping over one eye, evidently aspires to the position of class clown.

"Well, obviously, reality TV," I agree, poker-faced. "What else?"

They confer amongst themselves, and finally someone tentatively offers me "ritual."

"Precisely, and the point of all these aboriginal rituals is the survival of the community, isn't it? We dance, so that the gods may send rain or the return of sunlight. But if you're making a deal with someone, you have to give something in return—sacrifice."

"The Legend of the Five Suns," says a slim boy who had not so far spoken up. I ask him to explain to the others, and he does, very articulately, but also a little diffidently. Note to self: remember to encourage the shy ones.

"What about religion?" asks one of the eager beavers.

"We've just been talking about religion," Jocelyn with the bandana rebukes her.

"No! Proper religion! Christianity."

"Sure, same thing." Jocelyn is obviously willing to take control of the discussion, and I step back and watch my first class session crash and burn.

"Christianity isn't one of those primitive, bloodthirsty rites!"

"It is so! You have a god, or the son of a god, and he is sacrificed to save mankind. It's the same as in the Aztec legend, and there're dozens of myths like this, all over the world! In fact—" Jocelyn leans forward, and I feel a shiver of fear "—Christians *eat* their god every Sunday, in little pieces!"

There is a beat, and then a storm of outrage breaks. About half of the students are engaged in heated debate, but the other half are sitting quietly, and two or three actually look distressed. They are freshmen, after all.

"All right, break it up, people! Break it up, come on!"

Some appear to be relieved that I am taking control again; others are reluctant.

"You see how charged with controversy our topic is, and it is brilliant that we have discovered it all by ourselves, without any help from theorists or critics."

They have settled down again and are listening, and hardly any face shows the glassy lethargy that usually envelops a class two-thirds through.

"Okay." The muscles in my stomach relax. *Easy, now.* "So, this semester we are going to look at *comic* versions of this tale of sacrifice and survival. The plays we will read together accentuate the aspect of revival, but I think we understand now that even the brightest, fluffiest comedy suppresses its tragic twin, a tale of loss and sacrifice. Over every comedy looms the danger that the sunlight will *not* break through the clouds, or that the rain might *not* come. Can you think of dangers to the survival of a community that have nothing to do with murder or other forms of violence?" This stumps them. "How do tribes and peoples die out?"

"Not enough babies." This comes from Logan again, who is clearly hoping to throw me.

"And to produce babies, men and women have to have sex. *That*—and the ways in which these—um—negotiations can go wrong—is what early modern comedy is mainly about. Let's have a look, if you will—" I get up from the desk on which I had been sitting to distribute the first batch of hand-outs "—at how Shake-speare addresses this issue in his first sonnet."

"I don't think it's appropriate to discuss this sort of thing in class." A girl in a yellow silk blouse is holding the sheet of paper in her hand as if it were a soiled diaper. "In fact, I think it's very inappropriate."

"What sort of thing?"

"Sex and all that."

"We're not discussing sex," I say calmly. "But thank you for raising that issue—Marleen, right? I'd like to make this unmistakably clear: we're discussing a Shakespearean sonnet that happens to be about procreation. Okay, about sex. Our subject is the literary representation of the world, not the world itself. If you want that, stick to Political Science or Biology."

"I'd like to," she murmurs. "And my name is Madeline."

I smile at her, and I think she knows perfectly well what I mean but am not saying: you have three weeks to drop out, baby, and welcome to!

We read the sonnet quatrain by quatrain, but the language is too involved for them to catch its drift right away. Slowly I take them through the nature metaphors.

"You promised us sex!" Logan, for one, is unable to distinguish the tale from the teller or, in this case, the topic from the teacher. My impulse is to step on him, but I am supposed to be gentle with them, so I ignore him and the guffaws he provokes.

"This is a lookist poem," Jocelyn mutters. "Gorgeous people should have children so their gorgeousness lives on."

"Aren't the first sonnets addressed to a young man?" the shy boy, Lucas, cautiously offers. "And isn't the young man gay?"

Madeline flings herself against the back of her chair in an outbreak of exasperation; there are some audible groans in the room, and not of the good variety.

"No, no, hang on—it's not as bad as all that!" A sarcastic undertone creeps into my attempts to keep them calm. "You are right—Shakespeare played around with the traditional sonnet by replacing the poet-lover's unattainable lady with an unattainable boy. But this boy, the implied reader of the poem, isn't gay; that's not the point. What *is* the point?"

"He's a hoarder. He hoards food, the harvest produce, and other people starve." This comes from one of Logan's neighbors, a guy with shoulders like an action hero, who is evidently better at poetry than he looks.

"Excellent, now apply this metaphor to human beings."

"He's hoarding…no." He blushes and shakes his head.

"Yes." I grin at him. "Well, I've been suggesting to you that all this boy-meets-girl stuff in literature is, in essence, an enactment of ancient fertility rites. Renaissance England, being an agricultural society, was still closer to these realities than we are today, so we must expect Renaissance literature to be quite outspoken. The poet — in the persona of a fatherly friend or tutor — is encouraging the young man to settle down with a wife and procreate, to make sure that his beauty — Shakespeare might have said 'genes,' had he known about them — is passed on to new generations. But this isn't just a procreation sonnet. Let's be explicit about it: what is this 'self-substantial fuel' the young man is wasting?"

Jocelyn's eyes grow wide with comprehension, and of course she is not slow to name the taboo.

"Are you saying it's — he's talking about — *cum?*"

"Let's call it 'semen,' shall we? An Elizabethan word for it is 'spirit.' Yes, it's an anti-masturbation sonnet. Hey!" The noise level has spiked. "Don't blame me, blame Shakespeare!"

The noise is stifled by a movement that darkens the open door, first noticed by those in the last rows, then also by those who were watching my face.

"Oh — hey there, Professor Cleveland."

I'm so high on adrenaline and so pleased to see him that I lock my eyes with his and smile at him in complete innocence. First I think the shock that runs through me is one of embarrassment, but it isn't; it is an immediate, carnal thrill at the sight of that tall figure in dark jeans and shirt sleeves. "You'll be delighted to hear, sir, that we are discussing questions of genre!"

The students cannot know that this is a jab meant to remind him of our first encounter, but the obvious disingenuousness of my assertion sets them off into a roar of laughter.

His eyebrows shoot halfway up his forehead, and I can see that he is struggling to keep a straight face.

"As you were." A curt nod, and he is off.

One down, one to go. The challenges of a class full of English Lit graduates are very different from those of a general education class.

Surprise 'em. Stun 'em.

I hadn't planned to do that, but when I walk into the room — by now it's four o'clock in the afternoon, which seems to be a low point in almost everyone's circadian rhythm—I am suddenly incredibly tired. High on adrenaline all day, and now I crash. I slump into the chair behind the desk, blow air like an exhausted whale, and serenely scan the faces that are already registering confusion about my behavior. Sixteen names are on my list, and I count fifteen, audibly but under my breath, then sigh again.

"The first week of the semester is murder, don't you find? *Man…* I'm pooped."

They are very, very quiet.

"What say we watch something, hmm? I mean, you must have had a long day, too, and I think we all deserve some R&R…" I rummage in my bag and produce a DVD that I insert into the player, switch on the projector and, while I'm waiting till it's ready, I stretch out my legs under the desk, cross my ankles, and stifle a yawn. Good thing that at orientation they showed us how to work the classroom equipment.

"Right, here's the deal," I inform them. "I get to choose the video, and you get to watch it." I'm riding the wave of my impromptu performance, not sure how long it will carry me. "Are you okay with basketball? I hear Ardrossan ain't bad at basketball."

Tessa Shephard in the second row is watching me with an expression of fascinated horror, Selena O'Neal next to her has a pained half-smile on her face, others have started to whisper and giggle. I ignore their consternation and languidly adjust the volume level as moving images of a gym are projected onto the wall.

"Hey! That's Marv Albert!" one of the boys hisses.

"Who?"

"My dad says he was, like, the best basketball commentator ever!"

I settle in my chair and watch Marv announce, "Connie Hawkins, one-time Harlem Globetrotter, one of the most exciting players in the NBA, as a member of the Atlanta Hawks. And The Hawk will be opposed by Paul Simon."

As the camera cuts from six foot eight inch Hawkins to five foot two inch Simon, some of the students are beginning to laugh.

"It's *Saturday Night Live!*" someone whispers triumphantly.

"It's what? Who's the short guy?"

"Shhhh!"

Albert is asking Paul Simon about his uniform number, "decimal point zero two," and Simon explains, perfectly deadpan, that this had been his number since junior high school, and since it wasn't a number used by Hawkins, it would avoid confusion between the two of them. This has the students laugh out loud, and they relax into enjoying the sketch, reassured that their professor — although a little peculiar — isn't certifiably mad.

"So." I smile when I switch off the video machine. "What does all this have to do with parody and satire?"

The session goes like a dream. My unconventional opening gambit has jolted them into attention; they are lively and intelligent, and we have fun together.

Seems I owe Cleveland one.

On Thursday afternoon, as the two student journalists who interviewed me for the next issue of *The Folly Chronicle* have taken the inevitable photo of me and are just winding up, Tim sticks his head through my half-open office door.

"This is an intervention — oh, hi, Kirsty, Josh — oh, right — interview for *The Folly*! That's great!"

He seems jumpy, even for him. I understand why when I show the students to the door, and Tim steps out of the way to reveal Giles Cleveland and Tessa Shephard among the junk in the hall.

"This is…quite a crowd," I observe dryly, hoping to cover my confusion.

The students pick up the scent of a good story and are discreetly kicking their heels by the garbage container, but Cleveland makes short shrift of them.

"Off you pop, folks. Go on, on yer bikes."

He doesn't seem to see me. At least he sees no reason to acknowledge my presence in any formal way. Instead, he looks around my office, shaking his head.

"How long were you going to wait till something was done about this?"

"As long as *I* consider reasonable, in view of the fact that it is *my* office!" From the corner of my eye I see Tessa grimace at Tim as if to say, *Told you this was a crap idea!*

Cleveland seems unmoved by my belligerence. "And what kind of a cock-and-bull story do you tell the students to explain the state of this place?"

"Administrative miscommunication." I know I'm blushing. The students are visibly shocked when they enter my office and as visibly reluctant to swallow my cover-up tale.

"You can say that again," he mutters under his breath while staring at the pile of torn ring binders that sits crookedly on top of a crate with posters advertising a number of academic events that happened decades ago. "Well—out it all goes. Matter of minutes."

"So Elizabeth Mayfield said we can chuck it?"

"Elizabeth?" This comes with a frown and eye contact, suddenly.

"Y-Yes, she promised me to do something about—this—when I spoke to her last Friday. I assumed—I assume you're the relief force?"

Cleveland is gazing down at me, clearly at a loss, and I am so overwhelmed by his physical proximity in this cramped space that I feel my eyes flicker.

"Yes," he says. "We're the relief force."

He takes off his jacket and flings it across my swivel chair, and my little office is filled with the glistening light of a white shirt in the sun. When he undoes his cuffs and starts to roll up his sleeves, I have to look away.

We set to work, and apart from a slapstick moment with a moldering box full of fanfold paper—its bottom drops out and so do lengths and lengths of yellowed paper, tripping up both Giles, who was carrying it, and Tessa behind him—there are no mishaps.

"When you come across any slates and chalk, don't chuck them; the museum might want them," Giles says. "And the hornbooks, and the rolls of vellum."

"Actually, this is nothing," Tessa gasps, steadying herself against my desk. "Mel and I once got a look into his office, Professor Corvin's, I mean. Did you ever—? Well, it's the messiest place you ever saw! Actually, no, not all that messy, not like this, just completely stuffed full of...stuff. All the walls up to the ceiling, including the window! And piles of boxes, one in front of the other. You can hardly get into the room, it's like walking into a tiny closet full of clothes, only his is full of paper."

"Does he have family?" I ask. "Someone to look after him? He looks the type who'll lie dead in his apartment for weeks till the neighbors notice a smell."

"He once told me of a daughter, but she was then living in Vermont." Tim shrugs. "Keep your nose peeled, Anna."

"Morbid much, Tim?"

"This looks official. Are you sure we can just—?" Tessa is holding up a plastic folder. "It says nineteen seventy-five to eighty-four, A through L on the back. There's only the one, though, and the ink is—"

"I'll take that." Giles reaches over and, with a smile, wrests it from her hands. "If it's anything eggy, it had better end up on my face, not yours."

Half an hour later the container in the hall is spilling over, and my office is a dusty but *empty* room.

"Needs a good scrubbing," Cleveland observes, hands propped up on his hip bones. "And the walls need painting."

"I can do that tomorrow. Well, not the painting, but—thank you so much, this is—" I have to laugh out loud, I am so glad that he has bullied me into submission "—this is absolutely fabulous!"

"What it *is*—" he smiles "—now that it's out of this office and in the hallway, is a fire hazard. If they don't have it removed ASAP, they'll get into trouble with the fire marshal. Does your phone take pictures?"

"Mine does," Tessa offers when I hesitate.

"Mine does, too, but—"

"Tell maintenance to pick up the cart, and if they don't, send a picture of it to Health and Safety, and to the Dean."

"They'll be here faster than you can say asbestos," Tim adds.

"Whoa, hold your horses! I'm grateful for your help, sir, but I'm not going to bring out the big guns quite yet!"

"Why not?" Tim gingerly dusts off his pants. "I'm not coming up here every week to clean up after a crazy old man no one has the guts to fire, or after a newbie who hasn't the guts to stand up to admin!"

"It isn't a question of guts! But I don't want to make a fuss, and—"

"You're being too English about this."

"W-What?"

Cleveland is gazing down at me with an expression on his face that under any other circumstance I would call—no. No, no.

"The waiting game might work with Brits; in fact, there it's the done thing, and damnably inefficient it is, too. But it won't wash here. If you allow them to walk roughshod over you now, they'll never forget that you're…a soft touch."

"Well, I'm—I'm not," I stutter, valiantly suppressing the fantasy contained in those two monosyllables.

"I know that." He reaches across my desk for his tie and jacket, scooping up the old folder as if by the way. "But you have to make sure they know it, too."

Stunned and mildly agoraphobic I sit in my empty office and try to decide whether to go downstairs to the car at once to fetch my cleaning utensils, or leave it till tomorrow. An almost inaudible knock on the door interrupts me—but it is only Tessa.

"Sorry, Dr. Lieberman—I just had to come and check that you're all right."

Her freckled face looks apprehensive, and I am flooded with a rush of affection for her.

"Only if you drop this Dr. Lieberman nonsense once and for all and call me Anna!"

She grins, pushes herself into the room and shuts the door behind herself.

"You're not mad at Giles, are you?"

The tension drains out of my body, and I flop against the back of my chair, which gently rocks me on its springs.

"I was worried you'd think him a bully," she rushes on. "Because he isn't, really. That's why I chose him as my advisor. Well, partly; it's also that I wanted to work on Renaissance drama. I think he cares about you, that's why—"

"He *what?*"

"No, I mean—" She blushes so fiercely that her freckles disappear. "He feels responsible, and he is right, you know. You could write emails till the cows come home, and Hornberger would make all sorts of promises if you approached him in person, but—it's difficult, sorting out Professor Corvin, so he ignores it."

"Cleveland might have asked first."

"That's what I thought. But he said you'd only…um…put us off."

"What exactly did he say, Tessa?"

She grins. "He said, 'She'll only tell us to take a long jump off a short pier.'"

As Tessa and I are walking down the stairs, Madeline, the straight-laced girl from my Comedy class, approaches us from downstairs with two friends. The stairs aren't broad enough for five, and we slow down to pass each other. She seems uncertain whether to acknowledge me or not, so I smile at her and say hi, when she suddenly glares at me, eyes narrow and nostrils wide.

"You are *so* in trouble!"

"Pardon me?"

"Wait for it!" she shouts down at me, halfway up to the second floor.

I am too stunned to react quickly, but when I recover, my first impulse is to run after her to confront her.

"No! Oh, sorry—" Tessa blushes furiously for having grabbed my sleeve to stop me.

"What? What is it?"

She points her thumb in the direction of the great hall, and we walk down. "That's Madeline Harrison," she whispers. "*The* Harrisons?"

"You say that like I would say *the* Corleones."

"Well, not quite, but her uncle was governor a few years ago, and her father runs the family company, something biochemical, I don't know exactly, but Harrison Lab, down the road—they donated that to the college, like, fifteen years ago."

"Oh, no. Don't tell me I've alienated the one frosh who can get me fired!"

"Well, *have* you?"

"Are they very conservative and very religious? Of course they are, what am I asking?" I close my eyes to recall my chaotic first session with the gen. ed. class. "Christianity as a primitive religion; comedy as a fertility rite; homosexuality, except that wasn't my fault and we didn't expand on that; and masturbation in Shakespeare sonnet number one. Nothing much to upset anyone. Right?"

Tessa stares at me like she did when I sat down to make them watch basketball instead of teaching them about early modern literature.

"Wow!" she breathes. "You are *so* in trouble!"

The weight of having committed two *faux pas* drops to the bottom of my stomach: one, I misjudged what my freshmen can take in their first session, and two, I told a grad student about it. But I will not be moved.

"Oh, come on—surely not. Remember, this is a coeducational, non-sectarian liberal arts college! You don't get into trouble for talking about Shakespeare's sonnets!"

"Hi, Mom."

I wedge the receiver into the crook between neck and cheek as I lie on my sofa like a slug and stare catatonically up at the ceiling fan. Its swish-swish is the only noise in the room, punctuated by birds chirping. This is what I have been doing for the past half hour or so, ever since I came home, kicked off my high-heeled sandals, and grabbed a soda from the fridge.

"Listen, Anna, I only got a minute. I talked to Mrs. Krevitz at the grocer's this morning, and guess what? Her nephew is a professor at Ardrossan, too! At the Psychology Department. He moved there last year, so he will be glad of some company, too. Do you have a pen? I'll give you his number."

"Whoa, Mom, not so fast. I only got here four weeks ago and already you're trying to hook me up? And speak slowly, please. I can hardly move a brain cell, let alone a limb."

"Sorry, darling." She relents and dutifully asks, "Did you have an exhausting day? Teaching hasn't started, has it?"

"Yes, this was the first week." Silently I count to ten to overcome the temptation to unburden myself to my mother.

"Okay, *shadchan*," I sigh. "Do your thing."

"Well, like I said, he's doing what you're doing, only in psychology. Mrs. Krevitz says he had a girlfriend here, but they broke up a while ago, and—"

"Mom, if you think I'm going to call a guy who doesn't know me from Adam—or Eve, for that matter—think again. I'm not that desperate. In fact, I'm not desperate at all."

"Why, have you met someone?"

"Mom…"

"Anyway, what's desperate? You're new, he's new, but maybe he already knows a few nice places to eat—what's desperate about that? His name is Bernard Cogan. That's C-O-G-A-N—"

"Bernie Cogan? Bernie Cogan who lived on Ingram Street? I went to school with Bernie, don't you remember?"

"You did? Well, so much the better. You'll have things to talk about!"

"Mom, that was more than fifteen years ago! Bernie used to bully me into giving him my homework to copy."

He also taunted me about my short hair and my absence of cleavage and once gave me a Chinese burn that bruised my arm so badly I couldn't wear a t-shirt for two weeks because I didn't want to have to explain how I got it.

"You didn't give Mrs. Krevitz my number, I hope."

"Yes, I did. Now, don't shout at me—there's really no harm in it. There's more harm in only ever seeing your own colleagues and talking about work all the time. Some change will do you good."

No doubt about that. The idea of sitting in a quiet restaurant in the Real World and making Observatory-unrelated conversation has a definite appeal, but with Bernie the Bully?

"Yeah, maybe. All right, if he calls me, I'll go, but I won't call him first. I'm too old-fashioned for that kind of thing, Mom."

Chapter 9

To celebrate the completion of my first week of teaching at Ardrossan, Tim takes me bicycle-shopping. He claims to "know a little" about bikes, and unlikely as it seems, he is well known to the bearded, tattooed guy who runs the store.

"Hey, professor. If you came to get spares for your Colnago, gotta disappoint you, man."

"No, I'm not here for myself today. Anna, this is Chuck—Chuck, Anna, a new colleague of mine. She's looking for a bike to commute to work."

Chuck assesses my biking credibility which, since I'm wearing a skirt and ankle-strap sandals with heels, can't be impressive. "What you been riding before?"

"Uh—nothing."

Now Tim, too, is staring at me in disbelief.

"But you *can* ride a bike—or are we talking training wheels?"

"Look, I used to ride a bike to school all through high school, and I had a bike in Cambridge, and I shared one when I lived in London. Yes, that means it's been three years since I sat on one, but—well, is it true or isn't it? That you never forget?"

My words echo in silence. Chuck gives himself a mental shake and turns to Tim.

"Gonna do her for a Jamis, a 700c—over here." The men converse in low voices about my options and present me with a choice of three bikes, which I try out on the parking lot behind the store.

"This one, I think."

"Good girl. Helmet."

"Awww…do I have to, Mommy?" I wail, but pipe down when Chuck gives me a stern look.

"Sure don't look purdy, does it? Well, neither does brain matter on asphalt!"

When Tim lifts my new acquisition into the trunk of the Subaru (mental note: send photo of bike in car to derisive Liebermans in Queens), I can't help grinning from ear to ear.

"This is so cool! Thank you very much!"

"You *look* cool on it, too. Now, will you be all right setting it up, or are you going to thank Uncle Timothy by inviting him to the tomato farm for pizza?" The round blue eyes are all innocence.

"Tim, I appreciate your help, and you're welcome to come round to the farm any time you want. But if you were straight, I'd be thinking you're coming on to me — big time. So what's with the attention?"

He groans and contemplates the traffic rushing past for a few moments. "Martin's parents are visiting."

"Martin?"

"My…partner."

"But being nice to the in-laws is part of being married, so — "

"I am not *married!*" he snaps. "I only moved in with Martin because my building was sold and the lease expired, and I didn't want to commit myself to anything, property-wise, before my promotion is through. This is a temporary arrangement, completely unofficial, and I see no reason to become all lovely-dovey with his mom and dad!"

Lots of strong feelings, and none of my business.

"Well — " I shrug " — if you're really up for the drive, and you know a good take-out pizza place between here and there — because the farm ain't got no delivery service, dude — I got beer, and I got soda, and I got a porch to sit on and trees to look at. All yours for fixing the handle bar and adjusting the saddle."

Judging by the cars clogging up the parking space on the farm, the Walshes are having friends round. Tim and I park as best we can; I carry the pizza, the pump, and the helmet; Tim pushes the bike.

"You. Are. So. Weird," Tim breathes as I open the farmyard gate. Dolly and Jenny are playing with a girl their age and a toddler on the swing hanging from the chestnut tree, and Pop, Howie, and two other men are getting the barbeque going. Pop sees me, sees Tim, and I make sure to nod a greeting. First time the new tenant is bringing home a man — that will be food for gossip.

"Weird for wanting to live here? *Living in Ameeeerica*…suits me down to the ground. Along here." I direct him past the main house and the steel barn. The cottage comes into view, blue as the sky on this warm evening, and my heart glows with proprietary pride.

"Mind you, Cleve lives in the sticks, too." Tim shakes his head. "More remote than this, even. Without the farmers."

"Why do you call him Cleve?"

"Oh, from when we were at school. I don't see the appeal, myself, of this rural living."

"You were at *school* together?"

He grins. "I bet that gives you all sorts of salacious fantasies, doesn't it? Foreigners invariably think English boarding schools are hotbeds of adolescent sexual depravity."

"Aren't they?"

"No more than other establishments that lock up several hundred males with each other. *I* had a good time."

"You can't have been there together long," I try with an objective handle. "He's quite a few years older than you are."

"Swee'pea, I'm not as young as I look. Although I obviously prefer being older than I look to looking older than I am."

"Well, three or four years older than me. Right?"

"I'll be thirty-eight before the year is out." Tim is actually blushing. "This is what Shakespeare and I have in common: there are six lost years in our biographies. I doubt, though, that Shakespeare spent them on tenure track at a reputable American university and failed his five-year review."

"You didn't!"

"Let's just say there is a reason why I prefer to keep my closet door carefully closed. Hey, this is neat!"

"Eat your words, city boy, and get comfy. Bathroom, if you need it, is here, but there's a pile of girl's laundry in there, so be warned."

While the pizza is in the oven for quick warm-up, Tim sets up my bike and I exchange my skirt and heels for jeans and Birkenstocks and get rid of my contacts.

"Try this for height," he says when I come down the porch. "And tell that kid to stop staring at the whoopsie."

I look up to where he is pointedly not looking and see Jules sitting on one of the tractors, watching us.

"Hey, Jules!" I shout assertively, because I'm not going to be stalked by the Calderbrook Cinderella. "What's up?"

She jumps off the seat, but instead of making herself scarce, she comes over.

"Is something the matter, Jules? Not to be rude, but you see I have a visitor. So why don't we each look after our own, hm?"

Something clearly *is* the matter. Embarrassment and the desire to make mischief are fighting it out on her face.

"The men are wondering whether he is the man who raped the girl!"

"*What?*"

The shockwave of Tim's reaction makes even Jules flinch.

"Don't shout at me!" she says defensively. "I'm just saying what they're saying!"

"*No* is the answer to that one, kiddo!" Tim seems even more upset than I am.

"Jules," I intervene, "what do you mean, the man who raped the girl?"

She glowers at Tim, who seems absolved from the original accusation but is now in disgrace for having shouted at her.

"Lorna O'Neal—" she cocks her head into the direction of the main house "—works as a secretary at the Folly, and she said that there is a student who was raped by a professor."

"But—when?"

"How should I know? Yesterday, last week?"

"Yes, but recently?"

"Yeah, like—she—or her boss, dunno—found out only this morning!"

Tim shrugs his exasperation. "But that could be anywhere in the college. *If* it's true, that is!"

"It *is* true!" she flings at him. "And it was an English professor! I'm not stupid, you know!"

I am so stunned I have to sit down on one of the steps leading up to the porch. Tim leans on the bike saddle as if he was going to be sick.

"*Jesus F.*—"

"Hey, *pas devant les Chrétiens!*" I turn back to Jules. "Jules, this kind of information would be top secret, absolutely and totally confidential. Your parents' friend wouldn't be allowed to share this."

"It's all confidential," Jules says petulantly. "She told my mother. I overheard them. And Bill O'Neal told Grandpa and Howie."

"And you told us." Tim and Jules are no dream team. She glares at him, her cheeks dark with resentment.

"Okay, I'll go back and say it *is* you! I'm a rat, after all, so what do you expect!" She stalks off toward the group of men who have been watching us.

"Honestly, Tim…"

"The little punk. How come she's black? Is she adopted?"

"Sort of. The daughter-in-law was married before, so Jules is the, uh, black sheep of the family. Be nice."

"She isn't really going to tell them I'm a rapist, is she?"

"I doubt it. And even if she did, they wouldn't believe her."

"Because that would be really ironic, if I was lynched by a mob of rednecks who think that I raped a woman!"

"The Walshes are no rednecks, Tim!"

He looks at me like a very troubled baby, his convex forehead deeply lined. "Let me get my phone."

In the shade of my living room, the news seems even more ominous than in the bright sunlight outside.

"Just because someone was accused doesn't mean someone else was really raped," I think aloud, somewhat incoherently. "I hate to say this, but—it might be a trumped-up harassment charge, filed by some snowflake to be revenged on a professor who gave her a 'C' for her essay."

Tim looks up, and I have not yet seen him so grim. He actually looks his age for once.

"I wouldn't have said it if you hadn't," he admits. "But ten to one it'll turn out to be something like that. Boning student totty is one thing, but actual *rape?* I don't believe it."

"Oh, snap! You know what we're doing, don't you?"

"We're blaming the victim."

"Exactly. For shame! Who are you calling?"

He sits on my sofa with his phone in his hands. "Who'd know?"

"Ma Mayfield knows, for sure, as Dean of Studies, but—"

We stare at each other, overawed at the thought of phoning Elizabeth Mayfield on the little matter of a scandal involving a student, a professor and a count of sexual assault. Then we collapse in a fit of hysterical laughter.

"You call her Ma Mayfield?" Tim asks. "That's perfect! Why does it ring a bell, though? *Ma Mayfield...*"

"*Brideshead Revisited.* The nightcl—"

"The nightclub Charles and Sebastian go to in London, where they get sloshed and pick up those two prostitutes! Ma Mayfield is the proprietress! Oh, that is *perfect!*" Tim cackles. "Wait till I tell Giles!"

"Oh, no! No, Tim, please!"

"Well, whoever he is, and whatever he did, Ma Mayfield is going to have his balls for this!" he says gleefully. "And God have mercy on his degenerate soul!"

"Actually, whatever he did or didn't do, God is his best bet, because his career is finished." As the implications sink in, I'm beginning to feel nauseous, with the shock, with hunger. "Heck, I forgot the pizza!"

I bolt into the kitchen, which is already thick with the smell of burnt dough, though not yet with smoke. I save what can be saved, put it on a tray with two bottles of beer, and find Tim on the sofa, still immobile.

"And?"

He shakes his head. "Don't know. First things first. Cheers!" He takes a long pull. "The thing is, we don't want to be hasty here. This may still turn out to be a misunderstanding. I never heard of a sec called O'Neal, so she isn't one of ours. If she works at the Observatory, I'm sure I'd know her name."

"Hang on—why is the name familiar to me but you say you don't know her?"

"O'Neal? Selena O'Neal is one of our students. She's one of—"
He stops dead.

"—one of the new grad assistants recommended by Nick Hornberger," I complete his sentence.

"Holy shit!"

"Yes, but—no, Tim, that—no, come on! Would the whole family be visiting friends and having beer and barbeque, if the daughter had just come home with the news that her professor had molested her? That isn't likely. In fact, whoever it is, it's not the O'Neal girl."

"You're right. Anyway, she's hardly Nick's type." Absentmindedly he reaches for a piece of pie and starts chewing.

"*Does* Nick sleep with students?" I despise myself for using this opportunity to find out the dirt about my colleagues, but not enough to shut up.

"Does the sun rise in the east?"

"With Natalie? America's Next Top Model?"

 Tim grins through his pizza.

"You're quick. Yes, Natalie's the current flavor of the month."

"Current?"

"Nick and I don't share our weekend score over a beer on Monday nights. But to the best of my knowledge he's had one on the go most times since I came here. Everyone knows, everyone looks the other way, even Elizabeth, Dancey, and Ruffin, because he has never been reported and because he's an Ardrossan alumnus and knows all the important people, both on and off campus. Plays golf with the dads and then goes and does their daughters. You gotta admire the guy. In a way."

"Yeah, right."

"As long as they're of age—"

"I keep having this conversation with people! I don't care who Hornberger sleeps with, as long as it's consensual and he remains able to do his job efficiently and impartially! But *is* he? And if he *isn't*, is that because he has sex with the daughters or because he plays golf with the fathers?"

"Have you ever…" Tim peters out discreetly.

"Played golf?"

"Noooo…"

"No, Tim, I haven't! And yes, I'm almost as cynical about it as you are. But this—apparently—wasn't consensual! And I'm not even sure that I know what consensual means, if it's a case of a professor sleeping with a student!"

"Nick isn't the raping sort." He dismisses my objection and my heat.

"And who, in your opinion, is the raping sort?"

"All right. It's impossible to tell. Joe Banks had a fling with a grad student, but she left a while ago, and she was good people. And it can't be any of my brothers in the closet, unless it's a really, *really* devious double bluff."

"Is Dolph Bergstrom in your closet?" I ask, curious.

"Ha! No. But doesn't Dancey wish he were! Mind you, I have sometimes wondered how far Doofus would go, brown-nosing the alpha male. But that would be self-prostitution, not rape."

"Hm. I think I'll decide you don't mean that. Could it be one of the male teaching assistants, or one of the adjuncts? I know Jules said professor, but that may be a misunderstanding. A drunken party at a frat house—wouldn't be the first time."

"That—yes!" Tim sits up, obviously relieved at the thought. "That's perfectly plausible. Bad enough, very bad, but—hell, yeah! It's one of the frat boys! C'mon, let's hang out on your porch. Maybe they'll come over and tell us."

I get him another beer—he assures me he can have another one, for the shock, and still drive home—and offer him the rocking chair, which triggers an extremely funny *shtick* in the character of Laura Ingalls on how she went a-studying in the big city and fell for her handsome professor.

"So, tell me about Martin," I challenge him, innocently.

"What Martin?"

"Don't be an ass."

"I'm not an ass, I'm an arse," he quips but fortunately decides, upon reflection, not to elaborate. "Martin's my man."

"So the moving-in is a temporary arrangement, but Martin isn't."

"No, he isn't temporary. I think."

"And you're really not…out…to the department?"

"I'd say I'm neither out nor in." He shrugs after a baleful pause. "He—or she—who has eyes to see, will see, but I'm a professor on tenure track, not a gay-rights activist."

"Was that the problem the first time round?"

He dismisses the episode like he would swat a wasp away from his face. "With hindsight I'd say that homophobia played into it but that it was only one factor—the most actionable factor, though, which of course made the lawyers focus on it in a way that—ah, well. The whole thing was a nightmare. I don't want to ever be involved in anything like that again."

"And the Winchester connection?"

"You mean, did Cleve get me in here because we were at school together? No, I got this job fair and square!"

Cleveland must have been on Tim's search committee, and among the things I learned about private schools like Eton, Rugby, and Winchester when I was in England is that "old boys" smell each other out like stoats. But I understand that Tim and Cleveland have to pretend to each other, themselves, and the world that this played no part in Tim's appointment.

"So, do tell. *Tim Blundell's Schooldays*. Director's cut."

"Forget it, you salacious little fag hag!"

"Hey! If I wanna know about that time Cleveland rogered you behind the Fives' Court, I'll ask, okay? *Geez!*"

"You don't even know what Fives is, you colonial."

"Whatever. Something posh and brutal to do with a ball!"

He laughs. "Sorry, then. I know Giles had his chances at school. Don't know whether he ever took anyone up on an offer. Of course I had a bit of a crush on him; lots of us did. He was academically top-notch and a member of Lords—the cricket team—and something of a dish, as you can imagine."

I say nothing.

"Well, maybe you can't, but he was. *Is*, I would have thought, although I know he doesn't necessarily appeal to American women."

"He doesn't?" asks Puts-Her-Foot-In-It.

"Well, no—too reserved. The understated charm of the English upper middle-class male is lost on your sisters. There is nothing understated about the sides of hung beef favored by American women."

"Speak for yourself, dear."

"Tell me, Lieberman—" Tim chuckles "—what's the type *you* go for? By the way, I like you in your glasses. The sexy librarian. Have you started looking for some light diversion yet? Nice Jewish Boys are few and far between around here, I'm afraid. There's Freddy Katz, but he's orthodox with half a dozen children. His wife's an assistant professor in the music department. Then there's — oh, *incoming*, eleven o'clock!"

Karen and a woman about ten years older than her are walking toward us from the direction of the main house, their heads bent toward each other in rapid exchange, and I can sense their discomfort from here. As so often in my dealings with the Walshes, I am unsure of protocol. It seems impolite to remain seated till they have come up to us; on the other hand, getting up and walking toward them might be misunderstood to mean that I don't want them on my porch. I take my cue from Tim, who rises from his chair, and together we walk down the steps and wait there.

"Anna, I'm — I'm so sorry!"

"You mean because of Jules? Don't worry, Karen!"

"I'm so tore up about it, sir, I hope you weren't — well, of course you were offended, how could you not be!"

"Don't give her the satisfaction of having riled you," Tim intervenes, and I nod my agreement, but they stare at him as much for the authoritative way he has inserted himself into the exchange as for what he said. Hastily I launch into the introductions, and of course Karen's friend is Lorna O'Neal.

"Your Selena is in one of my classes, isn't she? I'm only just getting to know everyone."

"Well, she mentioned *you*," Lorna says sternly, and I don't know whether this is good or bad. She is a big, tall woman — what fashion magazines nowadays call "full-figured" — with blond highlights and a little too much color around the eyes — but striking, and clearly a very pretty woman when she was younger. I wonder how she gets on with her studious, mousy daughter, and then I wonder how mousy Selena would look if she straightened her shoulders and put on some age-appropriate clothes.

"Selena's a marvel," Lorna continues, "so hard-working and ambitious! I know you wouldn't think it on account of her being so quiet. She has to show more personality, I keep telling her, because she has every right to be confident. I don't mind telling you that she is the first in our family to go to graduate school! That's why the girls talk about you, Dr. Lieberman. You're an example to them."

A Jewish agnostic who talks to first-years about masturbation? I think not.

"Thank you, Mrs. O'Neal, you're very kind," I murmur mechanically. "But about this…rumor."

"Bless you, I'm sure I needn't to stress how very confidential this information is!" She is a self-assured woman, not easily shaken, but she knows perfectly well that she has committed a serious professional blunder that might even be cause for dismissal.

"So, who is it?" Tim asks bluntly. "If it's a secret that can be shared with the general populace, I don't see why you should be cagey about telling us."

"I suspect Mrs. O'Neal feels she oughtn't to tell us," I supply helpfully.

"*Can't!*" she insists. "And that's the truth! I know no more than that, Dr. Blundell. No names, no details. *But,* as right is right, this is too shameful a crime to be swept under the carpet by the college — dearly as they'd like to, I have no doubt!"

"Neither have I," Tim agrees.

I jump in before Tim can go on. "We'd best leave the matter to the authorities and interfere as little as possible. We appreciate the difficulty of your position, Mrs. O'Neal. Please give our best regards to Selena. Is she here, too?"

"No, she — " Lorna can't quite get herself to release Tim from her glare of mistrust. "She decided to stay behind to study."

Tim leaves shortly after the two women, promising to let me know if he finds out anything over the weekend. Through the shock and confusion I feel the pull of the woods. I could take out my new bike, but cycling would distract me from thinking, so I walk. Once through the poplars and across the creek, I cut left, away from the path that will take me past the pickers' camp and round to Calderwood Lane. No more people!

When Tim demanded to know whether I ever had an affair with a professor, I could truthfully answer in the negative. Alex Gresham was no professor. He was a rabbi.

Now *there's* a secret.

About half a mile along a path I never took before, the trees are thinning out and a grassland hill comes into view. Hare Hill, as I learned from the map of the surrounding area that I bought at the gas station. Today I will walk up Hare Hill, although it feels oddly uncomfortable to leave the cover of the forest and to venture out into the open grassland. Why do hares do that?

Alex and I weren't exposed. Not that we did anything wrong, or *morally turpid.* It is just that a recently widowed rabbi, on a curative exchange from Manchester, England, will always prefer for his affair with a twenty-one-year-old volunteer tutor at the temple to remain undiscussed by the yentas. I preferred it, too.

He was the first man I ever made love with. I'd had sex with boys, two or three — but I had not made love with a man. His grief made him both needy and unavailable at the same time; the combination was irresistible to me. We both knew that come August I would leave for the marshy plains of East Anglia, and neither of us ever called that event into question. I was in love, but I was also ambitious.

I sit down on a grassy knoll on top of the hill — no hares to be seen — and rest my chin on my hunched-up knees. The surrounding tree tops, in differing shades of green, have begun to turn yellow and red. Soon it will be autumn.

Why do I have to think of Alex now?

I rang him up when I went to live in London four years later. His phone number was not difficult to find, and I could hear that his first reaction was one of pleasure. But when I suggested a meeting, he backed off. Said it wouldn't be wise, what with my work and all. A week later he turned up, unannounced. We spent the weekend in bed, and I don't believe I have it in me to be happier than during those few days, even though at the end of them he told me that he was getting married again.

That evening I wrote him a letter. What I needed to say was that I loved him and wanted him to marry me. For the first and only time in my life I laid claim to another person, a man. Nothing by return of post; nothing within the week. Then, a small parcel and inside it a small box and inside the box a gray pebble, the size of a child's fist. No note, nothing. His answer to my question was engraved in the pebble: "&".

I have never seen Alex again or spoken to him. There is nothing left to say. I understood what he tried to say, and the pebble is among my most treasured possessions. I broke my heart over him and went back to having sex instead of making love, this time with Ciaran, a man whose wife and child were not dead. For a while I smoked a lot of dope and got little writing done, then I had a sort of breakdown and got no writing done at all. Dark days.

So lost am I in memories that when I hear faint grunts and moans echoing between the trees, I at first think I am hallucinating. That, in turn, worries me enough to make me tread more carefully and to survey the gray-green stillness around me. I have only taken one more turning of the way when off to the left, behind a huge uprooted tree, there is movement. The rhythmic movement and sound of hips smacking against each other.

One of the many things my dope-hazy affair with Ciaran taught me is a certain sang-froid in relation to casual sex. If you start sleeping with the owner of the house in which you share the top-floor apartment with a fellow student, and in which he lives with his wife and new baby on the second floor and runs a second-hand record store on the first floor, and if his wife not only knows about your affair but even claims to condone it, and if you spend an increasing number of evenings in their sitting room, smoking weed, eating Cadbury's chocolate fingers, and making out with your landlord, occasionally his friend and, on one best-forgotten occasion, even his younger brother, you do not flinch when you come across a copulating couple in the woods. I try not to step onto any dry twigs and make myself scarce.

"What the hell!"

Like birds flushed from a thicket, two bodies rush out of the undergrowth in front of me, limbs flailing, giggling, out of breath. They are as startled by my sudden appearance on the scene as I am by theirs, and it would be hard to tell which of us is more mortified when Logan Williams, the aggravating redhead from my Comedy class, and I recognize each other.

"Oh, shit!" He bites his lip, but the cocktail of adrenaline and testosterone in his blood spurs him on. "Dr. L.! What the fuck are *you* doing here?"

His companion, a blond hippy in a corduroy mini skirt and a grass-stained t-shirt, giggles and pulls him along, but as in class, Logan wants to see how I react to his provocation. I give him a sour smile and nonchalantly lean against the tree to my left.

"Not what *you're* doing here, fucking. Run along now. I hope you're using condoms!" I shout after them as they scurry off, giggling again.

What point is there in trying to teach this swaggering bundle of muscles and spermatic cords the subtleties of Renaissance poetry? He embodies the force of nature that comedy seeks to represent and tame, and while he is driven by the sexual energy of youth, he is not at all interested in its representation. And why should he be? Except that someone is forking out thirty thousand dollars a year to keep this kid in school.

I already wasn't looking forward to next week; now I'm looking forward to it even less. I wish the males at Ardrossan were a little less…ardent in their attentions to the opposite sex.

Chapter 10

On Monday morning I cycle to work expecting to find the Observatory shaken by a sex scandal as by a thunderbolt from a storm cloud. But the thunderbolt, insofar as there is one at all, strikes me. I guess it was naïve of me not to expect that there would be some fallout after Giles Cleveland's intervention in my office situation. Except that the fallout is more in the nature of a hurl-out, this time not back into my office — I give thanks for small mercies — but onto the floor space between my office door and the foot of the spiral stairs that lead up to the old observatory in the dome.

I call the janitor, Larry, who insists it isn't his job to clear out occupied offices. I explain that my office should have been cleared out in August, when it was still unoccupied, and that the content of the Dumpster, being mostly books and paper, poses a considerable fire hazard. In case he wonders why the contents of the cart are no longer *in* the cart, I refer him to Professor Andrew Corvin, room E-430. When I return from my library tour and a piece of carrot cake in the Eatery, the mess has disappeared off the floor, but the overflowing Dumpster is still sitting there. So be it. We have bigger problems now.

Upon reflection, I am not surprised that nobody talks to me about Hornberger. Although universities, like all close-knit communities, are rife with rumor, reliable facts are hard to come by at the best of times, and this threatens to be among the worst of times. If there are any fanciful stories at Ardrossan about professors guilty of, as

Tim put it so crudely, boning student totty, they do not reach my ears. Tim does not inform me of what he, no doubt, finds out in the course of the week, and if Yvonne has been filled in by Sam Ruffin, she doesn't let on. This is not a salacious tidbit like discovering two faculty members in the copy room during a Christmas booze-up. This is the violation of a taboo, and our instinctive reaction is to keep well away from it. A storm cloud has gathered above the Observatory, but we all pretend to each other that we haven't seen it.

"Right. Research. Anything in the pipeline?" Giles Cleveland asks me, drumming his fingers on the armrest of his chair.

Is this what the Faculty Mentoring Program calls "close and supportive mentoring of teaching and research activities?" I am the new girl in the Early Modern Studies graduate seminar, and we are assembled in a slightly ramshackle but cozy room across the road in the department of Art History. The floor is carpeted and sprinkled with chalk dust, the low chairs are upholstered and a little frayed. So is our host, Professor Harry Beecher, a potbellied figure in green corduroy and a blue tie, who handed round hot tea in college mugs and spilled sugar over the overhead projector. Eleven students have squeezed onto chairs, stools and boxes, and besides Beecher and Cleveland, there are five more professors from various neighboring departments. It was one of these, a guy with Franklin's "Join, or die" cartoon on his t-shirt and a long ponytail, who asked Cleveland to introduce "your new colleague" to the group.

"Um, well, I have three publications forthcoming, one of them my book. We're herding in the last contributions to a collection that I'm editing with a friend in England, and—"

"About?"

"Pregnancy."

Cleveland freezes, and the laughs are on my side.

"I take it you are speaking metaphorically," he says.

"You bet." I smile, something I find confusing and difficult where Giles Cleveland is concerned. "Pregnancy as a stage image, or a narrative trope, or narrative structure, even. It's a slightly off-the-wall theme, I admit, and we have some rather eccentric contributions, but—"

"The patriarchally circumscribed, ideologically enclosed female body-slash-narrative…" His face gives nothing away, but I know perfectly well that he is mocking me.

"Sometimes it works out like that, yes. But not as predictably as you might think. My main project at the moment is on illustrations in anatomy books, Vesalius and after, and how they adapt religious iconography, for instance that of the pregnant Mother of God, *Maria gravida*. I'm presenting that as work-in-progress at Notre Dame in November, and it—"

"Travel grant," he interrupts me. "Apply, ASAP. Ask Tim how—or Tessa, you could—"

"I can show you the forms, Dr. Lieberman. It's all online," Selena O'Neal offers, her cheeks bright red. She looks feverish, flushed, and pale at the same time, and once I see Tessa surreptitiously reach across and rub her shoulder in a way that strikes me as both comforting and concerned.

"I will, thanks. Listen, I don't know what the local customs are, but—" Just in time I manage to suppress the fatal phrase "*at NYU we used to*" and turn to Cleveland. "Would first name terms be appropriate?"

"Sure." He nods. "I'm Giles."

This time it takes about half a minute for the laughter to die down, and I realize that Cleveland's buffoonery is his way of providing a channel for the tension that thickens the atmosphere. Grad school is an anxious place.

"Hi, everyone, I'm Anna. Anyway, that's the article I'm mainly working on at the moment, the anatomies—"

"But that's out of your field, isn't it?" Professor Beecher interrupts me. He is turning the pages of a stapled document that, absurdly, seems to contain my CV and list of publications. "Your book is on Anglo-American Jewish writing. In fact, I fail to see how you qualify at all for a position in—"

"Dr. Lieberman's dissertation is on performances of civic culture in early modern English towns." Cleveland crosses his legs and shifts in his chair so that his long right leg is like a barrier to the room. "It'll be out early next year, with CUP. *That* one—" he nods at the sheets in Beecher's hand "—she wrote just for fun."

The students murmur amongst themselves, and I recognize the expressions of astonishment and worry on their faces. It is always worrying to hear what people a few years older than you have already achieved. Grad school is also a neurotic place.

For *fun*. Assclown.

Beecher appears to have sorted out my CV, but he is still skeptical. While Cleveland is lounging in his chair and, I suspect, watching me squirm like a boy watches a worm that is pecked at by a bird, Beecher continues to peck.

"But there is no link between either of these topics and the history of medicine. Is that going to be your third field of expertise? Because Jonathan Sawday dealt extensively with those images in the mid-nineties."

"In *The Body Emblazoned*, yes, I know. I wouldn't call it 'field of expertise,' precisely. It's an interest that grew out of my preoccupation with religious iconography. There is a…well, I'm going to *argue* there is an undercurrent of Protestant propaganda, or at least a Protestant impetus in these medical textbooks, particularly in the illustrations, and even more particularly in illustrations of the pregnant female body." I notice that in my eagerness to demonstrate that I am open to questions, I begin to sound as if I needed to justify my research. So I shut up.

"That sounds really interesting. Are you going to give a talk about that here?" Selena asks nervously.

"I don't know." I turn to Cleveland for guidance. "Am I? Would that be—"

"I think it would be extremely advisable to try that out on us before you ram it down the throat of a Catholic audience at Notre Dame."

"I'm not planning to ram anything down anyone's throat, thanks very much!"

Cleveland's lips twitch, and he looks down at his notepad as if he had to remind himself of the next step.

"Right, do you have any questions for Dr. Lieb—for Anna?"

"I do." The girl sitting next to Cleveland raises her hand. "Didn't you find it difficult to get a good job over here? With a British MA and Ph.D?"

"Yes, I did. I'm not going to lie to you. But—"

"And staying in England wasn't an option? Sorry, is it okay if I ask you that?"

"Oh, sure, it's —"

"Well, didn't you want to?"

"Well, I — I couldn't."

"Not enough prospects?"

"Not enough balls."

Cleveland lounges in his chair, watching me.

"You go to the UK to play, Jenna," he says. "And come back to the States to win the game."

"That is not quite how I would put it," I say firmly.

"How would you put it?"

We are looking at each other, and I don't know whether he is doing this on purpose. Cornering me.

"I think I…wouldn't. Put it. At all —" I falter. "I'm here. Hu-hurrah?"

Some of the students find this hilariously funny.

"Hurrah-and-hurrah." Cleveland nods, and then he gives me a smile of such sweetness that it takes my breath away.

After class, I try to get away as quickly as possible, but no such luck.

"Um, Anna, might I have a word?" Cleveland seems reluctant to talk to me, but he beckons me toward the first-floor hallway and I trail him like I trailed Elizabeth Mayfield five weeks ago. Then the place was flooded with sunlight; now the air is burning where the panes of stained glass add a red glow to the sunset. Cleveland pulls his office door hard into its frame, stretches past me, and switches on the light.

"Now, what's going on?" He doesn't even ask me to sit down.

"Pardon me?"

"Look, I know that jet-lag makes me stupid sometimes, but —"

"Oh, well done!" I burst out, remembering. "I read about it in the online *Guardian*. I assumed you didn't want me to say anything in front of the others because you didn't say anything in the faculty meeting, but — may I — *now?* First prize! Well *done*, sir!"

He is staring down at me as if he had forgotten who I am or why I am here.

"Don't call me that."

The ground is gaping wide in front of my feet. I take my heart into my hands and jump.

"Giles, then. You must be so proud of yourself!"

"Thank you. You're very…kind."

I can't tell whether this is an Englishman's habitual belittling of his achievement, or whether he finds me over-familiar and over-enthusiastic. Both, probably, and either way, I know I must back off.

"No, I'm not. Anyway, what was it you wanted to—"

"That's right, you were hoping I'd be trounced!"

"You knew I didn't mean that," I mutter gruffly, and I can tell that the blood is shooting into my cheeks. "What was it you—"

He strides over to the sideboard and dumps his books and laptop on it; I hadn't even noticed that he was still holding them in his hands. "I'm sorry to keep you from your…There is something wrong, isn't there? In the department? It's as if everyone is smelling a stench bomb and nobody wants to admit it."

"What makes you say that?" I ask cautiously, and my punishment is a darkling look across the room.

"Are you telling me I'm imagining things?" he asks bluntly.

"N-No, but I don't—You should ask someone higher up."

"I will. Now tell me what *you* know."

"All I know is that…well, what I heard is that one of our students accused one of our colleagues of sexual violence toward her. Rape, in a word. A professor from the English department allegedly raped a female student."

"Good Lord," he breathes. "Who?"

"I don't know."

"Now look here—"

"No, honestly, I don't know!" I give him a short, unvarnished report of the events so far, and he listens without interrupting me.

"So who else knows?" he asks at last.

"No idea. I haven't spoken to anyone about it."

"But the students know something."

"Selena O'Neal must have tattled. Of course—her mother is the fountain from which this muddy water has sprung."

"Perhaps. But when I went to the Eatery this afternoon, I saw Selena sobbing into her coffee and Tessa trying to calm her down. At the time all I thought was, I hope it's just a boy, and not that someone has died."

"Callous!"

"You think?" He strolls to the sofa and rests one buttock on the armrest. I begin to feel silly, standing where he left me, but at the same time I don't want to sit down. Standing is more formal. Formal is good.

"Sometimes the two feel the same," I point out, ruining my effect.

"Especially when you're twenty-three and a virgin."

"You don't know that Selena is a virgin! Or—do you?"

"Of course I don't *know* it! Perhaps that little crucifix around her neck and the chastity ring on her left hand are just a smoke-screen, and those buttoned-up blouses, and teaching Sunday school to the kids."

"*I* taught religious education at *my* synagogue!"

"And were *you* a virgin at twenty-three?"

"No, of course I wasn't," I snap at him, mortified.

He laughs. "At any rate, Selena is a good girl, and one of these days someone will pay for that. She herself, probably."

"But Selena can't be the girl…in question. Tim tried out that idea, and it makes no sense. Her mother was far too collected, and the family would never have gone visiting friends, if—"

"No, no, that's not my drift." Cleveland is gazing at me, and I'm not sure it's because he is waiting for me to catch up, or because he is using me as a screensaver while he is thinking.

"Natalie Greco didn't teach her class today," he finally says. Just that, no more. And because it's late and I'm tired, I forget to shut-the-fuck-up.

"You think Natalie's fling with Nick Hornberger has turned sour? And Natalie confided in Selena that she has accused her professorial lover of raping her, flunks off class, and Selena's world is in shreds because to feel secure, she must have the lion lie peacefully and chastely with the lamb. Selena in tears, hushed whisperings among the grad students. Have I caught your drift?"

"Yes."

"Damn."

"Yes. Only you don't know the half of it."

"Will you tell me?"

"No."

"Oh, unfair!"

Now he looks directly at me again, with a quick smile, as if he were surprised at something. As if he was surprised at me. But then he shifts on his perch and clears his throat.

"There's something else I need to mention. It appears there is a spot of bother about your Gen Ed class."

My stomach muscles, already tight in an attempt to resist his smile, clench with dread.

"Oh, no…Madeline Harrison?" Now I do walk over to one of the low chairs and flop down on it. "Of *the* Harrison family?"

"She went to see Hornberger. I'm to bring you in."

"Bring me in? To be hanged at dawn, I expect."

Cleveland says nothing, just gazes at me, his head cocked to one side.

"You really are…" He gazes, then shakes his head.

"A pain in the neck?" I offer bravely, not feeling very brave at all. "I'm sorry. It seems I misjudged them, and I also lost control a little, at one point. Am I in a lot of trouble? They're not going to fire me, are they?"

"No, they're not going to fire you."

"What, then? A lecture, a dressing-down, a note in my file, presumably?"

"Something like that."

As the shock waves ebb through my nervous system, I realize just how tired I am. It's not the tiredness of the second week of term; it's the deep exhaustion of an uphill struggle. When this feeling took over, four years ago, I fell into a lethargy that led me into some very irresponsible sex and the worst emotional and professional crisis I've ever been through. So with the exhaustion comes the fear.

"Did Hornberger say when? You needn't come with me, you know. To be honest, I'd rather you didn't."

"So you can become dewy-eyed and distressed to soften Nick's heart? Yes, that would probably work. He's a complete pushover for beautiful young women. As we have current proof."

So dry, so unexpected, so mean, this punch. And I'm reeling.

Whenever I have dealings with Giles Cleveland, I feel dejected afterward. Lonely. I don't know what it is about him, unless of course it is the mean, hurtful things he says to me. He *could* be a friend, I am sure he could, but he doesn't want to be. I, on the other hand, am summoned to appear before my department chair after just one week of student contact. I could do with a friend.

Interesting that Cleveland seemed convinced that Nick Hornberger is the rapist. *You don't know the half of it.* The truth is, I don't know a tenth of it. These people are all strangers to me. On Wednesday afternoon I see Hornberger walk down the Observatory steps accompanied by Ma Mayfield and an official-looking man. I give Elizabeth a diffident nod, but she either ignores me or doesn't notice me; when I peek back at them, they are walking toward Rossan House, where the Provost's office and central administration are located. It's the first time I have seen Hornberger in a suit and tie, and he may well be wearing them in his capacity as department chair, requested by the Sexual Misconduct Hearing Panel to speak for (or against) a colleague. His rattled expression is easily interpreted as dismay that his term of office will not be as uneventful as he had hoped.

That, or I have witnessed the Dean of Studies and a plain-clothes policeman escorting a professor accused of raping his graduate assistant.

This whole thing is utterly bizarre.

On Thursday morning I dash into the library for some last-minute photocopying for my Parody class. I'm late because I tried a short-cut from the farm to the campus that took ten minutes longer, and because I keep forgetting that this library is a still unfamiliar labyrinth. When I locate the book from which I want to copy an essay, it's two inches beyond the reach of my fingertips and there is neither a ladder nor an obliging basketball player in sight.

"Which one d'you want?"

As he stands there against the sunlight streaming in through the huge leaded windows, I finally grasp the echo of a resemblance that struck me when he sat down next to me at the faculty meeting: Dolph looks like Rocky Horror. I wonder whether it is because he's blond and brawny or also because he is the creature of some scheming mastermind.

"Uh, thanks, Dolph, I can manage."

He comes a couple of steps closer and peers at the books above my head.

"C'mon, allow a gentleman from the Old South to help a Yankee lady."

Another step, and he is so close I can smell the fragrance of his aftershave. Too close.

"Don't be a jerk," I say pleasantly.

This takes him aback, but not enough to actually step back. As if to support himself, he leans one hand on the shelf next to my shoulder and reaches up; he has, in effect, trapped me. Three or four seconds, then he steps back, a couple of volumes in his hand.

"Was it one of these? Swift's *Essays*?"

I don't believe this guy.

"Don't think I won't make a fuss while I'm on probation, Adolph! And don't kid yourself that just because we have a rape allegation pending, I won't complain about a colleague crowding me in the library!"

I snatch the book from his hands and make for the downstairs Xerox machines. Dolph comes running after me.

"What do *you* know about *that?*"

"Nothing. I'm just a rookie. I know nothing."

In the afternoon—I am up on the least wobbly of my chairs, wiping the top shelves and hoisting folders with teaching notes onto it—the phone rings. My first thought is that this is the Voice of Doom demanding to know why I consider masturbation to be a suitable topic for a freshman class. The plummeting of guilt into the pit of my stomach is followed by an even guiltier splash of callousness: faced with a rape allegation, Professor Hornberger would hardly be in a position to berate me for my morally turpid syllabus.

"Hi, uh—am I speaking to Professor Lieberman? Anna Lieberman?"

Oy, gevalt!

I know at once who it is, because none of my students or colleagues has so sonorous a baritone with a Queens accent.

"Bernie!"

"D'you remember me? Mrs. Schwartz's class? Zelda Krevitz's nephew?"

"Of course, Bernie, hi!"

"I hope it's okay I'm calling you at your office. I lost your number—the number your mother gave my aunt?"

A very sonorous baritone that raises the hope that pudgy Bernie has grown up into a broad-shouldered six-footer.

"Yeah, sure, I'm sorry, this is the first time someone's rung me on my office phone. Weird. Thanks, anyway. For calling, I mean."

"Well, I figured you probably wouldn't call me—strange man, strange city. I know I wouldn't, if I was a woman."

"Yeah, well, I have been extremely busy. A lot of work, being new at a place—well, you know that, of course." I hear him laugh. "What's the joke?"

"God, it's nice to hear you talk! You sound like home, you know that?"

The muscles in my stomach relax.

"Yeah, so do you…"

He does sound like home, and I am dismayed at how wistful that makes me. He suggests dinner in a Mexican restaurant he knows in Shaftsboro, and I accept with pleasure. Maybe an old adversary could become a new friend.

Chapter 11

"Showtime!" Yvonne murmurs when we meet at the top of the stairs three days later.

"Oh, poor you—do you have to teach Fridays? Maybe next—"

"*No!*" She casts her eyes round, but we are alone in the hallway. "The meeting this afternoon! About the—you have heard about it, haven't you?"

"About the…rape allegation? Is there a meeting? I didn't check my email."

Three hours later, and with half an hour to spare before showtime, I rush to the Eatery to grab something to sustain me through the meeting.

"Mind if I join you?" asks an English voice above my head.

I'm tempted to reply that I do not see why he would want to sit with a woman he suspects of making play with wet eyelashes when she is reprimanded by her department chair, but I manage to wave nonchalantly at the seat opposite mine.

"No, of course not."

Cleveland sets down his mug and a plate with a bagel on it, pulls out the chair and sits. His mug is less than a foot away from mine. When he reaches for it, I must not stare, even though the memory of that moment in his office when I noticed his hands still pierces me with the ache of guilty longing.

The man is married, and to a large-breasted blonde, and thou shalt not covet him.

Cleveland grins at me and bites into his bagel. It would be the most natural thing in the world to talk about Hornberger and the rape allegation, but my instinct tells me to steer clear of the subject. Tim, Erin, and Eugenia descend upon us, but the elephant in the room is making all of us tongue-tied.

"That carrot cake will be the death of me," Eugenia groans and nods at my plate with that slightly false note of exaggeration that betrays her effort to fill the awkward silence.

"I know what you mean." I grin. "Wanna bite?"

"Ah, no, best not—"

"Going, going…gone!" I push the last piece into my mouth and earn a burst of laughter for this lame bit of clownery.

"What do you make of the food here, Anna?" Erin picks up the cue. "Better than at NYU? Worse?"

"Wee-e-ell." I hurl myself into an answer. "You really want to try and compete with the variety of food available in Manhattan? No gluten-free, lactose-free, low-cal cookies in the Eatery, and there must be a place to get decent *cawffee*, because this potation here is undrinkable. And not for nothing, but the only pizza I've had so far tasted like cardboard with bits of tomato on it—honestly, how *do* you people survive?"

Cleveland, grinning with appreciation, leans forward on his elbow and rests his chin in his cupped hand.

"On pork and peanuts," he says earnestly.

"This coffee isn't so bad?" Erin looks round for corroboration. "I never found it so bad."

"Oh, I don't eat peanuts." I force myself to look into the seawater eyes and affect regret. "They're *very* high in cholesterol…"

Tim snorts his derision, while Erin and Eugenia wave over Kristen Thomason and Brenda Dampier and make them sit down at their end of the table.

"Do you eat pork?" Cleveland asks. "I'm just wondering."

I bite my lip.

"I don't eat any meat at all, if I can help it. I was kidding about the peanuts, though."

He grins and glances down at his plate.

"People here find vegetarians very…*New York*…"

"I'm not actually all that good at being a New Yorker, I think."

"That's true," Tim butts in. "She's a sweetie."

I pull a face at Tim, and Cleveland ponders Tim's assessment of my character.

"But you *are* a vegetarian," he says.

"Mm. My landlord showed admirable composure the other day when I wouldn't eat fried chicken."

"Your landlord—" He looks up, very intent all of a sudden; and I can see that he is on the brink of further questions.

"You'd love Anna's place, Cleve," Tim says. "She lives in a cottage by the woods. Think *Lady Chatterley's Lover*. Didn't you say there is even a patch of bluebells?"

"N-No, they can't have been bluebells," I stutter. "It's too late in the year, my landlord says."

"You'll have to wait for the wild daffodils in spring." Cleveland isn't teasing me anymore. His bagel lies half eaten on his plate and he is watching me, holding onto his mug as if his hands were cold. "The wild daffs…and the forget-me-nots."

"Well, if I've ever been tempted to run around naked in the rain, it is in this place, that's for sure." I know we are both thinking it, so I decide—foolishly—that spelling it out might still the frisson between us. It doesn't.

"Now this *is* a surprise," he admits. "I would have bet any sort of money that you despise D. H. Lawrence."

"I do despise him. Any woman must. But I also love him. It. The novel."

"I hope you realize," Tim supplies *sotto voce*, his eyes trained on our chatting colleagues, "that the female focalizer in *Lady Chatterley's Lover* is merely a tool to allow Lawrence to describe male beauty. What he's surreptitiously doing there is rewriting Forster's *Maurice* with the sex left in."

"Well, the author is dead," I say dryly, "and I don't care what motivated him to describe male beauty like that. I'm a heterosexual female, and I think it's a lovely book. And if you quote me on this, I shall swear I was drunk!"

Both men burst out laughing, and his hilarity does nothing to disperse the warm glow that surrounds Cleveland whenever I glance at him.

The events that follow do.

The Sperm Room is still locked when we arrive, so I decide to make a dash for the john while someone goes for the key. When I return I have no choice but to take the seat Tim has kept for me between himself and Cleveland, who is sitting several seats further down than last time. Our hands are resting on the table top with less than the length of a sheet of paper between them, his fingers twiddling with a university regulation-issue ballpoint. The sight of that lean, restless male hand—contrasting so poignantly with the pale pink cotton of the open shirt-cuff, with the deskworker's accessories and with my smaller, paler hand next to it—strikes me as so erotic that my belly floods with longing, a sharp, lingering shock of desire. Instinctively I shift my butt and at once curse myself, because Cleveland might think that I feel uncomfortable sitting next to him. He is watching Matthew Dancey welcome Dean Ortega, a tall woman with a boyish figure and an unruly mop of hair, who is accompanied by a judicial affairs officer and someone from Equal Opportunities. My fidgeting makes Cleveland turn round to look at me.

Something is wrong.

I don't know what it is, but his expression when he turns and sees me sitting there next to him—as if he hadn't noticed me earlier—is at once scornful and anxious. Cleveland is upset. Upset, and trying to hide it. I have the irrational impulse to clasp his hand and draw it close to me.

Dean Ortega does most of the talking, and what she has to say does not visibly surprise anyone now. She regrets having to inform us that Nick Hornberger has been suspended from his university duties for an indefinite period. This much, precisely, and no more, we may impart to the student body, should we be approached with questions. Any further speculation, spoken or written, runs the risk of being slanderous or libelous, and she trusts that the college can rely on our discretion at this time, as always.

Within these four walls, however, she will tell us that charges of sexual assault have been filed against Hornberger both with the Sexual Misconduct Hearing Panel and with the Shaftsboro police department. He was arrested on Wednesday (so it *was* a plain-clothes policeman!) and released on bail a day later. It is to be expected that the local news will report the case, but we would be well-advised not to believe everything they print. It goes without saying that under no circumstances may we discuss the matter with outsiders, especially not with journalists. She adds that although Ardrossan University's zero-tolerance policy on sexual misconduct applies to faculty as well as students, we ought also to recall that the accused is innocent until proven guilty—a principle difficult to maintain when so heinous a crime has to be investigated.

"Are there any questions?"

Several hands go up. Erin Gallagher wants Ortega to reassure us—"unofficially, of course!"—that Hornberger has denied the allegation. Immediately the noise level spikes as some people groan at her apparent naïvety, and Ortega evades an answer.

"May we know the plaintiff's name?" Brenda Dampier asks, and I am surprised that she seems surprised when Sam Ruffin, under cover of the murmuring at Ortega's refusal, leans over and whispers something into her ear.

"The students are likely to know a lot more about this than we do," Kay Chang says. "Does nobody else find that a very awkward situation to work in? Is this, for example, a race issue as well as an issue of sexual violence?"

Several nods support this as a valid point, but it is passed over by Dancey, who seems to feel it is time to put in his oar and promptly proceeds to deflect all questions.

"One of this incident's unfortunate consequences is that we need to find a new chair. A new search committee will be installed in the next few weeks, but you know how long the process takes. Meanwhile I would be prepared to step up from associate chair to interim chair."

"Having said that—" Ortega raises her voice above the low murmur "—it is customary to ask the department to name an interim chair or to ask whether there are any other nominations. I would then forward this list to the Provost for further negotiations." Something like a wan smile appears on her haggard face when she adds, "I say 'list,' but things being what they are, I'd be content with a list of one. One volunteer."

"I'm sorry, I don't understand." Sam Ruffin looks round, frowning. "Surely you don't mean *now*."

"Since we are rather pressed for time, yes, I would appreciate it if you would consider the matter here and now. Obviously there will then be talks in private with the volunteers, to sort out the details."

I do not wonder that Dancey, who is salivating at the prospect of institutional power, advocates this gun-shot method. From Ortega I would have expected a more delicate form of personnel management.

The tail of the table is very quiet as the head breaks into subdued but anxious tumult.

My eyes are fixed on Cleveland's cheekbones. If he clenches his jaws any harder, they will crack.

"Well, if no one else can see their way toward taking one for the team, I would offer my services once again." Dancey leans back in his chair, trying and failing to suppress a smirk. I realize with a lurch that if Dancey becomes chair, he would make maximum use of all student complaints against me. Dancey as chair is my personal worst-case-scenario.

Go on, Cleveland—volunteer!

So far he has said nothing at all.

Ortega turns to him. "Giles. Could we prevail on you?"

"I'm afraid not, no."

She raises her eyebrows at his calm but categorical reply. "Some people might feel that you owe the college one or two favors, Giles. Would you care to explain why you won't even consider offering your services in your department's hour of need?"

"No, I'm sorry, Holly, but I don't want to explain. I have my reasons, and they weigh heavily. Perhaps we can leave it at that."

Something *is* wrong. I *knew* it! He is now as immobile as he was fidgety before. Very still, he sits there, one hand clasping the wrist of the other as if he had to steady himself. I can tell that he is desperately trying not to offend Ortega. But I can also tell he will not budge.

"Giles, you were going to go up for full now, weren't you? Maybe the college will scratch your back a little over that, if you scratch theirs." Elizabeth Mayfield has largely kept out of the debate, and her voice is as placid as always, but she clearly agrees with Ortega that Cleveland ought to feel obliged to take over from Hornberger. Perhaps to protect the department from Dancey's rule?

Cleveland says nothing. But because I am sitting next to him, and because I am looking toward the head of the table as if I were interested in *them* rather than *him*, I can see a dark patch appearing under his left armpit.

"This does look like a rather blatant case of cherry-picking, Giles."

I don't know how Cleveland is able to withstand the combined glares of Elizabeth Mayfield and Holly Ortega, but he remains silent. Shrugs his shoulders.

"You have to count me out. I'm sorry, Elizabeth."

Never in my life have I more keenly craved inclusion among a group of knowledgeable insiders than after Ortega and Dancey send us on our way with the strict reminder not to encourage rumor, and we disperse toward our various floors and offices. As if accidentally, I trail Tim, Eugenia, and Erin, and halfway through the great hall Yvonne and Joe Banks catch up with me.

"Anna, I'm taking bets on how long before the full story appears in the papers," Joe says. "I give it twenty-four hours."

We laugh, and Erin turns round.

"Nervous tension releasing itself in laughter?" she guesses.

"I need to release my tension into a beer or three," says Tim. "You coming?"

The following two hours in the Astrolabe are far and away the most informative I have yet spent at Ardrossan, even if afterward I feel I need to take a shower to rinse all the sleaze out of my hair and off my skin.

"In a way it doesn't matter what happened and whether it was a rape," Tim says. "If there's a stink and the media smell it, the damage is done. It's very clever of Hornberger's bit of stuff to go to the police as well as to the campus authorities."

"*Clever?*" Erin lashes out at him. "Honestly, Tim, could you possibly be more biased in this matter? We're talking about a *rape* allegation!"

"Or a rape *allegation*," he points out.

I throw myself between them. "It is certain, though, is it? That it's Natalie Greco?"

Apparently so, and Joe and Erin not only confirm that she is by no means Hornberger's first fling with a student, but that his reputation preceded him when he came to Ardrossan twelve years ago.

"Nick may not be able to keep his hands to himself, but I cannot believe he's capable of violence." Joe lifts his glass to his mouth, sighs, and sets it down again without having drunk. "What do you think?"

It is no fun, gossiping about rape.

"I cannot believe even Nick is stupid enough to use violence," Tim says.

"In other words, you believe Natalie is stupid enough to ruin her own reputation by pulling this preposterous allegation out of thin air?" Erin is a forthright woman, but I have not yet seen her so vehement.

"Why should he force one into bed if three others will hurl themselves under him? It makes no sense!"

"You only say that because you refuse to understand, Tim! Rape isn't about sex. It's about power and humiliation!"

"Who knows what kinds of power games Nick and Natalie had been playing," Eugenia agrees. "If he really raped her, it was to degrade her, and to satisfy some perverse impulse that has little to do with… ordinary sexual desire. Whatever that is."

"Well, I'll be sorry if she turns out to be the victim in this—" Tim shrugs "—but Natalie Greco is a spoilt, manipulative little bee-yatch who brought the chair and the Dean of Studies down on me in her very first semester here because I wouldn't accept her essays after the deadline."

"But that doesn't mean she would fabricate a *rape* allegation!" Erin is exasperated. "Did you never see *The Accused*?"

Was it predictable that the men would doubt the truth of Natalie's charge against Nick Hornberger, while the women tend to believe it? Like television detectives we argue all sides of the case, and—for all its fruitlessness—cannot bring ourselves to stop speculating.

I make an ingenuous bid to steer the debate into another direction.

"So, will Dancey get the chair, do you think?"

"What *is* it with Giles?" Erin promptly fires up. "Someone needs to shake some sense of responsibility into that man! Elizabeth is right, he's been picking the cherries out of this job, and now he won't pull his weight!"

I catch Yvonne watching me, and I'm almost sure that she is covering up for me when she asks, "How do you mean, picking cherries?"

Now everyone is looking at Tim, but Tim—and I must say, I love him for this—shrugs and purses his mouth.

"It isn't a secret," Erin takes over, clearly annoyed at Tim's misplaced loyalty. "A year ago they gave him leave to teach at Stanford for a semester to see whether he liked it well enough to stay there—this is extremely unusual and set a few tongues wagging! And last semester they allowed him to bring his sabbatical forward, and he spent that in England."

"Well, he can spend his sabbatical anywhere he wants, can't he?"

"Yes, of course he can! It's just a little galling to see how some people get break after break, while others—I mean, I used my sabbatical to prolong my maternity leave by a semester!"

"Each to his—or her—own, Erin," Eugenia says gently. "That was your decision, and Giles did a lot of admin before he left, you know he did. Sure, the Stanford fellowship was a favor, but I know for a fact that he only got half his salary during the semester in England, although theoretically he might have had a full one."

"Big deal—for those with private funds!"

"Maybe it's just as well," Joe says. "You say you'd prefer him to Dancey, but Giles has a pretty idiosyncratic way of doing things, and if he took the chair and decided to go all English on us—that wouldn't exactly be helpful either."

"How do you mean, go all English?" I ask.

He was away for a whole year? What about his wife? But this I cannot ask.

"Well, as long as it's just his own research and teaching, it doesn't matter—after all, Diversity with a big D, right? But I'm not so sure his style is really suited to leading this department. Just my two cents, guys."

"You might not notice it so much, Anna," Eugenia adds, "coming from British universities yourself—Tim, are you not eating those nachos?"

"Help yourself."

"I'm shameless, I know," she sighs, pulling Tim's plate toward herself. "He comes across as not caring very much. Giles, I mean."

"It's the traditional British policy of non-interference." Tim can't, after all, stay out of the fray. "What you call caring, he calls mollycoddling."

"Non-interference by a nastier name is appeasement!" Erin snaps.

"Laissez-faire," I correct her, trying to keep my voice neutral. "Disastrous in world politics, maybe, but in education there's a lot to be said for it. I don't know whether Cleveland is like this, but I know a number of lecturers in England who don't believe in…well, in teaching."

"*I* don't particularly like teaching, either." Joe shrugs. "Necessary evil."

"No, I don't mean it like that." I fumble for an explanation. "I mean that they don't believe in teaching as organized, explicit instruction. In fact, they believe that good students shouldn't need teaching. They expect their students to get on with it, and they only interfere if you go off the rails or find yourself in a hole. They're catchers in the rye. Sort of."

"Sounds like a well-reasoned excuse for laziness, if you ask me." Erin frowns. "And it's exactly the sort of bull Giles comes up with."

Joe leans his elbows on the table and puts his fingertips together in a gesture I find irritatingly complacent. "It's two fundamentally different systems and cultures. And if he doesn't want to adapt to those differences, he can't teach at an American university — simple!"

"Well, they are wooing him to stay." Erin drains her glass and reaches for her purse. "I understand why, he's tipped for the top, ya-dayada. I like Giles — don't get me wrong. But he's totally biting the hand that feeds him, by being so stubborn about this. If Bob Morgan doesn't come back, Dancey will make sure that Medieval Literature is taken out of the curriculum and the next professorship goes to modern American Lit. But why should I care about that if Giles doesn't?"

"He got another break at the beginning of the semester, remember?" Joe reminds us. "Not having to be here for the first week of term?"

"Yeah, but—" I look at Tim, and again he shrugs. "He was in Scotland, Joe. He won a prize for his book on Sir Walter Raleigh. A quite prestigious prize, actually."

"Then why didn't he say so?"

"Because there's something devious about Giles."

"*Erin!*" Tim explodes.

"All right, not...*devious.*" She lifts her hands in a gesture of capitulation. "But he's not *straight!*"

"Yes, he is," Tim mutters.

"No, I mean — infuriating boy!" She cuffs Tim on the shoulder. "Up-front! You can never tell whether he says what he means, or whether he means what he says. And all he cares about is his own research! His crop of graduates is consistently smaller than that of any other subfield because he can't be bothered to waste time advising. Well, *he* would feel it's time wasted!"

Tim shakes his head in exasperation but decides to let it go.

"And Dancey, what does he—"

Erin interrupts me. "Now *he* is all bad."

I look at the others for a rebuttal of this blunt assessment.

"He thinks he's God," Joe says. "He wants to shape the department in his own image. Don't they all? And wouldn't you?"

"He keeps dropping these ominous hints about Medieval and Renaissance Studies, and Erin, you said this is about Bob Morgan's job, but is there more to it?"

I can tell just by the expression on Tim's face that there is more to it.

"Listen, guys," I add a little severely, "one of the reasons I applied for this job is the excellence of Ardrossan's Early Modern Studies program. If Dancey is scheming to pull the plug on the English Lit side of that, where will that leave me?"

"It's a game of dominoes." Tim at last seems ready to give me a comprehensible answer. "For twenty years and more, Rich Westley and Bob Morgan were a fixture in this department—Bob with his Medieval English Language and Literature, Rich with his Native American Culture and Dialects. Cultural Studies was big. These days—who cares? The pendulum is swinging back to hard science. The worst-case scenario—from your point of view, Anna—is that the professorship of Medieval English Literature will be re-designated as something like Aesthetics and Cognitive Science, to operate as a docking station for the new Center for—whatsit?"

"Institute for Cognitive Science, Linguistics and Psychology," Joe says.

"Hornberger's baby." I nod. "Dancey told me about that. He suggested Dolph and I convene a conference there, about Renaissance art and neuroesthetics."

"He did?"

"Yeah, but I mean…like hell."

"Don't be stupid, Anna!" Erin reaches over and grabs my wrist for emphasis. "This was Dancey's offer to join his camp! With Dancey, it's very simple. You're either for him or you're against him. And you can't afford to be against him." She turns to her colleagues. "Don't you agree that was an offer Anna can't refuse?"

They agree. Reluctantly, but unanimously.

"I don't think it was an offer," I say, drowning. "It felt more like a taunt. And the whole idea behind it is to pull the rug out from under my own discipline!"

"If we want to remain at the cutting edge, we need to reinvent ourselves!"

"Wait, so are you telling me that Dancey and Hornberger will trade in Medieval Literature and the Piedmont Center for Area Studies for a share in this new Institute for Cognitive Science? Is that the deal?"

"Can't make an omelet without breaking some eggs." Joe shrugs, and the others avoid my eyes.

"If any of this can still be stopped, it's by a department chair who will take on Dancey and make sure that Medieval and Renaissance Studies isn't bled dry." Erin counts some money onto the table and slips on her jacket. "It would have been in Giles's own interest to take the chair. See what I mean when I say he doesn't care?"

Maybe it's because I had too much coffee too late in the day—one before the faculty meeting, two in the Astrolabe—or maybe it's because the events of the day are whirling around in my head and gnawing at the lining of my stomach like tiny lampreys, but it's almost two in the morning, and I am still at my desk, brooding over the pregnant anatomies. Like Christian martyrs who present to the worshipping observer the body parts that they have sacrificed for their faith, these female figures peel away the layers of skin, fat, muscle and tissue from their bellies to present a view into their wombs. The point of these images is not the fact that babies grow in women's bellies; the point is that they show *how* they grow. The gift that these naked, dissected ladies make to the beholder is the gift of knowledge, both physical and metaphysical.

Gift, in German, means poison. The etymology is not as crazy as it appears: *geben* means "to give," and "that which is given or administered" is a *gift*. Could be a lump of money, as in *Mitgift*, dowry—or could be a dose of poison. A gift can be an ambiguous thing, a two-edged sword; a donation can have strings attached. Donation, my foot. *Hornberger was instrumental in acquiring the necessary funds.* What Dancey neglected to mention, of course, was that the new Institute for Cognitive Science has poisoned the atmosphere in the English department. How would I have voted on this issue, assuming there ever was a vote? Not sure. At any rate, I would have examined this gift horse's mouth extremely carefully.

Hang on—gift, present. That reminds me of the text my mother promised to send me about my father's birthday present, and that reminds me that on my way home my phone slipped off the passenger seat when I braked and under the seat when I accelerated again. An excellent excuse to go downstairs, grab the flashlight from the key rack in the hall, and take a stroll to my car.

It isn't as dark as it usually is. There is light and the sound of a car and voices. I tell myself that burglars would not leave the motor running, but it seems very late, on a weeknight, for the Walshes to have guests. Cautiously I peer round the corner of the main house and see Howie behind the wheel and Pop assisting Karen from the door to the car. Karen is wearing an anorak over her nightgown, woolen socks, and boots; Pop is in his pajama jacket and jeans, and I know that this is not good. They are keeping their voices down, presumably on account of the girls, but I can hear Karen's panic when she tells him to put one towel down on the seat and to hand her the other one.

The car drives off, and when Pop turns to go back into the house, he sees me standing just outside the pool of light cast by the porch light.

"I'm sorry—I wasn't prying—I forgot something in my car." I feel I must justify my presence at such a dramatic moment in the lives of people I hardly know. He looks at me, an aging man in jeans that slip down his paunch, his face gray and deeply lined, and he nods his permission for me to pass.

"Sir!" I can't help but whisper when he is about to disappear into the house. "Is it…the baby?"

I'm wary of his anger at my intrusion, but he looks at me again and nods. Just that. He has done what he can do, and now it's out of his hands—like the seeds that he plants and tends and that may still be blighted.

I feel very sad and foolish as I retrieve my phone and slowly walk back to the cottage. I haven't the heart to return to my desk and the images that are covering it. Sometimes my academic pursuits reveal themselves as precisely that: purely academic. Real Life is happening elsewhere, and it frightens me.

Chapter 12

Like a creature being born, New Year pushes itself into time and space head first. *Rosh Hashanah* means "the head of the year," and this year it falls on the fourth weekend in September. Like all new life it chastens those who watch its arrival and resolves them to do better in future. Purification, repentance, atonement, until, on the tenth Day of Awe, Yom Kippur, God determines whose name will remain in the Book of Life and who will be cast out. It may be a really stupid idea to give in to it, but when I wake up five hours later in the same subdued, chastened mood, I feel the pull of my past.

Freddy Katz's synagogue is across the river and about three miles due west. There are a couple of minibuses parked on a small lot nearby, their drivers smoking and listening to the radio, and about a dozen bikes and mopeds. I can't bring myself to park in full view of the entrance, flaunting my non-observance, so I guiltily drive round the corner and walk back. Temple Beth David has an open-door policy for Rosh Hashanah, so I have to stand in line for ten minutes to get in. The doorman narrows his eyes at me.

"*Ba'alat teshuvah?*" he asks.

That's a very good question, mister!

"*B'ezrat HaShem,*" I reply. This doesn't soften his expression, so I explain that I am a new colleague of Freddy Katz's and that he invited me. This does the trick, and he points me toward the stairs. I pick up a prayer book, squeeze into a back row on the balcony, smile bravely at the women who glance over at me, and wish them *L'shana tova.*

The New Year prayers and their melodies are familiar to me, but it's such a long time since I studied them, such a long time since I heard any Hebrew at all, that I well up and give thanks for the humility that made me come here today. Could not this be my home? I settle into a reverie of listening and praying and translating and meditating on the words, which totally gives me away to the *frum*-from-birth women around me who sit quietly chatting and nip downstairs to the restroom or to check on their children.

Hours later, when I slowly and stiffly inch out of my seat and wish my neighbors that God may inscribe them in the Book of Life for another year, the comforting familiarity of the service is superseded by the unfamiliarity of the faces. I feel overwhelmed and out of place and give up any thought I may have had of trying to find Freddy and his family in the crowd. But I'm glad I came. I feel much more grounded than I did this morning, much more confident that I will find my place in this part of the world and that the next few years, though stressful, will be a good and rewarding period of my life.

Although to an orthodox Jew this would be pointless at best and an abomination at worst, I stop at a grocer's on my way home and buy eggs, yeast, and flour to bake a *challah*, the round, braided, yeasty bread eaten on religious holidays. With honey, apples and wine, this makes up my solitary, candle-lit Rosh Hashanah meal, and I even say the prayer over the apples and honey.

May it be Your will, Lord our God and God of our ancestors
That you renew for us a good and sweet year.

Physically I am tired but my mind is supple and awake, and I manage to finish the book review for which I had allowed myself the whole weekend. Sunday morning, still calm and concentrated, I write two coherent-sounding pages for my Notre Dame paper. Then I begin to wobble. I eat the rest of the *challah* for lunch and decide to honor the late summer day by taking out my bike.

Pretending not to have a fixed destination, I cross the main road and wind my way slowly to the suburb of Ardrossan, where I explore the side streets and keep my ears open for the sounds that waft toward me on the soft breeze from the river.

And there they are. The horns.

The secondary but historically older meaning of the New Year holiday is that of Yom Teruah, "Day of Blasts," on which the *shofarot*, the rams' horns, are blown to alert Israel to the fact that the Highest Judge is in session and will rule over their lives. Many communities combine the *shofar*-blowing service with the *tashlikh* ceremony, a symbolic casting off of one's sins into a body of flowing water. Parents who made their children sit through the long prayer service are particularly grateful for a more relaxed outdoor activity, and the park by the stone arch bridge that connects the college and the suburb looks like an unusually leafy elementary schoolyard. The children run about, laughing, shrieking, blowing their little *shofarot,* some real, some made of plastic. A group of elderly people shelter on the wooden seats by the clump of trees, chatting in Yiddish. The college on the other side of the river looks magnificent in the afternoon sun, and my heart beats fast at the sight of it, but I don't know whether it is with pride and gratitude or with anxiety and foreboding.

Freddy Katz is one of the first people who notices me; he greets me very warmly and introduces me to Rabbi Ostrowicz, the youngest of the three rabbis I saw at the service yesterday, and Cantor Young, a handsome man in his early seventies who grins at me above the din made by the children and tells me that he retired six years ago and that *tashlikh* is his last remaining challenge. Freddy explains who I am and bounces off, I assume to find his wife. Rabbi Ostrowicz, looking straight past my face, asks me whether I am "a beginner."

"Oh, no, not quite," I stutter and wonder whether I could possibly explain to this diffident young man (well, he must be my age, but he seems younger) about Anshel the Yeshiva boy. "Well, my family is not very observant, but—"

"*And* a Yankee," Cantor Young decides in lugubrious accents. "We have another one of your sort."

It takes me several mortified moments to realize that he is teasing me, and I feel a right klutz for being so slow. Freddy returns with his wife and Mrs. Ostrowicz in tow. I do not have the impression that Margalit Katz is in any way interested in making my acquaintance, but perhaps I am being unfair. There are five little Katzes to rein in, the eldest *bar mitzvah'd* last summer. *And* she is about to make associate professor at the Music department. Maybe I don't much like *her,* either.

Everyone is *davening* and watching the children and listening to the *shofar* players—one of whom is proficient, the other one sucks but has a sense of humor about it. I go in for a minute of soul-searching to see whether all these little kids make me wish that one of them was mine, but I cannot in all honesty identify such a wish. Karen's unborn baby comes to my mind, and for her I pray:

We ask for a piece of sand
And God gives us a beach.
We ask for a drop of water
And God gives us an ocean.

There is the occasional glance into my direction, one or two smiles, but one man is staring at me in a way that makes me uncomfortable. He seems to be there with his wife and young son, and I wish I didn't have the feeling that he is more interested in me than in them. I turn my back to him and concentrate on the bread crumbs in my hand.

Our sins float on the waters of the Ouse, only to be engorged and digested by the ducks and swans that have congregated by the embankment.

Staring Guy appears next to me at the railings and stares again. And grins.

"*What?*" I snap, as if we were waiting at a bus stop in New York.

He flinches a little, but the grin on his face does not waver.

"Anna-Banana!" he says. "You still haven't got any tits."

Now it is my turn to stare.

"Oh, fuck off, Bernie!"

It is, as they say, as if we had never been apart.

Bernie, one year ahead of me, came to Ardrossan and did the prudent thing: he joined Temple Beth David. There he met Elvira, a recently divorced single parent; last summer the three of them moved into a new house together. I am not surprised that I didn't immediately recognize him; he is one of those rare people who are more attractive as adults than as children. Pudgy Bernie has not quite grown to six foot, but he is very fit and evidently takes care of himself.

"Ah, you found each other!" Cantor Young comes toward us.

"Better than that, Avi — we already knew each other!"

Avi Young fully appreciates the little *shtick* — presented by Bernie and me as a comic double act — in which we sketch our history for him, Chinese burns and all, and soon we are standing in a little huddle with Avi Young, Freddy Katz, and two friends of his.

"Who is that woman who is making all the men laugh?" one of Freddy's daughters asks her mother.

"Never mind her, honey. She came to shul by car this morning. She's from New York."

Oh, and you're straight from Lyubavichi, are you, Margele?

In contrast, Elvira — a buxom, Sephardic-looking woman who I'm guessing is a few years older than Bernie — welcomes me, literally, with open arms. And with a plan.

"Anna, would you like to come to our house-warming party? Might be nice for you, get to know a few of the locals? Danny, hmm — what do you think? Or Jake?" She turns to Bernie and gives him a significant look.

"Listen, I thank you both, but I'm not actually…I've only been here for a few weeks, it's a little early for a *shidduch* date!" I squirm.

"Anna's right." Bernie nods. "Anyway, a party isn't really a good occasion to catch up. Should we take her to *Los Viejos Amigos* first, after Yom Kippur, for a quiet glass of wine? That's our favorite Mexican place here in Shaftsboro," he informs me, as if I didn't know that already, and as if we hadn't already agreed to meet there in two weeks' time. Bernie, it seems, is a bit of a heel, still. But I don't mind. I like him much better now than when we were fourteen, and I am looking forward to knowing him a little better, too.

Chapter 13

The very next Monday morning I bump up against the realities of what it means to have Matthew Dancey take over the department chair because *other people* are shirking their administrative duties. When I check whether I have any snail mail, I come across Tim, squatting on a big box of Xerox paper and apparently meditating into a letter.

"Hey! All right?" I have learned that Tim is liable to lash out when pressed, but I also want him to know that he can confide in me.

"It's…nothing." He shrugs. "They've re-shuffled my committee."

"Your tenure committee?"

"Mmhm. Hornberger is out, obviously, but Dancey is in. That's…not so good. The good news is, the first paychecks of the semester are here!"

"Oooh—yay!" I make a beeline for L in the wall of pigeonholes. "This, my friend, is a moment I've been waiting for since I started college and realized that I would rather be a professor than a rabbi!"

Tim stares at me with his mouth open like a cartoon character.

"A *rabbi?*" he echoes. "But, babycakes, you wouldn't look at all hot in a whachamcallit—that prayer rug—what? Anna? What's wrong?"

I should shut up, but I can't.

"This is wrong," I say, and my voice sounds odd in my own ears. "My monthly net salary should be more than this. Almost two hundred dollars more than this, actually."

"Probably just a mistake," he says, almost too calm to sound confident.

"Maybe I should…my contract is in my office; I'll go and see whether Dancey is in."

"Or wait till next month?" Tim cautions me. "See whether by then—"

Let us cast away the sin of vain ambition, which prompts us to strive for goals, which bring neither true fulfillment nor genuine contentment.

The verses from the *tashlikh* service linger in my mind, but I do not see how it is evidence of vain ambition to insist on the salary that I negotiated. Those extra two hundred may not bring me genuine contentment, but being cheated out of them would make me genuinely discontented.

"Professor Dancey? Sir? May I ask for a couple of minutes of your time?"

"Sure, Anna. Go through." He points me to his open office door while he continues his exchange with Mrs. Forster in a low voice. I walk in and wait next to one of the two broad metal-and-leather chairs in front of his desk. He makes me wait for about five minutes before he comes in.

"You should have sat down, Anna! Or do you find us so very formal here at Ardrossan?"

Matthew Dancey. Always a master at the "Have you hit your child today?" sort of question. I smile politely and sit down.

"Thank you, sir. It's kind of you to make time for me at such short notice. I'll come right to the point: there's been a hiccup about my salary—"

"Oh, while you're here, Anna—sorry to interrupt you." He looks at the collection of Post-it notes on the cupboard door and peels one off. "Anna's shoes," he reads.

"Pardon me?"

"An odd request, isn't it?" He smiles. "Indulge me. Would you show me your shoes?"

Utterly baffled I stick out one foot from under the chair. I am wearing Victorian-style lace-up half-boots, what I think of as my Mary Poppins boots.

"Very nice." Dancey nods, like a benevolent uncle. "But they are hard-soled, aren't they? And so many floors of our building are stone-tiled—"

He seems to be saying that my heels are too noisy, but at the same time I cannot believe that this is what he is saying, because I have never heard anything so absurdly petty. So I shake my head to signal my puzzlement.

"I'm afraid to say, Anna, that I've had a complaint about the noise your heels make. It's always a question of what our neighbors are willing to tolerate, isn't it? When I was a graduate assistant at Princeton, there was a very senior professor who used to listen to Wagner in his office—drove us crazy! I'm sure you wouldn't want any of your colleagues to feel that you disrespect their right to a quiet work environment."

"Of course I wouldn't, and I'm sorry to hear this, but—"

"I just felt I ought to give you a little hint, Anna. You will know best how to respond in this case. Now, you came to see me about…?"

Choose your battles.

"My paycheck, sir. It's just a misunderstanding, I'm sure, a mistake, but I wanted to first consult with you how best to proceed to get it rectified. It doesn't match my contract."

Downplay your annoyance.

Appeal to wisdom of higher-ups in sorting out your life.

"Salary issues are always sensitive."

"Well, simple, too, in this case, I hope." I cast a beaming smile at him and extract the sheets from the folder I have brought. "The contract I signed in June specifies my salary and the major benefits… here. My check, however, doesn't match. By a fairly substantial margin, in fact."

Dancey eyes me with evident misgivings before he takes the documents that I'm offering him.

"I consider such a mistake highly unlikely."

"Well, sir, if you'll compare the two sums—"

He begins to suck in his lower lip and chew his beard even before he can have found the relevant passages in the two documents.

"Ah, well, this—" he waves my contract in the air "—was signed by Greg Newburgh. He was interim Provost, after Clement Hills died.

Were you told about Clement? Such a tragic story. He was one of the best administrators I ever worked with. We were undergraduates at Princeton together. He dropped dead in the middle of a meeting. Cardiac arrest. Such a loss, that man."

"Sudden deaths are always especially shocking."

"So naturally everything was at sixes and sevens over at Rossan." A row of teeth gleams inside the beard, although his eyes do not crease at all. "I'm afraid I cannot help you with this, Anna." He hands me back the two sheets. "This is a good salary for someone in your position, a first-year assistant professor, so maybe you want to consider your next step carefully."

"I do — that is why I came to see you first, to ask for your advice in this matter."

"Well, you heard my advice. Salary re-negotiations are invariably time-consuming and generally frustrating for all involved." He gets up to show me out. Throw me out.

"I see that, sir." I have no choice, I must rise, too. "But I'm not looking to re-negotiate at all. I believe a mistake has been made, which can easily be corrected. Surely this is in the best interests of everyone involved."

"And surely it will be, next month. I suggest you wait for the next check, instead of kicking up a great fuss now."

"I'm not—"

"Anyway, given that in your opinion Ardrossan is not a top university, I wonder how you can expect a top salary."

For a moment or two, all I can do is stare at him.

"Sir, I — what can you mean? Of course I consider Ardrossan to be a top university!"

"You do? I'm glad to hear it." He registers my loss of composure with satisfaction. "Have you seen the article about you in the *The Folly*? A very nice photograph, if I may say so."

"N-No, I haven't. Thank you, sir."

He pulls a copy out from under a pile of folders and leafs through it.

"They found the opportunity to speak to some students after your first classes…this bit was interesting: 'Dr. Lieberman brings a kind of energy and intensity to the classroom that some Ardrossan students may need time to get used to. A taste of academic life in the Big Apple.' Well—" he looks up at me "—I wouldn't call that negative feedback, would you?"

"Certainly not, sir. Energy and intensity are good things, in my book."

"Oh, talking of energy—Dolph has been talking to some people who will have the running of the ICSLP, and it seems that if you get a bid in quickly, you may well manage to be among the conferences sponsored next year. Next fall, probably. You two better stick your heads together and start writing a call!"

His voice is at its most sonorously patronizing, and I am painfully aware that I am in the hands of a master rhetorician who has outmaneuvered me.

"Yes, thank you, sir. Then I will next ask for an appointment at the Office for Faculty Affairs. May I refer to our talk today in my discussion with the Dean?" Mistake, mistake. And yet.

"Of course you may. But I doubt that Holly Ortega will have time to concern herself with such a trifle!" he says coldly. Now I have really annoyed him, but at least he has understood that I mean business. Irene is right; sometimes you have to piss people off if you want to stop them from messing with you. Sometimes the boomerang comes back, though, and hits you right in the teeth. We'll see about this one.

"The wrong salary? But that sounds highly unlikely," says a blithe female voice in the Dean's office when I call them.

"Nonetheless, I was wondering whether the Dean has time to see me briefly this week or next week. That would be so very helpful!"

"This week is all full up, I'm afraid."

"And next week? It needn't take long. I'm sure it's a simple mistake."

"Hmmm…nothing again, I'm afraid. Dr. Ortega is busy right now, as you can imagine."

"Well, then perhaps she isn't the person I should see about this at all? Could you possibly advise me who the best person to contact would be? I'd be really grateful."

"Oh, I couldn't say," she pipes back. "It's not my job to know these things, you see."

"Yes, I see. Well, since it's a matter involving my contract, perhaps the legal department would be the best place to try? What do you think? One of the legal advisors in HR?"

There is a short silence in the line.

"Can you make Wednesday at eight fifteen?"

I assure her that I can and dash off into the west wing (*clackety-clack* go the Mary Poppins boots), where I'm about to miss the beginning of my Comedy class. A crowd of students is loitering in front of my classroom.

"It's Dr. Bergstrom's class," Jocelyn says. "They haven't finished yet."

"Oh, good, I thought I was late!"

"Well…" She checks her phone. "In fifty-seven,-six,-five,-four seconds, you would have been."

At three minutes past the hour, Dolph has not looked left once, even though his students see me watching him through the glass pane in the door. I knock on the door. He turns his head, feigns surprise, raises his hand in a gesture that could mean anything or nothing, and goes on talking. At five minutes past my students have started giggling and joking that we should relocate to the Eatery, so I knock again and open the door.

"Apologies, Dr. Bergstrom, for interrupting what seems to be a spellbinding monologue, but might I ask you to wrap up now? We have a very full program, too."

"Yeah, sorry, I'll just finish this thought."

Just finishing this thought takes him another three minutes at least, while his class, half packed, and my class, half unpacked, sit and stand in awkward disarray. I vaguely feel that I should assert myself against Dolph, but my anxious mind is worrying the exchange with Dancey like a cat worries a dead mouse. On the whole it is perhaps just as well that I am in no mood to go for Dolph, the chair's pet.

"For the moment," I announce when Dolph and his students have left and I have settled down my class, "I'm more interested in figuring out how metaphor works than in defining what it is. How far do you take a metaphor before it becomes too far-fetched? Let's use Wyatt's sonnet 'Whoso list to hunt' as an example and be very simple and visual about it. Imagine all the features, all the characteristics of 'deer' as constituting one set…you know, like in third-grade math. Like this." I draw a bubble on the board. "And imagine all the features of 'lady' in an overlapping set, like this—" I draw another bubble "then the question is, what's in the intersection?"

"What? Reading, 'Riting, 'Rithmetic? And that's what I got out of bed for?"

"Mr. Williams. Having made it so far, perhaps you can go one step further and sit down?"

Logan lingers in the doorway—scruffy, cocksure, his ginger mop standing on end—and scans the group before he sits down in the row behind the last occupied seat. Knowing full well that I want people to sit in the front rows.

"In structuralism," I continue, "these bits of meaning are called *sememes*; from the Greek denoting meaning. Semantics. So in the cut set we collect all the sememes that the deer and the lady have in common."

"Semen? Do we talk about sex *again* today?"

I would ignore Logan, but several of the other students start sniggering.

"Actually, yes, we do—if you recall, we found out in the very first session that comedy is about sexuality, and a love sonnet is a sort of mini-comedy in one voice. So brace yourselves. Wyatt obviously uses 'deer'—and the integrated pun, 'dear'—as a metaphor for his beloved lady. But what do animal and woman actually have in common? How does this metaphor work?"

"Both run away from the speaker."

"They run away because they are shy and wild."

"No, they run away because they are being hunted."

"Both are objects of desire to others besides the speaker."

I fill the intersection of the two bubbles on the whiteboard as the students name similarities between a hunted deer and a lady at the court of King Henry VIII.

"Right, these are some of the similarities that Wyatt is encouraging us to consider or, to avoid the intentional fallacy, this is the area of overlap between these two semantic fields. Now, in a second step—"

"Sorry, ma'am, how do you spell that? P-h-a-l-l-u-s-y?" Logan is looking at me with fake innocence.

"Pardon me?"

"Well, you said it was all about sex, so I thought, phallus—phallusy…"

A groan of comprehension fills the air, and before I can muster the energy to relax, I snap.

"You *thought?* All we've had from you so far is adolescent wise-cracks!"

The perpetual sneer on Logan's lips wavers as the corners of his mouth tremble.

"And all we've had from you is ball-breaking—but I expected nothing less from a J.A.P.!"

"*What* did you call me?"

"What everyone calls you." He grins, back in his comfort zone. "Haven't you heard? Though it's a shame not all high-powered Jewish princesses wear tight little skirts and low-cut blouses when they boss others around. I can see you in a little skirt, you know…"

There is an ugly expression in his eyes, and for a few seconds something happens that ought never to happen in a classroom: I am just a woman, he is a man, and he's threatening me. That's what it feels like. He's hitting on me, with all the violence that expression implies.

"Dude, you're rude!" Ross the football player cuts in, but affably.

"Shut up, Logan, and let's get on with it!"

The support from the other students helps me calm myself, but inwardly I'm so furious I could slap his self-satisfied face.

"Mr. Williams, if you find us boring, I'm sure we'll survive your absence."

"Are you throwing me out?"

The room has gone very quiet.

"Well, you were tardy in the first place, so we can't be all that high up on your list of priorities."

"Okay, fine! I'll be counting how many balls you break in your first year, princess! You know what *you* need, don't you?" He glares at me, his cheeks flaming, grabs his rucksack and storms out.

In the corridor, on my way—flight!—back to my office after class, I run into Yvonne; and in a burst of confidence I blurt out what happened.

"Honey—calm down! Why do you let them upset you like this? They're just kids!" Her good sense makes me feel that I'm totally over-reacting, as of course I am. "What did he say, anyway?"

"He—ah, it's too asinine! He called me a Jewish princess. A ball-breaker! Oh, and I'm to wear shorter skirts."

Now I have impressed her.

"He said *that?* Anna, that's sexual harassment. You have to — well, you have to —" She stares at me, thinking fast. "That's sexual harassment *and* anti-Semitic stereotyping! You should talk to Elizabeth Mayfield about this!"

"For heaven's sake, don't start. It was sexist, yes, but not — look, I don't want to make a big thing out of it. Sorry, Yvonne, I'm seeing a student at my office, uh, five minutes ago, so — but thanks!"

I talk the student waiting in front of my office through her essay; she's from the graduate class, unrelated to the recent troubles. But I lost it with Logan Williams back in there, and the fear of retribution from my superiors is like a scorpion in my guts.

Before you get any salary at all at Ardrossan, Dr. Lieberman, you ought to consider a class in anger management!

Am I breaking down?

I cannot. I can't break down.

There is a knock on the door.

"May I come in?"

Oh, no! I can't face him now! Not now!

He opens the door a little wider and steps into the room. The sight of those lean, broad shoulders and that silver head of hair makes my chest expand with longing.

"By all means!" I jump up from my swivel chair and indicate one of the two other chairs in my dingy little office. "It's not very —"

He doesn't sit down. Leans against the bookshelf, one hand in the pocket of his pants. When I at last manage to look at his face, I realize that his awkwardness has nothing to do with having ventured upstairs into the servants' quarters.

"A lot of essays, those." He nods at my desk. "How are you getting on…with the students and all that?"

I sink back onto my chair, limp with defeat.

"Yvonne has been talking to you."

"Not talking, no. We passed each other in the hall just now, and she said there had been an incident in your class. She said you seemed upset."

"It's Logan Williams," I say, taking a deep breath. "He's been trying to undermine me from the start. You know, butting in, making snide remarks under his breath, generally being a right PITA — even his posture, he slumps in his chair, *sooooo* bored, and he's always a few minutes late, always! And of course I know I shouldn't let him get to me, but…"

"Why did he, today?"

It is so hard to fight the impulse to trust him.

"Come on, Anna. Spill."

Giles doesn't care.

Erin's verdict echoes in my mind, but he is here, and I must trust somebody. So I tell him everything; how I came across Logan and his girlfriend in the woods, about the "semen," the "phallusy," the reference to Jewish-American Princesses in tight little skirts, and even the suggestion that I'm a sexually frustrated ball-breaker. He is leaning against the shelf and listens impassively. When I'm done, he crosses his arms in front of his chest and sighs, I think in despair over my rashness and inexperience.

"I'm sorry it had to come to this," I continue hotly, "but a student was disrespectful to me, in a blatantly sexist manner, and I'll be damned if I'll take that sort of provocation—"

"—lying down?" His lips twitch, then he shrugs his shoulder in apology. "Sorry."

"Oh, that's—you know what?" I hear my chair bump noisily against the wall as I jump up again. "Thanks very much for your 'understanding'! If you've only come to—to be English about it, then this is a kind of mentoring I can do without!"

As I stand, quaking with rage and embarrassment, Cleveland moves over to a chair in front of my desk and sits down. His long legs crossed at the ankles, he pushes both hands into his pockets and frowns up at me.

"I haven't come to *be English* about it. Logan Williams' behavior is inexcusable, and we can think what to do about him later on. But more important is how you dealt with him. And how you will deal with him and his like in future, because I bet this sort of thing has happened before, and it will happen again."

"I can assure you that I've never been addressed like that by a student, ever! Not at NYU, not when I first started teaching university students six years ago in London, and not when I taught Hebrew to twelve-year-olds!"

I know I'm shouting because the alternative is crying, and I would much rather Cleveland thought me aggressive than pitiful. My throat muscles hurt from suppressing the tears that keep shooting to my eyes, and I stare down at the papers on my desk, surfing the wave of my emotions. If I blink, the waters will rise over the banks of my lower lids and drop down onto the pile of essays in front of me.

Cleveland doesn't move, and he doesn't speak. Bless him.

"I'm sorry," I finally manage to say. "I know the whole thing is absurd, but he really got to me. I mean, phallusy—that's—it's funny…" I giggle. Maybe I am sliding into hysteria after all. "I know I'm being defensive! I've never felt so defensive in my whole life, and—and I shouldn't, I mustn't! I know that I have to sort it out by myself, and I will, only I had to talk to someone about it, but… but if I had known that Yvonne would tell you, I wouldn't have told her, because I really can't afford to look like a dud…like a rookie… to half the faculty as well as to the students!"

When I dare look at him, my heart leaps at the expression on his face.

"First of all, I'm not half the faculty. Secondly, you *are* a rookie, and there's no shame attached to that at all. You are right to discuss these incidents with your colleagues. Choose your confidantes carefully, by all means, but don't feel you have to be able to wrestle with the slings and arrows of college teaching all by yourself, because that is the sure way to a burnout. Yvonne only told me because she was concerned, and she feels that as your mentor I should try to help. I've had my run-ins with Mr. Williams, if that's any consolation."

"You have?" I breathe with relief.

"He's what at school we used to call a complete dickhead. Do you want me to have a word with him? Only—"

"No, that would—"

"—I don't think that would increase your authority in the classroom."

"—look as if I needed help from the big boys. Yes, that's—I mean, no, thanks. I can deal with him, it's only that today—"

For a second or two I am tempted to give it all up and tell him about my paycheck, but—no. Not important enough. Not important enough to risk Cleveland's impatience.

"It doesn't excuse his behavior," he adds, "but Logan's biography isn't quite what you normally see in our students. He went to a community college after school and did exceptionally well there. Ardrossan has an agreement with the state to offer places to one or two of these students each year; that's how Logan got in. Since then he's floundered, and it's hard to say whether he is intellectually intimidated or feels culturally displaced. The social and cultural diversity on which we pride ourselves so much is, after all, of a very… er, circumscribed nature. What does your father do for a living?"

I'm too wrapped up in what he has been telling me about Logan to stop and think whether I want to answer that question.

"He's a cardiologist."

"See? Logan's father is in and out of prison. Forgery, embezzlement, stuff like that, nothing heavier. But I didn't tell you this."

"Oh, man." I rest my elbows on my desk and rub my forehead with the balls of my hands. "Now I can't even dislike him?"

Cleveland grins. "Yes, you can. Although I don't know about you, but I am usually more lenient with kids whose lives have been so much less privileged than mine. That's when my middle-class guilt sets in. It's the snooty, entitled ones who set my back up."

"But I *had* to wallop Logan today! He was asking for it!"

"As far as I can see, you did all the right things, only you shouldn't let him provoke you. But that's the high art of teaching, and for you it's early days yet. Now, in time—" He pauses, then continues with a twitch of the muscles around his mouth. "'When in eternal lines to time thou growest,' these incidents will become less frequent. Even if you were plain, you'd still be young. So be patient. Grow middle-aged. Don't dye your hair when it begins to go gray. Gain a couple of stone in weight. None of them messes with Elizabeth Mayfield, I can tell you that."

"That is preposterous!"

"It may be preposterous, but it's the best advice I have for you. Take it or leave it. The rest is an occupational hazard." Again he sighs, but he doesn't seem impatient with me anymore, lounging on his rickety little chair. "We are pissing into the wind. All of us who uphold the fiction—or maybe it's a dream, or worse, a hubristic fantasy—that by acquainting young people with, well, as Matthew Arnold has it, 'the best that has been thought and said in the world,' with *art*, which is always the fruit of intellectual subtlety and wit and compassion and tenderness, something that is bigger and better than us ordinary folk, so we have to expand our minds in order to grasp its brilliance and beauty—now I've lost the beginning of my sentence."

The seawater eyes release me from their deadlock; he looks round my office, bewildered. So passionate, when he lets his guard down, and so vulnerable.

I'm so in love with him I can hardly breathe.

"I was pissing into the wind," I remind him quietly. The eyebrows shoot up, but he doesn't smile.

"So you were." He seems to conclude our conversation by getting up from his chair. "There is nothing you can do to stop these young men from checking you out. And if they are the kind of male that bristles at women in authority, particularly in authority over *them*, they will seek relief from their discomfort by turning you into a sex object — a pretty little co-ed. If they become disrespectful, keep note of these incidents, mobilize witnesses, and report the offenders, but there's never any point in throwing a temper tantrum. Send Elizabeth an email about Logan, and then drop it."

All my tender feelings for him drown in the wave of blood that rushes to my head.

"Temper tantrum? That is so — patronizing! And where the hell do you get off calling me a *co-ed?*"

"I'm merely stating the obvious. You're — what, five-three? Five-four? A half pint." He appraises me dispassionately. "There are substantial benefits to be reaped by pretty, petite young women, as you no doubt know full well. But claiming authority over a gang of twenty-year-old males is harder for you than for some other types of woman. Boo-hoo and all that, but there it is."

"Will you stop calling me pretty!" I mutter through clenched teeth.

Cleveland's eyes glisten. He is hell-bent on provoking me, and I couldn't bring myself to back off if my life depended on it. We are both standing now, on either side of my desk, and the space between us is filled with crackling ice, or crackling flames, I can't tell the difference any more.

"When we're alone…I'll call you anything I like, and you'll stick it." He pauses for effect, and into the silence crowds a cornucopia of terms and phrases. "Not because I'm a male and more powerful than you — I'm not, by the way, more powerful than you — but because I'll not call you anything that I don't believe to be true. In company, rest assured it'll be 'Doctor Lieberman, my esteemed colleague.'"

I open my mouth to rake him down, but he cuts me off.

"And while we are having a heart-to-heart, I'll just enrage you a little bit further and give you some entirely uninvited and no doubt undesired feedback on your, er, garb. You tend to look like lamb dressed as mutton."

He pauses, as if he were waiting for me to lunge forward and slap his face. Since physical violence and stunned silence are my only options, I opt for silence.

"Of course I see that you dress conservatively to compensate for your youth," he goes on. "But in my opinion that's an error in judgment. It's quite easy to impress these youngsters, and your Noo Yoak toak and your Columbia degree do impress them, even if they don't admit it. Many of them are—well, maybe not *scared* of you, but a little in awe. The cool girl from the Big City. Make the stereotype work for you! You gotta slap them right if they don't act right…bitch."

His gaze holds me, and the word—its vulgarity, his low, gravelly voice—is as transgressive as his hand on my body would be. I can only gaze back, torn between fascination and fury, until I eventually manage to rally in my defense.

"Listen, don't…don't bitch me, buster. And maybe you can tell me why guys always think that women can be *goaded* out of the dumps? Because I got news for you: it's a *crap* method of cheering us up! It *never* works, and it *pisses* me off!"

His face lights up in that way that fools a girl into thinking she is his only joy and delight, but his shoulders do not relax, and our eyes do not unlock; in a moment of panic I lose my bearings and almost my balance, because what I see in his eyes is that he is *this* close to striding over to kiss me.

My clash with Logan Williams in front of the whole class has me panicking about my end-of-term evaluations, about my prospects at Ardrossan, and about my aptitude as a lecturer. If Giles Cleveland were to come round that desk, grab me, and kiss me, every cell of my body would hurl itself toward him with all the kamikaze force of which I am capable. I would forget all the Logans and all the Madelines in the world. I would even forget about my paycheck.

It would be the end of life as I know it.

Chapter 14

I'm running, stumbling over stones and the roots of trees, trying not to twist my ankle, trying not to fall. Trying to run off the adrenaline that sears all the nerve endings in my body, threatening to tip me into a vat of panic. What am I doing wrong? *Everything* is going wrong!

Not everything, not quite everything.

Dancey must not have been informed about Madeline Harrison's complaint about me, or he would surely have slapped me with that, too, the same way he feels it necessary to inform me that one among my colleagues considers the noise of my heels an attack on his personal freedom. Corvin. Or Dolph Bergstrom. Who else would complain to the department chair about a new colleague's shoes? *Shoes*, for Chrissakes, half-boots, not Louboutins! I'll be damned if I'll be bullied like this! They can underpay me, and they can fire me for treating students like liberal-minded adults, but they can't make me take off my heels! This battle I will fight.

And upon reflection I doubt that Logan Williams will report me to the chair, or worse, the Dean of Studies. Does he really want to tell Ma Mayfield about "semen" and "phallus"? Not freakin' likely. So I'm safe, for the time being.

As long as I don't fling myself at Giles Cleveland.

I must keep my distance, or I will fall for him like an egg from a tall chicken. Like an egg shot from a sling. Destruction upon impact. That was a crazy moment, earlier today. *Crazy*. At the time

I could have sworn that he was about to come for me, but now, in hindsight—impossible. Maybe what I saw in his face was his consternation at what *he* saw in *mine!* I can only hope and trust that in hindsight he, too, has decided that he was wrong.

The adrenaline ebbs out of my body, leaving behind a sense of nausea. Like a virus that crawls up my spine from the pit of my stomach. I would be fine, here, in my little cottage, with my new job and my new bike and my new colleagues. I would be fine, if it wasn't for Giles Cleveland.

Smoke.

I'm jogging along, deep in thought, and I couldn't say for how long I have been smelling burning wood, but it is very distinct now, and it's getting stronger. Feeling like Davy Crockett, I sniff and listen and peer through the dusky trees, and soon I can hear the sound of a guitar and of voices. The pickers' camp. I hadn't noticed it before when I walked past the clearing, but there is a knee-high stone circle designed to hold a fire. Several figures are sprawled round it, and on the wind comes a familiar whiff as of Catholic churches. I wonder whether the Walshes know of the depraved activities that go on here, the sex and drugs. But at least it isn't sex and drugs among illegal Mexican laborers; maybe that is all that counts.

One figure disengages from the group around the fire and walks toward me, or rather toward the path that leads back to the farm, and it is now so dusky that we only recognize each other when we're just a few yards apart.

"Hey, Jules," I greet her serenely.

She isn't as composed, but she manages to fake it, and she has no choice but to walk back together with me.

"Not for nothing, Jules, but you do know that if I ever happen to see you smoking dope, I'd have to tell your parents, right?"

"I wasn't smoking anything!"

"I'm not the Drug Squad. I don't need to know what you did or didn't do, and by the way, I could tell if you were stoned, and you're clearly not. I'm just saying. If."

"Have you ever—"

"Nice try, girlfriend, but hardly the issue."

"That means yes," she says quickly, and we both have to laugh.

"I confess nothing, Jules! I hope you heard me!"

"Yeah, yeah."

"More importantly, how's Karen?"

"How do you know about that?"

And why did I think I would get a straight answer out of a teenager?

"I had to get something from my car last night, and I saw them driving off. Is Karen at home again? Is she all right?"

"They're keeping her at the hospital for a day or two. To find out where the blood came from."

"That's okay, no need to tell me the gory details." A fifteen-year-old shouldn't have to talk about the vaginal bleeding endangering her mother's pregnancy.

"This would be the third miscarriage since the twins," she offers as if she were talking about the weather. That, of course, explains the hushed excitement when Karen told us the good news. "But she's only thirty-five; she can try a little longer." I have the uncanny feeling that she is giving me a sound bite from home.

There is a lot of bitterness here, and again I wonder whether it wouldn't improve Jules' lot if there was a little tomato princeling to shoulder his elders' expectations. But it wouldn't be appropriate to share this with her, particularly since there may well not *be* a princeling. Instead, I give her what I hope is an encouraging smile and let her jump first across the brook and onto the grass verge of the dirt track leading past the farm. In a cloud of dust a car approaches, a pick-up about ten years more beat-up than Pop Walsh's. Jules seems to recognize it; she gives a little yelp and starts waving. The pick-up slows down, and out the window leans my favorite student.

"Hey, ladies—going home already? The party's just starting!"

Jules giggles and says something about a curfew. I wonder whether her admiration is as obvious to him as it is to me, and my heart sinks.

"Who's your friend?" Logan asks Jules and hesitates only for the tiniest moment before he looks over at me, bold as brass. Looks me straight in the eye, daring me.

"Oh, this is Anna!" Jules responds eagerly. "Lieberman, Dr. Lieberman. She is an English professor at the Folly, too—don't you know each other?"

"Yeah, the name rings a bell."

Against my will I am a little tickled by this display of *chuzpah*, but if he thinks he can play me, he better think again.

"Logan is in one of my classes this semester, Jules."

"He is? That's so neat!" she exclaims. "That's so weird, though! Don't you think that's weird?"

"I do." My tone is dry enough to register with Logan, but not with Jules, whose attention is focused on the boy.

"Stranger things happen at sea," he says breezily and drives off.

Great. Logan Williams and Jules Walsh exchanging gossip about his new professor and her family's new tenant. This you do not get if you teach on a large urban campus.

"How come Logan hangs out with the pickers?"

"He has a job here! He's a regular, been picking for, dunno, four or five years?"

With a dysfunctional family and the transition from a community college to Ardrossan University to digest, Calderbrook farm may well be a comforting factor of continuity in Logan's life. He's welcome to it, too, as long as he keeps his mitts off my landlord's underage step-granddaughter.

Chapter 15

Kay Chang was right to suspect that the students know far more about the *affaire* Hornberger than we do after the evasive briefing by our Dean and our new chair. There appears to be no other topic these days on the fourth floor of the Observatory than Greco vs. Hornberger, and the hub for all information is Natalie's and Selena's office. Natalie keeps coming to school with an air of wounded but stubborn pride that I secretly admire—no matter whether it is real or a show.

Unfortunately, as a junior professor I must not be seen to allow or encourage familiarity with students. All I can say after a few days of walking purposefully (and noisily! *In-yer-face!*) past their open door on my way toward the stairs is that there is word of at least half a dozen other students who have, over the years, enjoyed Hornberger's attentions, that he got a kick out of seducing them in all sorts of places on campus including his office, the library, and the elevator at Rossan House (this I assign to the realm of the fantastic), and that nobody seems to be openly contesting Natalie's version of events.

They—she and Nick—went to a conference together in Los Angeles shortly before the semester started; he lured her into his room, plied her with drink, and forced himself on her. This is more or less the story that I expected, and I'm ashamed to say that my first thought is that Natalie will find it difficult to explain away her friendliness toward Hornberger since then. It is easy to imagine how the same events are being related by Hornberger himself, probably with as much claim to subjective truth. This affair will occupy our thoughts and time for months to come, money and administrative resources will be wasted, and in the end nothing will emerge but the two irreconcilable narratives that we already know today. Just because an aging male professor can't resist the opportunities that offer themselves to him in the nubile shapes of young women eager for approbation.

The sleazy talk is momentarily interrupted the following Wednesday when I turn up early on the fourth floor of the Observatory to prepare for my hard-won appointment with Dean Ortega.

The air at the top of the marble stairwell is unusually crisp, and I mentally congratulate the cleaning staff who must have left some windows open. But what Martha Borlind, Steve Howell, and a couple of students are examining seems to be the result of vandalism. Three window panes, each in a different dormer window, have been smashed.

"Could it have been birds?" Martha wonders.

"Then you'd have the shards *inside*, on the floor here!" Steve brushes her off. "But most of the glass is — " He cautiously opens one of the broken windows to peer down onto the inner yard. "Well, I can't see anything; it's bushes down there. But either the pieces were swept up already, or these were smashed from inside!"

I slowly walk along the corridor checking each hole, the last one in the window closest to the Dumpster that is still sitting under the stairs. Now and again people add some waste paper or some cookie wrappings to the pile of junk, and the other day I fished half a sandwich out of it — don't want to encourage the rats, on top of everything else. What I find in there today is a blood-drenched ball of tissue paper. I nudge a pile of plastic folders over it and saunter back to the others.

"Has anyone called maintenance?"

Larry the janitor is, if possible, even more appalled than we are at this evidence of wanton violence. He calls his young man, and together they are taping plastic sheets over the holes in the window panes as I leave to make my way across campus to the Dean's office at Rossan House.

"That's funny," Larry observes cryptically.

"What is?"

"All happens in front of your office, ma'am."

"What does?"

"Mess. Junk. Now this—" He nods at the windows.

"But that has nothing to do with my office!"

He looks past me at the cart and scratches his grizzled head. I'm waiting for him to explain himself, but after staring and scratching for a while, he turns back to his work.

"Anyway, you promised two weeks ago that you'd have this… thing removed," I add sharply. "You know better than I do that it's a fire hazard!"

"Central maintenance's job, ma'am."

"Yes, but it's your job to see to it that central maintenance do theirs! And I believe I've asked you not to call me ma'am, Larry!"

He glances over at me, and I could project any kind of disdain into his expression, but I don't have time for this.

Holly Ortega is apparently starting what is going to be a very busy day—during the ten minutes that I am in her office, her secretary comes in to hand her a sheaf of faxes, but she is very focused and friendly as she listens to my plight. I was right to come and see her, she tells me, but unfortunately she can't do more than make a phone call for me.

"Morning, Liz. Holly Ortega here. Listen, I have a young colleague here with some discrepancies in her paycheck. It's one of the contracts Newburgh signed…that's right. Can Amanda see her next week? Tuesday?" She looks at me. "Tuesday at ten thirty any good? Great, Liz, the name is Lieberman, Anna. Thanks very much. Bye!" She puts the phone down and smiles at me, her thoughts clearly already on her next task. "There you are, Anna—Amanda Cleveland will sort you out."

Oh. My. God.

Yes, I'm sure Amanda Cleveland will sort me out good 'n' proper. Especially if I tell her that I am lusting after her husband.

Well, all right. I admit it. I'm curious about the woman who is allowed, by some cosmic coincidence of time and temperament, to run her hand across those broad, boyish shoulders. Slip her fingers into his and draw him close. Undress him. I am still wondering why he was so dead set against becoming department chair. There is more to it than "Giles only cares about his own research." Amanda knows. *I* shouldn't even *want* to know.

When I return to the fourth floor of the Observatory, business seems to be going on as usual. The office doors are all open—we received a memo from Dancey reminding us to leave our doors open as much as possible and without fail when we are in our offices with a student—and the makeshift plastic window panes are softly flapping in the wind. How much more pleasant it is, despite the frustration, to wonder about Giles and Amanda Cleveland, if the depressing reality is a blood-drenched hanky in my Dumpster and the janitor's muttered suspicion that the recent mishaps on E-4 have one common denominator: the location of my office.

That's got to be nonsense.

As usual, my bunch of keys is hiding at the very bottom of my purse, and when I've found it and grab the door handle, my hand slips off and I smash bodily against the door.

"What the—"

The handle—and now also the palm of my hand—is covered in a thick, oily substance. Viscous, oily, and evil, smelling of rotten fruit and airports. Engine oil? Lamp oil? Maybe Larry did something to the door hinges while he was up here, and a little got spilled? But there is no oil on any of the metal parts of my door.

Slowly it drips onto the floor in front of my Mary Poppins boots.

No. I will not lower myself into the bog of paranoia.

It must be Corvin. I would totally believe that Corvin has complained to Dancey about the noise my heels make. But would a seventy-five-year-old emeritus professor, no matter how aggressively senile, smear lamp oil onto the handle of colleague's office door? And what's with the broken window panes?

There are two rivaling theories about the windows, Martha Borlind informs me when I invite her, a little disingenuously, for a coffee in the Eatery. One, favored by Martha herself, is that this was the act of vandals, the same individuals who last semester smashed some glass cases with *libri rari* in the library and sprayed graffiti on the front façade of Rossan House. The second—and Larry vowed to make enquiries—is that a party at Modern Languages yesterday evening got out of hand.

I don't tell Martha about the oil on my door handle, or about the bloody Kleenex. When I come back from the restroom along the corridor into Modern Languages, it is still sitting there, underneath the plastic folders, possibly the *corpus delicti* in this case. Without really bothering to examine my motives, I slip it into a clean plastic bag and lock it into the drawer of my desk.

Thursday after class I do what I consider to be the main part of my job: I spend an hour in the library and then work at my desk till my eyes cross with exhaustion. I may not be able to sleep eight hours at a stretch, but I can and do fall asleep anywhere. My three chairs pushed alongside each other make an adequate cot, and I'm dead to the world seconds after lying down. When I wake up, with a crick in my back and swollen eyes, it is almost eleven o'clock. The view from my window is a panorama lit by moonlight, sparsely dotted with the light from other offices, other night owls, and I can see the straight line of Victorian-style street lamps that illuminate the river promenade. I've never been in the Observatory so late in the evening. The hallway looks picturesquely dark except for the dim light from the windows, and it is exciting to feel that I have the building to myself. A little eerie, too. When mid-term grading is upon us, I'll be surprised if by midnight this place is empty. We will be keeping ourselves awake with green tea and gymnastics in the corridor. Two essays, one jog up and down the staircase, another two essays; that would be a good routine, guaranteed to —

Oh, snap! There is someone upstairs in the dome!

I'm as scared as I would be if I saw two thugs walking toward me in a deserted alleyway. This huge old building sitting on a hill, with its dome designed to look out into the night sky, empty except for some light and some voices at the very top, under the roof, one of the highest points on campus. The immediate associations from films we have seen are inevitable. A chair rocking gently, the creaky voice of an old woman talking to her son.

Every step I take will go *clackety-clack* on those stone tiles. I take my shoes off and creep up the first couple of steps of the spiral staircase, my shoes in one hand. A male voice and a female voice. It may simply be some students who've picked the lock and think it cool to have midnight sit-ins under the dome. Who else *could* it be, really?

The vandals!

In a flash I feel more protective of Ardrossan than ever before. My vigilante spirit awakes, and I have to hold on to the grubby metal handrail to stop myself from charging upstairs and demanding to know, like Malvolio in *Twelfth Night*, whether the intruders have no wit, manners nor honesty, to gabble like tinkers at this time of night. My compromise is another two steps, but as I creep up, my heart stops — the female voice grows loud enough for me to distinguish words.

"But it's wrong! I know it is! I shouldn't be doing it!"

"Charity, Selena! You're the only thing that keeps me going! Hey… hey, come here…"

The man, whose voice I can't place, continues to murmur and hush the agitated young woman. I recognized her voice at once; there is a strained, mewling quality to it that is very distinctive. I rode up in the elevator with her the other day, and she forced herself to talk to me although I could see that she was both shy and preoccupied. What Selena O'Neal is doing in the dome of the Observatory late at night is anybody's guess, but the one thing she is *not* doing is planning acts of wanton destruction. I would wager the missing sum on my paycheck that Giles Cleveland is wrong about Selena's virginity.

Overcoming parentally-imposed obstacles in order to have a sex life may be a drag. Presenting one's work-in-progress in the graduate seminar of one's academic program may be daunting. But neither warrant the sort of spectacle that Selena makes of herself when next we gather for an EMS meeting. She sits at the front desk like an Allegory of Misery, her face a sickly green above her demure jonquil blouse, trying and failing to unscrew the top of a water bottle by wedging it between her arm and her body. I can see from where I'm sitting how cold and sweaty her fingers are.

"Here, Selena, let me help."

She hardly looks at me, let alone thanks me, and I begin to wonder whether she is in too much of a state to do this.

"Selena…Selena?" I have to raise my voice to arouse her attention. "Are you all right? What's wrong with your arm?"

"Oh!" She stares at me, then at the arm as if it didn't belong to her. "I changed from touchpad to mouse. It's just a little sore. The doctor says it's like tennis elbow."

"I'm sorry to hear that. Shouldn't you be wearing a sling?"

"No! No, it's not that bad, really. I'm fine!" The skin between her brows puckers. "Thank you, Dr. Lieberman."

She is dutifully polite, her little silver cross dangling above the tiny triangle of skin visible at the neck of her blouse. I can't help finding this one a little creepy. Having seen the mother, I see the same large chest, luscious hair and full mouth on the daughter. Selena would actually be a much better candidate for America's Next Top Model than Natalie because she would give Tyra Banks the chance to do magic. Even a day's shopping and grooming with Irene Roshner—heck, even with *me!*—would go a long way toward turning this pasty-looking duckling into something swan-like. But Selena doesn't want to be a swan. Good for her, but I do wish she weren't such a drippy duckling. She makes me want to shake her, pull back her drooping shoulders, and send her out on early morning runs. Or better still, a course in kick-boxing. I'm convinced she goes up to the old observatory to have sex, but it doesn't seem to be enough to get her circulation going.

"She's not fine, you know." Tessa has shifted on her chair so that she seems to be commenting on the people filing into the room. "She's sick almost every morning, and I don't believe for a minute that it's flu or a bug. You don't have a stomach bug for more than two weeks."

"Not normally, no."

"Well." Tessa is still looking neither at me nor at Selena, and I'm actually not sure what she is driving at, or that I want to hear it. "Grad school isn't for everyone, that's all. It isn't just about working hard. You gotta be able to stand the pressure, mentally. I'm not the toughest cookie myself—cried for two days when Beecher dissed me for my paper, although I knew he would; he always does. But next to Selena I'm hard as nails."

I could say a thing or two about being hard as nails, or ever wanting to be hard as nails, but this isn't about me.

"Do you know whether she has seen a doctor? Other than about her elbow, I mean."

"Why would she? To be told it's bad for her and she should stop doing it?"

It dawns on me that Tessa and I have been talking at cross-purposes. I was thinking about nervous stomachs; she was talking about bulimia.

As it happens, *I* have a nervous stomach. How acute of Giles Cleveland to call me a co-ed. That's exactly what I feel like, a nineteen-year-old airhead fidgeting in her chair because her favorite professor is about to enter the room. So embarrassing. The other embarrassing thing is that I decided to go a little way toward heeding his advice about my clothes. The black turtleneck may conceal a lot of skin, but it is tight-fitting, as are my jeans. This is not one of my teaching days, so I thought I could risk jeans. And a tight sweater. And silver pendant earrings. Let's just say that this ensemble has worked before, okay?

It is so easy for men. Charcoal jeans, a white dress shirt with very thin dark stripes, a tweed jacket—delicious. He takes off the jacket, and his shirt cuffs are undone, as usual, but he does not roll them up to expose his arms. The smooth cotton tightens across his shoulders as he welcomes us and introduces Selena, and I get sucked into a sexual fantasy in which I slip my hands underneath his shirt, run them up his chest and around those shoulders that look so severe and vulnerable at the same time. Push the shirt up over his head, ruffling his hair, his beautiful, soft, silvery hair, sink my teeth into the skin over his pectoral muscles.

I'd be so gentle with him. Use my teeth on him so gently, ever so gently, just hard enough to make him moan and close his eyes and roll his head back onto his shoulders.

Would he like that? Does he like being undressed? Or is he a control freak who must be in charge at all times? I wonder what Giles Cleveland is like as a lover. Whether I'd think he's a good lover. Whether that *shiksa* of his thinks he's a good lover. I know that this is a trick that Mother Nature has evolved in order to safeguard the procreation of the English—the sense that an Englishman's reserve hides a volcano of passion. Not the case, in nine cases out of ten, but the poor deluded non-English female is hopelessly intrigued.

I rejoin Selena's talk when she looks up from the sheets she has been reading, so much like a deer caught in headlights that I feel guilty for not having paid more attention. Her project—at once predicable and disturbing, coming from her—is a cultural history of Satan, from medieval grotesque to sophisticated player. It could be summarized, although she does not do so in so many words, as the question, Since When Has Evil Been Sexy? It is a catchy topic that might spark a lively discussion, but Selena is making a hash of it because she does not approach it with the playful yet sophisticated mind it requires. She is right to observe that this shift, which culminates in Milton's grandiose rebel, happened during the early modern period. But exactly by what method she is going to combine the analysis of synchronic aspects like popular culture in conflict with scholarly teachings, and of diachronic aspects like developments in and of the various genres, from the dramatic to the theological, is unclear both to her and us.

"Yes, uh…Selena," Beecher interrupts her, "we can see that you read a great many texts, which is, uh…commendable. But could you perhaps summarize for us your main conclusions so far?"

She explains, haltingly, that she has not reached any "conclusions," but that her main observation is that the medieval devil is merely an instrument by which temptations are presented to the tempted, a go-between, while the seventeenth-century devil begins to *embody* temptation, as an object of sexual desire himself.

"There is no suggestion at all that Mephistopheles in *Doctor Faustus* is himself temp*ting*, he is merely a temp*ter*; but Othello, for instance, is a figure of temptation in this double sense. Another example—"

"Now we're back with examples. Does your, uh…hypothesis go further than postulating that devil figures, along with practically all fictional types that survived from the Middle Ages into the Renaissance, were rendered more psychologically realistic? This would be true of kings and maidens as much as of the devil."

"Well, I…I would try to show *how* this is done, sir, not just… postulate." Selena reddens but soldiers on. "If I may…Othello, for example, accuses himself of loving his wife too much, and this is also what Milton's Adam is guilty of, loving his wife more than he loves God. But in most other respects, Othello is characterized as a satanic figure—black, and so forth. In a recent study about racism in intertexts of *Othello*—" Now it is Cleveland who groans and fidgets. "Yes, I know, sir, you don't like the author, but—"

"Whether I like her or not isn't the point; the point is that her book about *Othello* is—" he seems to fumble for the right word "—utter tosh. You should only read it to disagree with it."

"But Othello—"

"—has satanic features and is guilty of idolatry. You are perfectly right about that." He nods. "Carry on."

It is obvious to me that Selena would benefit much more from an hour or two of individual tuition with her advisor than from this plenary interrogation. Why Cleveland allowed her to hurl herself into a methodological and theoretical quagmire like this, I cannot understand.

Giles does not care.

Here we have it.

Making the best of a mess, I suggest to Selena that her analysis might become more dynamic if she distinguished different genres of devil narrative. "Your second type of devil, the sexy seducer—" Selena flinches a little, as if she had made a wrong movement with her elbow "—is a new figure on the Renaissance stage, but he does not immediately replace the older, medieval kind of devil, the malevolent but inept bungler who assumes the shape of a black dog and promises riches and revenge to guileless old women."

I'm gratified to see that Selena is making some notes, though none of the professors acknowledge my comment in any way.

Jenna, the girl who had asked about my British degrees, raises her hand and waits for Cleveland to give her a nod. "I was wondering, does that mean that in stories with a sexy devil—" Again there are some giggles at the phrase, and Jenna blushes. "That these stories are always about a woman—an Eve—who has to choose between an Adam and a Satan? A lot of love stories are like that, right?"

"Yes, the theme…the theme is temptation. The satanic figures that I want to look at aren't just…evil. They tempt. That's their defining feature." Distress is making Selena's strained voice rise in pitch, and I suddenly remember what I overheard the other night.

It's wrong!

It's charity!

"Charity" is an odd word to use for a young man who wants to get a girl in the sack, unless he understands how she ticks and is using her Christian morality against her. Satanic indeed.

"What about *Gone With the Wind*, though?" Tessa speaks up. She is nervous, as students usually are in these seminars, and very earnest. "Within the framework of a formation novel, Ashley Wilkes is the immature…like, the idol of the adolescent girl, while Rhett Butler is the man, the real man, she must grow up to appreciate. But isn't our theory that the satanic figure is the immature fantasy? That the heroine has to overcome the temptation posed by the devil in order to marry Adam Ordinary and be happy with him?"

"Selena, I think Tessa has outlined an interesting line of inquiry." I turn to her with the most encouraging smile I can muster. But Selena has lost it. Instead of composing herself, she has been following our exchanges with apprehensive eyes, and she is not ready to respond. So I ad-lib to buy her time.

"Actually, I tend to think the opposite. Rhett Butler is the immature fantasy, not Ashley Wilkes, although the film would have you think otherwise, because it equates masculinity with the ability or willingness to dominate women, and other men. With Rhett you can be as irrational and high-maintenance as you want, and he'll laugh at you, first, then bitch-slap you, then rape you. Which is all you wanted in the first place, of course, only you were too much of a princess to admit it."

Cleveland is quietly chuckling in his seat, but I am warming to my topic.

"Ashley Wilkes, on the other hand, apart from being far more beautiful than Rhett Butler, in my humble opinion, has no time for bitches. The truth—" I wait for the commotion to die down. "The truth is that Ashley is bored by Scarlett on every level except the sexual, just as any other grown-up man would be bored by an adolescent girl on every level except the—well, anyway."

I cut myself off when I see several alarmed faces staring at me and Cleveland hiding a grin behind his hand as he leans forward to cup his chin. I know him well enough by now to be able to tell that there are all sorts of inappropriate things he is not saying, and while I am struggling not to respond to something he has not actually said, I have a sudden vision of Cleveland in a gray Confederate uniform, or a brown cutaway, vest and white collar, or a blue flannel shirt, the sleeves rolled up to his elbows to display his long, sinewy arms, his long, sinewy fingers…and that lean face, so sensitive, so intelligent that I am itching to grab him and fuck him till he begs me to let him come.

Oh, I hate Englishmen.

This one in particular. After his customary flippancy early on, he does nothing to protect Selena from Beecher and his henchmen, who round on her till she caves in completely. That she does not burst into tears is about all, but her monosyllabic answers become so painful that I have to withdraw my mind from the situation and keep thinking *shut the fuck up* to stop myself from intervening. It is like a deer being baited by blood-crazed hounds, with the rest of us standing by, careful to keep away from the fray.

When it is all over, we disperse quickly and quietly. I find myself walking back toward the Observatory with Cleveland, fuming.

"Why didn't you say something?" I burst out.

"Sorry?"

He looks down at me as if he was only now realizing that I'm here.

"Back in the meeting! Why were these…*historians* allowed to annihilate Selena like that?"

The gray-dappled green eyes focus on me and narrow, with condescension or impatience, I can't tell.

"Because no one stopped them," he says.

"That's what I mean! Why didn't you stop them?"

"Why didn't *you* stop them?"

I stare at him, confused. He's evidently trying to provoke me, and I really don't see why he should be doing that.

"I couldn't!"

"Why not?"

"Because I'm nobody! Because Beecher wouldn't listen to me anyway! But if you had told him to belt up —"

"It was Selena's job to do that."

"Well, she tried — you could see that she was trying! It was our job to protect her! *I* have to shut up, but *you* could have shut *him* up!"

"Bring in the cavalry, you mean?"

We walk up the steps to the entrance and almost come to a halt. Is he going to open the door for me, or am I going to go first? Or have we decided to dispense with polite gestures altogether? My level of adrenaline is so high that I step forward and hold the door open for him; he walks in, and when he catches my eyes and cocks a sardonic eyebrow, my blood reaches boiling point.

"You were the only one there from whom Beecher would have taken it! Which means that you were the only one there who could have prevented the last ninety minutes from being a complete nightmare for one of our grad students, and a complete waste of time for everyone else!"

"You are making my knees buckle. Such a weight of responsibility."

"Which you refuse to accept!"

"I do. Because I, unlike you, know how to choose my battles! Now listen! Listen, once and for all!"

The tone of his voice makes me turn round on the stairs, and my blood runs cold. Face to face with him, because he's two steps lower down, I can see that I have managed to upset him. His lips are tight with anger and his eyes hard as green glass.

"I do not believe in letting graduate students paddle about the shallow end with water wings on! Sel—" He hushes himself, but that only seems to make him fiercer. "The student insisted that she was ready to present, and it was not for me to veto her! And before you point out that her paper was feeble, permit me to say that I knew that! I knew it, and I told her, but she would not listen! I have told her on two different occasions that she should not attempt a doctorate degree, but she would not listen!"

"But it was a shambles!"

"Yes, it was," he agrees, breathing hard. "But so is the job-market situation in the Humanities. Even if she pulled through, she would never find an academic job out there that would suit her. She can't teach, and she is neither mentally nor intellectually equipped to do top-notch research. That said, she is neither dumb nor lazy, and that was sufficient to secure her an excellent first degree. But she is simply not good enough to continue!"

"But how must she feel right now? It was irresponsible to let them trample her like that!"

"It's equally irresponsible to allow someone unsuited to an academic career to waste her time in grad school. So she failed! She will go home, think it over, talk it over, and revise her dissertation! And if she doesn't, she'll fail again, and if she keeps failing, she'd better come up with Plan B, because she won't make it in academia!" He pauses and looks at me, oddly. "What's your Plan B?"

"Plan B?"

"What are you going to do if this doesn't work out?"

"Are you talking about what if I don't make associate?"

"Well, for the syntax of that sentence alone you should be blackballed."

"No, but—but this isn't about me! And it isn't about this particular student's potential as a young academic! This is about common decency!"

"Oh, bollocks!"

And he stomps past me, two steps at a time with his long legs, up the stairs and along the hallway to his office. Just leaves me standing there, swaying with adrenaline. A student comes down the stairs and avoids my eyes so clumsily that I know our fight was audible all through the staircase. I hurry up two flights of stairs to my office, hoping that I will make it into my little sanctuary before I burst into tears. I am in such a state, my hand is trembling so badly I can't even fit the key into the lock.

What's with this freakin' door?

The key does not fit the lock. It isn't my trembling fingers at all. The lock has been changed. I hadn't noticed it right away, in my rush, but the handle is different, newer; the whole thing, lock, handle, and all, has been changed. Thirty-six hours after I scrubbed it to get the stench of motor oil off it. And no one told me.

If a last straw were needed, this would be it.

Up the stairs…up the spiral staircase. The door to the old observatory under the dome will be locked, too, bound to be; Selena and her demon lover won't have left it open, but at least it'll get me out of sight. I crouch at the top of the stairs by the heavy carven door that looks as if it had not been changed since the eighteen fifties. Lean against the wall among broken chairs and wooden casks, and slide down into a pathetic bundle.

It is pouring out of me. Floods of silent tears, when I hate crying, when I haven't cried since my *bubbe* died last spring, and why the hell does Cleveland keep reminding me of my *grandmother?* When he looked at me back there on the stairs — *What are you going to do if this doesn't work out?* — for a split second I saw my grandmother's anxious face. But no one is going to look at me ever again with such affection-ate concern and say "But are you happy, *lemeleh?*" It would be foolish, the supremest of all follies — to think that anyone will. Or would.

Or just did.

Tears of fury — God, yes! But not about Cleveland.

And I don't even have a — I wipe my face and nose with the sleeve of my blouse, and detect, in the dusky light of the landing, a box of tissue paper wedged between two moving boxes. Chances are, there's a rat living in there. Or a huge spider. Gingerly I push my fingers in and have to bite on a squeal; something hard touched my fingertips. A key. Not a flat key like the ones on my key ring; a metal skeleton key, like the key in a fairy story.

It does make me feel childishly implausible, but how can I indulge in a fit of *Weltschmerz* when I may be holding the key to the fabled Ardrossan observatory in my hand?

It is like stepping into the apse of a church. The dome is a ribbed vault divided into eight segments, each designed to be slid open by a long crank handle. The windows are as high as the ceiling—long, slim lancet windows all round, in keeping with the neo-gothic style of the building, the walls between covered by high bookcases. This is a marvelous space.

The bookcases are full of junk; there are piles of broken office chairs, a musty old sofa, and a few old tables. Wooden stepladders, half a dozen or more, to reach the telescopes and the higher shelves of the bookcases. I instinctively scan all visible surfaces for evidence of violence or debauchery; I don't know what I thought I would find. In fact, there is nothing, nothing that I can see in the dusky light of early evening. Except—

I've still got the box of tissues in my hand, and what I thought was a white carton with little flowers on it is in fact a white carton with specks of dried blood on it.

Okay, so…what? All sorts of people with all sorts of clandestine or nefarious intentions are using the old observatory as their base? Whoever broke the windows on the fourth floor mopped up the blood from the gashes on his hand with tissue paper from this box, then hid the box on the top landing—why? Why not throw it into the Dumpster, too? Selena and her boyfriend have late-night tête-à-têtes up here, so it must have been they who hid the key in the box of tissues. Why not just take it away? The only reason for Selena and Mr. X not to pocket the key is that they know that other people are also using it and that these other people would become suspicious of them if the key went missing. At the same time—what if this third party suddenly happened upon them when they are in the middle of a tryst? Awkward. They hadn't even closed the door behind them, yesterday evening, or I wouldn't have seen the crack of light.

I don't give a hoot. I couldn't care less about who is doing it with whom in the various attics, basements, elevators, or broom cupboards on campus. Let them all go to hell. I want my bag and my coat, and then I want to go home.

Except I don't know where that is.

Chapter 16

Next morning I do not set off for New York City. Instead, I get my bike out of the shack, pump up the tires, pack my little rucksack with sandwiches, chocolate, and a thermos of coffee, and start cycling. I wish that I could jump out of my skin. Out of my life. But I can't, and running away is not going to solve my problem. Maybe I'll just go on pedaling along the Piedmont till I reach Hagerstown, Maryland. Or southward, toward Chattahoochee National Park. Why should I head northeast? There is nothing for me there. There is nothing for me here, either, it seems, but this is where I'm marooned, so I might as well reconnoiter the area.

The first five miles are bad. I'm listless and bored. The idea of cycling all day seemed better in theory than it is in practice. But I am not a quitter. That's what this is all about. The first stretch along the Ouse riverbank is thronging with families and couples whiling away the time before lunch. From a distance it's a sight that sinks my spirits even further, but as I thread my way slowly through the crowd, I pick up snatches of bickering and *kvetching* that cheer me up a little, malevolent bitch that I am. I'm profoundly glad when I turn off toward the lake that is tucked into a bend in the river.

The monotonous pedaling and the wind on the water calm me down. On a bench with a view I have the most delicious cheese sandwich I've ever eaten and two plastic cups of tepid but equally delicious coffee. Hardly anyone is around and the few elderly stalwarts that I meet smile at me with open, friendly, weather-beaten faces.

It's invariably couples that I see. Their average age seems to be about seventy-five, and more than one couple is holding hands.

"Come in and have a nice warm muffin!" one of them says to me, walking past my picnic.

"Oh, thanks! But no thanks. I…I just want to be alone."

What sort of a reaction to the kindness of strangers is *that?*

I am almost thirty years old, and I have never met a boy, or a man, who made me dream of walking along a lake with him holding hands when we're seventy-five. Except Alex Gresham, of course. Is that evidence of bad luck, of choosiness, or of immaturity? My mom has an opinion about this, but *I* don't think I'm too fastidious. I'm just not particularly interested, most of the time, and then, for no good reason, I fall for one.

Cleveland's face when I shouted at him on the stairs.

A wave of anxiety washes over me. I seem to be shouting at him a lot. In my office, in the main staircase of the Observatory. I know why. And if he is not a complete dunce, he knows it, too.

God, he was *furious* with me!

By the time I had washed my tear-stained face and composed myself enough to go downstairs and find someone to unlock my office for me, Larry the janitor had long since gone home. The night watchman knew about the new locks — apparently all offices on the fourth floor were due to have their locks changed — but couldn't tell me why I had not been informed, or where I might get hold of a new key. So next week, which already features my appointment with Amanda Cleveland, will begin with a show-down between self and Larry, to be followed by a set-to between self and Dancey, if I know anything about Larry and his refusal to take responsibility for anything at all that happens in the Observatory.

Next week I'll ask Selena O'Neal to have lunch. It was eminently prudent of me to keep quiet during the meeting, but if Cleveland won't talk *tachlis* with her, somebody else must. He recruited me for grad advisement, so advise her I will. Perhaps I can salvage that dissertation of hers, even if I seem unable to salvage my own career.

The stench and the noise of the Shaftsboro bypass clash painfully with the quiet of the riverside path, and I cut into the woods again with only a vague idea about how to find my way home. It should be due north, but how's a girl from Queens to know where north is when she's cycling through a densely forested area and the sky is gray?

In the same moment that I see water glisten among the trees I also see evidence of human life, or rather canine life. Two large dogs of indeterminate breed are speeding across the path onto a clearing to my left. At first I'm a little alarmed when the second one catches up with the first and they turn summersaults among the dry leaves in a bundle of legs and tails and fur, but as there is no fierce growling or painful yelps, and they immediately pick themselves up and start chasing each other again, they are presumably just playing. It's a pleasing sight, the animal exuberance, two creatures enjoying the energy of their bodies, and I stop and lean against a tree to watch. The dogs break out of the narrow, overgrown path on the other side of the main track, and I think I can hear twigs crack under a foot. Is there any danger? I'm still finding it hard to get my head around the fact that country lanes might be as dangerous for a lone female as empty urban alleyways.

A man appears from between the trees, stamping his foot to get a clump of wet leaves from his hiking boots. He's wearing frayed corduroys and a thick blue Royal Navy sweater, which strikes me as oddly ominous. Then he lifts his head to look for his dogs, and it's Giles Cleveland.

Giles. A sense of dread swamps me, almost like fear and my first and spontaneous thought is, *I hope* she *isn't with him!* I can bear seventy-five-year-olds holding hands on Sunday lakeside walks, but the sight of Giles Cleveland in affectionate physical contact with his wife would do something to my precarious emotional balance that I won't even analyze.

I see him before he sees me, so I have a couple of seconds to adjust my face before he freezes. His reaction makes me feel that I ought to apologize for being here, on his turf, in his way. Luckily I can stop myself from so abject a gesture.

Be cool. Be off-hand.

"They belong to you?" I nod toward the dogs that come bounding up to him and, having ascertained that all is well with him, begin to examine me on my bike.

"Yes," he says slowly, doing the same, but with his eyes. "Are you okay with that?" He means the dogs' attention.

"Yeah, sure. Ignore them, right?"

"That's right."

The smile that has been lurking in his light eyes now reaches the corners of his mouth. He looks different, in his old corduroys, his hair windswept into his face; younger than in his working-day suits, and again I see the college athlete in his long legs and broad shoulders. Why the hell isn't his wife with him? Perhaps she's at home, preparing Sunday dinner for her man. Lighting candles. Slipping into something soft and gauzy that she will slip off again when she has undressed this strangely diffident, successful university professor. "What are their names?" I'm watching the dogs, who have already lost interest in me.

"Feel free to scoff. This one, the Alaskan Malamute-plus-who-knows-what, is Toby, and that one, probably Beagle-plus-Spaniel-plus-something else, is Andrew."

"As in Belch and Aguecheek? And does Sir Toby have Sir Andrew under his thumb, and pinch his food, and send him into fights with puny poodle ladies?"

Cleveland grins. "Toby's the boss, yes, but on the whole Andrew doesn't mind that. No cakes and ale for either of them, though."

Two English Lit nerds discussing dogs that are named after Shakespearean characters. But even that doesn't ease the atmosphere.

He nods at the bike.

"So, you've been getting some exercise."

"I've been round the lake."

"Really. Wow."

"Yes, but now I'm lost. Could you tell me, kind sir, the way back home, please?" I bat my eyelashes at him, only twice, but it feels as dangerous as if I had reached between his legs to feel his crotch.

Cleveland flashes me a deliberately lecherous grin.

"As it happens, my cottage is just up there, along the track. There's a nice fire burning, and tea's a-brewing, just right to warm the cockles of *bicyclistes* in distress." He says the word in French, as if they were a breed he takes a special interest in. *Bicyclistes in distress.*

"You know the fruit farm about a mile beyond the old bridge road? That's where I live. Now, if I keep close to the lake here, that should get me near it, but I don't know how best to cut off from the lakeside path. I don't want to go round and round again…"

With perfect composure Cleveland gives me directions, clear and precise, easy to memorize, easy to follow, and I cycle off. *Calm.*

Calm. Did he just ask me…have I just refused…what? A cup of tea with a colleague, a peace cup, since neither of us seems to smoke, sorely needed after last week, after the last few weeks. I'm cycling straight toward a two-story cabin. It is built into the slope that leads down to the lake. Its lakeside half sits on stilts; there's a wraparound porch, a shack that seems large enough to double as a garage, and a breathtaking view of the lake directly behind it. I can't stop and admire it, though, because Cleveland must be following me, and the last thing I want is for him to catch me goggling at his house. He'll be thinking that I'm waiting for him. He'll be thinking that I want to come in after all.

"I bet you get a ton of mosquitoes," I say when he has reached the little footpath crossroads on which I've stopped.

He pushes his hands into pockets, frowning.

"Visitors usually respond a little more favorably."

"I'm Jewish." I grin. "You see a bagel, I see a hole. No, seriously, this is…a dream."

If he asks me to come in again, I will.

He looks at his house as if it wasn't his at all.

"You think?"

"Hey, Cleveland, one compliment is enough! If you want to go fishing for 'em, the lake is right there!"

This makes him smile. "Well, you're evidently hiding out, too, on that farm."

I am stumped, for the second time within ten minutes.

"At first I only rented it, but when—" He hesitates and seems to reconsider. "I was able to wheedle some money out of the college about nine months ago, and I decided to buy it."

"Oh—nice! What's the secret?" I laugh. Playing for time.

"Get offered a job at Stanford and hope your college will bribe you to stay!"

He glances over at me, smiling. Looking very handsome, but not like a man who is going to ask stray females in for cups of tea. Not like a man about to cross any lines. The moment has passed. We're just making conversation.

"I had heard that about you. That you refused a job at Stanford. Me, I didn't even apply for any jobs on the West Coast. It's just too far away."

"From?"

I finish that thought, and to my own surprise the answer is, "From England."

He's still looking at me, but he's not laughing any more. "Mmhmm."

"Why didn't you go? To Stanford?"

"I tried the idea on for size," he says readily, "but I think it's fair to say that both sides realized that it wouldn't have been a match made in heaven. But it seemed probable enough to allow me to put pressure on some people here."

We are gazing at the cottage again, and I briefly debate whether I'm going to regret giving in to the impulse that makes me say, in a sportscaster's voice: "Aaaand yesterday we heard that Giles 'The Brains' Cleveland is talking to Stanford Cardinal, oooh, that's going to mean trouble with his home team, the Piping Plovers, they won't like that at all, not to mention his fans—question is: can they top the Cardinal's offer? Stay tuned; we'll keep you posted! And here's the latest on Cleveland's transfer to Stanford Cardinal: it's all off! Seems he doesn't want to leave the East Coast after all!"

He looks so lovely when he laughs! I've made him laugh; he's laughing out loud, and I know that he would never laugh like this if he didn't like me.

"It's not that I didn't want to leave." Now he is no longer laughing. *Wait, what? Why?*

"But then you bought a house," I manage, hoping that this is an innocent enough comment.

"Maybe I shouldn't have. Andrew! Toby! Come here! They think we're going for a swim. *Toby!*"

I wish I could go on asking, but I can't.

"Well, would you mind not selling it till I can afford to buy it off you?"

It was meant to be just a joke; but when he looks over at me, surprised and curious, I realize what else I have said. And I'm actually okay with that.

"So…a decade, do you think?" he teases me, but gently. "Or am I insulting you by saying it'll be a decade till you can apply for a job at Stanford?"

"I told you, I wouldn't move to California," I remind him. "Too far away."

"Ah, yes, that's right. But maybe you've moved too far away already?"

"By coming to Ardrossan?"

"By not staying in England."

"Yeah, maybe. Giles?" My heart is beating high in my throat.

"Yes?" He is very quiet.

"Why won't you take the department chair?"

My question surprises him, but I don't see the shutters going down. He looks down at his boots, gives a spurt of self-deprecating laughter, shifts on his feet.

"I can't tell you that."

I think he almost did tell me, nonetheless.

"It's getting dark. I better be on my way." I am sad, suddenly, and I don't want to be. I made myself better, pulled myself out of the dumps. I don't want that spoiled.

When I get home I feel strangely woozy. Sleepy, drugged, almost, with oxygen, lulled into physical tranquility by several hours' pedaling. The small, bright, sizzling restlessness in the middle of my stomach has not disappeared, though. I put the kettle on and have a melancholy cup of tea on my sofa while I'm filling the bath tub with hot water and orange-scented foam. In a little while I start glowing from the inside, and my skin begins to tingle. I undo the zipper of my anorak, which I haven't taken off yet. Then I undo the zipper of the cardigan I'm wearing underneath. It feels sexy, undoing zipper after zipper. So I undo my jeans as well. A glimpse of belly, the skin still gratifyingly taut. My breasts, what I call my BBTs—barely B-cup tits—seem gratifyingly large, but that's because I'm about to get my period. Maybe that's why I shouted at Cleveland. Pre-menstrual tension. I put the mug down and clasp my naked breasts in my palms. The nipples pucker and harden into little crimson hillocks; it's been ages since I've touched myself. Why don't I do that anymore? It's bad enough that nobody else is touching me; I should at least look after myself a bit more. I've been too busy, that's all. Too tense.

I look down at my breasts and recall the image of Ciaran's blond head pressed between them. Huh, no. I guess a girl can say that she's over a guy when the idea of having sex with him is no longer distressing but merely boring. I try another fantasy, a newer one. I imagine myself on another sofa, the sounds of the lake wafting in through an open window. My anorak undone, my cardigan undone,

my t-shirt pushed up over my breasts and a mouth suckling me…
soft, silky, silver hair between my fingers…gray-dappled green eyes
full of tender amusement…large, sensitive hands on my skin…I
shift in my seat to pull my jeans a little further down over my hips.

When I hobble into the bathroom, pants round my knees, the
overflow drain is just about to start sipping hot water and foam
from the tub.

Chapter 17

Sunday is the loneliest day I have yet spent in the South. I try to be honest with myself. Am I hankering after the owner of a certain lakeside cabin, or do I feel sick at heart because this afternoon Freddy and Marga, Bernie and Elvira, Avi Young, little Rabbi Ostrovicz and all their friends will gather at their shul for Kol Nidre? There are few things that make one feel more of a social failure than sitting home alone on a holiday. This is the first Yom Kippur eve on which I don't at least have dinner with friends or go to my parents' house, but before I jump into the mire of self-pity — while the men at Beth David are immersing themselves in the waters of the *mikveh* to wash off their sins — I call myself to order.

In the spirit of the day I do what I should have done days ago, I walk over to the main house to visit Karen. My news of her is almost ten days old, and apart from the fact that she is at home again — which I know because I saw her feeding the chickens — I know nothing. And it's none of my business, of course. I would never do this in New York with a neighbor I know as little as I know Karen Walsh. But we are not in New York, and after all I was present when she announced the pregnancy.

These German-Scotch-Irish are a hard-to-read bunch, though. I don't think I am welcome at the kitchen door yet, so I walk around to the front. Literally one second after I ring the bell, the door is yanked open by a twin dressed in a frilly gown — *they are all fixin' to go to church.* Trust the silly Jewish Yankee to come visiting at ten on a Sunday morning. Pop Walsh seems to consider his reaction for a few moments while everyone is staring at me, then he nods his head into the direction of the kitchen.

"'Morning, ma'am. Karen will be at the back, if you'll go through."

No idea whether I'm welcome or whether he's merely too polite to slam the door in his tenant's face.

Karen, at any rate, is glad to see me, but she looks drawn and anxious. She sits me down with a mug of coffee — she has herbal tea herself — and I make no bones about the fact that I saw them drive off the other night and that Jules told me about the two miscarriages. She seems taken aback by my straightforwardness, but if I'm going to visit the complicatedly pregnant, I'm not going to make small-talk. And as before, my blunt approach works and she pours out the story of her failed pregnancies. Apparently this time the problem is a blood clot in her uterus that may be leaking blood needed to nourish the fetus. It is inoperable, and the blood thinners that could be prescribed have the downside of bleeding out not only the blood clot but possibly also the fetus, so they are not an option until a later stage of the pregnancy.

"So I can only pray and take things easy." She smiles wanly. "Neither comes naturally to me, I must confess."

Maybe that is why Karen and I understand each other. Once she has opened up, she doesn't stop talking, and I listen.

I am, in a tiny way, atoning for my cowardice. I would lack the courage to do what Karen is doing, endure pregnancy after pregnancy (there was a miscarriage before the twins as well as the two after), complication after complication, weeks and months of fear. I encourage her to talk, but neither of us mentions the monster at the horizon: what if the baby dies?

When I stroll back to the cottage, Jules is sitting on my porch. She has her feet propped up against the table and her hands hitched up inside the sleeves of her sweater with only the tips of her fingers peeping out, and she is texting. This is not the first time I…well, do I say *caught* her? It is not a word that her behavior suggests. She sits on the steps of my porch, sometimes on the porch, sometimes on the big sawn-off tree trunk at the back, and when I look out the window and see her or when I come home and she is hanging out in what I consider my backyard, she doesn't seem to feel that I have any cause to feel irritated. Perhaps the tree trunk isn't part of the lease? The porch certainly is.

"Hi, Jules. Did you want something from me?"

She shrugs in the manner of a fifteen-year-old, without putting down her phone.

"I just couldn't stand it at home any more. They don't talk about anything else any more but the…baby. It's always the same—no, actually, it gets worse each time." She shrugs again, pushes the phone into her kangaroo pocket. "And it always ends the same way."

I lean against the railing and cross my arms. I sympathize with Jules, I do. But I don't much feel like switching on the psychotherapist each time I talk to her.

"How's *your* life going?" I ask, cheerfully. "How's the driving coming along?"

She gives a hollow laugh. "Been grounded."

"Why? Were you caught…" I end that question on three dots, because I suspect there may be several things she might be caught doing, particularly at the pickers' camp, that wouldn't amuse her family at all.

"No! I told you, I don't do that stuff!" she insists hotly. "They're making me help my mom cook and clean. School is allowed, but no fun."

"You know this means an awful lot to your mom, right? It's a really big thing you can do for her at this time, helping her and—you know, playing along. I understand that from where you're sitting, all this sucks."

"Sure does."

"But you're almost grown up, and you'll begin your own life soon, and your mom will still be here, growing tomatoes and…well, being a wife and a mother. That is her job, and you gotta allow her to do that job."

I'm impressed at how well I put that, and even Jules has no retort ready.

"Sweetie, not for nothing, but I gotta ask you to—"

"Oh, hiya!"

Her face lights up, and she bounds past me toward the steps. Startled, I turn round, and like a stray ginger dog, Logan Williams has appeared in front of my cottage.

"Nice place, Dr. Lieberman." He smirks up at me.

"Come on." Jules pulls at the sleeve of his over-sized sweater. "The others said twelve o'clock!"

Making sure that I see him grab hold of Jules' hand, he follows her around the cottage and toward the pickers' camp. It's almost deserted now, except for a trio of Poles in a camper van. The boys I see working on the farm, the girl is the blond hippy I saw with Logan in the woods. If that's the arrangement—sex with the Polish hippy, holding hands with Jules—fine. Presumably Logan knows that I know that Jules isn't legal yet and that he is more than six years older than she is. If he were committing a felony, he wouldn't flaunt it in my face like this. I hope.

"Hey, Jew girl."

"Hey, gay boy."

Over the music of some public place I hear Tim chuckle into his phone.

"Listen, you said you weren't going with Freddy Katz to his synagogue, so my compassionate heart was rent at the thought of you sitting all alone on the tomato farm, in the Southern diaspora, pining for your people."

"*G'mar chatimah tovah* to you, too. Tim, are you drunk?"

"It's twenty past seven, how can I be drunk? I'm at Mairie's Pub in Beanes Road, that's off James, near that pizza place. D'you wanna come out? Or is that a terribly goyish thing to ask?"

"Would you stop getting at me for my religion?"

"Sorry, sorry. I just thought, if…if you're lonesome tonight," he starts crooning. "Are you?"

"A little, yeah," I say. Understatement of the semester.

"Then come out! We're sitting at the back, underneath The Pogues."

"We?"

"Oh, yeah, I forgot, Cleve is here, too."

I'm going from G'mar to Gehenna in a glass of Guinness.

The second thing that hits me when I push myself onto a three-legged stool in a corner of Mairie's Pub is that Tim is, notwithstanding his protestations, on a fair way to being plastered. There is one empty pint glass on the table, one almost empty, and one half full. The latter one is Giles's, who has just been brought a sandwich with fries.

Tim says he'll do like they did in the olden times, have beer instead of solids, but what am I having? His innocent question makes me sigh. Well, since I'm obviously not doing Yom Kippur this year…

"You're supposed to fast, aren't you?" Giles states rather than asks.

"Moses supposes his toeses are roses."

"But Moses supposes erroneously. So, *not* fasting. Have some of my chips." Unfazed, he inches his plate toward me. "The sandwich is grilled chicken, so you can't have any of that."

It's not as if he had looked up to greet me. Giles Cleveland doesn't do greetings. I'm getting used to that, particularly since I am also getting the impression that he is very attentive, very tuned in to me. Without really looking at me. I can't really look at him, either. His face has been so vivid in my mind, and I have been imagining such things that he would be embarrassed if he knew. Angry with me, maybe.

"I'll have half a Guinness, please, Tim, and a veggie pie or something like that. Whatever. But veggie."

"I'll go." Giles jumps up and blends into the crowd at the bar. He is wearing frayed light blue jeans, a dark blue hoodie, and sneakers. I think he looks lovely, but then I always do. He does not, however, look like a guy who dressed up for a Sunday night out, and I am disappointed that meeting Tim and me in a bar doesn't even merit a change of clothes. Maybe my choice of a pleated tartan skirt, knee length, with opaque black pantyhose, Mary Poppins boots, and a black sweater was a naff idea for an Irish pub, but at least I made an effort. Cleveland, on the other hand, couldn't care less whether I think he looks nice.

What am I *saying?*

He returns with three beers and three small bags of potato chips.

"Compliments of the bartender." He grins.

"What's the joke?"

"He wanted to know who the girl is with, and did she know that she's wearing a County Leitrim tartan."

I smooth the pleats of my gray-and-red crisscrossed skirt, a little awkwardly because squatting on this low stool I am showing more leg than I had intended.

"Well, at least I get a compliment from *some*body…"

"What did you tell him?" Tim takes the pint off him.

"Sorry?"

"Who the girl is with."

"I said she's my wife." Giles shrugs, utterly poker-faced, and Tim cackles into his beer.

Yeah, big joke.

I am still not sure why the boys want me with them tonight. Tim asks me a few things about Yom Kippur, and Giles listens but doesn't contribute any questions, except hadn't I celebrated Rosh Hashanah at Freddy Katz's synagogue?

"I did, and the crazy thing was, I met a guy I knew at school, at home, and my mom recently met his aunt and gave him my phone number—you know what mothers are like. Well, Jewish mothers, anyway. Maybe you don't know."

"You met your childhood sweetheart from Queens in a synagogue in Shaftsboro?" Tim squeals. "God, your people really *are* few but well organized!"

"Bernie wasn't my sweetheart! Quite the contrary. But yeah, it was weird."

Giles is watching me, and I am ashamed. I know why I tell them about Bernie (and neglect to mention Elvira), and it has a lot to do with the woman who was waiting for Giles in their cabin by the lake yesterday. It also has a lot to do with his long, hard, be-denimed thigh next to my pantyhosed one.

The whole conversation is a little desultory. I eat my quiche, finish my beer, insist on getting the next round—Coca-Cola for Giles and me, more Guinness for Tim—and have the barman hit on me, playfully, in a charming Irish brogue.

"Eh, lass—why did you throw yourself away on a stuck-up Englishman?"

I push my money across the counter and give him my sweetest smile.

"Oh, but he's a fantastic shag!"

I am still grinning when I set down the drinks, and Giles avoids my eyes so sheepishly I have to grin even more.

"So, what's the, um, beef?" I ask.

"What do you mean?"

"Well, not for nothing, guys, but I'm assuming there is more to come, apart from, 'Will you really fast all day?' and 'How does atonement work?' Don't get me wrong, I appreciate this. I was getting a little lachrymose at the cottage, to tell you the truth. But there's more, right? Has something happened?"

Giles glances over at Tim; Tim inhales and slumps against the wall behind him.

"They've drafted me onto the Sexual Misconduct Hearing Panel!"

Apparently three of the six members of the current committee have resigned over the investigation of Nick Hornberger's misdemeanor, and procedure in the case of resignation is to immediately replace the former members.

Now I see why Tim is deliberately getting legless tonight.

"But—you're in such a vulnerable position, with your tenure review pending! You shouldn't be made to involve yourself in this kind of thing!"

"You'd think, but their logic works the other way around. I'm vulnerable, so I can't refuse. And we've been taught all the legal stuff, and there's no time to train new members. Besides, imagine the noise when it becomes public that a new hearing panel had to be appointed because half of the current members wanted nothing to do with it! Worse and worse. No, it's all hush-hush, business as usual, normality at all times."

"But why do people volunteer for these committees in the first place if they're going to cave in the moment a really distasteful case has to be heard?"

"Oh, Anna! Such innocence!" Tim mocks me. "They're afraid the evidence will mean they'll have to fire Hornberger, and they want nothing to do with that!"

Innocence, indeed.

"In that case, shouldn't they stay on the panel and see if they can bail him out? By hook or by crook?" The two men look at me blankly until I have caught up with them. "Oh, you mean, they know he's a lost cause? *Oy!*"

"*Oy* is right. I don't know how else to interpret this mass resignation. Presumably they know more than we do. He must be in it up to his neck."

"But," I say for the third time, "I just don't see it! It's evident and plainly obvious that he and Natalie were having an affair—who knows for how long? Maybe since her undergraduate days! But she was friendly with him in the Astrolabe, after the first faculty meeting. I saw them! I sussed them *because* they were so natural and familiar with each other!"

Tim stares at me and blinks.

"It totally kills me when you use British slang in that Noo Yoak voice of yours. I would so do you, Anna, if." He looks at Giles for corroboration.

"And I will so gag you, Timmy-my-man, if you don't watch your mouth," Giles says.

Tim, three-quarters drunk at this point, seems offended at this unambiguous announcement, but Giles smiles at him in a way that shows how little amused he is.

And I am sick at heart.

Because the *first* thing that hit me when I walked up to the two men huddled around the small table underneath a poster of The Pogues was the lamentable but undisputable truth that I have fallen in love with a married man who is also a tenured colleague.

For the sin which we have committed before You by improper thoughts.
And for the sin which we have committed before You by a confused heart.
For all these, God of pardon, pardon us, forgive us, atone for us.

Chapter 18

Since Monday is not a teaching day for me and I have no set appointments, I could stay at home, slip into a white sweater, white sweatpants, and woolly socks, abstain from food, drink, and sex (ha!), and have an informal, private Yom Kippur. Obeying the letter of the law would be easy this year. I'm too dejected to have appetites of any sort, and in a sullen way I would even enjoy the ordeal of enduring thirst. But in view of the past days' events, it seems hypocritical to do *teshuvah* — pray to return to God and to a stricter observance of His laws — when I know that tomorrow I will still be sadly and stupidly infatuated with Giles Cleveland.

So I drive in. It is pouring down rain, and my butt is still a bit sore from my bike ride on Saturday. My plan is to sort out the mystery of the lock on my office door. I start with the department secretary.

"Lorraine, hello. Listen, you wouldn't happen to have a key to my office? E-four twenty-nine."

"Oh, sure, dear — forgot yours at home, did you?" She unlocks a cupboard in which there is a locked chest in which are stored all the keys of the department.

"No, I mean, a key to the new lock on my door. There's a new lock on my office door, but I never got a key for it."

"But that's…not yet," says Kathy, her assistant. "Remember Central Maintenance wrote an email saying some of the older locks will be changed?" She clicks open some emails, finds the one, and says triumphantly, "Yes, November, and it will affect offices with the numbers E-four-oh-six, E—well, anyway. But that's next month."

"Well, the lock on my office door was changed last Friday. Any idea how I might get hold of a key? Preferably today?"

"This is funny," says Lorraine, rummaging in the key chest. "E-four-twenty-nine, you said? There's no spare key here for E-four-twenty-nine."

"I know, right?" Kathy pulls the metal box toward her. "It's a mess in here. Professor Dancey was looking for a couple of keys last week, and they were missing, too."

Dancey was looking for other people's office keys?

Lorraine tells me that Dancey teaches on Monday afternoons but usually comes in just before his class starts, so it would be better if I spoke to him afterward. But my patience has run out.

"Professor Dancey? I know you're teaching now, sir, but I spent the better part of the morning trying to get into my office. A new lock was fitted on Friday afternoon, but I never received notice of this, nor a key. So I'd be extremely grateful if—"

"Oh, then this must be it!" Dancey, who had been hanging up his coat and cleaning his black woolen sweater with an adhesive roll, reaches across his desk to where a padded envelope is sitting on top of a pile of books. He picks it up and rattles it. "This arrived on Friday afternoon when Lorraine had already gone."

The envelope, baggy and dog-eared like all recycled office material, has *Central Maintenance* and *Urgent* written on it. Not urgent enough to inform me, apparently.

These are my plans for getting my ass fired from my tenure-track position at a national research university. Plan A: alienate the big-donor, conservative Christian clientele. Working on that. Plan B: start an affair with a married and tenured colleague who is also my academic mentor. Unlikely to be realized, as said colleague does not progress beyond very mild flirtation and comes to Sunday night drinking spree in his dog-walking gear. Plan C: drive into town, find a locksmith, and have the ancient key to the old observatory copied behind admin's back. Check. I don't even know why I want a duplicate of the key to the dome. Ineffectual spite, I guess. Why am I so determined to piss off my employer? Well, Your Honor, *they started it!* Armed, at last, with the key I fingered out of the (sealed and re-sealed?) envelope on Dancey's desk, I enter my office with as much suspicion as the weakest link in the tenure chain may allow herself. What does it matter if anyone's been in my office while I was locked out? It isn't my private home, and if I keep anything private in my workplace, it is at my own risk.

Except that someone *has* been in my office. As far as I can tell, nothing has been taken, but why would someone lift up and turn over the library books on my desk? Someone picked up all the items on my desk and did not realize that my system of working through library books is that I put the ones I'm done with face down. I know for a fact that there was a face-down pile of four; the pile is still there, but it is facing up. Knowing that Crazy Corvin had a key to my office made me uncomfortable, but this is a brand-new lock. It wasn't Corvin who snooped around in here.

Wonderful. So now I have a choice of at least four stomach-churning scenarios to worry over: my paycheck disaster, the intrusions into my office, the fact that I have not added a single sentence to my Notre Dame paper since Rosh Hashanah, and my imminent encounter with the woman I envy more than anyone else in the whole wide world.

"Ms. Cleveland is upstairs, but she knows she's seeing you at half past."

Liz, her administrative assistant, opens a door from the landing area into a waiting room with a suite of slim beige armchairs and a sofa. The office itself can be partitioned off by a sliding door, which is already half open. There is another sliding door, currently shut, on the opposite wall—evidently the other legal counselor's office. It's like being at an expensive dentist's, including the Picasso prints on the walls and the potted ficus by the window. Actually, some root-canal work doesn't sound so bad. I hear the door open and close in the adjoining room, and my stomach turns.

"Look, you can't simply walk in here and assume that I'm going to make time for you! I'd like to see your face if I barged in on one of your lectures!"

"Would you prefer me to ring up your secretary and make an appointment? I can do that, if that's what you want!"

Oh, please, God—don't make me witness a fight between Giles Cleveland and his wife!

"Anyway," he says, "this is urgent. Holly Ortega and the department want me to take over the chair from Nick."

I should leave. I should wait for Liz to return and inform her that Ms. Cleveland is seeing someone else first, and discretion dictates that I wait out of earshot.

Do it. Get up. Leave the room.

"But you haven't made full professor," Amanda Cleveland says. She sounds defensive now, less exasperated than she did at first.

"Well, I sort of have, as both Holly and Elizabeth hastened to point out. I got the salary boost before I went to England. They're promising me the full package now, if I hand in my stuff by Christmas."

"Why can't someone else do it?"

"Any suggestions?" he asks sardonically. "The only one who wants to do it is Matthew Dancey, which would be a disaster, particularly for MedRen Studies. I think he's planning a putsch of some sort."

"Then do it." I don't have to see her face to know that there is no conviction in this counsel.

"To clean up after yet another one of Nick's messes? Like hell I will. And no, I do not relish the idea of revenge, gratifying as it was for about fifteen seconds."

Revenge?

"I do not see why revenge needs to come into it."

"Oh, it's just a thought. Many a man would feel tempted to kick his wife's lover in the balls if he gets the chance."

Jumping cats!

Right, that's it. If they find out I've been sitting next door and soaking up every word like a shamefaced sponge, Cleveland will get me fired before I can say "tenure review." He will get me fired, and my body will be found years from now in the river, a bloated, water-logged corpse with a couple of volumes of the *Oxford English Dictionary* tied to its feet. Folio edition.

"So don't take the chair. Giles, I am really busy. I'm supposed to be seeing someone right now. She's probably—"

"I'm going to explain to Holly Ortega why I won't do it."

Another pause. I can only guess that Amanda is speechless with horror. I certainly am. Speechless and rooted to the spot.

"You can't do that," she says flatly.

"Yes, I can. To Holly, and to as many of my colleagues as necessary, because they are all convinced I'm merely shirking a tedious job."

"You know as well as I do that Nick didn't force himself on that girl! She's just a hysterical little attention-seeker!"

"On the contrary, it would amaze me to hear that Nick has evolved enough to adhere to something as sophisticated as a sexual code of honor. But of course you have more insight into the matter than I have."

"Giles…"

"No, forget it. I've been as civilized about the whole thing as I can — maybe too civilized. But this is where I draw the line!"

"You were glad I gave you an excuse to leave me!"

"That's ridiculous!"

"You weren't even angry!"

"*Then* I wasn't! I was too busy feeling like a complete failure because my wife cheated on me with the biggest wanker on campus!"

He's sure as hell angry *now*.

"I didn't think…about how much it would embarrass you, Giles," she says in a very level voice. "And I never thought it would go on. I certainly never thought we'd be caught."

"One never does, I suppose." Giles, too, is calmer again, though still sardonic. The steam seems to have gone out of him a little. My stomach muscles unclench.

"If you'd taken the job at Stanford, none of this would ever have turned into a problem!" Amanda is audibly nettled by his acquiescence.

"I can't believe you are seriously suggesting that it would have saved our marriage if I'd gone to California! It would have turned it into even more of a travesty! For fuck's sake, Mandy!"

"Look, Giles, I know you're riled, but this is my office and I won't have you using that kind of language!"

"I'll swear as much as I like, thank you very much. And to make this as petty as possible, I was here first. I'm not saying you wouldn't have got the job on your own merits, but the fact remains, you were a spousal hire! I made way for you and Nick by going to Stanford and by shifting my sabbatical forward, but enough is enough. I will not chair the English department while Nick is accused of raping one of our students! And I want my name back."

"I don't understand."

"My name. I want you to use your maiden name again."

"Why? This is pure malice!"

"Not a bit of it. You're not my wife anymore—well, as of any day now you won't be my wife anymore, and you didn't want to be my wife anymore. We're done, and I think I may ask you to give up the use of my name without being accused of gratuitous cruelty."

"But why do you have to advertise it all over campus?" She sounds more annoyed with him about this than about anything else so far. Frankly, I can see her point.

"What, our divorce or your adultery?"

"Oh, stop wallowing in self-pity just because you're the wronged party in this, Giles!"

"I am not wallowing! I just want to be free of it!" he says stubbornly. "The whole bloody thing! And I don't want people to think I'm married."

"People? You mean students! So now *you* are going to—"

"Fuck," he says. "Go on. Am I now going to fuck our attention-seeking little snowflakes? No, I'm not. But anyone who looks up *Cleveland and Ardrossan* on the Internet will find us both and assume we're married, and that irks me. So if you wouldn't mind, I want to see *Amanda Saunders* on that door next time I look."

"Giles, what is *wrong* with you?" Her voice, remarkably calm so far, rises in pitch. "You wouldn't just be harming me but also yourself! Everyone would *know!*"

"No, they wouldn't," he says, ignoring her tone. "The last thing Holly and Elizabeth want is to besmirch Nick's fair name any further. They wouldn't blab. Nor Dancey, if he must know. Dancey least of all, no matter how much he'd like to drop me in it. They've been amazingly generous about my leaves of absence, so I need them to understand why I'm not going to help extinguish this fire."

"Give me time to think. I need to—to talk to Daddy about this."

"There is nothing for you to think about, and I don't care what Robert says. I am merely here to give you warning that I am going to do this. Complain to Nick about it, not to me. This isn't about revenge. I don't give a flying toss about the whole thing anymore."

"The breakup was your fault! I never wanted a divorce! If my parents hadn't made me—"

"*My* fault?" There is a loud thump; I think it was his fist on a table top. "*You* suck the campus dick in your office, and *I'm* supposed to take that on the chin and shut up about it, just to save appearances? You always did take me for a blundering idiot, didn't you? Is *that* why you married me, Amanda?"

Instinctively I check Liz's silhouette through the glass pane in the door. She can't *not* have heard Cleveland's flare-up. Her head turns, she peers through the glass, sees me sitting on the sofa where she left me. For one tense second we stare at each other, and with all my might I will her to sit down again. No such luck.

"What's going on here? Where's Ms. Cleveland?"

"Ms. Saunders," I correct her weakly. I'm toast anyway, so it doesn't matter. Hurried murmurs from the next room, the sound of a chair scraping along the floor.

Giles stops in his tracks as if he had collided with an invisible barrier.

"What the hell are *you* doing here?"

The mysteries of sexual attraction. How—*how on earth*—could any woman even contemplate sex with Nick Hornberger when she can have this man? It's clearly not true that he doesn't care anymore. His blood is up, and it is shocking to me how intensely I respond to that. I expected to be mortified with embarrassment, and I am. Embarrassed, a little afraid, and mightily turned on. Giles Cleveland has come out of his shell.

"Don't let 'em screw you!" He darts his finger at me as if he wanted to recruit me for military service.

I nod obediently at this harsh order and—while I am still looking up at him, half startled, half playing at being startled—the air congeals between us.

Will you?

No, I didn't say it out loud. But I might as well, because he heard it, and it flusters him terribly. His chest is heaving with emotion, and he is staring at me as if panicked by what he read in my face.

This time I am sure. I am calm. Not physically — my hands are cold with sweat, my chest hurts with excitement — but in my mind I am calm. I mean it.

If you want, I will make you forget your humiliation at the hands of a silly woman and a man who thinks with his cock. Oblivion may only last for a few minutes, but I promise you it will be sweet and intense.

Screw me, Cleveland.

"How much of that did you hear?" Amanda asks the big white crystal on her desk when we have sat down.

"Not much. Almost nothing, in fact," I say deliberately. "I am very hard of hearing…well, *can* be."

It works in mobster movies. I wonder whether it also works in the office of an Associate Vice President of Finance and Administration. Apart from the heightened color in her cheeks, Amanda Cleveland, née Saunders, betrays no sign of agitation. My natural sense of tact made it difficult, at first, to look her in the face when she asked me to take a seat at her desk; she would join me in a couple of minutes. And she did. A couple of minutes later she entered her office from the hallway, and if I didn't know that she was just involved in a shouting match with her soon-to-be ex-husband, I would never have guessed it. This is one cool chick.

Chic, too, in a tight-fitting, pale green skirt suit and a charcoal top underneath that shows off her cleavage. And she may actually be a real blonde, styled in that medium-long way that looks as if she was wearing spaghetti tongs on her head, its teeth framing her jaw and chin in a many-layered wave. *Put together* hits it precisely. She is very slim, very good-looking, well-groomed and self-assured: exactly the sort of girl I envied at school and college. Today, if I were a man, I wouldn't even attempt to get close to her. No point, no joy.

And yet this is a woman who had quickies in her office — *in her office!* — with Nick Hornberger. I try to picture her, hot and tousled, her slim legs wrapped around Hornberger's no doubt hairy football player's torso. Or maybe he would hike up her skirt, bend her over her desk, and take her from behind? Did she actually enjoy having an affair with him? It seems so improbable. And what is it with that man, anyway? What kind of potion does he ply them with to make these females — babes, all — lift their skirts for him? I think I understand what draws a certain kind of student to a certain kind of philandering professor. But Amanda Cleveland is no attention-hungry co-ed who knows that she carries her best assets in her blouse. No, I don't get it.

She is a professional. I show her the original letter stating salary and benefits, my reply bidding for a higher sum in view of my publications, a print-out of the email that agreed to this higher sum, my contract and my paycheck. She takes her time reading everything, and I wonder whether she is merely very thorough, buying time, or finding it hard to focus.

"This was signed by Greg Newburgh," she informs me, and I shrug and nod, too preoccupied to talk.

Irene would slap me if she knew how little I am interested in the material issue here — my money! — because I can't help wondering, is this what Giles fancies, or is this what Giles doesn't fancy? Used to fancy, but not anymore? No matter, really, because I couldn't be like her if I tried, and the hair and the cleavage are the least of it.

Ex , ex , ex!

The syllable had been drowned out by the shouting and the aggravation and the sudden flare of sexual energy and the necessity to concentrate on figures and contracts. But in the hush of rustling paper and the clicking of her keyboard as she opens my file, it is echoing in my head like an alphorn.

Giles Cleveland is getting a divorce.

"You're right, Dr. Lieberman. There is a discrepancy here, and I am for the moment at a loss to account for it. I must ask you to give me some time to look into it."

What a self-righteous cow I've been, taking sides where I had neither the right nor the necessary information to do so! Wife cheats on husband with senior colleague, colleague flutters on to graduate student in the manner of a testosterone-driven butterfly. Said student accuses him of sexual violence, husband is given the opportunity to be as unhelpful as a department chair can be in such a case. Husband refuses, preferring the opportunity to come clean about his wife's fling to the college authorities.

WTF?

Giles must still be mightily pissed off about his wife's infidelity to prefer humiliating her to settling his score with Hornberger. I think he overestimates his colleagues' discretion. Someone always blabs. He will be known as a cuckold all over campus, cuckolded by the very man who is currently suspected of having raped a student. How is that better than chairing the department and washing his hands of Hornberger once the case is dealt with in a court of law, as it surely will be? He must be driven by revenge. No other motive makes any sense at all.

Why won't you take the department chair?

I can't tell you that.

What he also didn't tell me is that he is divorced. About to be divorced. Separated from his wife, a free man! And indeed, why would a man who doesn't even change out of his dog-walking pants before he meets a woman in a bar tell that woman that he is as good as single? No wonder he looked so disconcerted just now when I gave him my best come-hither look! Whoever he is dating now that he is rid of Amanda Saunders, she is sure to be cool and blond and enormously stacked. And who was that big-mouthed *yuchna* who told him that she saw the hole while he saw the bagel? Well, the hole in this bagel is that he did *not* invite me into his home for tea! Whatever it was that sparked the impulse, he regretted it almost instantly. He did not want me to know that he is divorced.

> *O soul, be changed into small water-drops,*
> *And fall into the ocean, ne'er be found!*

I cannot remember when I was last so comprehensively, so painfully ashamed.

The last thing I need right now is another clash with Dolph Bergstrom. He overruns his sessions most weeks, but usually he just runs into the transition time, not into my class period. Today my class is once more still loitering in the hallway when I turn up. The light of a beamer is flickering in the darkened classroom; I recognize Peter Fonda in his psychedelic shirt pressing his face against the stone statue in the cemetery. I mentally re-run the film and calculate it is at least another five minutes until Wyatt's bike is blown up. Five more minutes of film, wrapping up, packing up—what the heck does Dolph think he is doing?

Whatever I do, I must do it with conviction.

"All right, people—we can't barge in on the ending of *Easy Rider*. Wouldn't be cool. I'll start the session in ten minutes sharp. See you back here in seven."

Seven minutes to hide in the toilets, my fists pressed into my eyes. When I return, I can tell by their silence and their faces that my apparent sangfroid has created a certain sense of expectation, gleeful in some cases, apprehensive in others. For a moment I feel like the narrator in George Orwell's story about a police officer in Burma who is goaded by a crowd of natives into shooting an elephant. But my job is to teach them Ben Jonson's *The Devil is an Ass*, not to mud-fight a colleague.

A "colleague" who, five-and-a half-minutes into my class period, is still holding forth about the contradictions of avant-garde film-making in late nineteen-sixties Hollywood.

"Excuse me, Dr. Bergstrom—so sorry to interrupt. You'll have noticed it's way past the end of your class period."

Without waiting for his reply, I usher my lot in but almost lose my cool when he says that he has been showing a film and needs another couple of minutes. My students, with the deference to authority that doesn't cease to amaze me, stop in their tracks and look at me for their cue.

There is never any point in throwing a temper tantrum.

"But a couple more minutes won't do justice to *Easy Rider*, now, will they? Maybe leave it till Thursday and discuss it properly?"

Dolph is in my face as if I had interrupted him at a particularly tricky bit of brain surgery.

"Now you're telling me how to teach? Listen, if I want your advice, I'll ask you!"

My instinct is to go for him, but my bad angel has been doused so effectively by the icy water of eavesdropping that it lacks the élan to egg me on to a foolhardy confrontation.

"I wouldn't dare. But this isn't your time and place to teach, I'm afraid, Dolph, but mine, and I'd be glad if you gave me the chance to do so."

A good speech, if I say so myself. It makes Dolph close his laptop with an angry *klop* and his class sigh with relief. My New York students would by now have formed a ring around us, chanting for their champions—well, metaphorically speaking, anyway. Ardrossan students are made uncomfortable by clashes between their authority figures. Ignoring me completely, Dolph packs up the projector and turns around to wipe the board as if he was alone in the room and had all the time in the world. Then he picks up the board markers, one by one, and sticks them into his back pocket. It doesn't help that bubbling up through my stupor I feel the urge to laugh about his absurdly territorial behavior.

"Wait." I hold him back very affably when he finally collects his papers and books and shoves them into his bag. "You forgot to pee on the desk. Go on. You know you want to."

This provokes a double-take as he stares at me, thunderstruck. Then he grabs his belongings, storms out and—get this!—slams the door behind himself. His last remaining students rush out meekly, and Logan, of all people, gives me a cheer of triumph that makes me bite on a smile.

Asshole.

I drive home at a snail's pace. My brain has slowed down, my whole body has slowed down in the attempt to come to grips with what I learned today. Not that I have fallen in love with Giles Cleveland—I knew that already. But that there is no limit to how wrong I can still be about a man, at the great old age of twenty-nine years and three hundred and forty days. How selectively blind to his signals. This is a man enjoying his new-won liberty! Yes, he made that little joke to the barman about me being his wife. Yes, he enjoyed, for a moment or two, the idea of picking up a young woman in front of his cabin at the lake. But that whole conversation at the lake, which made me feel so warm and happy—which for the first time made me feel as if he actually liked me—is now overshadowed by the glaring absence of one simple sentence.

My wife and I are getting a divorce.

I don't know how long I've been sitting in my car in front of the farm's gate when my phone bleeps.

Call me! Great news! Deb.

Oh, God, no. Not another pregnant woman! Debbie has been joking that if editing the pregnancy essays isn't going to make her conceive, she will go for IVF. I would be very happy for her if she could save herself that whole ordeal, but this is not the best moment for me to rejoice with her. But I owe Debbie. So I go inside, get a glass of wine, and call England.

"Queen Mary College is going to advertise a full-time position for someone who does Ren. Lit. as well as something modern to do with Anglophone literature! I spoke to Ewan Buchanan; he says Anglo-Jewish definitely qualifies, and he says hi, and you would be a fool if you didn't apply!"

Debbie is a little breathless after this outpouring. As am I.

"Woah, hold your horses, Crocker. Did you tell Ewan that I have a tenure-track position at Ardrossan?"

"Yes, I did. He said, *Where?*"

"God, you Brits are so arrogant."

Debbie chortles into the phone but says nothing.

"'Kay."

"What?"

"I'll apply."

"Seriously?"

"No, I'm kidding. Yeah, seriously!"

"Anna, is something wrong?"

"Yeah." I don't want to talk about it. I just want to sit on the couch in Debbie's and Dave's living room with a mug of milky tea and a biscuit, or stand and *shuckel* with the half-asleep Jonah against my shoulder. "D'you think I'm pretty?"

"Oh, Anna," she sighs. Then we both burst into laughter.

I give her a sixty-second version of events, and Debbie points out that Cleveland has evidently turned out to be the jerk I took him for at our first meeting.

"No, see — he isn't. Me refusing to read the message he was sending doesn't make him a jerk. Not fancying me doesn't make him a jerk."

"Yes, it does!"

"Bless you, but no, it doesn't. He's probably seeing someone else, that's all. Spoiled for choice, that one, for sure."

"So what was your plan before you found out he didn't tell you he is divorced but seeing someone else? Start sleeping with a senior colleague? If that was the idea, I suggest you find yourself a Southern pothead and do a repeat performance of Ciaran, because—"

"Please, don't. Look, I'll apply for that job at Queen Mary and meanwhile I'll lust after my mentor a little, okay? No harm done, either way. End of debate."

Chapter 19

True to the resolution I made on my bike ride, I try my hand at sorting out Selena O'Neal. *Muscle in on grad advisement*, Giles said. Okay.

"Hey, Natalie. Hey, Selena."

The two young women are sitting and working at their desks, facing each other, framed by the window and the blue sky behind them. An academic idyll.

"Be great if we had weather like this at the weekend, huh?" I'm about to ask whether both girls' families will come to Ardrossan for Family Weekend when it occurs to me that this would hardly be tactful. Natalie is showing great strength of character (or a great deal of *chutzpah*, depending on who you listen to) by showing up in college like this, but Family Weekend is a very different ballgame.

"All weather stations say it'll be sunny," Natalie informs us archly. "So it'll probably be pouring with rain!"

"Mmhmm. Selena, I was wondering whether you had a moment?"

Selena jumps up onto her feet. "Of course, ma'am. Dr. Lieberman."

"Anna."

She bobs her head and twists her shoulders in a way that makes her look like a cross between Princess Diana and Rapunzel. This will be much harder than I thought.

"I tell you what, if you have half an hour or so, we could get ourselves a coffee and walk a little?"

Natalie's beautiful face clouds over. I doubt that coffee with Dr. Lieberman counts as a special treat in Natalie's eyes, but she is peeved that Selena is getting it. Not that Selena is keen. If she could think of an excuse, she would wriggle out. But I smile at her in the manner of a kind but firm professor, and she has no choice. Ten minutes later we are walking between the box hedges, each nursing a paper cup between her hands.

"Selena, I felt bad about—hey, what happened to your hand?" When she took a sip of the coffee, her sleeve, pulled down to her fingers, shifted a little, and I caught a glimpse of raw flesh.

"No, it's nothing."

"Yes, it is, let me see that!" Doubly alarmed, I become vehement. "Have you been in a fight, or what?" The knuckles on the backs of both hands are red and glistening with lymphatic fluid; these wounds are fresh. Four round red marks on each hand.

"I…fell," she improvises. "I was carrying something and scraped against the…wall of the garage, at home. It's nothing." She hitches her sleeves over her hands like oven gloves and nurses her coffee.

"Selena, I'm not stupid. How you deal with stress is none of my business, so I won't probe. But I feel all the more urgently that I ought to say this, about last week's grad seminar. Things got a little out of hand, and you may have walked away from it feeling that your topic doesn't make sense or that your approach doesn't work. But all you need to—"

"Oh, no, I wasn't bothered by that," she interrupts me. She may be shuffling alongside me in her sensible skirt and sensible shoes, ducking her head so as not to have to look down at me, but she is perfectly capable of interrupting a professor.

"Weren't you? Well, that's good. What's your…what did you take away from it, upon reflection?"

Not much, it seems. She tries to convince me that like a good little grad student she listens to all criticism and tries to use it constructively, so appreciative of all the help she gets, such an opportunity, graduate study at a place like Ardrossan—

"Yes, but. Selena." Aha, there it is, the mulish set to her mouth and jaw. I've seen it a few times, but I keep forgetting it because the impression of her dowdy diffidence is so overwhelming. "I spoke to Giles Cleveland about your paper, and it seems to me that you and he do not exactly see eye to eye on the question of whether you should go on to do a Ph.D."

"You fought with him about me. Natalie heard you."

If I had a wall to bang my head against, I would.

"We didn't *fight*, we had a—never mind that! We are discussing your—"

"I was admitted as a graduate student, therefore I must have the academic ability to succeed," she interrupts me again. "To tell me I shouldn't be in grad school when I *am* in grad school is another way of saying that Ardrossan's admission policies are determined by the financial situation of the university, and not by the academic potential of the students."

She is right. She has summarized, in a few brutal sentences, the situation in graduate schools all over the country. But if I agree with her and she repeats it, I am toast. On wheels. I'm in enough trouble as it is.

"These are very general statements. I would like to hear what you feel about your personal situation. Are you enjoying grad school?"

"I couldn't imagine doing anything else in the world!" she states in a hollow voice, and her cheeks flame.

Oh, of course. The young man in the observatory. Perhaps I should cast a beady eye or two over the male grad students. I briefly consider asking her what her parents would say if they knew that they are coughing up thirty thousand bucks a year so that their daughter, a girl chastely reared in the fear of God, can have it off with some guy in the attic of her department. She would presumably tell me, and rightly, to mind my own freaking business, and anyway, she is paying for her own tuition, isn't she?

"That is not really an answer to my question."

"I'm fine!"

"No, Selena, you're not fine! But it's your life, and you have—"

"That's right, it is!"

"—and you have been brought up with a strong sense of right and wrong. All I can encourage you to do is to trust your own judgment and to be honest with yourself about what you truly feel about something. Or someone."

Good speech. I should memorize it and tell it to the mirror tonight.

"I am! That's exactly what I *am* doing!" She seems almost pleased with me for putting it so well. Her face, bare of make-up and exposed by that demure blue headband, beams with relief, and up close I see how white and soft and smooth her skin is, and how her lips are trembling a little.

Well, all right. So this vulnerable, headstrong young woman has fallen into the hands of a scoundrel. But the sex has intoxicated her, and people as inconsequential as a new assistant professor or her study advisor have no chance of getting through to her. Hey, grad school's a bitch and then you get fucked by a bastard. Been there, done that. Wait till you are on tenure track. Tenure track is an uber-bitch, and you fall for a lovely man who doesn't even tell you he is dating another woman before you fall in love with him.

Contrary to Natalie's cattish prediction, the weather on Family Weekend is dry and sunny. The campus appears in its full glory of undulating shrubbery, surging, orange-yellow-brown masses of leaves, and green lawns already dotted with orange and white shirts, banners, and hats. "Pipe, Plover!" is Ardrossan's war cry, and apparently the Plovers are expected to trounce their traditional rivals, the Lynxes, who are traveling over from the other research university on the other side of Shaftsboro for tomorrow night's football game. I'm proud to belong to the Ardrossan Family, despite all the squabbles we recently had, and I bought a long-sleeved Ardrossan U t-shirt especially to go with the dress pants I dug out for this day.

When the door of the elevator opens onto the fourth floor, I almost push my bike into Tessa, who comes running around the corner from the hallway.

"You must come," she says, heaving, pale as a sheet. She grabs the handlebar, pulls my bike out of the cab, and lets it slide against the wall. "Come, quickly."

"Tessa, what—" Another smashed window? What?

Oh. My. God.

Now it is graffiti. Across Natalie's and Selena's office door, in red capitals about two feet high:

WHORE!

And on the opposite wall:

IF A PRIEST'S DAUGHTER DEFILES HERSELF BY BECOMING A PROSTITUTE, SHE MUST BE BUR

"Jesus fucking Christ on a cracker…"

"I don't think more cursing is going to help!" Tessa flings at me, then bites her lip. "Sorry."

"No, I'm sorry, Tessa. When did you see this?"

"Thirty seconds before you did? People will be up here with their parents today, and—oh, dear!" She is fighting down tears, and I can understand why. We are standing in the middle of the empty hallway, red hatred screaming at us from the walls.

"And what's that stench?" I walk further along the corridor, where a foul, pungent smell—

"Fish," Tessa says, sniffing like a pointer. "Rotten fish. Gross."

"Well, I guess that sort of fits the general idea. If you're into vulgarities of that sort."

"Yes," she says, "but it comes from your office."

It does. A biting smell emanates from my office door, which has been liberally sprinkled with some sort of fluid. I peek into the plastic box that is screwed against the door to hold essays and notes, and in it are nestling some stinking chunks of pickled herring.

"Here," Tessa says and holds up a glass jar, using a Xeroxed journal article like an oven glove. "'Kranz's Kosher Pickled Herring.'" It had, of course, been thrown into the cart that is still, on the morning of Family Weekend, sitting under the stairs. Smelling of rotten herring.

I dial Lorraine Forster's number, but the voice that answers is Matthew Dancey's.

"Anna—are you out of your mind? It's Family Weekend! I have to make a speech to the parents in less than an hour!"

"Yes, sir, I understand. But unless you want to make a speech explaining why the top floor is displaying graffiti that says—sorry, I'd like to give you this verbatim—" I pull the phone's cord out from under my desk and walk into the hall. "'*If a priest's daughter defiles herself by becoming a prostitute, she must be bur,*' I guess he ran out of paint here—I suggest you send someone up here pretty damn quick. Oh, and it says 'WHORE' across one of the office doors. Pardon my language, sir, I'm only quoting. And there is the further damage of spilled herring, moldy, pickled herring, which has been slopped all over my office door, so the place reeks to high heaven. Actually, maybe it would be easier to think of a reason why the fourth floor will be closed to all visitors today, only you'd have to inform Modern Languages of that, because—well, it's their corridor, too."

I can't deny that I am enjoying this a little. The customized insult in the form and smell of kosher herring will earn a place in the Lieberman Hall of Fame, and as such it is here to stay. The opportunity to tell Dancey that a wall in his department is displaying the vilest kind of obscenity *re* the pending rape case, however, is too rare and too delicious not to be savored.

Two minutes later Dancey is surveying the evidence for himself, surrounded by everyone else who has arrived.

"I hope you weren't planning on showing your kids where Mommy has her office," I murmur next to Yvonne's shoulder.

"Well, not today, that's for sure," Yvonne says with a grimace. "This smell is making my throat hurt, do you want to—"

"Good kosher herring is making your throat hurt?" I exclaim in mock outrage. "You anti-Semite! *Oy,* what next?"

"Stop it, Anna. This is not the right moment."

"On the contrary, this is exactly the right moment."

She scans me through narrowed eyes. "You're furious, aren't you?"

"Yeah, I'm furious. Sorry, I'd love to get out of here, but I have to stay and see what they're going to do with my door. I didn't tell you, did I? A week ago they replaced the lock on my door. No one told me, no one left me a new key. I spent all of Monday trying to get into my own office. And now this. Oh, and there was some sort of oily goop on my door handle before, a couple of weeks back."

"That's mobbing, Anna, and it's anti-Semitic. I told you from the first!"

"Well, it's general assholery. And the only thing I hate worse than mobbing and anti-Semitism is general assholery, so…we'll see how this plays out."

"Anna, if you do meet Teddy and Alethea later on, you will mind your language, won't you? You have the mouth of a ghetto queen on you." Yvonne looks at me like a stern mother who understands why her overstrained toddler is screeching but nonetheless has to shut her up.

It is amazing to see how fast the administration of a private university can move if the objective is to shield parents from any knowledge that might confuse them as to where to send their next child. Within minutes of Dancey's phone call to maintenance, a phalanx of men in overalls has appeared on the fourth floor. The graffiti is not a problem; a fresh coat of beigy-gray might look odd on old grubby beigy-gray, but not obscene. The letters on Natalie's office door resist the solvent that is used on them, so some posters are found and strategically placed over them. My door is taken off its hinges, placed on a large plastic sheet and scrubbed, using liquid soap and language that would make any ghetto queen blush. I try to keep in the background, but when Larry glares at me, I glare back.

"Will you now stop thinking that I'm doing this myself, Larry?"

"I never said you was doin' it, ma'am. I'm sayin' you was havin' it done to you. Take that Dumpster down, two of you," he mutters to his young men.

"What, already?" I pout, pushing out my lower lip. "Can't I keep it a little, to look at and smell?"

He snorts and pulls his mouth to one side. I think I have made Larry the janitor grin.

"Anna?" Tessa appears in the doorless frame of my office door. "Are you coming to hear Giles talk about Raleigh?"

There is a series of pre-lunchtime events in the university book store, and although I know I shouldn't, I am longing to see Giles. He doesn't want me, but I know that the sight of him will calm me down.

"You bet! Will you run ahead and keep me a seat?"

Ten minutes later I shunt the men out of my office, push the bike into a corner, lock the door, and gallop down the stairs.

The contrast between the fourth floor and the rest of the building, not to mention the rest of the campus, is surreal. It is warm enough for people to sit in shirts and sweaters on the steps of the stately entrance to the Observatory, on the lawns, and the low brick walls that mark off plots all over campus. This is probably the happiest day of the academic year for the largest proportion of students, and I can't help but smile at the sight of all these smiling people—nostalgically, because it is now a decade since I was part of this kind of happiness.

On my way to the book store I am stopped by Ross Maher, the football-playing hunk in my Gen Ed class, who in the first session didn't have the guts to say that Shakespeare's Sonnet Number 1 was about masturbation. You can usually tell parents who did not go to college themselves and for whom it is a big deal to send their child to a place like Ardrossan. Mr. and Mrs. Maher are forthright, unaffected people, and there is no way I will snub them by hurrying off. They tell me that Ross says I am the teacher who first taught him to read properly.

"That's what you say, isn't it, Ross? Read *properly!*" his mom ribs him, and Ross grins in that endearing way only well-brought-up nineteen-year-olds have.

"Mom! You're embarrassing Professor Lieberman!"

We all laugh, and I protest, "Not at all, tell me more! I can assure you that freshman professors feel as insecure sometimes as freshman students!" This is exactly the right thing to say, and they are very pleased with me when I allow no doubt at all that the Plovers will thrash the Lynxes and wish Ross the best of success in tomorrow's game.

A group of people seem to have been watching us from the other side of the street. I cross, assuming that they have been admiring the view, but a stentorian male voice addresses me.

"Professor Lieberman? One moment, please!"

Frank Harrison, one of the triumvirate that runs *the* Harrison family's business, needs no college deans or department chairs to convey his considered opinion about his daughter's professors. How, he wants to know, did I intend to respond to the fact that a large portion of the students I was teaching this semester found the material disturbing and my manner abrasive and intimidating?

He is a big man in a brown blazer and a white-and-orange tie who made sure to position me in such a way that he has the sun in his back and I have to squint up at him; the oldest trick in the book.

"Well, sir, intimidating is a very subjective term, isn't it? Some people might experience your behavior right now as intimidating."

There is no way I can stand up to this man. He is literally standing on his own turf, in front of the Harrison laboratory of biochemistry.

His family has probably been coming to Ardrossan since it was founded, rising in the world as the university rose in it. I don't believe for a second that Madeline, who has linked arms with her mother and her older sister like girl football players in cashmere, has felt intimidated by me. I will believe, however, that she has felt pissed off and bored.

"Sir, I'm sure you are aware that since Madeline is of age, I am not allowed to discuss her academic concerns with anyone but herself. If she feels unable to appreciate my class, she may say so at the end of the semester in her evaluation of the course. And now, if you'll excuse me, I wish you an enjoyable weekend."

All the seats in the book store are already taken when I squeeze in. Tessa waves at me from the second row and shrugs; I signal that I perfectly understand that she was powerless against the two middle-aged women sitting next to her. The bar tables holding cheese, crackers and white wine in coolers are as popular as the chairs, and one back of a curly head looks very familiar.

"'Candy is dandy, but liquor is quicker,'" I whisper into his ear.

"Jesus, Anna!" Tim gasps. "Hey—glad you could make it. Will you stand at the back with me and be bitchy?"

"I came here with no other object in mind. Actually, that's not true. Can you reach one of those clean glasses? I need a drink."

"Wassup, lady?"

"I'll tell you later. Who's on first?"

I get a very straight look from the baby blues over the rim of a wine glass.

"No, I mean—" I have to giggle "—is Giles on first?"

"Naturally," Tim says. "Oh, no—assholes incoming."

Dolph Bergstrom and Steve Howell, both in orange football jerseys, are edging their way into the store. They seem to be scanning the small crowd, whispering to each other, and I look away a second too late. Steve sees me, nudges Dolph, and both quietly start sniffing. Scrunch up their noses. Sniff again. Inflate their nostrils. Steve gets out a hanky, fluffs it up in a theatrical manner, and pretends to blow his nose.

"What the fuck are they doing?" Tim frowns.

I turn my back to them, because I am actually close to tears for a moment.

"Adding insult to injury. God, they really are assholes!"

"Why, what—"

"Shh. I'll tell you later."

The manager of the book store comes on and introduces Giles, whose legs are very long and awkward as he steps onto the stage, and who looks so English in his light gray suit, blue shirt, and burgundy-and-blue-striped tie that the cold hand crushing my heart now digs its fingernails into it.

Tim bends closer to my ear, and I can hear his glee through the whisper.

"The tie…"

Everyone is wearing white and orange and sporting little plovers everywhere, and Giles-sodding-Cleveland comes in his Cambridge college insignia?

Gotta love the man or hate him.

The audience loves him. He keeps his talk about the book short and humorous, belittles the prize he won for it by pointing out that it is awarded by a small group of Scottish academics who otherwise occupy themselves eating unspeakably horrible food, being insufferably arrogant about the English education system, and doing unmentionable things to their sheep. He stresses the good account to which professors put their sabbaticals but advises university provosts to conduct themselves more in the manner of Renaissance monarchs.

"King James I got the first volume of a *History of the World*; several treatises on politics, warfare, trade and economics; and piles of poetry out of Raleigh by the simple expedient of locking him into the Tower of London for a dozen years. And with that thought…"

Amid the laughter, a second chair is placed on stage for Loren Bonner, host of the ABC Shaftsboro morning show, and the cameraman crouches next to the stage to get a better view.

"Can't she see that she's making him cringe?" I speak through clenched teeth, unable to avert my gaze from the spectacle of Giles crossing his arms and legs into knots of discomfiture as Loren sets to work on him.

"She's enjoying it," Tim murmurs back. "He has brought out the praying mantis in many a female. My grasp of heterosexual coupling behavior is tenuous, but I think they sense something in him that needs a strong woman."

"Not all strong women are dominating bitches."

"Granted, but he attracts the bitches. And they snap at his soft tissue till he yelps."

With a tiny jerk of his chin he points at Loren, who is leaning in and has wrapped the ringed fingers of one hand around Giles's wrist. Her long fingers disappear in the gap between his naked wrist and the cotton of the shirt; the claws of her rings must be pressing into the skin of his chest.

If this were a scene in *Ally McBeal*, I would be Lucy Liu, spewing fire. I am the dragon, Giles is the virgin, and I'm saving him from the clutches of the Wicked Witch.

Giles has rid himself of the transgressing fingers by gesturing with one hand while keeping the other wrapped firmly around his waist, hugging himself. Because he is so articulate, speaking in beautiful, well-turned sentences, and because he holds his long limbs in that blue cotton and gray wool so very still, apart from that expressive hand, he does not come across as uneasy. Reserved, yes, that goes with the accent, introverted, intellectual, but also amusingly self-deprecating, which Loren doesn't get at all. I think it is perceptive of Tim to have picked up on the vulnerability in Giles that alerts the praying mantises and the dominant bitches.

So where is the reason he has not told me he and his wife split up? Is she here? *Who is she?* I daren't look around to see whether I can identify a woman in the audience who is watching him with that look of tender amusement that I am trying so hard to keep from my own face.

Jenna, the fan from the graduate seminar, has a question.

"I read on the IMDB website that the book is going to be turned into a film? That is so awesome!"

"Thank you—yes, since the hype of all things Tudor seems to continue, the BBC is thinking of jumping on the bandwagon and doing something similar. A mini-series, something along those lines. I say *may*." Giles gives his answer in as neutral as voice as possible; not arrogant or condescending, just as if he were genuinely uncomfortable with it. Tim whistles under his breath.

"The sneaky fucker," he murmurs. "This is the first I've heard of it."

Tessa, too, turns round to us and makes the face of an astonished cartoon character. I roll my eyes and shrug back.

"That sounds wonderful," Loren says, picking up her cue. "Is that something you will be involved in? Will you be writing the screenplay yourself?"

"Lead actors?" one of the ladies next to Tessa butts in. "Perhaps you might convey the preferences of the reading public to the casting officer!"

Giles smiles at her. "Well, what are the preferences of the reading public?"

This leads to cheerful palaver among the audience as they debate the question. The bookstore manager and her assistant appear next to Tim and me.

"I thought this one would be a dull Brit," the manager says. "If I'd known he'd charm rings around them, I'd have put him last!"

I have to hide the delighted smile on my face from the store manager on my left, from Tim on my right, and from Dolph and Steve across the room, so I check my phone.

Know that bust of Abigail Adams?

"Oh, my God! Tim, I have to go. I think my friend is here, my friend from New York!"

I jostle my way out of the store, as eager and excited as if I were a freshman and my parents had come on a surprise visit. The campus is very crowded now; the smell of tailgate barbeques is wafting through the air (I fight down the memory of rotten fish), in the distance the band is playing the Ardrossan song; someone seems to have brought a banjo. I run across Library Square, and the tall figure with the glowing red hair sticks out a mile.

"Reenie! *Irene!*"

She sees me, and I could cry, I am so relieved to have her here, a familiar face, someone who knows me.

"But, Professor Lieberman! This is so sudden!" She grins and catches me as if I were her little sister. I know I am overreacting, but I can't help myself.

"Oh, Ashley, take me away! I'm sick of it! I'm tired of it! Oh, Ashley!"

This makes us both laugh, and although she is playing it cool, I can see how pleased she is that her surprise was a success.

"That bad, huh?"

"No, no, it isn't. Well, today is—wait, what are you doing here, anyway? You should have told me, I could have—"

"Didn't know till Wednesday. Listen, I don't want to rain on your parade, though. What were you doing when I burst onto the scene?"

"Never mind—you're here! You're here!"

We get one or two odd looks, Red Irene in her dark teal skirt suit, strutting at five foot ten inches in her heels, Anna-Banana in her white Ardrossan U t-shirt. We are both used to it. I can persuade her not to go back to the book store—I wouldn't mind her meeting Tim, but there are other dangers—but to stroll along the river promenade toward the stone arch bridge instead.

"*Gee, Anna, you were right. This place is beautiful!*" I cue her.

"Well, it ain't too bad." She nods graciously.

"Thanks, that's all I wanted to hear. So how *are* you? How is everyone? What are you doing here?"

She is accompanying Jacques on a business trip to Washington. He flew in on Thursday and has meetings all day today; she took the first flight to Shaftsboro this morning and will join him there. I guess it would be ungrateful of me to be disappointed that she has not come down merely to see me.

"But tell me how *you* are!" she exclaims. I am always a little suspicious when Irene starts exclaiming, because it is often a cover for something that is troubling her. But I know she isn't ready to tell me, and there is too much to see and too much else to talk about.

We amble up the hill toward the Observatory, and I decide not to tell her of the fishy events of this morning. I am still too upset and confused to talk about it to an outsider, and to one who I know will tell me she told me so. I don't need that. I show her round the Observatory, including—with bated breath—the fourth floor; and she does not comment on the fresh paint and the bouquet of solvent intermixed with Eau d'Herring. The garbage cart is gone, too, so there is nothing that needs to be explained away.

"What's up there?" she asks, pointing at the stairs to the dome.

"The old observatory, but it's not—actually, why not. It's pretty cool. Come on."

Making light of the fact that the key to the dome is kept in a box of tissues in front of it, I unlock the door for her. The dome is flooded with sunlight, beams of dust are dancing in the air, and the old glass panes distort the light so that the air itself seems to be whirling.

"Wow…" She turns on the spot, her head tilted back.

"I know. I wonder why the college hasn't spruced it up, as a museum or something. These things—" I run my hand along one of the telescope stands "—must be a hundred years old, maybe more."

"This is a place for secrets."

"Well, Reenie, funny you should say that…"

Of course she relishes the story about Selena and her night-time lover.

"He's bound to be an absolute assclown," she says definitely. "And she's writing her thesis about the devil? Bound to be the guy. Anyone devilish among your male grad students? Unless she's making it with a professor, too."

"Oh, come on. They can't all be having affairs with professors! Anyway, Selena isn't—"

I had been wandering aimlessly around the room, curious to see what it was too dark to see when I first came up here. There are two folded rugs on the old sofa; they look new and smell new, too. And on the little washbasin there is a small wash bag with a toothbrush sticking out of it. A bar of soap, and a disposable razor blade.

"Someone sleeps here?" Irene asks, looking over my shoulder.

"Possibly, although this doesn't look like—eew!" I drop the razor into the washbasin.

"What?"

"This was not used to trim a beard," I say through clenched teeth. "Come on, let's get out of here."

"Blood?"

"Naaah…don't ask."

At the bottom of the stairs, as if to illustrate my story, Selena O'Neal is staring up at us, white as a sheet.

"Dr. Lieberman! I thought—"

"Hmm? You thought I was someone else?"

"I thought there was no key to the observatory!"

"Oh, but everyone knows where the key is kept!" I say airily. "Even I do! Sorry, Selena, could we just get past?"

The hallway is empty, except for Natalie Greco, a couple of girls I don't know, and Mrs. O'Neal. They are viewing what is left of the evidence, and one of her friends sees me and whispers something to Natalie. She casts me a quick glance, undecided whether to address me or not.

Mrs. O'Neal has no such qualms.

"And what do you make of all this, Dr. Lieberman?" she demands of me.

"I'm sure my guess is worse than yours, Mrs. O'Neal," I reply smoothly, glad that Irene has disappeared into the ladies' room.

"Someone hates this poor girl! As if she hadn't been through enough!" She bends down to me and lowers her voice. "Father's dead, you know, he was much older than Natalie's mother. She—the mother—has taken up with a new man. He's a bank manager in Shaftsboro. Plenty of money, but—well, you can imagine."

"Was her father a clergyman?" I ask on a hunch.

"Yes, why?" Lorna appears not to have been told about the quote from Leviticus on the wall. "Yes, he was a church minister, a highly respected man, and a very charismatic preacher. Lung cancer, bless him."

Natalie has made up her mind to step in front of me. All these towering females, I'm getting tired of having to look up at everyone.

"What do *you* have to do with this?" she blurts out.

"Nothing at all, I would have thought. What do you think?"

"I'm sure I don't know what to think!" She flicks back her long mane with a sound that is close to a "Humph!" Natalie, I am beginning to suspect, is a little annoyed with me for stealing her limelight.

"It must be two different…things." Selena has followed us and offers her opinion, possibly to erase my impression of how flustered she was just now. "Unconnected. It's possible."

"I don't see how they *could* be connected," I point out.

"You think it's a coincidence?" Mrs. O'Neal asks, still belligerent.

"That seems equally unlikely, I agree." My non-committal friendliness frustrates them, but I will not be drawn out.

"What was all that about?" Irene murmurs when we are walking down the stairs.

"Hate graffiti on Natalie's office door this morning."

"Which one was Natalie? She's the one who says she was raped, right?"

"The one in the sexy dress. Selena's the one in the attic."

"Odd. I would have said the other way round."

It strikes me for the first time how odd it actually is. Ninety-nine out of a hundred uninvolved bystanders would guess that Selena was raped and Natalie is having clandestine sex in unconventional surroundings.

"That dowdy girl, the one who has sex in the observatory, has fallen for a very bad man." Irene clicks her tongue. "She would never have given in to the nice boy in her poetry class. She hates herself for what she's doing. She's has self-hatred steaming out of every pore."

"You can tell that at a glance? You're quick."

"I'm a family lawyer. I have to be able to tell that sort of thing."

"She does hate herself. Harms herself, too, she scraped her knuckles—wait. Oh, *wait a minute!*"

I run back up the stairs, four flights, and arrive panting on the fourth floor. Selena is standing alone in the corridor looking down toward my office.

"Selena, would you mind—" I hold out my hand, and because I am so rattled and out of breath, she obeys automatically and gives me hers. I clasp her wrist tightly so she can't pull back when I push up the long sleeve of her tunic, all the way up over her elbow. When she sees what I'm doing, she struggles and her wrist slips from my grasp. But I have seen what I thought I would see.

"Dr. Lieberman! What are you doing?" Mrs. O'Neal hovers in the door of her daughter's office.

"Nothing," I say, still heaving. "Selena?"

Selena's face is like cast iron. "It's nothing, Mom."

"I worry about you, Banana," Irene remarks when I pick her up on the second-floor landing.

I'm too upset to trust myself to speak. In the great hall a tour of the campus is just about to start, and a crowd of people is milling about, waiting, looking at the paintings by students from the art department that are shown here because of the light. A tall, blue-shirted figure stands out, and every fiber in my body rushes toward him.

"Wait a sec, Reenie."

"What, again? Okay, I'll get myself a coffee over there."

"Giles—"

His face lights up when he sees me, and through all my shock and anger I am desperately sad that this smile doesn't mean what I thought it meant.

"I know this isn't the right moment, Giles, but could we—sorry. I should first say—you were really good, earlier, in the…in the bookstore. Very funny."

"Thanks. Sometimes Americans like me."

Last time I looked into his eyes, it was to offer him sex. I think he remembers that.

"A BBC series, huh?" I have to say something, or we'll stand here forever, gazing into one another's eyes.

"It may all come to nothing."

"Tim was a bit miffed he didn't know about it."

"He called me a sneaky fucker. To my face."

"Yes, to my face, too. But I wasn't going to repeat that."

"Not to hurt my feelings?"

God, I wish he'd stop smiling at me like this!

"Actually, not to get Tim into trouble."

"Speaking of trouble," he says, turning serious.

"Giles—could we talk about Selena again? You know the other day some windows were smashed up on the fourth floor?"

"Yes, Tessa said—"

"That was Selena. With her naked elbow, like this." I punch the air with a sharp, horizontal jab.

"She did *what?*"

"And there's more. She—sorry, I don't want to pour this out here and now, just to ask, can we talk about this? Soon? And there's more, still—not about Selena, but—well, I'm—"

"Flapping."

"Yeah, I'm flapping."

And I'm so in love with you, and I want to tell you my worries and hear what you have to say, and I want to share my life with you!

"Talk now. I have time till the concert."

"No, I can't. I—have a friend waiting." I will not introduce him to Irene.

"Right, then, let me know when it suits you." Withdrawing almost imperceptibly.

"I will, thanks. I appreciate it, Giles!"

"Who is that?" Irene, a cup of coffee in hand, is staring past me across the crowded room as if she had seen a ghost.

"Who is who—oh. The gray-haired guy?" But she knows me too well. If anything, my harmless reply makes her more suspicious.

"Yes, the gray-haired guy! Are you sleeping with him?"

I know my face is flushed with the wine and the rush and the mayhem, but at this, my temples start throbbing.

"No! And will you *please* keep your voice down!"

Irene sets her jaw, but goes on staring.

"Who is he?"

Flustered, I turn my back to Giles, who is doing the agreeable with a group of parents.

"Giles Cleveland. Stop interrogating me, Reenie. And stop staring at him."

"And who is Giles Cleveland that I have heard so little about him? Nothing, to be precise. Zilch. Zip. Nada."

"A colleague."

"I met him before." I can hear the bombshell in her voice.

"Don't be absurd. You can't have."

"Excuse me, but I have. Here, I can produce evidence: he has a thin scar that runs from the corner of his eye to his ear, like a crow's foot, only longer. Sort of like a professor of literature who was in a bar fight. Sexy."

"Yeah, I know." My own voice sounds hollow to me. "Okay, tell me—where?"

"At that conference about whatever-it-was in London. When we were supposed to be on a girls' trip around Europe and you schlepped me to school because you had to give a paper."

"Anglo-American Writing Between the Wars?"

"That's the one. I'd been sitting next to this cute guy—chap, don't you know, something of a dish," she says, imitating a posh English accent, "who was really impressed with your paper. Don't you remember? I tried to point him out to you afterward, but he was gone, like Cinderella, and didn't even leave a slipper."

"That was Giles?" My stomach churns as if I had eaten rotten herring for lunch. "What was it he said? Something—wasn't it something about young academics giving better papers than the big names?"

"Yeah, I outed myself as a totally clueless tourist, and he laughed at me for wasting my time at stupid conferences instead of going shopping or sight-seeing. Wise guy. Sexy smile, though."

"Tell me something I don't know."

"Well, he said that your paper was the only worthwhile one he'd heard that conference, and that one could tell that you loved what you were talking about, unlike the old codgers who just do it because they have to and bore everyone stiff."

My fingers are trembling so badly I have to set down my cup for fear of spilling the coffee.

"He said that?"

"Yes, I definitely remember he said 'bore everyone stiff,' because that made me wonder whether he's the type who goes—what do you call that? Conference hopping. Mind you, he wasn't hitting on me or anything. I sort of expected him to hit on you afterward, but apparently his pumpkin was waiting. Speaking of which, *is* he married?"

"Divorced. But—"

"And is he hitting on you now? Come on, I could totally see that he is!"

"Irene, he doesn't even—I'm not even sure he—where are you going? *Don't!*"

She storms past me, and before I can wrestle her to the ground and kick her under a table, Giles—who is momentarily between parents—has seen us. I think it is fear that I see flickering in his eyes for a few moments, and I don't blame him.

"Hey, there!" Irene charges at him, hand outstretched. "Remember me? I guess not, why should you? London, the July before last? A conference on—what was it again?" She turns to me, pulling me closer by my sleeve.

"Queen Mary, Lockkeeper's Cottage. I do remember," Giles says, and I can tell that he does. A line from *Lady Chatterley's Lover* comes into my head. Sir Clifford, her husband, says something—can't remember which scene this is from—*with the suavest English stiffness, for the two things often go together.* I doubt Irene can tell, but Giles feels extremely uncomfortable, either because she is doing her loud-mouthed New Yorker, or because she caught him being complimentary about me. I can't even process that yet, on top of all the other events of the day. *Giles knew me?* Well, not *knew*, but Giles heard me give a paper, in London, last year? So when the search committee shortlisted me, and when we first met and I was so insecure because I thought he hadn't been involved in my appointment, and when he was a condescending jerk about my work—he knew all along who I was?

"We weren't introduced at the time," he says to Irene. "Better late than never, eh? I'm Giles Cleveland."

They shake hands, and before she can make things worse, I butt in.

"Giles, this is a *yuchna* from the planet Klutz, who is impersonating my friend Irene from New York."

"Is that so?" He smiles blandly, but I can tell he is mustering his defensive troops. "And from that far away it is you've come to see Anna at Ardrossan?"

"Was he…making fun of me?" Ten minutes later Irene still has not recovered from being stumped.

"Yeah, well. *A biseleh.*" I could not suppress the beam of delight on my face if my life depended on it.

"He's like…an eel! A gray eel with a stick up his ass!"

"No, he's English, that's all. It's partly an act. The upper-class English schoolboy. They grow into six-footers, hone their bodies with all that rugby and rowing, and then play on our maternal instincts with their awkward charm. On British women it doesn't work half as well as on us. You either can't stand them because you think they're effeminate and moody and emotionally constipated, or you fall for them."

"I must be more British than I thought," she grumbles. "Have you fallen for him? But why am I asking? I can see that you have!"

"I don't remember the falling. Where do you want to go for dinner, Reenie?" I pointedly change the subject. "Bernie recommends a Mexican place to which I haven't been, or we could try Cajun, then you'd have something to tell Jacques about, or—"

"I can't." Irene doesn't often look embarrassed, but now she does. "I gotta be back at the airport by four thirty."

"You're not flying back today!"

"Yup. Sorry, Banana. Jacques wants me at this working dinner he has tonight."

"Well, call him and say you've found me in a madhouse and you have to stay the night at the tomato farm to set me to rights again. You haven't even seen the tomato farm yet!"

"I would so much love to, really I would!" She's not lying, either. "But these people tonight are really important for Jacques, and things have not been going so great between us, so…this is our quality time. Our quality time together is a business dinner he has in Washington with two guys from San Francisco. Care to guess what our problem might be?"

This is where the exclaiming earlier came from, and the brittle gaiety that she's had all day. I would have wormed it out of her earlier, if—well, if I hadn't spent the day in a madhouse.

I am very sorry to let her go so soon, but I can't pretend that it is Irene that I brood over when I cycle back home. Or the herring, or the graffiti.

Giles knew me?

Chapter 20

Matthew Dancey has a lot of questions. Is the difference between my New York students and my Ardrossan students very considerable? Am I finding the transition hard to make? Do I feel that Ardrossan students and I, in modern parlance, have "clicked"? Is it perhaps my experience with the British university system that made me neglect the crucial mainstay of private education, that is, the cultivation of good relations between parents and faculty?

"These are largely rhetorical questions, sir. I take it you do not mean me to answer them."

"And I take it you don't have any answers! After Friday's events you must be aware of the fact that your settling-in period at Ardrossan is rather more problematic than we had hoped!"

"It is more problematic than I had hoped, too, sir, and I'm sorry for it."

Contrary to my expectation that Dancey would try to file Friday's vandalism under the heading of *Wear & Tear (Misc.)*, he phoned me in my office half an hour ago and summoned me to a meeting. He had cleared this with my mentor, with Maxine Emerson from Employee Relations, and with Jerry Poplar, an officer with the campus police. He caught me unprepared. I am still in the phase of fermentation, strangely unable to stay away from the scene of the weekend's bizarre events and revelations. After my first impulse to pour out to Giles what I had found out about Selena O'Neal, I stalled. Or maybe I stalled because I haven't figured out what to make of the fact that he knew me, had seen me present a paper, but never mentioned it. Wasn't it worth mentioning? And why do I seem to be in a state of perpetual turmoil about the things Giles Cleveland might have mentioned to me but didn't?

Ten minutes before we were due at Dancey's office, Giles called me. Would I please come downstairs and explain what all the fuss is about? Now he is sitting opposite me round the table, digesting the news bulletins I threw at him on our way there.

"Well, Anna, this question is not rhetorical." Dancey glares at me. "Do you have any idea who might be responsible for the damage done to your office door?"

"No, sir, I do not. I suspect someone, but I have no evidence."

"Dr. Lieberman." Jerry Poplar clears his throat. He is a big man in a shirt a size too small for him, with two necks bulging over the collar. "Your reluctance to accuse an innocent person, or innocent persons, is commendable, but we are dealing with someone who has displayed considerable violent energy, and — not to scare you — considerable aversion against you. It is in your own interest to identify the culprit."

"I have reason to believe that the department would not act against the person who is, if I may use the term, my prime suspect. Naming this person might harm me, but it would not lead to disciplinary action against…said person. Plus, I might be wrong. It is not in my best interests to name names."

"Dr. Lieberman, it is in your very best interest not to obstruct justice!" Jerry is a little flustered at my speech.

"I never thought I would ever be in a position to say this to a police officer, but are you going to slap me with a subpoena?" And because I am smiling at him very sweetly, and because I am a pretty (argh!) young woman, and because he has a sense of humor, Jerry laughs.

"For not telling me who you think slapped a can full of fish against your office door? No, ma'am. As long as you're not withholding actual information from us."

I mentally cross my fingers and try not to think of Selena's purple-and-yellow elbow, lined by crusty lacerations.

"No, sir, I have no actual information in this case. Besides, I have not been threatened with violence, unlike Natalie Greco. So your first priority should be to identify *that* culprit. Not that I am taking the herring lightly, of course. I was and am *appalled*."

"Sorry — threatened with violence?" This is news to both Maxine and Jerry, and they both look to Dancey for information. Giles widens his eyes at me, and I could kick myself — but how was I supposed to know Dancey would keep that detail from the police?

"Professor Dancey, I believe you reported — let me see — " Maxine checks her file " — here: 'scurrilous phrases, applied with spray paint to an office door and the opposite wall.' You did not mention threats of violence."

"No, because — threats of violence, goodness me, that does not adequately describe the facts at all!" I don't suppose I will ever come closer to seeing Matthew Dancey blush and stutter. He will have my head for this.

"May we have the precise wording of the graffiti, please, sir?" Jerry clicks his pen into action.

"I'm sure I can't remember. I think it had the word 'whore' in it again. I really can't — "

Jerry and Maxine look at me.

"Sir, I can't pretend not to remember," I say to Dancey.

"Nobody is asking you to pretend anything!"

"Matthew…" This is the first time Giles speaks, and Dancey hears him.

"Very well," I sigh. "Across the door it said WHORE in capitals; you can still see some of that because the paint hasn't come off properly. And on the wall it said, 'If a priest's daughter defiles herself by becoming a prostitute, she must be bur — '"

"She must be what?" Jerry glances up from his notepad.

"It's Leviticus twenty-one nine. 'She must be burned in the fire.' It's about the rules for priests at the Temple."

"And you were alarmed enough to look this up?"

"Um…no, I recognized it. I read the Bible."

Jerry stares at me.

"Lieberman. *Lieberman?*"

"That's a part of the Bible that we have in common," I explain.

"Oh. Well, this is serious indeed, and more serious, I agree, than the fish. Sir, will you share your thoughts about…the fish?"

I am surprised that Dancey has any thoughts about the fish at all. He flicks through his own notes and informs me that Mr. Frank

Harrison asked to speak to him on Saturday and complained on various counts about my behavior in and out of class.

"This aspect of the matter does not really concern us, Professor Dancey. Maybe you could come to the salient point?" Jerry Poplar is fast shooting up the list of my favorite people in the world.

"In short," Dancey says, his voice tight, "and this is extremely confidential information, Madeline Harrison came to Ardrossan with a record of destructive behavior at her previous school. She was educated at a very select private academy that refrained from contacting the police provided that Madeline's institution of further education is informed of her history."

"Does her history include arson?" Jerry asks matter-of-factly.

"It does include two counts of arson, yes."

"But that—" Giles and I object in one breath.

I complete the sentence when he sits back in his chair again. "That makes no sense! We're dealing with two different people here, the graffiti artist and the herring slopper! Did Madeline ever use fermented herring against her enemies at school?"

Dancey shifts in his chair, and I am paralyzed by the fear that he'll say yes.

"Excrement." And for the second time this morning a rosy hue spreads across his bald pate.

"Oh, for heaven's sake! Teenaged girls are the *worst!*" Jerry Poplar shudders, expressing what we all feel.

"I will take on board your suggestion, sir, that Madeline's dislike of me is violent enough to make her, um, deploy rotten fish against me. It is a sort of speaking punishment, actually, because her main complaint is that I occasionally mention sex in class. So the use of fish in an attack against me makes sense. Symbolically speaking."

Maxine Emerson chokes and looks down at her notes. Dancey and Jerry Poplar stare at me as if I had produced a fish and slapped it on the table between us, and Giles…Giles is chewing the inside of his cheeks to stop himself from grinning. Then he clears his throat and intervenes.

"I might say, Matthew, that I witnessed a few minutes of Anna's first class session, which she conducted with great verve and tact. Yes, it involved the mention of—"

"Christianity as a primitive religion predicated on cannibalism, fertility rites, homosexuality, and masturbation!" Dancey reads out from his notes in rising cadences. "In the first session of a general education class full of freshmen! This is either an example of inexcusable provocation or of astonishingly bad judgment! What *were* you thinking?"

"I thought I was introducing a group of open-minded, broadly educated young adults to a class on comedy!" I turn to Giles for support. "Would you teach comedy without mentioning sex?"

"I wouldn't. But don't shout at Matthew, no matter how much he deserves it."

"Masturbation?" Dancey repeats, angry with me for having to mention this word at all in public.

"We were looking at Shakespeare's Sonnet Number One. It's about—"

"I know what Shakespeare's sonnets are about!" he barks. "In the first session?"

"They enjoyed it," Giles intervenes again. "I happened to be passing, the classroom door was open, and—sorry, Anna—I stopped to eavesdrop a little because the class seemed very lively. You saw Anna's teaching presentation when she applied, Matthew, you know that she—" He looks at me, and my feelings for him rise like a dolphin out of stormy waters. "She has zing! Snowflakes like this Harrison girl may find that uncomfortable, but it's good for them. Builds character."

"In other words, Anna adheres to the British school of higher education, also known as the principle of sink or swim!" Dancey states sardonically. "No wonder you're defending her in this, Giles! I had my doubts about appointing someone not properly socialized in the American academic system, but I was not heard!"

"Pretext!"

"Three students have complained about Anna's conduct in class, and it isn't even mid-term yet!"

"Freshmen always complain. You know that, Matthew! Are their parents alumni? I bet they are!"

"Can this debate perhaps wait till my one year review?" I assert myself with the vehemence of the deeply exhausted. "There is no point in wrangling over it now, and I'm sure we all have more pressing matters to see to."

Maxine and Jerry seem glad to get out of here, but Dancey asks me to stay, and I sit down again very much with my tail between my legs. I am more dejected now than I was before the meeting. I don't know what to think, about the fish, about the complaints, and I don't know where I stand, except that I am beginning to realize that it isn't in the same corner as the college.

In the monologue that follows, Dancey affirms this last point far more explicitly than I think is necessary. He does not say anything new, but he is angry, and he is a vindictive man.

"This is two-thousand six, Anna. No one deliberately endangers their position on tenure track. It would be the supremest of follies. You seem, therefore, to have committed an error of judgment, and this I find most upsetting, because it shows how your cultural background clashes with that of your students. You are not in control of your classroom. I do not need to stress what a fundamental problem this is, for you as well as for us who must assess your suitability for this job!"

I don't say anything. He just wants to vent, not to discuss this constructively. I ought to tell him about Selena O'Neal's act of self-harming vandalism, but I would sooner bite off my own tongue.

When I am back at my desk twenty minutes later and the phone rings, I'm tempted to rip out the plug from its socket. Of course I can't. I'm on tenure track.

"Me. Could you come downstairs, please?"

"Giles, I don't—"

"I want to talk to you, and your place is too crowded."

"Yes, well, I don't want to talk to you, so—hello—?"

He has hung up on me.

I slink past the open office doors and the students chatting by the water fountain and take the elevator down to the first floor. There are people around here, too, but I keep my eyes down and head straight for the door at the garden end, which is open just a crack. I step in, just far enough so I can see him sitting bent over his desk. The shirt across his shoulders looks like a thin, translucent skin gleaming against the dark leather of the chair. I would be all right if I was allowed to run my hand over the strands of muscle and the bumps of bone of his back. Lay my cheek against it. Utterly ridiculous how social conditioning works within me to associate the pure, fine strength of a male back with protection and safety.

"Anna." He jumps up, impatient, or—something. Edgy. "Come in."

"Really, I don't—"

"Door. Will you—"

I do, although I have no intention of staying. "I've been shouted at enough for one day, thanks, so—"

"Shout? Why would I shout at you?" He is upset, and my defensive attitude draws him toward me with a couple of quick, long strides before he thinks better of it and retreats back to the sofa. "Come. Sit down."

"Why? I've had my lecture. And—" I find it difficult to keep my voice steady, suddenly. "And thanks for—"

"Interfering? Yeah, thanks very much for nothing. Won't you sit down, just for a second?"

He's too impatient to wait out my sulks, or my obstinacy, or my—what? God, I wish he would give me a hug. He is so tall and full of pent-up energy, and his office is quiet and dusky, like a hideout, even though it's only mid-afternoon. I want to hide from the world, and I want to hide in Giles Cleveland's…office.

"Listen, don't—" He comes toward me again, as if he meant to grab me and make me sit down. "Don't let them get to you. That's all I want to say. You know that, don't you? You know admin are all full of crap. Don't pay Matthew any attention. Just do your thing."

I'm still standing with my back against the door, my palms flat against the cool wood.

"But that isn't what they want." I have to swallow a pain in my throat, but it's better to speak than not. "They don't like…my thing. They don't like me here."

"See?" He stabs at me with his hand, vindicated. "That's why I had to talk to you! I knew you'd turn this into a great big stick to clobber yourself with! Don't do that!"

"Don't *you* turn me into a neurotic female, Giles! I'm not a good fit at Ardrossan! First the rumpus about my contract, then Logan Williams, now all this—and Dancey can't stand me, you saw that, didn't you? Time to face facts! I'm walking the plank here!"

He has come close enough to see that my eyes are stinging, and it adds to his exasperation.

"Balderdash!"

"It is *not* balderdash!" I interrupt myself, suddenly tickled. "*Balderdash?* Who says balderdash these days?"

This takes him aback, and he stands gazing at me with a watchful frown, scrutinizing me, checking whether it is plausible that I have calmed down.

"'Atta girl." His face clears, he nods. "Laugh it off. Best thing to do, believe me."

My smile is a little wobbly, because I really need to sit down somewhere and have a good cry. I should go home with a bottle of Merlot, have a hot bath and a good long cry. Be right as rain afterward.

Giles reaches out, and his hand on my shoulder unclenches all the muscles in my body so suddenly that I sway against it.

"But you're not laughing it off, are you? I wish you would."

Did he feel my body lean against his hand for half a second? I try to catch myself, mortified, and launch into false swagger.

"Hey—there's plenty of time to find my feet! Just because I'm having a rocky start doesn't mean I'll…fail, does it?"

How simple it is. How simple, an arm around my shoulders, a warm hand cupping my neck. I can't believe he is actually doing this, that he has actually done this, gripped my shoulder more tightly, taken that one step closer toward me, drawn me against himself, into his arms, against the smooth cotton of his shirt, the solid body underneath, and that he is holding me tightly, not politely. This is not a gesture. He wants me to feel it.

"I'm sorry." His voice is so close, in my hair, against my ear. No idea what he means, and I don't care, either. But I have to pretend. I have to disentangle myself from his arms and my longing, and look up at him, although my eyes are swollen with exhaustion.

"Why sorry? This has nothing to do with you."

He steps back from me.

"Yes, it has. I helped to get you in here."

For the first time since I entered the room, his eyes fall from my face. He is standing in the middle of his office, in his black pants and white shirt, staring at the pattern of the rug on the floor.

"And here's me thinking it was my qualifications that got me in. Duh."

"No—yes, of course!" He actually drives his fists into his pockets, he feels so awkward. Sorry, maybe, that he touched me.

"Or my sex and my religion. After all, Dancey told me in so many words that I had, quote, 'sailed in here on a diversity ticket,' so—"

"*What?*" Within a second Giles's expression has gone from troubled to suspicious to furious. "God, he is such an arsehole! No, they weren't sure about your UK degrees, and Elizabeth wrote to me, in case I knew anyone in England who had worked with you. Well, since I had just seen you at the conference, I told them that you were by far the best fit, and that I would strictly veto any of the other candidates."

I am too tired to manage my anger.

"And why didn't you tell me this earlier? I thought I had been dropped into your nest like a cuckoo's egg! You were horrid to me!"

"I was not!"

"You were an arrogant jerk!"

With a crack of laughter he flings himself into the low upholstered chair at right angles to the sofa. That's a lot of arm and leg to dispose of, and one hand is back in his pocket, the other elbow on the back of the chair.

"Anyway, when you came down, people liked you much better than they liked that Wright woman, and Bergstrom never had a majority anyway, so Elizabeth decided it would be best to go for the third candidate. And although none of that is your fault at all, several of my esteemed colleagues, Dancey among them, were so miffed that they've taken it out on you. But that's just a little hazing, and it'll pass once they've got it out of their system."

"Gee, that's so comforting." But now I sit down, too.

"What I want you to understand," he goes on, undeterred by my sarcasm, "is that this isn't how it's going to be. They'll find a new grudge and forget about you."

I contemplate his angular posture in the chair, the hunched shoulder and the ankle resting on the opposite knee so that his shin forms a horizontal bar between us.

"You don't believe that," I say. Down comes the ankle, but his legs are still crossed, and he shifts uncomfortably in his seat. "No, Giles, I think you're beginning to realize that what with the resentment I caused simply by having been the laughing third party, and the resentment I'm causing now by scaring your snowflakes and by attracting haters, there's a real possibility I won't be renewed next year. C'mon. Do admit."

"No." He shakes his head, but only after a long silence in which he goes very quiet. "It's not for a while yet. You just have to get used to each other's ways, you and Ardrossan. And you will! I'm just sorry that you're not having a better time of it."

This sofa is preposterous. I've edged up against the back, which is high enough to support my neck, and my feet are dangling half a foot off the ground. Thirty seconds alone on this sofa, and I'd be fast asleep.

"So you summoned me to apologize for having recommended me for this job? That is terribly silly of you." It is so dark in his office now that we cannot read each other's faces anymore, but since I can hear the tenderness in my voice, I assume that he can, too. I force myself to sit up and scoot forward. "To be given a chance to prove myself at a national research university? I'm grateful to you, and if it doesn't work out, it's…just one of those things."

"No, no, come on!" He, too, sits up, and the earlier tension is back in his body. "Be philosophical about it, by all means, but there's no reason to be pessimistic! Are you worried about Dancey? He won't fire you, I'll see to that!"

"Giles, that's…that's not how it's supposed to work."

He straightens in his seat and pushes his clasped hands between his knees.

"I wasn't proposing to thrash him. Smack him about a bit, maybe."

The quiet dignity with which he says this fools me for three seconds, then we both break down in whoops of laughter. There is a precarious moment when the laughter dies down but our energy is still up. This can go either way…forward…or backward…advance… retreat.

"Giles?"

"Hmm?"

"Have you told them?"

"Told them what?"

"About—your horns." *About the time Hornberger fucked your wife.*

"Oh, that. No."

Any moment now he will brush me off. But until he does…

"And will you?"

"On the whole I think I will, yes. Maybe not this week. Maybe not next. Or maybe not ever. It depends a bit."

"I should have left Amanda's office." I stand up, and my heartbeat almost chokes me when I have to step past him on my way to the door.

"Just as well that you heard. I didn't quite know whether to tell you."

When I get home, I go straight to bed, huddle against the mattress, pull the comforter tight around my body, and pretend I am still in Giles Cleveland's office. In Giles Cleveland's arms.

Chapter 21

Amanda Cleveland is very near the top of the list of people I do not want to see this week, or ever again, but no such luck.

"Might I ask you to come over to my office, Anna? It's difficult to discuss this over the phone."

What's difficult to discuss? *There was a mistake about your paycheck, it has been rectified, the college is very sorry about the inconvenience this caused you.* That's the only thing I want to hear about this.

And that's *Doctor Lieberman* to you, sorority girl!

There is, unfortunately, a great deal more. Amanda, in a beige turtleneck and tweed skirt (we have *those* in common, it seems), picks me up at her assistant's desk. Embarrassment doesn't come easily to her, but there is an aura around her that doesn't bode well.

Ten minutes in, I am having trouble keeping my temper in check.

"Look, I understand that my contract was signed by the interim Provost, but surely his signature is still legally binding!"

"It is and it isn't. I understand your disappointment, Anna. The situation is less than satisfactory." Her poise seems more natural than last time we sat opposite each other at her desk; and this time it is up to me to listen, read and digest at the same time. "Provosts used to have the authority to fine-tune starting salaries according to the new hire's qualifications. In keeping with this custom, and on account of your publications, Newburgh slotted you into the highest salary category for first-year tenure-track appointees. However, this policy was changed during Clement Hill's last term, and Newburgh was apprised of this change — theoretically."

"But surely my contract was not the only one signed by Newburgh according to the old policy. How have you proceeded in all the other cases?"

"So far I've had to deal with three, and they all accepted the college's gesture of goodwill." She pushes a contract form toward me.

"Gesture is right," I agree after studying it. "This is still almost one hundred and fifty a month less than the sum promised me."

Amanda nods. "Yes. Your stipulated salary was the highest of the four."

"And the college would not consider honoring these contracts?"

She purses her mouth in a way that may be intended to signal regret.

"I would advise you to discuss this with your department chair and the Dean. When they submit their annual merit evaluations they may recommend salary increments that would get you up to the sum on your original contract quite quickly. Within three or four years."

Yes, I can just see Matthew Dancey recommending me for a raise.

"I will consider that, thank you."

"I think it only fair to mention that you may, of course, sue the college for the full sum in your old contract. But—" She doesn't have to complete the sentence.

"But that would be professional suicide. I know. Well, I can think of pleasanter ways of shooting myself down while on tenure track. Thank you, Amanda, I appreciate your candor." I get up to leave because I am irrationally angry with the messenger, and there is really nothing left to say.

"Since candor seems to be the new watchword," she says when I am about to open the door. "Has Giles told you he can't father any children?"

I swing round to stare at her, and I can see how far she has moved out of her comfort zone to land me this facer. But candor is an impulse hard to suppress.

"Listen, he didn't even tell me you were getting a divorce, so don't get your panties in a wad, lady!"

It's just as well that you heard. I didn't know whether to tell you.

I don't even want to think about this.

Does he have a low sperm count? Is he the carrier of a horrible congenital disease? Is he — perish the thought! — erectilely challenged? And *why* did she tell me? Jealousy? Spite? Did she mean to thrust a spoke into a wheel that she saw turning in Giles's mind when she saw us together? Impossible. Our encounter in her office lasted about twenty seconds! On the other hand, she knows him well, so if Amanda thinks Giles likes me, then maybe…maybe Giles likes me. *Like-likes* me.

No. I refuse to think about it. I refuse to account for the flash of relief that ran through my body when my brain had processed her question and its implications.

I still have not told anyone about Selena O'Neal's self-harming spree, not even Giles. Irene says I should talk to Ma Mayfield or someone from the Counseling Center, but definitely not keep it a secret. I don't particularly like Selena. But I don't think that being sued by her college for damages incurred when she broke three windows with her bare elbow will help to stabilize a girl suffering from bulimia and the throes of what is presumably her first love affair.

If it *is* bulimia. Maybe it is really just nerves.

The week after Family Weekend has an anti-climactic feel to it because students have to hand in their midterm essays. After that, we tumble into fall break like into a life raft. Compared to previous fall semesters, my stack of essays is miniscule, and I rejoice at the prospect of two whole days to work on my paper for Notre Dame.

That is before I realize that seven of the Comedy essays and three of the Parody essays show evidence of what the Honor Code calls Academic Misconduct, in this case plagiarized sentences, passages, or thoughts. Grading twenty-eight essays, if you do it conscientiously, takes about two working days. Checking twenty-eight essays for evidence of plagiarism takes frustratingly longer.

Logan, at least, seems to be clear. His essay is sloppy but not without sparks; I am not magnanimous enough to ask him to come and discuss ways of improving it, as I might otherwise have done. My biggest headache is Madeline Harrison. My syllabus states explicitly that a) extended deadlines have to be approved by me beforehand and that b) essays handed in late will be downgraded. The essay that Madeline sends me three days late does not, fortunately, show evidence of plagiarism, but it is so badly written, both in style and in content, that downgrading would make it fail.

So do I go against my elaborately wrought syllabus just to avoid further trouble with the Harrisons? The answer, I'm afraid, is no. No, I will not be bullied, even if it means another trip to Matthew Dancey's office.

When Tim calls and asks if I want to meet Giles and him for an absolutely confidential report about the first sitting of the Sexual Misconduct Hearing Panel, I leap at his offer before I remember that I had resolved to limit my contact with Giles to the Observatory-based minimum. And because this secret intelligence meeting can't take place in public, and because the mysterious Martin, too, is sitting at home grading essays and can't be disturbed, Tim decides that it is time Giles was invited to the tomato farm.

I panic. Then I run over to Karen to ask whether I can scrounge a few apples. I need to bake a cake. Apple and almond.

"I should say straightaway that I disapprove of this," Giles says when he has got off his bike and is ascending my porch. Unlike Tim, who comes in bright professional cycling gear, he is wearing jeans and his Navy sweater. I am glad — even Giles would look silly dressed as a canary. I wouldn't mind, though, if he was a little chirpier.

"You do?" I ask, crestfallen, and look around me.

"Not of the farm, or — this! This is very cozy. Very nice, indeed."

I am learning to hear what Giles doesn't say, and what he doesn't say about my gamekeeper's cottage makes me blush under my cake-baking flush. It is very nice to have him here. Very nice, indeed.

"No, I disapprove of this habit Tim has developed of feeding you classified information!"

"Giles believes that I'm corrupting you." Tim shrugs and disappears into my bathroom. "You don't mind, do you?"

"No, I don't mind." I peek up at Giles with my most helpless *bicycliste*-in-distress mien. "Please corrupt me!"

This hits him like a blow to the body, and his reaction is anger.

"You!" He points again, like Uncle Sam. "You shouldn't even be making jokes about that sort of thing, in your position and what with…with what's been happening at the Observatory lately!"

Now I'm stumped, because I suddenly can't remember whether—

"Did I *tell* you about Selena? I thought I hadn't…"

"Selena?"

"That Selena is having sex in the dome? In the old observatory? I didn't. Damn, I didn't mean to."

Giles checks Tim's whereabouts—he's still in the bathroom—then gazes down at me. This is why I didn't want him in my cottage. Now that he's here, I don't want to let him go again.

"Who with?" he asks.

"Don't know. Some guy. Strictly speaking, I don't even know for sure that she's having sex. Well. Yeah, I do. I think. She must be."

"Is that what you wanted to tell me last Friday?"

"Last Friday. What was last Friday? Oh God, was that only last Friday? No."

"There're all sorts of things you're not telling me, aren't there?"

I nod, so nervous I have to swallow before answering. "But so are you. Not telling me things."

"That's true. Too dangerous."

This is why Giles so rarely looks into my eyes. When he does, the earth moves.

The men are perfectly happy to be plied with coffee and cake and are very complimentary about both. Since each of them has three slices in the course of the afternoon, even as neurotic a housewife as I will believe that they enjoyed it.

"They postponed my tenure review," Tim explains his cold-blooded violation of confidentiality. "The committee was all set and supposed to meet next week, Monday, but it has been deferred for the time being."

"'Organizational problems,'" Giles adds. "That's all I was told, at any rate."

"Just to keep the sword dangling over my head! They are so screwing me—I don't see why I shouldn't squeal!"

"Who's on the sexual misconduct panel now, anyway?" I ask. "Elizabeth—"

"No, Ma Mayfield is only sitting in. The Provost decided since she's biased, being English Lit and all that, the Assistant Dean of Studies should chair the panel. Young guy, more hair than sense."

"It would have been better for Natalie if it had been some old, cynical bastard with nothing to lose," Giles remarks. "He might have stirred things up a bit."

"Nobody is interested in stirring things up, Giles!" Tim snaps. "It's not as if Hornberger is a pedophile or anything! He is one of the college's best cash machines, with lots of extramural connections. The girls he has sex with are grad students, which makes the dependence and power play worse, but it seems he's wise enough to stick to the older ones."

"*Older?*" I jeer.

"Twenty-one or older! Look at what the athletes get away with, and the frat boys!"

"That is no excuse."

"Well, there is no excuse for forcing untenured assistant professors onto a committee that could potentially blow up the college! All three faculty members on the panel are on tenure track—Sandy Rohde from Biology and Bernard Cogan from Psychology. That shouldn't even be allowed, in my opinion."

"Bernie? Oh, but I know Bernie! He's my friend from—well, not *friend*, exactly, from school. The one I met at Freddy Katz's synagogue. Bernie. He does turn up in the oddest places!"

"Used to bully you, didn't he? Yeah, he said." Tim grins. "He was dragooned into this by his chair because he's published stuff on sexual abuse in families or something. He's in his second year on tenure track, so he's vulnerable, almost as much as me. Sandy is up next year, and the Big Boss in her section is Carl Gissing, who is like *this* with the Biology alumni, not least among whom is Frank Harrison, who is like *this* with our Nick, because they were in the same fraternity back in the seventies. It's a farce!"

"Of course it's a farce," Giles agrees placidly. "Bureaucracy always is."

"The irony is," says Tim, "that in this day and age, colleges have to demonstrate their political correctness by having a fair number of sexual-assault cases to adjudicate each year, or they run the risk of appearing to discourage their female students from confiding in college authorities. If this case involved a frat boy and a sorority girl, most likely both pissed out of their heads, they would be on the 'rapist' like a pack of hounds. But it's one thing to make an example of a drunken twenty-year-old who can't even recall, the next morning, in which and how many holes he came the night before. It's another to have our golden boy Nick up there. They'll get him off, mark my words. The only one openly baying for his blood is Lorna O'Neal."

I almost drop my fork at this. "Lorna O'Neal is a member of the Sexual Misconduct Hearing Panel?"

"That woman is a bulldozer!" Tim groans. "If she had her way, Hornberger would be strung up by the larger of his two testicles and left to rot! She is *rabid!* Just as well, maybe, because the rest of us are chicken."

"You just said Nick doesn't deserve to get it in the neck," Giles reminds him.

"Well!" Tim swallows a mouthful of cake and puts on an expression I assume is supposed to evoke Hornberger. "'I'm a full professor. My students are of age and of sound mind. It's nobody's business how many of them I fuck, how often I fuck them, and where I fuck them.'"

"He did not say that!" I gasp.

"Oh, boy, did he ever." He grins. "The moment had a certain element of grandeur, I can't deny it. I think he is trying to scare them. And it's working! Another gem was when they read that passage about moral turpitude, and Hornberger said something like, 'Son —' I do believe he called the Assistant Dean of Studies *son* '— there is nothing turpid about the body of a young woman. Turgid, yes, if you know what you're doing, but not turpid.' Can I say *gross?*"

I glance over at Giles and see that he has made a decision.

"Tim, you know that Mandy and I split up when she had an affair, don't you? Note that I'm saying 'when,' not 'because.'"

"Y-Yes?" Tim clearly doesn't know where this is leading.

"The affair was with Nick."

"Oh, Christ!" Within seconds, the blood seems to drain out of Tim's face. "Oh, my sainted aunt! But how? *Why?* No, never mind." He manages to collect himself, but it is with difficulty. He laughs. "Sorry about this. *That* was…unexpected."

"I'll say." Giles hesitates. Then he bends forward and briefly lays his hand on Tim's thigh. "Sorry, mate. Didn't mean to rattle you. I've been wanting to tell you for a while and never quite got round to it."

Tim stares across the table at me. "You knew this?"

"Not officially." I try to evade him. "I heard something I wasn't supposed to hear."

"How does Ma Mayfield handle herself when Nick comes out with *bon mots* like that?" Giles changes the topic back to Hornberger's most recent affair. "Or is she not allowed to speak?"

"Oh, she's a complete dude! Very from-the-hip."

There is a beat, and we are in convulsions of laughter.

"But why does Hornberger—oh, man…" I wipe some water out of my eyes. "Why does Hornberger provoke them like this? Is he not worried he'll be fired? Ruined? Publicly shamed?"

"You have to hand it to the man, he is a cool motherfucker. Sorry, Anna. His defense—apart from insisting that he did not force himself on Natalie that night at that conference, or ever, which he can no more prove than she disprove, because she did not go to see a doctor afterward, so there is no official testimony to support her version. There are two photos." Tim gives an eloquent shudder. "I didn't look very closely, because she cannot conclusively prove that those photos were taken that night."

"His defense—" Giles starts Tim's sentence again.

"Oh, yes, his defense—and I have to say, even Ma Mayfield was shocked by this one—is that he has been having sex with students for twenty-five years, and he has never been accused of sexual violence by any of them."

"That's bullshit," I point out. "That's like saying, 'I've been driving for twenty-five years, officer, and I've never run anyone over before.'"

"It doesn't make rational sense, but the effect was stunning. Besides, Natalie insists that he told her that there was at least one other incident where he was accused of rape, when he was younger. Maybe that's more than twenty-five years ago."

"Hmm," Giles says, chin in hand. "I'm beginning to wonder whether perhaps Natalie is responsible for the graffiti. You know, like the CIA attacked the Twin Towers."

"Yes, Cleve, but that is a conspiracy theory cooked up by crazy people," Tim states flatly.

"*Because*, if Natalie has no proof, what else can she do except make herself look victimized and vulnerable some other way? Writing herself public hate mails would do it."

"But the second graffiti wasn't a hate mail. You agreed it was about…well, about sex. Maybe a defloration, even." I grab a cushion and hug it to my chest.

"Self-absorbed, obsessive, maudlin!" Giles says disparagingly.

"I wouldn't describe Natalie as 'maudlin,'" Tim says, and Giles shrugs skeptically.

When the cake is gone, the men proceed to beer. I stick to water.

"I'm saving myself for Erin's end-of-midterm-grading party on Sunday," I explain when Tim looks down his nose at my glass. "Talking of which—how do I deal with plagiarists?"

"You send them to Ma Mayfield to have their nails plucked out with red-hot pincers," Giles says. "Or you could keep them standing by to mop up whatever that Harrison girl next slops against your office door."

"Homecoming will probably be her next opportunity." I nod, darkly. "They've told Natalie to stay away from the college, did you hear? Especially from events like Homecoming. For her own protection."

"They should tell the Harrisons to keep their degenerate daughter locked up. Tim, Matthew thinks Anna's hater is one of our spoilt brats, one who's too Christian to read Shakespeare's sonnets."

"I don't…" I sigh and shake my head. "I don't buy that."

"So who do you think it was?"

"Well, Corvin."

All things considered, I still think that Crazy Corvin, Corvin the Invisible, is behind all my troubles. The complaint about my heels, messing with the mess in the garbage cart, the oil, and now the fish. I don't know how he got hold of the new key before I did, but doesn't searching my office smell of the same paranoid, secretive mind? Ironically, Natalie's hater might know. He or she may well have seen Corvin apply the herring. It is not that I don't believe Madeline Harrison capable of this kind of adolescent malevolence, but it strikes me as improbable that she would advance these two very different weapons against me on the same day, rotten fish and her bully of a father. No, I think it was Corvin, and I must decide what to do about him.

While Tim is pulling on his cycling boots again, Giles takes the plates and mugs into the kitchen and re-emerges a few seconds later, a little bewildered.

"Were you aware of the fact that you have two youngsters copulating in your backyard?"

"*What?*"

I don't even bother to look out the window. I rush out the back door, but on the other side of the brook there is no one. The men follow me, both looking alarmed, and Tim finds the message they left for me dangling from a low-hanging twig: a semen-filled condom.

"*Logan Williams!* This is middle-school humor, you…*douchebag!*" I yell into the shadows between the trees.

"Anna, come." Giles takes me by the arm and draws me away, his shoulders shaking with laughter.

"Did you recognize him?"

"No, it was just two figures, er, moving."

"I'm sure it was him! If I catch him fucking my landlady's daughter, I'll make chopped liver out if him!"

"Long, blond hair?"

"No. No, that's…she's okay, she's a tomato picker from Poland."

"D'you want me to get rid of…that?" He tries to suppress it, but his face is gleaming with wicked laughter.

"What, that? Thanks, but I'm not having my guests dispose of other people's disposed-of condoms."

Our eyes meet only for a fraction of a second, but again I feel a seismic wave travel through the earth, up my legs and into my womb.

I am in a panic of indecision. I can't orchestrate a reason for Giles to stay. Do I even *want* him to stay? If he really wanted to stay, he could cycle off with Tim, lose him at the next junction, and come back. I am too shy to even look at him again to see whether he would like to come back. No, we are both carefully looking past each other.

Just as well. Who would prefer sex to grading essays, anyway?

Chapter 22

On Monday I cycle across the Observatory parking lot, across Library Square, past Harrison Lab, along the river promenade, across the stone arch bridge into Ardrossan. When I hand the manila envelope to the elderly woman behind the counter in the post office, she says, "To England? This one's sealed with a kiss, am I right?"

"Yes, you're right. Wait—" I take it from her again and quickly kiss it for luck. "Oh—have I smudged it now?"

"No, it's fine, dear. If half the love letters in the world were mailed with half the dedication as these…" She weighs and franks it. "That's three thirty-one, please."

Every other year the English department hosts its own Homecoming reception—what Nick Hornberger called "the black lining on the cloud of Family Weekend." For two hours on Friday afternoon we will be welcoming English Lit alums, and they are sure to be interested in one thing and one thing only: the sex scandal. Hornberger *lui-même* will be conspicuously absent from this occasion but not, more importantly, from the opening ceremony at the new Institute for Cognitive Science, Linguistics and Psychology. Apparently there was a ruckus about this amongst the President, the Provost, and the Board of Trustees, but Hornberger insisted that he was innocent until proven guilty, and as such—that is, innocent—he had every right to celebrate the coming to fruition of a several-hundred-thousand-dollar project that he had been working on for over a year. Fair enough. Meanwhile the men who had to clean up the E-4 hallway on Family Weekend are now posted at strategic corners of the Observatory to prevent a repetition.

I shake a lot of hands that afternoon and smile so much that my cheek muscles begin to tremble. Dancey steers us through the official program with professional efficiency, but he cannot stem the flow of gossip afterward. I say gossip, but the term disparages the experiences and memories of these women—more than three-quarters of English Lit alumni are in fact alumnae—that span a period of more than forty years. Those who were here five or ten years ago confirm that Nick Hornberger was notorious in their days for his favoritism and his affairs.

"He was in charge of assistantships, scholarships, fellowships—tedious paperwork for his colleagues, so they were happy to leave all that to him," Annie, class of nineteen ninety-six, remembers. "And boy, did he pick 'em! The fourth floor looked like the catwalk of a beauty pageant!"

"The one good thing you can say about him, he is color-blind." This information comes from a very attractive African-American woman, who adds hurriedly that her then boyfriend, now husband, was a member of the basketball team, so Hornberger never hit on her. "But I know of several girls who—well, he was charming, so they were rarely offended. I never heard worse of him than that. Flirting, I mean."

I catch Yvonne's eyes and I can see what she is thinking, but we had better shut the fuck up.

A woman whose nametag says *Elaine Shaw, '77, Tulane* has been standing in our circle without commenting, and her silence becomes so conspicuous that I apologize to her for talking about a person unknown to her.

"Oh, I know Nick," she says grimly. "Except he wasn't called Hornberger then. He took his wife's name, didn't you know? Ex-wife's, now. He was born Nicholas Eagleson."

This is news to everyone, and Janice, the black woman, wonders what on earth possessed him to change his name from Eagleson to Hornberger.

"You may well ask," says Elaine.

After an awkward silence, I speak for all of us. "I think we *are* asking."

"He raped a girl in my dorm. Nick was on a football scholarship, confident, popular, going places. Mary-Lou was biracial, not conventionally beautiful, but striking—tall, very beautiful hair, and… well, these days it's called curvaceous. But she never quite found her feet at college; first-generation student, you know how difficult that can be, especially for girls from underprivileged backgrounds. In short, he exploited her vulnerability. Befriended her, helped her with her coursework, that sort of thing. She was flattered, felt she owed him. And don't forget, this was in the mid-seventies. The world was a little different then. Mary-Lou was persuaded to file charges with the college authorities—" Elaine flushes a little "—which was entirely the right thing to do, politically speaking! Imagine it, one of the first female students of color at Ardrossan, and what happens? She's raped by a football star!"

"What became of her?" asks Janice.

"The college kept stalling and stalling. They listened to her and they believed her, oh, yes, sir! And then they did nothing. She dropped out after her third year. Started working as a sales assistant somewhere and got married soon after. Then I went to Rice for my doctorate and lost contact with her."

"Of course there's no statute of limitations on rape in this state," Annie says, spelling out what we are all thinking. "If she came forward now—"

I remember Tim's report of Natalie's report of an earlier case of sexual assault, but I dismiss it at once. Pillow-talk can be very unguarded, but is it credible that Hornberger told Natalie that he raped a fellow student three decades ago? I don't think so.

It had been made very clear to us that our attendance at the opening ceremony at the new institute is required. All assistant professors have shown up, and about a quarter of the tenured faculty. Nick Hornberger, who looks older and a little sallow, is not among the triumvirate—this is not, alas, an institute for Literary Studies. But he is a deserving member of the steering committee, and there is no discernible awkwardness at all in the way the other middle-aged, dark-suited men include him in their self-congratulatory circle.

"You know who that is."

"Some rich guy." I don't feel like encouraging Martha Borlind, who has been supplying me with a running commentary on the speakers.

"That's Natalie Greco's father. Stepfather, that is."

Dagnabbit, but that Martha Borlind is sure worth listening to!

"What, the one standing next to Hornberger? The one that looks like Hornberger's *brother?*"

Martha and I stare as the two men shake hands and laugh at the remark made by a third.

Innocent till proven guilty, and we wouldn't have it any other way, would we? Maybe what we just witnessed was an example of consummate professionalism. Nonetheless, it makes me feel sick to my stomach.

About a dozen speeches later we are invited to a buffet lunch, and by a stroke of misfortune I end up waiting in line with Dancey and Dolph, who can hardly bring himself to look at me. Dancey enthuses about the new directions the Arts and Humanities are taking and has several proposals as to how Dolph and I might sub-section our conference.

I inspect the potato salad for evidence of sausage.

"Dolph, what do you think?" I ask conversationally.

He launches into an enthusiastic response. "I think these are all excellent suggestions. If we could position ourselves at the forefront of research aided by the cognitive sciences—"

I cut him short. "Oh, you're such a creep. Matthew—Professor Dancey, sir, even if the moon turns to cheese, I will not organize a conference about neuroaesthetics. Let me rephrase that. Even when all the little devils put on mittens and shawls because hell has frozen over, I will not organize a conference about neuroaesthetics, with or without young Adolph here. Have I made myself clear?"

Dancey collects himself to speak, but I interrupt him.

"And yes, sir, I do want tenure at Ardrossan. But I will not organize—see above. And now we can all be very calm in our minds and concentrate on our food."

After this reckless but gratifying stand against bullies and hypocrites, my Homecoming Saturday continues somewhat adversely. Yvonne and I have just taken position on the Observatory garden wall to watch the Homecoming Parade when I feel that tell-tale tightening in my stomach and a vaguely painful pressure in my lower back. Four days early! Must be all that adrenaline. This is how Ardrossan messes with my body.

"Sorry, Yvonne, I forgot something upstairs. Back in a sec!"

If I don't take that first ibuprofen quickly, it will be too late and I'll be doubled up with pain for hours. I enter by the side entrance to Modern Languages and take their elevator up. The last time I saw the fourth-floor corridor so deserted was the night I overheard Selena and her lover in the dome. Of course this, too, is a moment convenient for an illicit rendezvous, with everyone out on the streets for the Parade. I am wearing soft-soled boots, so I am not very noisy, but I tread even more carefully and listen up the spiral stairs opposite my office. Take a few steps up, listen again. Nothing. And besides, do I *want* to know? As if I didn't know way too much already about way too many people in this department. When all I wanted was to sit in my neat little office and write lots of articles about early modern English literature.

"What the—"

My office door springs open the moment I push my key into the lock. Crouching in front of the locked drawer in my desk is Nick Hornberger. With a screwdriver in his hand.

"*You?*" My first impulse is anger at this constant intrusion into my space, but when he gets up—two dusty patches on the knees of his suit—he is a big, heavy man with a pointy metal object in his hand. Anger is not my main response any more. I back out through the door.

"Anna." He follows me. "Don't overreact, okay?"

"What are you looking for in my office?" I yell at him, still retreating. "What the *fuck* do you think I am hiding in my office? What have I to do with your—*fucking mess?*"

"Will you stop shouting, you little bitch!" he snarls at me.

"You must be crazy to come up here—did *you* have the lock on my door changed? And was it you all the time, with the oil and the fish?"

"The oil and the fish? What, are you—you're raving, woman! And be quiet! *Be quiet!*"

His voice is much louder than mine, which somewhat undermines his command, but I am not about to start arguing with a cornered, desperate man twice my size. At this point, I am ready to believe him capable of anything.

"Look, I understand you're shocked." He makes an effort at controlling himself. "You don't understand what is really going on — how could you? You know nothing about us here at Ardrossan. So be a good girl, hand me your keys, and stand over there by the window."

I throw him my keys and retreat to the window in the corridor, watching him.

"We talked about you yesterday."

"At the reception? I'm not surprised." He fiddles with my keys; it is the smallest of six. "It's quite a fantasy, isn't it? I bet those dried-up alumnae pretend to be all aghast. Nick Hornberger, the rapist professor. *They wish.*"

My blood runs cold at this blatant brutality. Maybe he knows he is finished, maybe he knows this time he has gambled too high and lost. I really don't know what my evil angel thinks he is doing when he whacks his spurs into my flesh.

"Nick Eagleson, the rapist football player, actually."

The effect is all I could have hoped for. Like Lot's wife looking back at Sodom, he seems to turn into a pillar of salt.

"So you did find it." He stands up slowly and leans against the back wall. He is huge in the small space of my office and in the gray afternoon light. His eyes focus on me through the doorway. "Where is it? Why haven't you handed it over?"

"Handed what over? What are you talking about?"

We both realize in the same instant that he has said too much and betrayed himself. A strange movement runs through his body, and although I can't consciously decode it, it activates my flight instinct. On a very short distance, I have a chance.

I bolt, darting along the corridor toward the staircase, never bothering to look back. "Help! Security! Up here! Security!"

In the great hall I find them, four watchmen standing at a bar table drinking left-over coffee. It strikes me that if I shriek at them to do their damn job and catch the intruder on the fourth floor, and they rush up there and intercept Professor Nick Hornberger, I'll have a great deal of explaining to do. Have I thought that through? His word against mine?

Suddenly there is a shout behind me, from the second-floor landing.

"Guys? Guys, up here, quick!"

They charge past me and I follow them, but instead of running up the stairs, they turn off into the professors' hallway. It is full of security men and the half-light of an over-cast late October afternoon, so I hear before I see.

"*Shit!*" one of them shouts and kicks something along the floor. It is an empty can of spray paint. Its content — red, again — is on the walls around Hornberger's office door in the form of stenciled poems:

THE WHOLE MOON TURNED BLOOD RED, AND THE STARS IN THE SKY FELL TO EARTH AS FIGS DROP FROM A FIG TREE WHEN SHAKEN BY A STRONG WIND.

"He'll be writing a feckin' novel next," says Rich Westley, whose door is two along from Hornberger's.

"Sir, did you hear nothing?" The security chief is torn between embarrassment at his team's incompetence and impatience at Westley's vagueness.

"Sorry, no — sleeping off the effect of too much lunch at the new Institute for Clap-and-Trap."

I catch a strong whiff of his liquid lunch, but no other olfactory disturbances. Unless —

My office door is closed but unlocked; the bunch of keys lies on the desk. The drawer is hanging open, but since there was nothing in it, nothing is missing. I grab an ibuprofen, swallow it with one gulp from the water fountain, and send Tim a text.

Wanna see some more graffiti? E-1.

When I get downstairs again, Tim is already there, and he has brought Bernie Cogan.

"Hi, honey. We met at the Parade, and Tim thought since I'll hear about it in the Hearing Panel anyway, I might as well see it, too. Never a dull moment, huh?"

"You can say that again."

"And this happened just now?"

"Was discovered just now, anyway. What do you think?"

We survey the blocks of stenciled lines.

"What's your first impression, both of you?" Bernie asks matter-of-factly, and this is a side I have not yet seen of him.

"Red," Tim says.

"Love," I say. "It's a labor of love. Cutting out—oh, look, there it is!" One of the security men has found the stencil, an extra-large sheet of carton. "Look at those letters. This must have taken forever. This is different than the hate graffiti on the fourth floor."

"Love and hatred require equal amounts of energy," Bernie says. "What else?"

"It's about sex," I say slowly. "Upstairs was about hate and sex; this is about love and sex. It's about a girl losing her virginity."

Rich, Tim, Bernie, and two security men stare at me.

"Trust me, boys. I'm a girl, and I read poetry."

"Who is your favorite?" Giles asks later that day when I find him in the statue garden, where he is apparently listening in on the concert in the nearby amphitheater. He has a glass of wine, a small bowl of cheese crackers, and an apple with him—"My supper!"—and I can't believe that he is alone and that he seems pleased to see me.

"Hermes." I don't need to think about that answer. "I like that he is the god of travelers, thieves, liars, and poets. I also like that he isn't quite as brawny as the other male gods."

Giles turns his head to look at me and smiles.

I am very happy I found him.

"How did you like your first Ardrossan Homecoming?" he asks. "Did it have enough pomp and circumstance for your taste?"

I haven't often seen him in a chatty mood, and as the muscles in my stomach relax, I wish I could just snuggle up to him and chat the evening away. It's grown chilly and the sun is beginning to set.

"My taste doesn't much run to pomp and circumstance. Mind you, Ardrossan's foolish, fairy-tale Gothicism is a much less daunting backdrop to processions and trumpets and flags than the neo-classical grandeur of the Morningside Heights campus. That always gave me the creeps, to be honest."

He gazes at me as if he wanted to comment on that, then he offers me a cheese cracker.

"Two different people, then," he says when I have told him about the new graffiti. "Corvin, or maybe that Harrison girl, threw fish at your door, and someone else writes graffiti about Natalie Greco and Nick Hornberger."

"But this is about first-time sex, don't you agree?" I unfold the piece of paper on which I copied the verse.

"Without a doubt."

"It isn't really, of course. It's from the Bible, like the other one. Revelation, this time. Don't know whether that is significant. Anyway, so much for your theory that Natalie herself is the graffiti artist. She would hardly produce such a labor of love for a man she has reported for sexual assault, and apparently her mother and her step-brother testify to the fact that she was at home with them all day."

"It was a good theory." He shrugs and offers me another cracker.

"Thanks. By the way, I saw Natalie's stepfather at the opening ceremony of the new institute. His bank is one of the sponsors. He shook Hornberger's hand! Can you imagine that?"

"Wine?" Giles isn't interested in Nick Hornberger. He is offering me his glass, and I can see that he is shy about it, which in turn rouses my maternal instincts. Amongst others. If I kissed him now, the tangy aroma of the wine would be on both our lips and tongues.

"Oh, and the other mind-blowingly surreal thing that happened today: I caught Hornberger going through my desk! No idea where he got the key to my office, but he has one. So it probably wasn't Corvin who broke in before, but Hornberger!"

Now he *is* interested. More, even, than in coming on to me.

"Did he threaten you?"

"Um…obliquely, I'd say. I didn't know what he was looking for, still don't, but he didn't believe that. But one of the alums at the reception, I think she's a professor at Tulane, told us that he raped someone, a friend of hers, when he was a student here. *Allegedly* raped someone," I correct myself.

Giles gazes at me, waiting. His eyes are very bright and warm.

"What? *What?*" I nudge him.

"Do you really not know what he was looking for?"

"No! Something to do with the allegations, but—"

"I thought we'd found it. Tessa found it. And it *was* in your office."

All I can remember when I think back to that day is Giles in his white shirt, and his shirtsleeves, and how he stumbled when —

"The folder. God! I'm thicker than shit in the neck of a bottle!"

Giles laughs. "Yes — *the folder.* The file that went missing when Nick was hired. DeGroot was held responsible, because he was Dean of Studies back in the seventies and had done his utmost to sweep the case under the rug. It explains why Nick was dead against the idea of a Homecoming reception at the English department. But Ruffin and a few others carried it; they may not even know why Homecoming is Nick's most hated event in the calendar. Too many ghosts!"

"And the allegation? Did he really rape the girl back then?"

Giles shrugs and offers me the glass again; I shake my head.

"No idea," he says. "His case isn't in the file. Corvin must have taken it out, maybe taken it home. If you want to know what I think —"

"I do."

"I think he did it. Then and now."

"You have reason to think badly of him."

"Badly, but not the worst. He didn't hold a knife to Amanda's throat." Giles's jaw clenches and relaxes. "Hornberger gets off on bending people to his will, but brute force isn't the kind of triumph he wants. I'm sure he calls it seduction, but he messes with their heads. It's part of his fun that the women afterward hate themselves even more than they hate him. I'm sure he hates women."

He inhales as if he had a load of boulders on his chest. Who knows what scenes were played in the *affaire* Saunders-Hornberger-Cleveland. If Giles was a friend of mine, I would advise him not to tell his colleagues about Amanda and Hornberger. What purpose could it possibly serve? Dancey has the chair between his teeth now and won't let go. Giles can take over from him when Horny Horn has had his horns clipped.

"Not *Hornberger!*" I exclaim, jumping with the sudden recollection. "Giles, where's the file?"

"Why? What is it?"

"You do know he wasn't called Hornberger then, don't you?"

He stares at me, very still. Giles becomes very still when he is startled. "What *can* you mean?"

"He took his wife's name when he married! He was called Eagleson! Is there a Nicholas Eagleson's case in the file?"

Giles is still staring, thinking fast. "I only checked for Hornberger."

"Well, come on then!" I draw him up by his hand—surely in an emergency, innocent physical contact is allowed?—and to my surprise he holds on to it.

"I don't want you involved in this," he says.

"I *am* involved! He rifled my desk for it!"

"That's incidental."

"Giles!" I fairly shout at him, all excited and impatient to have at least one of my Ardrossan mysteries solved.

"It's no use yelling at me. Do what you like when you're tenured, but for the next five years you must be as untainted by scandal as a newly hatched spring chicken!"

The implications of this harsh statement hit me as if one of the stone statues had been knocked against the back of my head. But this is a piece of his mind that I will have to chew in private, and not in the middle of the garden, in the middle of campus, still holding hands with him, for Chrissakes!

"Be that as it may," I say, pulling my hand from his clasp. "I must know about the file! Is it in your office?"

"No," he says mechanically, but he is in as much of a hurry to get back to the Observatory as I am.

"Hey, sir, you're going in the wrong direction!" some students shout across at us. We are swimming against the current because everyone is now streaming toward the stadium for the evening game.

I am almost running now to keep up with his long strides.

"Anna, go and powder your nose!" he says curtly when we have reached the first-floor hallway.

"Unfair!"

"Boo-hoo. That's tenure track for you." He pushes his hands into his jacket pockets for his keys. "Off you run. Will you be at the—and you needn't make Bambi eyes at me, *Miss* Lieberman! I'm immune to 'em! Well," he corrects himself punctiliously, "maybe that's overstating the case. But I don't hold with corrupting vulnerable young women, and I won't let you read that file. Stop that!"

He turns away from me, and I can see his ears have gone red. I only did as he said—opened my eyes at him, fluttered my lashes, pushed out my lower lip, and pouted.

"What if I sit across the room from you, and you just tell me whether it's there or not?"

This makes him laugh, but he is still barring my way into his office. Just as well that the hallway is empty and nobody can see our ridiculous mating dance. Non-mating dance.

"What if I sit across the room, with my face against the wall and my eyes closed?"

"Anna—"

"If I touch you, you can scream," I challenge him quietly.

Our knees almost do touch as we sit at his low sofa table perusing the file that records the alleged sexual assault of one Nicholas George Eagleson upon one Mary-Lou Tandy. The scenario, it seems, was humdrum. A dorm party, drugs and alcohol, the assumption of implied assent on the part of the male. What makes this worth breaking into offices for is the eye-witness and ear-witness reports that—if genuine and accurate—seem to leave no doubt that Mary-Lou resisted him and that she had severe bruising on her arms and the inside of her thighs afterward.

"'They always say no. They have to, because of their reputation. If they let you feel them up, it is okay to go ahead anyway.'"

Giles looks up from the sheet he is reading, the vertical groove between his eyebrows deep and angry. "What?"

"Said one Tommy-Lee Konig, twenty-one, student of geography."

"It's incredible that this was kept inside the college." He surveys the evidence. "It's as conclusive as it can be, short of a video film. He would almost certainly have been convicted."

"*Would be* convicted, you mean," I correct him. "This would still stand up in court, in this state. It wouldn't in New York, you see."

Giles sneers in triumph, and for a moment I can see how much he truly hates Hornberger.

"'And that's what I love about the Soooouth…'"

Chapter 23

This is not the first end-of-grading-period party that I have been at, and maybe it is just me, but it seems to me that we have all gone a little crazy.

"No shoptalk!" Erin declares when we arrive. "Whoever mentions the Observatory, or essays, or students—"

"Studnets!" Eugenia interrupts her. "Nine times out of ten when I type the word, it comes out as 'studnet'! I just call them 'studnets' now."

"*Nomen est omen*," I say darkly. "Very appropriate, under the circumst—"

"SHOP!" Tim shouts. "SHOT!"

"*What?*"

"Down in one, please, Ms. Lieberman. *Doctor*, I should say, a.k.a. Anna-Banana, but don't call her that, she doesn't like it!" Tim, already a little ahead of the rest of us, hands me a small glass full of some colorless liquid. Egged on by the others, I shrug and down it without asking what it is. It is straight vodka.

"Fix your hair in bunches with little butterfly clips, and you don't look old enough to drink that." Vern, Eugenia's husband, looks into my eyes just a second too long. I am tired of jokes about how young I look, so I smile and say nothing.

"You are the baby here, aren't you, Anna?" Erin is our kind hostess, so again I smile and say nothing. But Erin doesn't allow people to slip from her grasp. "How old are you? Absurdly young, I remember that from your application."

"Only at heart," I say wryly.

"Oh, come on—have you crossed the Rubicon yet?" Kirsten Thomason leans back and fluffs up her hair. "That was my worst, so far, thirty."

"Almost."

"Almost thirty? What does that mean? This year? Next year?"

"Tomorrow."

This, predictably, creates something of a hullaballoo. "It's your birthday tomorrow, and you'll be thirty? Why didn't you *say?*" Erin is almost angry with me.

"Because it isn't important! Really, guys, don't…don't make a big thing of it. This is nice, isn't it? End of grading, yay!"

"SHOP!" Tim shouts. "SHOT! Down in one, please, Thirty-Years-Old-in-Three-Hours-and-Seventeen-Minutes!"

The evening progresses from there.

At midnight they congratulate me and sing for me, and the women hug me, and the men awkwardly shake my hand, all except Giles.

"Did you get any exciting birthday presents?" Eugenia asks. "I would have gotten you something, Anna, if I'd known!"

"I bought myself a seat on a plane. That's my birthday present to myself!"

"Aaah! Where to?"

"London."

"Of course, London! Nauseating anglophile," Tim adds for good measure.

"Yes, I am," I admit sadly. "I know I am."

"Maybe one of these days Anna won't come back from England," Erin jokes. Almost.

"No, no, I'm here. I'm back," I assure her, or myself, or my mom. I've had far too much vodka.

"Would you have stayed for a man?" she keeps needling me. "It usually hinges on that, doesn't it?"

This question goes too far, and the others are beginning to be embarrassed by Erin's insistence.

"I'm guessing that when Anna did her MA at Cambridge, she met more than one bona fide English toff or knob who would have kept her there. In England." I'm surprised that Giles joins Erin in baiting me. Or maybe I'm just too drunk to decode his signals accurately.

"Not really. Jewish girls from New York tend not to hobnob with the nobs." I have to giggle about my own pun. "Oh, wait—a friend took me to a party at Trinity College once, and there I, um, met an Etonian."

"We shan't enquire further," says Giles.

"Oh, yes, we shall." Tim grins. "Spill, baby."

"Well, he was drunk, and he told me his uncle was a duke. I bet he told that to all the overseas students he wanted to pull."

"Did it work?"

"Naaah. But he was cute, sort of."

"You must have been drunk, too," Tim decides. "Etonians are not cute. They are fearful oiks. Repeat after me—"

"—fearful oiks."

"Would that not have appealed to you?" Giles asks, playing with his shashlik skewers. "A posh English boyfriend, meeting his nice parents in their nice house in Buckinghamshire, sailing off the Sussex coast where they have a nice little cottage, nights out at the theatre, tickets for all the exhibitions at the London galleries…"

"Shut up, Giles, you…rotter. I hate you. Anyway, he couldn't kiss," I splutter, so disoriented for a second or two that I lose control over my words. "And I was in love with somebody else, and all the posh English boys in the rough, rude sea could not have washed that love out of my heart. So there! There you have it."

"There we have it." Giles nods. "No posh English boys for you, then."

"I'm okay," I protest as we get up, several hours later, or so it seems to me. Here I am, on my thirtieth birthday, and it comes as a surprise to me that although sitting down I felt only slightly befuddled, standing up I'm reeling.

"Anna, you're welcome to stay over, if you don't mind the patter of tiny feet at six in the morning." Erin hopes I won't accept but feels obliged to offer.

"I'll be okay! Just gimme a—second…"

Amidst the laughter—I am *not* drunk, and I demonstrate it by walking unaided into the hall and toward the coat rack—Kirsten Thomason comes up to me.

"Anna, we could drop you off. Do you live along the river or across?"

"Hm? Oh, thanks, but—I live—thataway." I point into the direction of the kitchen, which I take to be roughly east. "Behind the college. I can take a cab."

Several coats have buried mine, and it isn't easy to put the wrong ones back onto the hooks, what with the loops so tiny and the light in the hall so painfully bright, after the candles in the living room.

"I'll drive you."

There is a pause of about two seconds. Or two minutes. I'm not sure. I have to think about this.

"Calderbrook is on my way." Giles takes the pile of leather, quilted nylon, and wool out of my arms. "Which one's yours?"

I know perfectly well that I can't drive anymore. Instead, I must focus. Focus on walking straight, talking straight. Balance. Posture. Must. Not. Bump. Into. Him.

The cool night hits my head like a hammer, but I am not nearly plastered enough to be oblivious to embarrassment. More rounds of good-bye, and Giles motions me across the street and into a cul-de-sac. Our heels clack-clack on the asphalt and echo back from the house fronts; it is the loudest noise around.

This. Like this, Mr. and Mrs. Cleveland would be leaving a party. Walking back to the car. He, tall and handsome in his blue Barbour and his Oxfords; she, in her tailored woolen jacket and knee-length pleated skirt. Not quite knee-length, actually, and I know that I look nice in it. But what is that to the purpose, if the purpose is to take him home, rip his clothes off, and jump him? Mr. and Mrs. Cleveland on their way home to make love all night with an uninhibited abandon that belies their composed, academic exteriors.

"Anna?"

It's like getting your naked toe caught under a door. You have time to expect the pain, and then it shoots through every nerve. He calls me so rarely by my name, it's like a physical shock rushing through me.

"It's this one."

Car. I had been walking past his car. No idea what make it is; I am still not used to paying attention to that sort of thing. Cars are yellow cabs or not; that's the only distinction necessary in Manhattan. I climb in, feeling strange in the passenger seat. The seat belt is unfamiliar, but he doesn't help me with it as I fiddle it into the lock.

"I'm afraid the car smells of dog."

"I don't mind. How does this — oh, got it."

"All right?" His eyes glitter in the light of the street lamp. He is as keenly aware of this unprecedented privacy as I am.

"Yes. Sorry."

He reverses out of the lane and onto the street, fast, and for a dismayed moment I worry that he may be trying to impress me with his driving.

"Sorry? What about?"

No, stupid. He is simply a much more experienced driver than Lame-Duck Lieberman. Calm down.

I am not calm. How could I be calm, with Giles Cleveland's hand on the gear stick, jerking it unexpectedly toward my knee as we speed along the main road? I'd like to ask him about manual transmissions, but I daren't draw attention to the fact that I have developed a fetish for his hands.

"You're not sorry you got a bit sloshed, are you? You had to."

We come to a halt at a busy junction. The car is flooded with red light. He looks over at me. "You had to make yourself a little vulnerable, you know. Now all is well."

Green.

"I thought I did that when I came here in February and jumped through all the hoops that were held up for me!"

He chuckles, and this time I am ready for the moment he will accelerate. Inches. His hand inches from my leg. I wish I were a Jedi knight. Then I could will his hand over onto my knee.

We have reached the beltway. He shifts into fifth and rests both hands lightly on the wheel.

"So…thirty." He casts me a quick glance, eyebrows cocked. "Do you mind?"

"Not at all," I reply sweetly. "I'm good. I've been thinking that when I'm thirty I can afford to be more…you know."

"What?"

"More of a bitch."

This makes him burst out laughing.

"Do you want to be?"

"Yeah…sometimes. Well, academia is The Place of Extended Adolescence, isn't it? And it's beginning to get to me. The most dumbass, moronic big-heads get to mess you about and you have to curry favor with them instead of telling them where to stick their bright ideas. And I have five and a half more years of having to shut the fuck up…if I'm lucky."

"Oh, you'll get tenure, for sure. Only take care never to get tipsy in the presence of the Provost."

"Hmm?"

He glances over, as if to see whether I am really not following. I am really not following.

"Language."

"Oh! Sorry…I'm sorry…"

"Don't be—I don't mind. And you're right, of course."

There is a pause. I'm glad. I want to enjoy the fantasy of driving home with a man who, when he has parked the car and walked the dogs, will follow me into the bedroom, undress me, and make love to me, because he likes it when I am a tiny bit drunk and in need of some tender loving care.

"Have you recovered from the recent…brouhaha? And having to shut up about it?" He sounds quizzical, but I can only see his profile, so I can't be sure.

"Oh, I told Dancey where to stick it!" I exclaim and report my violation of the prime directive at the ICSLP lunch. "I don't care. He can't deny me tenure because I wouldn't host a conference with his pet."

"No. But don't defy him too often, is my advice."

"What about you? When you were thirty?" I ignore his warning. "What was your STFU-factor? Probably lower than mine, because you're a *man*."

"Yeah, maybe. Although I wasn't brought up to speak my mind. Less than you, probably. Hang on, can I remember my thirtieth birthday? Oh, Lord…"

I don't know whether the groan means that it's so long ago he can hardly remember or that the memory is unwelcome.

"I'd just got married. I got married shortly before I turned thirty."

The realization hits him, and I can tell the groan was genuine. I want to groan, too. On a night like this, a decade ago, Mr. and Mrs. Cleveland did drive home and had wild, uninhibited sex all night. And then, presumably, there were many nights when they drove home in near-silence.

"You must have thought then that it was a good idea to marry Amanda. Sorry!" I glance at him and suck in my lips. "I'm drunk. Don't listen to me. Don't answer that!"

He drives on in silence.

"I was quite frightened as a young man," he says after a long pause. "And consequently, full of bravado, and anger." He glances over and smiles. "You wouldn't have liked me."

"Wouldn't I?" A minimal answer, not to distract him.

"No, I was insufferable. I didn't understand at the time that there is a good way of feeling safe with someone and a bad way. Amanda and I had a sort of…pact to pretend that the demons weren't there. The monsters. So we felt safe with each other. And then the monsters pounced." He sighs and laughs grimly. "*You're* drunk, and *I'm* meandering. I do apologize!"

"No, no…" If I'm impatient with him, it's because he is giving this madly fascinating information when I'm not able to process it adequately. "What became of them? Of the monsters?"

"Oh — I've chased the ringleaders out of town, and as for the ones that stayed, well, these days I know where they live." He laughs again, less sardonically. "And this is where *you* live!"

My heart is pounding so hard it hurts. "Thank you, Giles, that was — it was irresponsible of me to drink when I had the car."

"Hardly the most irresponsible thing you've ever done."

"Well, no."

We're looking at each other in the dim light shining in from the Walshes' porch, and we're thinking the same thing.

"I'm not going to do the most irresponsible thing — ever," I manage to say.

"Now what would that be?"

He actually wants me to say it. Then I will say it.

"Ask you in for coffee."

"I wouldn't come in, either. You know I couldn't. Not in this world."

His answer gives me a pang, but I nod. I know that he means it kindly, but of course the rejection is like a blade through my heart. I wish I could brush it off with a joke, but I can't trust my voice not to betray how pitiful I feel. It doesn't get any more pitiful than having to bite down the declaration that I don't want tenure, I don't want a career, I want this man naked in my bed! And if I can't have that, can he not at least kiss me to make it better?

He moves. His wax jacket is noisy in the silence of the car; he is undoing his seat belt. Good God, does he mean to come in with me, after all? But he leans across, cups my face between his hands, and kisses me.

It is not meant to be a sexy kiss. His lips are firm and soft and warm on the corner of my mouth, and they linger; it is not quite a friendly kiss, either.

"It's too dangerous," he whispers. His thumb brushes across my lower lip, across my cheek; his eyes follow its movement. He is so close I can see the black pupils in his light eyes. Feel his voice on my skin. I clasp his wrists to keep his hands in place, and kiss him back.

Properly.

I had forgotten what it feels like to kiss someone like this. To feel the incomparable softness of another person's lips and tongue, to gauge his kissing style, to begin to communicate in this intensely private manner. It is the tugging ache in my womb that makes me pull back. This is not supposed to happen, we've told each other that, but if we don't stop at once, it *will* happen.

His face has gone all soft and blank; he's not hiding from me at all, and I know I have the same look on my face. I'm still holding on to his wrists, and I push them together and hide my face against his cupped palms. Behind the double shutters of his hands within mine, I close my eyes, breathe, and try to think of the rotten herring on my door, that I must decide what to do about Selena, of Nick Hornberger snooping in my office. Of the Notre Dame paper that is waiting to be finished.

A long kiss into the hollow of his right hand, and I sit up. Shaky.

"Go now. Go quickly."

I don't know whether that was addressed to me or to himself, because he isn't looking at me anymore. He has withdrawn from me. And although that makes me want to climb onto his lap and kiss the desire back into his eyes, I am sober enough to understand that I have to let him be.

Chapter 24

Kissing Giles was the bizarre, dreamlike culmination of a sequence of bizarre, dreamlike events as the second half of the semester claims us. The second graffiti was painted over even more swiftly than the first, and since it didn't seem to contain a threat, it is regarded more in the nature of an eccentricity than anything else. "Seen any graffiti lately?" becomes the jokey greeting in the Eatery at lunchtime.

Now that I know what Hornberger was looking for in my office, I am more reluctant than ever to get involved. STFU. Giles never told me what he intends to do with the file. Hornberger's first hearing is over, and the second one has been scheduled for the week before Thanksgiving; the first meeting of Tim's tenure review committee has been shifted to the week after Thanksgiving. Now all the balls are rolling, and we will see where they land. I am a mere bystander.

In a strange kind of way I am glad that it was Hornberger who broke into my office, because—though turpid—I can understand his motivation; he's trying to save his neck. Corvin is a crazy old man who uses disgusting fluids to express his antagonism toward a new colleague. That is a lot more disturbing. I have not seen Corvin since the extraordinary faculty meeting after the rape bomb exploded. The image of this vindictive emeritus moray eel sitting in his burrow and waiting to dart out again to bite me when next he feels provoked is one that I push away.

Not that I have much time to brood. Mindful of Selena O'Neal's academic predicament, I am very conscientious and very candid when it comes to advising undergraduates which major to go for, whether to go for honors in the major, and in a couple of cases whether graduate school might be a good idea. This leads to hours of fruitless and draining argument with young people who have always been extolled for their academic abilities and are now bumping up against real resistance and their own unexplored limits. I am not impatient, though. This is very much the routine work of a college lecturer, and after all the hindrances of recent weeks, it is soothing and strangely validating to simply be doing my job.

The few hours I snatch to finish my anatomy paper for the Notre Dame conference are precious and stimulating. I saw Giles once in the past two weeks, and that was across the library reading room. Once I had a quick coffee with Tim. Yvonne and I supported each other in our first round of Ardrossan essays — she had more plagiarism than usual, too — but that was not exactly fun and games.

I have taken up my early morning walks again, which means I am out with my thermos between six and seven o'clock. At first I thought it must have been a Walsh or a forest warden who scratched the bark on several trees. But one morning, the gold-brown shape ahead of me turns its head, and the early morning sun is reflected in its eyes as by two small torches. A bobcat. This is why I came to live on a Piedmont fruit farm after living in New York City.

I am surprised the cat does not change its itinerary when I start waiting at the same crossroads in the wood each morning. I sit there; it materializes out of the undergrowth, casts me a pissy glance and strikes across the clearing. Once it has a small dark body in its mouth; its legs blur as it hurries past me for fear I'll rob it of its prey. Once, in the week before Thanksgiving, its approach seems slower and more cumbersome. No wonder: it got hold of one of the Walshes' chickens. The feathery white neck is dangling out of the cat's mouth; there is no point in trying to chase after it.

"Oh, man!" I sigh. "Okay, I'm not going to turn you in, but don't let me catch you doing it again!" That is a sentence I am saying far too often these days.

Chapter 25

"About tomorrow—"

Giles Cleveland materializes by my elbow, watching Dancey and Dolph caught up in some conspiratorial exchange as our colleagues file out of the Sperm Room. It is so like Dancey to schedule a faculty meeting one day before we break up for Thanksgiving. Nobody is concentrating, everyone is mulling over holiday menus or travel arrangements, eager to get away.

"Tomorrow. You're not—" Giles hesitates, and for a wild moment I expect him to announce that I cannot go because there will be a departmental putsch and we all have to be present. "Are you flying to South Bend or to Chicago?"

"South Bend. Why?"

An emotion flickers across his face, but I still think that it must be in reaction to the two men standing by the windows. Giles barely acknowledged me during the meeting; I assumed that is what happens when you kiss colleagues after drunken parties. In the cold light of day, they ignore you.

"I could take you to the airport, if you're on the eight-twenty flight." As if he was offering to lend me some books or get a marker for me from his office.

"Why?" I realize I am repeating myself, but in my confusion I value precision over variation.

"I'm going, too."

"To the airport?"

"To Notre Dame."

 I cannot help myself.

"But *why?*"

"Er…" He avoids my eyes and makes a show of fumbling to come up with a good reason. "I gotta see a horse about a man."

"Barton, Scherer and Nussbaum Legal Associates, Irene Roshner speaking."

"Help, Irene! *Help!*"

"Banana! What's the matter? Are you okay?"

"Yeah…no…can you call me back later tonight? I know you're busy, but—can you?"

"Sure, but tell me now! I'm alone in the office. I can talk. Tell me—what's—"

"He's coming to the conference!" I wail into the receiver, crouching on the sofa in my woolen pants even though I know that will make them go baggy at the knees.

"Who? What conference? Anna, no one has died, right? No one is about to die?"

"No! Well, my career."

"What the hell are you talking about?" Irene is using her resolute voice with me, so I settle down, straighten my legs, and try to be coherent.

"Tomorrow I'm going to present at a conference at Notre Dame. I bought the plane tickets months ago when—"

"Hey, I thought you were coming home for Thanksgiving!"

"I am coming home for Thanksgiving! Except I'm coming via South Bend. Anyway, today after a faculty meeting Giles Cleveland wanders up to me and offers me a ride to the airport. Tomorrow. Because he's coming to the conference. It's on iconography in early modern Europe, for Chrissakes! He isn't even interested in that!"

"Seems he has unfinished business to attend to."

"*Shut up!*"

"Why? You know where your priorities lie! It's okay to flirt a little. Might do some good, when you're up for your review."

"I don't want to — *flirt* — with him! I want to suck his brains out! And not by the shortest way!"

Irene groans into the phone. "Are you sure no one can hear you? You'll be fired for sexual harassment! You *and* Horny Horn!"

"I'm not calling from my office, you *nebbish*. And I am absolutely not planning on being part of Ardrossan's next little sex scandal."

"You only wanna suck the Englishman's *schlong.*"

"I want to do everything with him."

"Well, you can't. Way too messy, an affair with a senior colleague while you're on tenure track. Question is, how will he take a brush-off?"

I am trying to assess how Giles will react when I reject him, but my system jams at a point of grammar. *If.* How would Giles react *if* I rejected him?

"*Much virtue in 'if'…*"

"Huh? Oh, you're quoting again."

"Maybe I shouldn't go."

"Of course you're going! What's he going to do, fling himself on you in a dark corner of a Catholic campus? If you don't encourage him, he won't try anything. He'd be mad to!"

"Well, in view of the fact that I kissed him…"

One Mississippi, two Mississippi, three Mississippi.

"Reenie?"

"Yes, hello. Could I speak to Anna Lieberman, please?"

"It was after a party, and—"

"That kiss — what are we talking about here, anyway? When you say 'kiss,' do I hear 'blow job'?"

"No!"

"That kiss may have cost you and your parents tens of thousands of dollars. You realize that, right?"

"What are you talking about?"

"Because a fling with a member of your tenure-and-promotion committee will cost you exactly that: tenure and promotion. And if you think word won't get round why that promising young scholar didn't get tenure at Ardrossan, you know a lot less about academia than I do! If all you wanted was a teaching job at a third-rate school somewhere in flyover country, why bother with an Ivy League education?"

This is the heavy artillery. I am impressed that Irene would get genuinely upset with me. Irene Roshner. The arch-player.

"Anna, I gotta go. Ed Barton is giving me the evil eye. But one more thing. I've known you practically forever, and I'm going to tell you this truth about yourself: you could not handle an affair with Cleveland. I'm not saying that because I don't want you to have great sex again—I do. But Cleveland's not the one. You're hardly tough enough for academia as it is. You're way not tough enough to brazen out an affair with one of the shooting stars in your field. You said he is going to be big."

"For sure he is."

"Then picture it. All you'll ever be is the little girl Cleveland fucked when she was new on tenure track at Ardrossan. There are bitches who could handle shit like this, but you're not one of them!"

"Thanks, Reenie. You're making your point very clear."

"Love you, too. Bye!"

In a depressing kind of way I was more at peace when I still thought that Giles was married and that he disliked me. I bore the deep, blind yearning of my body for his like I bore Andrew Corvin's garbage in my office. A time of tribulation that I will always connect with my first months at Ardrossan. Eventually the situation would have resolved itself and become a hazy, even amusing memory: the crush I had on Giles Cleveland during my first semester. It is much, much harder to muster stoic self-denial now that I know what his lips feel like on mine. Now that I have heard him admit that in another world he would come to my bed. Does Indiana count as "another world?"

He won't try to seduce me. He could have had me on a platter the other night, and he refused. Politely, regretfully, but he refused, and he was right.

In the morning there is little time to brood, partly because — improbably — I oversleep. I scold myself out of bed and into the shower, where the sixty-four-thousand-dollar question presents itself. To shave, or not to shave? I do my armpits and shins, carefully, can't be doing with any cuts today. Trimming is allowed. I always trim. Nothing to do with the prospect of sex tonight.

Did I say "prospect?"

Tomorrow evening I will be sitting in my parents' living room. It seems surreal, and yet it will happen, and it will feel completely normal. There is just time to send a text to Gloria: *Wd love to go to Edelstein's. Will u book?* When I am in the middle of brushing my teeth, the phone rings.

"Anna, this is Mom. If I can still book a table for Saturday evening, I will, but they may be full. In that case I'll go for Sunday lunch — or do you have plans?"

"No, that's fine. Irene and I will work around that."

"Only you needn't think Nat and Jessica will join us."

Orange alert. Gloria is peevish.

"I hadn't thought of Nat and Jessy. Why?"

"Jessica announced to me yesterday that she and Nathan have decided not to go on their winter holiday together."

"What does that mean?"

"You may believe that those were my very words to her!"

"Mom — I'm sorry, but I'm about to leave for the airport, literally this minute. We'll talk about it tomorrow, okay? Don't worry too much!"

It is still dark, and cold enough for gloves. Karen and the girls are letting the dogs out as I wheel my suitcase past.

"Happy Thanksgiving!" she shouts over. "Going home for the holidays?"

"Yeah, ain't it great? Happy Thanksgiving."

"Have fun! Is that your taxi?"

As I approach the car Giles gets out, and I am relieved to see that he has the same kind of idiotic half-smile on his face as I feel on mine. Karen will never believe that he is a taxi driver.

"I do know, of course, that clothes are more of a challenge for women than they are for men, but —" He takes the suitcase and lifts it onto the back seat with an exaggerated expression of effort. The trunk is fenced off and lined with old rugs, for the dogs.

"I'm flying home afterward. To New York." Since "good morning" has apparently gone out of fashion. He checks my face when he hears this, but he doesn't comment.

"In."

Slightly disgruntled, I climb into the passenger seat, and he slams the door behind me. As I watch him walk round the front, I see Karen and the girls lurking by the chestnut tree. Well, that'll give them food for talk.

Giles accelerates down the lane toward the main road, and I cannot help feeling that he is not quite his usual sweet self.

"Are we late?"

"There'll be traffic on the road and queues at the airport."

Maybe he is not at his best in the mornings. I decide that I have too much on my plate today to start fretting about Giles Cleveland's mood, especially since this whole thing was his own idea. So I keep quiet and settle into enjoying the view. His Barbour is on the backseat, and he is wearing a dress shirt underneath a rust-colored pullover. I would say he looks particularly handsome in it, but I suspect he would look handsome to me in polka dots and purple flares. There is a slight scent of soap in the air, and I indulge myself with a fantasy of Giles stepping out of the shower this morning. As far as I am concerned we could drive to Indiana in this car. I would watch his hands on the wheel, and his long thighs, and dream the journey away.

Last time we sat together in his car, he kissed me. And then I kissed him.

"Are you nervous?" he suddenly asks.

"Huh? Oh, about the conference. No, not really. Well, a little. Yeah, you know what? I am. But that's part of the fun, isn't it?"

He glances across, and for the first time today smiles at me. Thank God—I thought he didn't like me anymore. But he does. He still likes me.

"Giles?"

"Hmm?"

"You're not going to make me pretend I won't mind if you come in, right?"

"Come in where? Ah." I can see that he knew this subject would rear its anxious head sooner or later. "But I've been delegated to assess how well you carry yourself as an Ardrossan representative."

I must have looked absolutely appalled, because he searches my face longer than the speed at which he is driving allows.

"I'm kidding. Anna—hey! Joke!"

"Oh, you horrible man! If I weren't afraid you'd land us in a ditch, I'd hit you! *Horrible* man!"

"Yes, I know." He grins.

I exhale noisily, still in shock. "Why *are* you coming, anyway?"

I would never have had the courage to ask if he had not wrong-footed me like this. But now the question hangs between us like a piece of lacy underwear pulled out from under the sofa cushions.

"To take you out to dinner tonight."

Again he looks over, and I can see in the tension of the muscles around his mouth that some of his nonchalance is fake.

"All right," I say quietly.

He looks straight ahead, and I really think that is all he will say on the subject.

"So your flight to New York is tomorrow." This comes a full minute later.

"Yes, of course. Tomorrow afternoon."

That has been eating him. I don't believe it. He has been sulking.

"To be honest, there's another reason I'm going," he says, and I hold my breath. "A friend of mine—we go way back, he was my tutor at Cambridge—recently got a job at Notre Dame. I haven't seen him for ten years."

"At the English department?" I ask. "Who is it?"

"Paul French. He was at UCL before. I don't suppose you know him?"

"We were never introduced, no, but I remember seeing him at various Shakespeare-related events. Ginger-haired, roly-poly. Exuberant."

"That's Paul. Anyway, how do you think your paper will go over?"

The butterflies in my stomach rise and flutter hectically, like a flock of pigeons flushed from the side of a building.

"I hope I've made it watertight enough to stand up under scrutiny, but there'll be a number of historians there, you know, proper historians, not lame-ass cultural historians like me. I wouldn't be surprised if they had a go at it. Or at me."

"You should have presented it in the graduate seminar, or better still, given it to me to read." He casts me a quick glance but looks away when I look back.

"You're very busy."

"I would have read it, if you'd asked me. I'm supposed to, as your mentor!"

"Thanks," I mutter, not very graciously. "Of course I discussed it with various people. I'm not that much of a frosh!" He raises his eyebrows to express skepticism, and out rushes the truth. "If I must be panned, I'd rather be panned by a bunch of strangers than by you!"

"But that's silly. Just silly." He deliberates for a moment. "Did Tim say I've been thrown off his tenure committee?"

"No! Why? And what does that mean?"

"I'm too close, personally and professionally. To be fair, I probably am. It's just that Elizabeth would not have objected, and Dancey has."

"But Tim'll be all right, won't he?"

Again he considers his reply carefully.

"I think so. His portfolio is too solid to deny him tenure, even if some people wouldn't claim that he's…their favorite person."

"Nobody can be everybody's favorite person."

He grins. "That's a wise thing to say. But everybody can and should make sure that their mentor approves their conference papers!"

I get the distinct feeling that I have just been officially reprimanded.

"Well, if they thrash me, you'll tell me that you would have told me so if I'd given you the chance!"

"At great length, and with plenty of footnotes!"

"Keep your eyes on the road." I nod toward the windshield, biting on a laugh. "We'll never find out if you wrap us round a tree."

"I just—" he starts, then stops. Relaxes his hold on the steering wheel as if he had been clasping it too hard. "I just don't want any of those arseholes—and there are bound to be some, there always are—I just think that you should have taken all possible precautions to shield yourself against boorish attacks, that's all."

"The more enemies, the more honor."

He casts me another exasperated glance. "You're very cool."

"I won't be cool if you come in to listen."

"Think of me as a claque," he says. "It's nice to have a friend in the audience, isn't it?"

Yes. It's nice to have a friend.

I disentangle myself from our dispute and force myself to watch the forest by the highway flying past. There was a road sign to the airport; shouldn't be longer than ten minutes till we're there.

"*You* don't care what people think," I say slowly. A harmless remark, like a pebble into the pond of our…friendship.

He glances over, with a snort and a lopsided smile. "It's hard for a young lion not to care what the alpha males say about him."

Giles doesn't care. That is *so* not true.

"My father was a soldier," he goes on. "An officer, during the war. He was fifty-one years old when I was born, and although he had an artistic side and was, I think, more naturally warm-hearted than my mother, he never quite reconciled himself to the fact that his younger son was a…a wuss."

"Wuss he?" I ask, and he laughs. I love that. I love that I can make him laugh.

"I felt like one, anyway. With a father who fought in Italy and Germany and was present at the liberation of Bergen-Belsen, and an older brother who had made his first million on the stock market by the time he was twenty-six, a First in English literature doesn't really cut it."

He would never be telling me this if he didn't have to concentrate on the road and couldn't pretend that we are only chatting.

"Are you sorry you didn't go into the City?"

"Lord, no." He scowls. "I would have made a complete hash of it."

"A nice house in Buckinghamshire, a cottage in Sussex, a sailing boat, tickets to all the fancy London premieres…sorry, *premieres*."

"No, that's your fantasy," he says, a little riled. "I emigrated to another continent to get away from all that."

"Well, if I had wanted *all that* so very badly, I could have stuck with the Etonian."

"Maybe you should have."

We are almost fighting.

"Do you know what is so depressing?" I ask when we have parked the car and are walking toward the terminal. I need to say this out loud, because I need to see how he will react. "That sooner or later a girl realizes that her good opinion means very little to a man. A woman can't boost a man's ego, not if he feels inferior to the big boys out there. Women don't count. They can undermine a man, sure, and he might take it out on her if he had a bad day at the office, but it's the boys' admiration that he craves, not hers."

"If you believe that, you're crazy!"

Whatever this is, it is not the notorious English reticence.

Our fellow travelers are all on their way south or northeast, so the departure lounge in which we wait for our flight is only half-full and quiet. Giles, ambling along the window front, both hands dug deep into his pockets, bag slung over his shoulder, seems to contemplate the airfield bathed in the pinkish-gray light of the rising sun. Seeing him there, out of his natural habitat, my face softens, my whole body softens.

I know in my head that making love with him tonight would be a really stupid idea, but my heart and my belly know not from reason.

His seat is on the other side of the plane, a few rows behind mine, but when I look up after extracting gum, pen, and manuscript from my bag and stowing it under the seat in front of me, he is standing above me, elbows propped against the overhead locker.

"I hope you wouldn't have preferred sitting next to that nice lady who changed seats with me."

I raise myself to look across the rows of seats and see a middle-aged woman in colored knitwear wave at me. I wave back and mouth a thank you.

"What did you tell her?"

His grin deepens and he slumps into his seat, suddenly no more than a few inches away from me, closer even than in the car. So much for the nap I had hoped to take during the flight.

"Oh, never mind." He pretends to be interested in my manuscript. "I can be very persuasive if I want to be."

I decide to let that one pass and go for small talk. "Have you ever been to Notre Dame?"

"'South Bend! That sounds like dancing, doesn't it?'" he says in a falsetto voice.

"Katherine Hepburn. In *The Philadelphia Story*."

"Well done." He crosses his long legs and squirms in his seat so that his back is half turned toward the aisle and his body creates a little cocoon of privacy for us. "If you can tell me who she says it to, I'll buy you a cocktail before dinner." He leans the side of his head against the head rest and watches me expectantly.

"Gin and tonic, please. She says it to James Stewart's character, the journalist. Mike. She asks Mike where he's from, he says South Bend, Indiana, and she repeats it in that high, affected voice."

I turn away from the window, ever so slightly, turn toward him, lean the side of my head against my headrest and smile. I am allowed to smile at him. The plane starts backing out of its berth, and suddenly the whole cabin is flooded with sunlight.

I am dancing on the edge of an abyss.

"Aren't you a little too young for screwball comedy?" he teases me.

"Are you kidding me? I had a whole shelf full of MGMs from the thirties and forties. Cary Grant, mainly. But I've never seen *Die Hard 17*, or *The Return of the Killer Terminator*, or *Saddles on Fire*, or any of those."

"You're a nostalgic soul."

"Yes, I know." Nostalgic for a time when the world watched as six million of my people were murdered. We all have contradictions in our lives.

"James Stewart or Cary Grant?" he asks.

The moment the plane accelerates to take us out of our rigidly circumscribed social roles, we turn into teenagers, lying on a beach or hanging out in the park, comparing lists. Bands, films, actors, writers. I know what this is. We are curious about each other, and we are talking as if we were going to have sex tonight, as if we needed to find out whether we would work. We are getting personal with each other although we have decided that there is no point in getting personal, because we can't get physical. This is like eating an irresistibly delicious piece of cake knowing that there is a bitter nut in there somewhere, so you go on eating but you chew very, very carefully.

"Cary Grant." I sigh like a foolish teenager, and he laughs.

"Thought so! Top three Cary Grant films?"

"No, no, my turn! Which Hepburn?"

He takes his time gazing at my face and smiles when I blush.

"Audrey," he says. "With Katherine's mouth on her. Now you. Top three Cary Grant films."

"Well, *Philadelphia Story* is high up there, and *Holiday* is a lovely movie. Most of the Hitchcocks, of course, except I think he shouldn't have fallen for Eva Marie Saint. He's very sexy in *To Catch a Thief.* Oh, my very favorite one is *Cha*—no."

"What?"

"I'm not sayin'."

Charade is my favorite Cary Grant movie. But he's so much older than Audrey Hepburn in that one, with his gray head of hair and his crow's feet, that I am ashamed to admit I have adored it ever since I first saw it when I was eleven years old.

"So you like Cary Grant but not Clark Gable. Not sure I get that."

"Dude! You totally underestimate the sex appeal of Ashley Wilkes!"

"Ashley Wilkes is a girl's insipid dream!" he exclaims. "The romantic hero of an adolescent! Reassuringly asexual, and when he does knock on Melanie's bedroom door, once a fortnight, you can be sure he'll take his weight on his elbows. Like a true gentleman!"

"I'm sorry to interrupt you, sir, but—would you like tea or coffee? Water?"

"Right, what do *you* think—" He peers at the name on her lapel. "Oh, come on—you're never called *Melanie!*"

The flight attendant, a slinky young woman with a tattoo peeking out of her blouse, grins. "My mom was a huge fan of the movie, and *she* liked Ashley Wilkes! For my money, I'd take Rhett Butler any time—if he's available without the cigar-and-brandy breath!"

I'm laughing so hard, I can hardly hold my plastic cup of tea without spilling it all over my manuscript.

"Of course a man with an English accent is always very sexy." Melanie smiles, pushing herself through the narrow gap between the drinks cart and Giles's seat.

"I know, right?" I agree a shade too heartily and rest one hand on his thigh in order to pass her two dollars. She narrows her eyes at me and turns to the other side of the plane.

"Oooh, I say." Giles flutters his eyelashes and sighs.

"Giles, what have you done with Hornberger's file?" I ask on an impulse.

"Boring!"

"It's not boring at all! It is nail-bitingly exciting, and you are an old meanie for not letting me be part of the adventure!"

"That's me. Ol' Meanie Cleveland. And you're a good little assistant professor working on her spotless, sparkling tenure file. End of adventure."

"You're talking through your hat, Cleveland." I'm genuinely annoyed with him. "And you're a hypocrite!"

"I'm what?"

"Well!" I look around me in the cabin of the plane.

"What do you—oh, I see what you mean." He grins. "But I said *dinner*. What did *you* have in mind?"

For the first time since he offered me a ride to the airport it occurs to me that I would be disappointed if he didn't try to seduce me. Talk about hypocrisy!

I make another attempt. "Did you, for example, try to find Mary-Lou Tandy?"

"I had a look in the Shaftsboro phonebook. She isn't there."

"That hardly counts as *trying to find*. Have you handed the file in to the police? Or to the chair of the Sexual Misconduct Hearing Panel?"

"No…"

"But, Giles! That's—" I instinctively lower my voice. "That's withholding salient information in ongoing legal proceedings!"

"No, it isn't. It isn't even a case. Had Mary-Lou ever filed charges with the police, yes, but she didn't have the mental or emotional stamina to do so. I don't blame her. But she didn't, and having raped her doesn't make it more likely that he also raped Natalie."

"Yes, it does!"

"No, it doesn't!"

"But you think he did!"

"I do, but that's neither here nor there."

"Cleveland, you're really starting to upset me!" I inform him, in case he hadn't noticed. "Don't you want to see him behind bars?"

"That's a very complicated question."

"It is? Guy rapes women, guy ought to go to jail. What's complicated?"

"Revenge." He shakes his head, gazing out the window behind me. "So difficult, that. You've read the plays. You know how revenge invariably returns to stab the revenger in the back."

"Yes, for plotting and scheming against his adversaries! You're not setting a trap for Hornberger; you'd only be exposing what should have been exposed long ago! And talking of revenge—never mind." I cut myself off, but he raises his eyebrows at me, demanding to hear. "Well, Giles, I don't know, but threatening to tell Holly Ortega and Elizabeth Mayfield about Nick's affair with Amanda—that was revenge, too, wasn't it?"

"The revenge element was incidental. I had another reason."

And more he will not tell me, so I try another tack.

"Why do you think Corvin hid the file?"

"Blackmail? We've all wondered how Corvin gets away with… what he gets away with. Maybe this is why."

"I hate to think *Hornberger* is getting away with it all!"

"There is that," Giles agrees. "That is in the balance. Justice and revenge. If he hadn't fucked my wife, I'd be the first to blow the whistle on him. But the fact that I hate his guts and would love to see him—how did Tim put it?—see him strung up by his testicles makes it more complicated. You think I'm mad, don't you?"

Madly fascinating. I want to crawl into his brain and find out how it works, and I am convinced I would not be bored for a second. Impatient—that, yes!

"Do you always dissect your emotions with a long-handled scalpel?"

He looks at me, and suddenly his face is English again, guarded and impersonal, his eyes like green glass in the sun shining in through the window.

"Always," he says.

I find it difficult to switch from playing at pillow talk with Giles on the plane to the effusive but superficial manner required at conferences. Mere acquaintances fall around each other's necks as if they had last seen each other in the previous century. People who have dissed each other in reviews since they last saw each other struggle to adjust their behavior. Having a paper to present means you walk around with a leaden weight in your stomach till it's over, and then you either start enjoying yourself or you get bored.

I am a little piqued when I arrive at the conference venue and Giles suddenly doesn't seem to know me anymore. But I have my own people to greet, and it occurs to me that Giles may simply be giving me space to do my own thing. After the first half hour of coffee, it is almost as if I were at Notre Dame by myself, my main objective being to sell my paper. In fact, this is the first conference that I am attending without also having to sell myself, Ph.D-for-hire. For the first time I am an assistant professor on tenure track. The world is my oyster.

We hear a keynote and two papers. Interaction is concentrated and critical, but collegial. My chest is getting tighter.

When we are being herded back into the conference room after the break, I crane my neck to spot Giles in the small crowd, sidle up to him, and push my hand inside the crook of his arm.

"Giles — wait!"

Through the cotton of his shirt I can feel the hard muscles of his arm and how warm his skin is. It is a good thing that I am flushed already. "Now would be a good time to go and have that chat with Paul French. Have a cup of coffee with him!"

"But I just had coffee. Besides, Paul wants to hear your paper."

"Giles! Not fair! You said you wouldn't do this!"

"Wrong. *You* said. If you think I'm going to miss this, think again, ducky."

We are standing very close while the audience is murmuring its way past us. I peer into the room and see Pete Kirkpatrick, who is going to give the response to my paper. Giles is watching me with unholy amusement, and I can tell that my plea is making no impression at all.

"Courage, *ma chère*."

I feel the gentle pressure of his hand in the small of my back. *It's nice to have a friend.*

Paul French comes bouncing up to us. "Come on, Anna. Don't be nervous!"

"Heavens, I'm *not*...yes, I'm coming."

Of course the anatomy illustrations have an immediate appeal; they make an audience sit up automatically, unlike broadside woodcuts, pewter pilgrim badges or city seals. There are giggles and groans when I start my PowerPoint presentation, as well as the inevitable "Eeeew!"

"As you can see, I am cheating a little today. I am trying to sell you my car with a hot, half-naked blonde sitting on the hood. Except in these cases, the blonde is pregnant and half-dissected, but I hope you won't be choosy."

Make 'em laugh.

"I would like to convince you, over the course of the next twenty minutes, that these illustrations are the Protestant answer to *Maria gravida*, images of the pregnant Mother of Jesus Christ."

Make 'em doubt you. And then reel 'em in.

I don't manage to catch all of them in my net; there are two or three historians who shake their heads and roll their eyes. I am too whimsical, too impressionistic for their taste. But I flatter myself that the discussion after my paper was the liveliest yet, and most questions were genuine, most comments helpful.

Yes. I can do this! I am good at this! *Team Lieberman!*

Giles, having insisted that he hear me, sat at an oblique angle to the panel so that I did not have to look at him during my talk. I force myself, afterward, not to check his face, and once, when my eyes flit over, I see that he seems hunched over. Reading something, possibly.

"I'm glad to see that at Ardrossan they continue their tradition of hiring bright young things." An elderly gentleman has come up to me, and because I saw him nodding and smiling during my paper, I don't take offense at being called a "bright young thing."

"Uh, thank you—" I peek at his lapel "—Dr. Prewitt."

"That was a very clever little talk, and I mean that in a good way. I expect great things from you, Anna Lieberman. I'll be watching you!"

Boosted by my success, I walk over to greet Kathleen Murray. We were in grad school together long enough to develop a deep dislike of each other, but personal animosities with colleagues in your field are never a good idea. Kathleen and I will periodically meet at conferences for the rest of our lives; we have to get on with each other.

"I see you're here with Giles Cleveland," she says crossly.

"Actually, no, I'm not here with Giles Cleveland. We left the same town this morning and came to the same town this afternoon, that's all."

The one positive thing I can say about Kathleen is that she is fully alive to Giles's brand of attractiveness.

"Anna, you have to introduce me! Come on, he's standing by himself!"

Groaning inwardly, I allow her to pull me across the room to where Giles is leafing through one of the new publications on the book table.

"Giles, meet Kathleen Murray. She and I were at Columbia together before I went to London."

"Professor Cleveland!" She beams at him. "I'm so excited to meet you! Your biography of Raleigh is wonderful! I'm going to use it to teach next semester!"

"Kathleen got the job at Brandeis that I also applied for."

"Did you? I'm so glad!" He gives her his blandest smile, and I have to hide in my coffee cup not to burst out laughing.

"Why do *you* never tell me things like that?" he murmurs when we file back in again for the third panel. I cast a speaking glance up at him, and he laughs quietly.

"So, are you happy?" He means my paper.

"Whatever," I grumble. "It's not as if you paid me any attention!"

"I did!" he protests. "You were very…sexy."

"Giles, you rotter."

He laughs, and his eyes are very warm and very bright.

He *has* come to Indiana to seduce me.

Paul French has a lot of fun with "my pupil, Cleveland, my creature, my single success story as a tutor!" He is a charming, buoyant Botticelli angel of a man, impossible to dislike, but by the time we adjourn to get changed for dinner, he has turned into a rival.

"Actually, Giles, I was hoping to abduct you tonight! I know a quiet little place downtown — we have such a lot to catch up on!"

No! Tonight he's mine!

Giles accepts. Smiles, accepts, and explains to the bystanders that he and Paul last saw each other in nineteen ninety-five, when they got vilely drunk on Sangria at a conference in Barcelona.

"Sorry — I'm sure you understand — older rights, and all that!" This is not addressed to me but to Kathleen, and I feel as if someone had hit me over the head with a Riverside Shakespeare. Worried that shock and disappointment are written all over my face, I turn away from the group, mutter something about the effect of the coffee on my bladder, and flee into the restroom.

What the hell did I say to make him change his mind about me? *I wanted him!*

To have dinner with, at any rate, since sex is…should be…out of the question. I'm so disappointed I could cry. Scream. Kick in the door of the cubicle in which I am hiding my humiliation from the world.

Rationally, I understand what is going on. The moment he becomes unavailable, I want him. I wanted him before, I've been wanting him — oh, who am I kidding?

But my career…

I want my career more than I want a man. Naysayers, detractors, even haters I can deal with. The more enemies, the more honor. This afternoon I convinced a roomful of scholars of my intricately woven analysis of Renaissance images of dissected bodies. Like a barber-surgeon's knife through the dead flesh of a criminal, my intellect cut through conflicting layers of discourse, isolated the semiotic codes by which these images hang together, and carved a coherent argument out of a mass of material. But the sense of triumph this gave me was short-lived. Now I am tired. And frustrated. And so lonely.

What is *wrong* with me?

Since I cannot run away, and since I do not trust myself alone in my hotel room tonight, there is nothing for it but to team up with Kathleen and a couple of delegates I know from other conferences. Project the successful young tenure-track professor. Wear the high-heeled boots.

"Anna!" Giles is hurrying down the hallway with long strides, Barbour still open, scarf hanging around his neck. "Where do you think you're going?"

"Out." I hitch my purse up on my shoulder and pull the door shut.

"But you're my date!"

"Well, that's what I thought until you blithely agreed to have dinner with Paul French!"

"Smokescreen, darling. I was sure you'd get that."

"No, I didn't get that," I mutter defensively.

"Do you have Kathleen's number? Tell her that you have a headache. Ask for the name of the place they're going to and say you'll follow on later. If you're feeling better."

"What did you tell Paul?"

"Headache." He grins.

On our way downstairs and across the lobby, I am still so overwhelmed by confusion, relief, joy, suspicion, and resentment that I am dumb, but outside on the sidewalk I snap.

"I don't know that lying was such a bright idea, Giles! If anyone sees us now, we're toast!"

"We're not going to be seen. They've all gone to South Bend, and we're going to Mishawaka." He hails a cab from the stand down the street. "Unless you'd rather stay in and order room service…"

He says it like something he didn't think he would have the guts to say, and then it slipped out at the first opportunity. The taxi draws up, and Giles and I are still gazing at each other, teetering on the brink.

"Get 'n the car."

I make my voice sound extra gruff, and the quick nod of my head would have done any mobster proud. He holds the door for me and exchanges a few words with the driver while I sort out my coat, then he climbs in after me. We drive along the southern edge of the campus and turn right.

"I'm—I'm sorry." He has to clear his throat before he can speak. "I can't believe I said that. It was crass and—God, I can't believe I'm such a…klutz!"

"Giles." I reach over and slip my hand into his; he claps it firmly, without hesitation. "You're not a klutz for spelling out what we both know is in the cards. I'm glad you did."

It's too dark to see his face properly, but he doesn't let go of my hand.

"You're much better at plain-speaking than I am."

"Well, I am still a New Yorker while you are a freakin' Englishman."

This clears the air a little, and I give in to the innocent—I hope—pleasure of linking my fingers with his and leaning a little closer when he lays our hands on his thigh. I am sinking back into my fantasy of being with Giles—of being allowed to be with Giles—like I would sink into a hot, foamy, scented bath. It is a drive of some fifteen minutes, during which we hold hands but do not speak. We pull up in front of a country club-style building, brightly lit, in what appear to be quiet, park-like surroundings. While he is paying, another taxi draws up, and I hold my breath for fear it might be conference delegates, but it's an elderly couple with what I take to be their college-aged granddaughter. They are chatting quietly and walk in before us. Giles is about to follow them when I grab his arm.

"Giles!"

"Hmm?" Immediately he swings round, stands very close to me and reaches for my hands. I love that he likes holding hands. I love everything about him.

"Giles, I'm…very tired and…and emotional, and I don't want to end up having sex with you tonight merely because it is something I can do horizontally."

He smiles and lets me go. Three nimble steps and he is up the front porch of the restaurant—light-footed, happy.

This is so dangerous.

The restaurant is generously laid out but feels cozy because the space has been compartmentalized by big potted plants and painted paravents. Giles hangs up my coat and takes off his Barbour, and although I am ashamed to admit it, the warm glow in my belly is fanned by the pride of possession. I managed to suppress this feeling all day today—at the airport, at the conference—but now that he is lavishing his whole attention on me, my heart swells.

The waiter is leading us to a booth with a window at the back of the room when a hot, painful rush of panic sets my skin on fire, and it takes me a paralyzed eternity to register the cause.

"I say, Cleveland! Over here!"

Paul French. At a big round table, with Kathleen, Pete, his wife, and several other people from the conference.

"*Varkackt*," I mutter next to Giles's shoulder, and he, lifting an arm to acknowledge Paul's salute, mutters back, "If that means what I think it means, I'll say *oy* to that."

He turns round to look at me. "I don't want them!" he pleads, with the pitiful but helpless frown of a thwarted boy. "I want *you!*"

"Let's run!" I whisper. We stare at each other, and I am so in love with him, all my resolutions have evaporated into thin air; if he grabbed my hand to run, I'd run with him. But we are both too responsible, or too cowardly, and we both know we won't run.

"Good, so you got my message! I wasn't sure it would reach you!" Paul pulls out the chair next to his, and his voice and behavior tell me—and I hope no one else—that he is covering Giles's ass. And mine. Giles glances over at him, too annoyed to play the game, and I greet the others far more enthusiastically than I would in any other circumstance, except possibly on a mountain top in the Himalayas. All I can do is prevent the ultimate frustration of having Giles sit next to Kathleen.

"Here, Paul, Giles—you haven't seen each other in yonks—" I push Giles into the chair offered by Paul and slip in next to Kathleen myself.

"I'm so glad your headache is better, Anna!" she trills sourly. "How boring it would have been for you to spend the evening all alone in your room!"

When Paul fills our glasses with wine, I drink.

"Anna? Anna, would you say you had a fair impression of your college after you'd been to your campus interview?" Vicky, one of the conference organizers, has to raise her voice to alert me.

"Oh, I—I don't know. How can I—" I gesture toward Giles.

"How can she answer that in front of a colleague?" one of the other women scolds Vicky. "Is Giles on your P&T committee, Anna?"

We glance at each other, and I hope my embarrassment is taken for the defensiveness of a junior professor. "That hasn't been settled yet," I say.

"Probably not," Giles says.

At first I am relieved when someone starts asking about the Hornberger scandal. Only a few of them had not heard of it, and so a censored version of life at the Ardrossan Observatory becomes a safe topic to pass the evening.

Once embarked on this salacious topic, each of them has a similar story to relate: of the eminent professor who got up in a faculty meeting to announce what she wrongly assumed was an open secret—her affair with an adjunct lecturer; of the female professor who married her much younger teaching assistant, who ten years later threw himself off a bridge; of the bright young female student who serially dated three professors during college, only to end up taking a job as secretary in a firm of car dealers.

Be quiet! I want to shout them down. *Does nobody know any stories with a happy ending?*

"I'm on the third floor—you, Anna?" Kathleen asks me as we are walking up the stairs back at the hotel together at the end of this fucked-up evening.

"Um, yup."

"Giles?"

"I think so." He rummages in his coat pocket and produces his keycard. "Three twenty-one. That's sort of round the corner and behind the sofa, underneath a potted plant."

Why doesn't he draw her a freaking map?

I am seething. *Seething.* It makes no difference that her room is near the elevator, while both Giles and I are further along the hallway and round a corner.

"See you in the morning," I mutter, slam my keycard into the slit on the door and throw myself against it.

"This is—" he says, as if he had suddenly remembered something important.

"Good night."

"This is the moment Grace Kelly turns round to kiss Cary Grant."

"Look, Giles, don't even—go there—" I shake my head, so distraught and disappointed I could cry.

"I know. Scandal-mongering is awful. Poisonous."

"It is! And I don't want to become the object of—"

"I wouldn't let them."

"You couldn't stop them!"

The tension leaves his body, his shoulders slump. He gazes down at the floor.

"I would do my best."

"Giles, I—I'm really sorry we didn't get the chance to have dinner together. I am. But I asked you not to do this. Hit on me."

"Not hitting," he says softly, looking up. "I just want a kiss."

He is very still, all flippancy gone. So handsome, in his suit and Barbour, melted snow glistening on his sleeves and in his hair. And at the same time—shy. He is shy, and neither smooth nor masterful.

That, or he is playing me.

"Hit me again," I say softly, mockingly. "Only this time, choose a better quotation."

He hears my softness, but he also hears the mockery. The tension around his mouth relaxes, and he smiles.

"'Hasn't it occurred to you that I'm having a tough time keeping my hands off you?'"

The sentence echoes in my memory and I have to laugh. "Much better."

I step up to him, glad of the high heels that have been pinching me all afternoon, because they make me tall enough to wrap one arm around his shoulders while I kiss him. On the mouth, and just deliberately enough, I hope, to send a spark into his belly.

You play me, I play you.

"More," he murmurs when I try to pull away.

"Giles, somebody might —"

He is not interested at all.

Very fuzzily I make a deal with myself: the second he begins to push me through the half open door of my room, I will push him away. Only he does not. He slips his hands underneath my coat and draws me firmly against himself, and although I could hazard a guess that it is not his phone that is hard below my navel, he is very still, as our lips and tongues slow down, find their pace. How much you can learn about someone by kissing him! I already had an idea that Giles Cleveland is a man who enjoys kissing, and enjoys it for the intimacy it allows. He is kissing me now to get to know me: my mouth, my tongue, my body and their responses to his. My courage. I want to do everything with him, I told Irene, and it is absolutely true.

"He said *what?* Noooo! And then what did she say back?"

"What did she say? What did she *do!*"

Loud, cheerful voices cut into my consciousness like a blade into skin. I jerk my head back and gasp for air, now listening hard. Voices approaching along the hallway. Voices about to turn the corner.

"Go!" I push him away frantically, push him into the direction of his room. "Go, go, quickly!"

"Anna…"

He could easily overpower me. I feel it in his body's resistance, in the way he clasps my upper arms, glances along the hallway and into my room.

"No, Giles! *Go, now!*"

And I tear myself away from him, dive into my room and slam the door.

The moment I hear the latch on my bedroom door, my rejection impulse is overcome by remorse. What have I done? What the hell have I just done? But I cannot be seen French kissing Giles Cleveland in a conference hotel hallway! I might as well fingerpaint it onto my forehead!

I slammed a door in his face.

Shame, as keen-edged as the panic before, rushes through my body like hard liquor.

Why did he give up so easily? Is Giles Cleveland a quitter? He certainly didn't stand by his woman, just now, and I am *furious* he didn't! He might have propelled me into my room, out of sight, easily! *Why didn't he?*

Maybe because I told him that I wouldn't enjoy this evening if it was all about getting me into bed.

Maybe because he doesn't want to have sex with a woman who has to be dominated and coerced into it, like a bashful virgin.

Damn!

Damn caution! Damn my career! Damn this constant, constant anxiety!

Do something.

Get drunk. Find a night club, drown in the noise. Dance your way through this need to stop thinking. I need to be part of something simple again.

My heart is beating hard and fast in my throat. I can't. I shouldn't.

I should take another shower. Flush the anger and the need out of my body.

It's a good shower, this. A big showerhead, a full, yet soft spray of water, hot, as hot as I can bear it.

I can't bear it.

I've never felt it so keenly, the two-edged sword of temptation. It cuts both ways. Damned if I do, and damned if I don't. I never knew that. Supposing I had an affair with Giles Cleveland. My career would crash and burn like a Japanese plane on the flight deck of a

US destroyer. But what if my plane from South Bend to New York crashes tomorrow, and I die without ever having been naked with him? What if my plane doesn't crash, and I die in my bed at the ripe old age of eighty-three, like my grandmother, without ever having been naked with Giles Cleveland?

Chapter 26

If any evidence were needed that I did not come on this trip with any thought of seducing anyone, my pajamas would do it. Baby-blue flannel with white sheep. Thick woolly socks. You never know how warm or cold these hotel rooms will be, and I hate cold feet.

Out the door, down the mercifully empty elevator, into the hotel lobby. It is past midnight, and residents have retired to bed or the bar. The receptionist is on the phone to a friend, talking in loud, over-emphatic cadences. No one notices me as I stroll nonchalantly toward the restroom. Like a child sneaking out to buy candy in a corner store, I clasp my coins in my hand. I have loose change enough to buy two.

Two, in different colors.

Hand deep in coat pocket, as if I had stolen them, I sidle back toward the elevator. Again I am lucky; no one rides up with me. I pad along the carpeted hallway, half-expecting to see Kathleen round the next corner. But the hall is silent and empty. And now…

I knock.

I knock, and the door gives a little, as if the door hinges were loose, or as if someone had very carefully not quite closed it. One false move and it will latch. I so dread being seen in the hallway that I slip in and quickly close the door behind me before I realize that there may already be two people in the room.

Why else would the door not be shut? Careless.

I force myself past the cubicle formed by the bathroom toward the dim pool of light round the corner—and there he is, lying in bed, propped up on his elbow, reading. Like a boy.

Not reading now, of course. He is watching me, waiting. He does not look as I would if I had just heard someone enter my hotel room in the middle of the night. Did he leave the door open for me? That must be nonsense, and yet it adds to the poignancy of the situation, because I know that in a pathetic kind of way this whole thing is about me wishing someone would leave the door open for me.

Giles closes his book and puts it on the bedside table. He is wearing a white t-shirt, and the light of the lamp shimmers on the knobbly bones of his wrist and elbow and on the long strands of muscle that connect them. He looks like a boy waiting to be tucked in, and at the same time it is one of those moments in which I am overwhelmed by how big he is. The swell of his shoulders and the sudden bulge of his bicep as he bends his arm to lift the corner of his blankets.

My flannel knee looks childish on the edge of his mattress, and he could touch it without moving his hand more than a few inches. But he does not. He is so grave he almost looks forbidding. No smile, no flippant remark to relieve the tension. Waiting. Watching me with those light green eyes. There is a low crackle of plastic in one of the pockets as I let the robe slide to the ground. But I still don't have the courage to climb into bed with him—the enormity of what I'm doing has rooted me to the edge of it. His eyes crease in a slow, wary smile, his shoulders relax, and his hand is warm and hopeful around my knee. The temperature in the room rises. He sits up and bunches his pillows against the headrest of the bed, scoots up so that he can lean against it and lifts his comforter to reveal blue-and-gray-striped pajama bottoms. I crawl up to him, into his naked arms, unsure of how fast this is going to happen. One arm is around my waist, and he pulls me onto his lap, astride, facing him. So near, suddenly. So close. So hard.

He slips his hands under my pajama top, up my back to my shoulders, his fingertips hard in the tense muscles, and for a swooning moment all blood drains from my brain. His eyes are glowing with pleasure at what lies ahead. His whole face is glowing, and I'm so nervous.

How difficult it is not to hide from what I want so much.

"I have to switch off the light."

Comprehension registers in an incredulous shake of his head. I understand the disappointment, but not the flash of fear that hardens his face when my words sink in. But I am afraid, too.

"You can't do this with the light on?" he asks in a tight voice.

"Not—tonight."

"Not with me."

"No."

He seems to shrink into himself, and his hands lie still on my pajama'ed thighs. He stares, without seeing, at something there. The back of his hand, my knee in flannel.

"I don't like that."

He sounds defeated, but I can't explain, and I can't argue. The truth is, I need to do this in the dark and in silence. I grope for the switch of the bedside lamp, and the room is dark. Not quite pitch dark; after a while we are able to make out the white patches of each other's eyes. I shrug out of my pajama jacket and wrap my arms around a phantasma. It is warm to the touch, substantial and alive, this fantasy of mine, and it smells like Giles Cleveland. It kisses like Giles Cleveland, too. Like a grumpy Giles Cleveland, at first, because he is annoyed with me, unresponsive. I love that he wants to see me, but I can't allow that. Can't allow him to see…me. See how much I want him.

The memory of the connection we made earlier is still glowing in his belly, too, and soon he is kissing me like he kissed me in the hallway. Only now I drive him on. He wants to be tender with me, but I cannot allow myself to feel the tenderness. There is nothing for me here except the fierce ache of lust. Impersonal and anonymous, in the dark, this naked male body, and I want to make it mine. This body is my fantasy of Giles Cleveland, and a fantasy is all he can be to me. I want to blurt out words, words to tell him what this feels like, what I feel for him. But the Sinatras are right. I won't go and spoil it all.

I draw him toward me, away from the pillows, so I can lean over him and pull his t-shirt up and over his head. So much naked skin, cool in the night air but heated from inside. One male body should be much like the next, shouldn't it? But this is the one I want. I lift his hands and cup them around my breasts, and he squeezes them lightly and chafes the tips with his palms. Half-heartedly, it seems to me.

"Too small?" A pointless question, but I can't help it. This is an insecurity I thought I had mastered, but apparently not. Not in this case. He gives a low spurt of laughter, and of course I can't tell, now, what it means, because I can't see his face. The top of his head brushes along my chin, then my left breast contracts almost painfully, his mouth is so hot and so deliberate in its caress. It feels like the ache of fear, and I know why: if he is going to touch me like this, I will lose it.

We grapple in the silvery darkness, and with this phantasma I can be bold in a way I could not be bold with Giles Cleveland.

"No, don't!" He pushes my head away. "I won't—last. Please. Please."

The skin of his belly is smooth and vulnerable under my lips, between my teeth; the soft, wiry hair tickles my cheek, and I simply *have* to take him back into my mouth. I wish I could be rough with him, just make him come fast and fierce, all control mine. Suck his brains out. I know I can make him come, and judging by the state of his hot, hard shaft, it would take about thirty seconds.

He scoots away from me, out of my arms, and jumps out of bed. Is he angry? What man gets angry when the woman he invited into his bed offers oral sex to him? He disappears into the bathroom and I hear him rummaging in a bag with a zipper. What is my cue? Should I just leave? When he returns, he makes for the window and opens the thick curtains with one swift movement so that the light from the street lamps illuminates the room enough to see the outline of furniture and bodies. Enough for me to see that he has left his pajama pants in the bathroom. Enough to see that he has not gone off the idea of having sex with me. Not at all.

Naked and erect he stands in front of the bed, waiting for my reaction. He doesn't want this to be the anonymous encounter of two naked bodies in a hotel room. I can't be mad at him for that.

"You do it." He holds out his hand.

Oh! That's why he went into the bathroom.

He reaches past me and takes something off the bedside table. There is a faint bleeping sound and then the display light of his cell phone dimly illuminates the scene.

And what a scene it is—the most beautiful cock in the world. Its length and thickness are in perfect proportion, the shaft is velvety and without blemish, and it is so hard that the foreskin has receded almost completely from the head, which rears up like a snake from the sheath it is shedding.

I scramble onto my knees and crouch in front of him; it is too, too beautiful, so hard and proud against the pale skin of his belly, and then like a smooth, lambent torch in my hand, and in my mouth.

"Anna—it's not as if this weren't a dream come true, but—"

This confession makes me grin, and with a plopping sound I release him. Gingerly I tear open the sachet and do what I have not done for almost a year—what I have never done in my life. I roll a condom over Giles Cleveland's cock. Admiring my handiwork, I cradle his balls in my hand. This is almost the most intimate caress of all, holding a man's testicles. So curiously heavy, so soft. So vulnerable.

I make him sit as before, with his back against the headboard, and he pulls me into a bear hug, nuzzles his face into what passes for my cleavage and exhales such a deep, heart-felt sigh that I have to laugh, though it sounds more like a sob.

"I know!" I whisper into his hair, against his shoulder. "Giles, I—" He freezes in my arms, so ready to expect a rebuke. "I don't think I need a lot more foreplay."

Again that spurt of laughter, and then he kisses me.

He runs his fingertips slowly down my spine, up my sides and over my breasts, over and over, like butterflies, like a length of silk, still kissing me. He is unexpectedly expert at caressing tiny tits, very unlike a man who is used to handling those sizable jugs that fill the former Mrs. Cleveland's blouse, very gentle, suckling them, flicking at them with his tongue, raking his fingernails along my back with just enough pressure to make me shiver. Now I *really* don't need any more foreplay. I raise myself on my knees, clasp the base of his cock—*he* doesn't need any more foreplay either, judging by the state of it—and—

Just a naked man. Just a cock. It will feel lovely, because I am burning to have him—it—inside me, but I mustn't picture us—Giles and Anna—in this hotel bed, me crouching over him, Giles clasping my waist with both hands, because if I could see that, his hands round my waist, both of us looking down although we can't see more than hazy outlines, looking down to where we will be joined and fused—if I could see all that, I'd panic.

Control. Keep mine. Make him lose his.

"Oh, sweet Jesus!"

He rears up as if in pain, and I gulp for breath but manage to do it soundlessly. It does feel like pain, the stimulation overload as he slides into me, just slides in, smoothly and easily, all the way, all in one simple, fluid movement. I am so ready for him, have been, for such a long time. And because that felt so good, I do it again. All the way up till he almost slips out of me, till we almost lose contact but not quite. His fingers tighten around my waist, and this time he pushes me down, bucks his hips in anticipation, and I can't suppress a groan of pleasure as he fills me up.

Fuck, yes. *This.*

"Make me last," he whispers when I start to ride him, not fast but thoroughly, to feel as much of him as possible with each thrust. If I want to pretend to myself that he is just a man, just a cock, I will have to close my eyes, because we can see each other now, in the silvery darkness. I can see his gleaming eyes and tousled hair and the slim, angular outline of his shoulders that feel solid under my palms as I am holding on to him. He feels so solid and strong, strands of muscle and sinew under warm, smooth skin, but he looks almost fragile, like a specter, like a phantasma. Like a boy. I remember watching the side of his neck in the car this morning, and how on the plane he made a little nook for us with his body, and the pleading expression in his eyes when he turned to me in the restaurant and said *I don't want them! I want you!*

"No," I murmur against his lips and set to work.

I am neither surprised nor disappointed that he comes about three minutes later. I meant him to. I made him. What does surprise me is how close I was to coming myself. I don't, usually, with a new man, not right away, not the first few times, not if it's someone I care about. Surely not with Giles Cleveland!

Almost. I am seconds away from an orgasm, but also seconds away from falling asleep; it is the most bizarre feeling. If I roused myself just a little more, just stretched that little bit further, I would crash on the other side of a huge climax and then…I don't know what then. Sleep for a hundred years.

I fall asleep. The last thing I remember is wrapping my arms around his neck and resting my cheek on his naked shoulder. No, the last thing I remember is the insidious bite of doubt whether he would want me to stay or to leave.

"Don't leave…" The bedclothes rustle; his fingers touch my thigh and close around my knee as I scramble onto my haunches. "In the fairy tales the princess always has to stay with the ogre till the morning."

"Ogre?" I can hear the smile in my own voice.

"To break the spell."

I am amazed at how well he understands what this is about, and yet I have to ask, "Is that what we've been doing here?"

"I thought that was the idea." Warm, gentle fingers are inching their way up my thigh. "I'll feel horribly lonely when you leave."

His hand slips round my waist, the flat of his hand against the small of my back; the mattress sags, and he pulls himself toward me. I only realize what he is about when I hear him groan and feel his cheek on my thigh and his face nestling against my naked belly.

Never in a million years had I expected Giles Cleveland would be so open, so trusting as a lover. It disarms me completely, and at the same time it exasperates me. What on earth *was* the trouble between him and Amanda? He is lovely. Just lovely.

Curled around me like a lanky dog, he offers me access to all parts of his body, and it is only because I am tenuously holding on to the resolution to go back to my room that I do not avail myself of this opportunity. One hand in his hair, the other on his neck, I try not to think of the long strands of muscle along his spine, and how easily I could run my hand down to the smooth, taut globes of his buttocks…*and the demesnes that there adjacent lie.* I drop a kiss onto the temple that is facing up, hoping that this will help me preserve a state of maternal tenderness.

"And there's another thing," he murmurs against my skin.

"What other thing?"

"In the fairy tales the magic number is always three."

The sensation of his lips between my breasts clarifies the meaning of this remark more efficiently than my addled brain can decode it.

"Giles—don't!" I clutch his hair roughly, but of course I cannot push away a man who has both his arms wrapped around my waist.

"Have you already had enough of me, after that pathetic little performance? Don't I get a chance at a make-up exam?"

"I haven't had enough of you." Saying it out loud sends a shiver of anxiety over my skin, but it is dark, and so I say it like it is. "But

I know I will be lonely tomorrow, and I want to go back now. To find out how bad the loneliness will be."

"Presbyterian mentality."

"Your lot doesn't have the premium on guilt, you know."

"Guilt-shmuilt," he murmurs, and a heartbeat later we are shaking with giggles like an eight-limbed blancmange.

"Oh, Giles!"

"I hate the idea of flying back home without you."

He is breathless with laughter, but there is defiance in his voice now, and a little resentment, too, but what can I say? So I bend down again and kiss the cool skin of his shoulder. What else can I do? There is nothing I can do about it. So we will both be lonely, but there it is.

"I hate the idea of a whole week's holiday," he insists. "And what I would do with you if I had a whole week to do it in."

"Don't…"

"And when you get back you'll pretend this never happened."

A sensitive man, who, inevitably, has moments of tetchiness.

"No, not pretend it never happened. But it can't happen again. We agree on that, don't we?"

His arms around my waist tighten and for a few seconds he presses his face hard into my belly. "Giles! We do agree this is a… one-off, don't we?"

"Please stay with me tonight. The whole night. Will you?"

I don't know about this. I am getting really cold — wouldn't be surprised if I am catching something, naked and sweaty in the cool hotel room — and after the first post-coital languor I can feel a wave of anxiety rolling toward me. I would rather be alone when it hits me. It will carry me far, far away from Giles, and I don't want to be in the same room with him, let alone the same bed, when it breaks.

"Someone once asked me to assess, on a scale from one to ten, my ability to make myself happy," he says. "I thought at the time it was about three and a half."

"Are you asking me?"

"Yes."

"I don't know whether this — coming here, tonight — falls into the category of making myself happy, or the opposite."

He raises himself onto his elbow and gently kisses me on the cheek.

"Happy," he says.

My cheek finds its place in the warm, fragrant crook of his neck; my shoulders relax in his embrace. He pulls me down, and our chests roll against each other, his ribs hard against mine, cushioned by the soft squishiness of my breasts, and our hips, pelvic bones colliding, and the smooth, musky skin of our bellies, and then our legs as we huddle under the blankets again.

"Come closer. While you're still here, come close…"

I worm one arm through the narrow gap between the mattress and his body, slip the other around his waist, and nestle against him as if I could by some osmotic process become one with him. He catches his breath in the darkness above my head, and a large, determined hand clasps my buttocks.

"Every bone in my body turns to jelly when you do that," he breathes.

I press my face against his shoulder and wonder whether he can feel that I am giggling again.

"And one bit of…um…jelly turns into a bone-er…"

A quiver runs through his chest and his hand on my ass squeezes in involuntary response.

"I had hoped you would notice…"

Leaning back on my trembling arms, I am mesmerized by the moonlit sight of our gyrating hips as Giles slams his cock into me, and because I am again half sitting on his lap, he has his hands free and puts them to good use on my breasts. Kneading them with his palms, tugging at them, a little harder now than before, as if he knew it was time. As if he knew I was riding the wave. Then he slows down, and frustration makes me want to cry out in protest, but I am determined not to surrender myself to him, to it—whatever *it* might be, my need for him—so I cautiously inhale, as calm as I can be while he is still inside me. God, this is so bizarre. Giles Cleveland's cock inside me, utterly bizarre.

He clasps my hips and moves hardly at all, only his thumbs, stroking the sensitive skin above my ovaries, inching lower—I can't believe he is doing this. Pushing my lips apart, away from his shaft, unfurling them to expose the swollen hood. I can feel it's wet because it's cool in the night air, then hot under the tender, tentative pressure of his thumb.

"Can I make you come…like this?"

"No," I lie, and just in time my clit and the sensitive surrounding area are released from the firm, circling attention of the ball of his hand. I gulp for breath, relieved, frustrated.

"Show me how," he says softly, but I can hear the tension and the excitement in his voice.

"No!" I almost don't have breath enough for that one syllable.

"Yes." And then, even more softly, "Please."

He gives me a second or two, and when I don't comply, he leans forward, and while he is kissing me, makes me fall flat on my back by the simple method of jabbing the crooks of my elbows. I try to protest, but his mouth is back on mine, and when he finally releases me and sits up, his cock still hard in my belly, he takes my hand and guides it between my legs.

"You're safe. I'll be watching you the whole time."

There is a faintly malicious note in his voice; he is still angry with me for switching off the light. He settles my butt on the mattress and stretches out next to me, his legs tangled with mine, careful not to slip out of me. Props himself up on one elbow, draws me closer with one arm around my waist. Clasps my uncommissioned fingers with his other hand. Pins my left arm above my head when I try to free myself.

"Giles, no! This really isn't—"

"You look extremely sexy like this, you kn-know that?"

I can tell that he means it; his voice close above my head is so strained it cracks.

"No, I don't!"

He thrusts himself into me again, slowly but deliberately, and it's as if a vial of hot oil had been poured onto his cock.

"Liar," he whispers into my hair, and I giggle and groan at the same time. I hate that he knows how much he is turning me on, hate even having to admit to myself how much it turns me on to be pinned down like this, by his body and his cock, held like this, exposed.

"Liar, liar, pants on fire…" he whispers. Hesitates, almost stops breathing. "…cunt on fire…Show me how to make you come."

I couldn't say whether he pushed my hand back between my legs or whether it crept there of its own accord, but I don't care anymore. I press my face against his chest. His skin is hot and smells of sex and fresh sweat.

And then I show him.

Sometime later, I float up from what feels like twenty thousand leagues under the sea to find that gentle fingers are caressing the back of my neck, kneading the muscles in my shoulders. A body lies warm and naked against mine, and a voice whispers like an echo from the deep.

"I can't keep my hands off you."

I grunt softly and arch myself against his fingers in languid invitation. They need no encouragement. Slowly but inevitably they work their way down the long strands of muscle next to my spine until a large, sure hand molds itself around the warm globes of my buttocks. It needs no more than that. Or perhaps it is because my defenses are down. I want to spread my legs, but at the same time I don't want to show my need to be touched so blatantly. Down my thighs his hand travels, to the back of my knees, and up again on the inside of my thighs. I only realize that I have lifted myself up and toward him when I hear a noise of amusement next to my ear.

"Here?" he whispers. "You want me here?"

His hand slips into the hot, slick cavity high up between my thighs, almost but not quite reaching my center. Still I am hoping he will nudge my legs apart to give him more scope, but he does not. I must do it, offer myself to him in the silvery darkness, hiding against the mattress. I moan when he slides into me, when he bites into my neck, plays with my ear. His loins feel so smooth and strong against my naked butt. The bed sags. He has taken the weight off his elbows.

This time I come against his hand.

When I wake again, my mouth is so dry I can hardly swallow. I was dreaming I was in an exam situation — fully clothed, at least — and I had to pick one from a table covered with hundreds of cards in wild disorder. I knew that the card held the question I would then have to answer, and I was terrified because I had not prepared myself well for the exam. Hoping against hope to pick a question I could handle, I turned one over, and instead of letters it showed an anatomy illustration: like one of Charles Estienne's or

Giulio Casserio's naked women, this figure looked vaguely Grecian, and she was holding up the folds of her abdominal wall with both hands as if it were a frilly petticoat.

I knew without having been told that it was my task to comment on what she displayed within her abdominal cavity, but hard as I strained my eyes, I could not seem to focus on any details. People were passing in and out of the room, and I grew ever more frantic because one of them would stop by my table and demand an answer. Finally someone did stop, and I, playing for time, began to describe the scene in the drawing. But the examiner reached for the card and began to pull it out of my hand. I tried to hold on to it, but he laughed. As he laughed, I looked up, and it was Ciaran Dyce. With an overwhelming sense of defeat, I let go of the card and woke up.

I cannot do this.

I have not lost myself in him, or in *this*. But if we do it again, I will crack. He will crack me open to the core.

Chapter 27

"So tell me already," Irene says, not wanting to know.

"What?"

"Well, so you fucked him. Now what?"

My heart begins to race, and it's not with pleasure at the memory. We're sitting in my former life, at Antonio's on Amsterdam Avenue, and are each having a panini and salad.

"I did not…*fuck* him."

She inflates her cheeks and exhales like an impatient balloon.

"Right, you had the most romantic night of your life with him. Now what?"

I don't want to fight with Irene. I want to slap her, yes, but then we would fight, and I am too dejected to fight.

"I wanted him, that's all. The truth is, I want him, and the truth is—"

But I'm not sure I will lay myself open to more jibes than absolutely necessary. Irene waits for me to go on, but I shake my head again.

"The truth is it was the best sex of your life. Cue violins!" There is no escaping the jibes.

"That's not what I was going to say."

"What, then? Talk *tachlis*. Why are you bent on ruining your career? I thought I'd—"

"Don't, Reenie!" I interrupt her, almost with my hands over my ears. "Look, there won't be any more sex, okay? I left him."

"How do you mean — *left him?*"

"Left while he was sleeping. Left for the airport first thing and bought a ridiculously overpriced ticket that someone else hadn't picked up."

"Wait — you did *what?*" Irene is genuinely shocked, and my throat is getting so tight it hurts.

"I panicked. When I went to his room, it was almost completely dark, but later the moon came round to that side of the building, and — "

"You had sex in the dark?"

"I made him switch off the light. I couldn't have — I wouldn't have been able to go through with it, with the light on."

"What are you talking about?"

"I know. But I can't even begin to tell you how beautiful he is to me."

"Hence the light. All the better to see him by."

"No, because — " I'm staring at my hands shredding the napkin in my lap, and suddenly tears are dripping down like from a leaky faucet.

"Anna, for heavens' sake!"

I swallow and swallow again, gulp down the tears, although I feel that there are many more, a torrent of salt water.

"All I could manage was sex," I manage to say, feebly but mercifully without sobbing, "and he…I think he wanted to make love to me!"

The first time I almost called him was in the departure lounge at South Bend Airport. Since then, I have been on the brink of calling him a dozen times. But what would I say?

You are a wonderful lover, and you're so beautiful it stops my heart. But don't touch me again.

I knew all this before I went to his hotel room.

"You'll never be able to stay away from him," Irene predicts after she has ordered two shots of limoncello and made me down mine in one.

"Oh, you can rely on Giles to stay away from me. I h-have — I have h-hurt him, and now he'll hate me!" My chin wobbles, and she pushes her own glass of limoncello toward me. "It's like a disease!" I rally against my tears. "Foolish infatuation! You remember what

Elinor says, in *Sense and Sensibility*? That it is foolish—no, I think she says 'bewitching'—that it is a bewitching idea to think that all our happiness depends on one particular person. Jane Austen knew it was wrong, dangerous, to think that! We all know it! And yet…"

"Why don't you come home?" Irene asks gently.

"Failure."

"No one would think that!"

"I would. Although that place, Ardrossan, is a madhouse."

Irene waves her hand in a gesture that says, *I told you so, but I'm not going to rub it in.* "You could even sleep with the Englishman, for a while, and then come home."

I should be annoyed with her for advocating an affair with Giles because the inevitable fallout will set me free to move up north again. But I feel guilty for not telling her about the letter I kissed in the Ardrossan post office, so I leave it at that. There is no point in discussing an affair with Giles, because there will not be one. It may even have been necessary to hurt him. I'm not at all sure that he agreed that we were having a one-night stand, and I'm pretty sure that I would not have been able to resist him if he had continued to…um, woo me. Now I needn't worry he'll woo me. He won't even speak to me.

"I haven't seen you cry since your *bubbe* died," Irene says after a couple of minutes.

"I know. And she had lived her life. I…not so much."

"Now you're being melodramatic! You have a life, you have a career!"

"I think I have a career so that I don't have to have a life. I know this sounds melodramatic and adolescent, but—" I shrug, too dejected to try further explanations.

"You're exhausted, that's all. You should have rested and gone hiking for three weeks before you started that job down there, not squeezed every drop of energy out of yourself to finish your book!"

I look up at her impassioned face and smile.

"That's what Giles said."

Chapter 28

feel tense and forlorn in New York, but I dread coming back to Ardrossan. I dread it so much that the night before my flight I can't sleep, and on the day itself I can't eat.

Even my cottage is no safe haven.

There are traces of cigarette ash on my porch, and I sweep up a crunched-up cigarette rolling paper. Perhaps Jules was sheltering here again and tried her hand at rolling her own. Whatever, I'm not having it. Events at the Observatory—Hornberger's intrusions into my office, Corvin's senile guerilla attacks—have affected me more than I had thought, and my nerves are still raw. This is what paranoia must feel like. How does this ash get onto my porch? Was this towel not clean when I left, and now it's limp and grubby? Did Karen not give me four brown eggs before I left, and now there are two brown and two white ones? There's nothing for it; I must talk to Karen about Jules.

"So I guess you've seen it. I'm sorry, Anna." Karen is crouching by the chicken pen with a pair of pliers. Sheltering criminals seems to have become second nature to me, because for a weird moment I think she is talking about the bobcat that got the chicken, and my impulse is to deny all knowledge of it.

"Well, have you spoken to her about it?" I ask.

"Lorna? No, I haven't seen her for weeks. But I know that she is terrible tore up about it all. She does have very strong feelings about… well, everything, really, but especially moral issues."

"Lorna? What are you talking about?" Never mind Jules rolling cigarettes on my porch.

Karen stands up and pushes her hands into her back as if it hurt her. Like this, standing straight and pushing her belly out, her pregnancy is beginning to show.

"The report in the newspapers?" Now she is as confused as I am. "I'm surprised the university managed to keep it quiet for so long; a professor accused of raping a student, and what's more, the stepdaughter of an important man in the city—that's a big story."

"Was it in the papers? No, I didn't know that! In the *Shaftsboro Times*?"

"Yes, Saturday. Everyone talked about it at church on Sunday—well, you can imagine." She pulls a face. "People around here are very happy to suspect the Folly of all sorts of moral misconduct and liberal laxity. Oh, that sounded poetic, didn't it? Liberal laxity. Anyway, I thought you meant Lorna. What *did* you mean?"

I can't bring myself to mention the grimy towel and the brown eggs, but the evidence of loiterers on my porch is no paranoid fantasy, nor was the condom dangling from the tree in my backyard like tinsel from a Christmas tree.

"I'm just putting that out there, Karen. No interference; none of my business. But Logan Williams is not the best company a fifteen-year-old malcontent could keep. I wouldn't trust him, to be honest."

But to my surprise, Karen brushes away my concern and vaguely promises to have a word with Jules about not sitting on my porch when I am away.

"*If* she really does that. Why would she, really? She has her friends in the pickers' camp, and they sit in their vans, or round the fire. She is allowed to walk past the cabin, you know." Karen pushes her little finger between the jaws of the pliers and pinches it.

"Of course she is. But what I have observed is much more than *walking past*. She seems to regard the cottage as part of the farm, while I regard it as my home. I would like to be able to decide who I invite into my home, and when—even if it's just the porch or the garden. I'm sorry, Karen, but her disregard of the fact that the cottage is my private space is not acceptable."

"Yes, well, I'll, um…I'll mention it to her, and I thank you for your understanding."

Maybe Karen's hormones are messing her up. Or maybe I am overreacting.

"It was in the *Washington Post*!" Tim splutters into the phone when I ring him later. "That woman has totally blown the whistle on us all! Where were *you* the past few days?"

"Busy. That woman. Lorna O'Neal? Do you mean to say that *Lorna O'Neal* spoke to journalists from the *Post*?"

"Our very own Deepthroat! 'According to anonymous sources,' the article said. Anonymous, not so much. Unauthorized, you betcha."

"No, wait—then how do they know it was Lorna?"

"We were all summoned to appear before the Prez and the Prov, individually, you understand, and she admitted it! Felt she couldn't, in all conscience, stand by while the university was doing its damnedest—my word, not hers—to sweep Hornberger's misconduct under the rug. Of course they *are*, and it *is* sickening. Do you know that they approached Nancy, Terry, Martha, and Warren for character assessments?"

"Of Natalie, or—"

"Of Nick! No, Natalie they want to have psychologically assessed. Martha came to my office the other day and told me that the Assistant Dean of Studies had phoned her at home and suggested that she volunteer to give Nick a character reference. He assured her that the whole thing would be handled most discreetly, anonymously, of course, and she would not regret having cooperated with the college in this delicate matter."

"And she felt she couldn't refuse."

"Right. Except he then read them out. Aloud. With the authors' names and everything. Martha thinks Hornberger is a mediocre scholar who has buttressed his position at the department by his extramural connections and his bullying techniques. How can she be stupid enough to be honest! After a phone call! If this doesn't scream, *You're being fucked here, baby, and there'll be no paper trail for you to prove it*, then what does?"

"Oh, man…"

"The other three followed their cues and produced wonderfully creative pieces of fiction. So with these glowing character references in the balance—"

"Tim, if…just supposing there was a similar case from way back, years ago. Would that make a difference to the way the hearing is going?"

"Do you mean the incident back in seventy-six? How do *you* know about that?"

Careful now.

"There was a woman from Hornberger's year at the Homecoming reception. She told us. How do *you* know?"

If *Greco vs. Hornberger* is all over the papers now, Mary-Lou Tandy may hear of it and come forward to testify. If she wants to go back to that traumatic time, if it is her own decision to get involved, I will make Giles throw the file into the ring. He cannot go on protecting Hornberger.

"Natalie said. She's full of lewd and lurid stories about Hornberger's past, including this one, but she can't prove any of them. Mark my words, Hornberger will end up looking like the innocent victim of a smear campaign!"

"I feel sick."

"*You* feel sick! What do you think *I* feel! I already had my fingertips on terra firma, Tenurica, the Land of Safety, when I was pulled back into the maelstrom of university politics by an over-excited snowflake and an aging, over-sexed macho! We don't know what our cue is, from one meeting to the next! Bernie says we should simply carve our signatures into potato halves and tell them to do whatever they liked with them."

"I'm seeing Bernie the Sunday after next at their house-warming party. I suppose I know nothing of this, right?"

"*Nothing* is already too much. Don't throw me under the bus now, okay? My tenure committee sits in two weeks' time. I want that to go as smoothly as a lubed cock into — "

"Eeek! Yes, you've made your point, Blundell! I won't say a dicky bird."

On Tuesday morning I finally get a reply to my emailed apology to Vicky Benedetto and Pete Kirkpatrick, the organizers of the Notre Dame conference. Pete, who sends the reply, does not bother to pretend that they were not offended by my sneaking out of the conference like that. Nonetheless, they are offering to include me among the selected papers that they plan to publish as a collection of essays. I see this as a confirmation of my paper's quality, but I also see how close I came to compromising myself professionally. It is like a near miss in the car—you're grateful worse was prevented and resolve to keep your eyes very firmly on the road in future.

The light-blue lambswool sweater is a trusty friend, but I have not yet had the courage to wear my short tweed skirt, and at the beginning of the semester I would not even have considered combining it with what I consider to be among my coolest articles of clothing: a pair of brown nappa, knee-high, lace-up boots. My classes go like a dream. The remaining twenty-one students in the Comedy class eat out of the hollow of my hand, and Logan Williams—on time, for a change—sits in the last row and gazes at me with a mixture of resentment and fascination. Well, baby, I know that half of you—the lower half—wants to see me flat on my back across one of the classroom tables. But life's a bitch and then you don't fuck your professor.

Mental note: You *do not* fuck your professor.

On Wednesday afternoon Yvonne knocks on my office door.

"Anna. I need to tell you something. Do you have a minute?"

"Sure, come in."

She closes the door behind herself very carefully and walks over to close the window. "I am violating someone's confidence by telling you this, so please promise me that you won't do the same? I know that sounds idiotic, but I simply have to talk to someone about it!"

"Is this about Hornbergergate? Actually, Tim calls it 'Hornygate,' but you know Tim."

"When is his tenure review?" Yvonne frowns. "It's not for me to say, but isn't he very careless with the things he says in public?"

"Look, the boy's under a lot of pressure in that damned hearing panel—cut him some slack. Anyway—"

"Yes, anyway." She inhales deeply and holds her breath for a moment. "There's this woman in the church I joined last year. She's divorced, too, lives with her younger daughter not far from me; the daughter sometimes sits with Teddy and Ally in the evenings. Last Sunday—and remember the story about Hornberger was in the *Shaftsboro Times* on Saturday!—we had a clothes bazaar, and she and I happened to have kitchen duty at the same time. I saw at once that something was bothering her, and eventually I asked, and she—God, I find this so upsetting! She told me that she knew someone who was a student at Ardrossan in the seventies and that this woman was raped by Hornberger!"

"A ghost from the past! You wonder how many there are. Will this woman come forward?"

"No, no, you haven't heard it all." Yvonne catches my hands in hers. "Anna, I do believe she was talking about herself! I know her as Louise Randall—Louise may easily have been Mary-Lou as a girl! I know that her mother was white, and she is clearly an intelligent, educated woman, and she told me once that her first husband was the manager of the store where she worked. That all fits, doesn't it?"

The skin on my arms puckers with goose bumps.

"Could it be a coincidence?"

"Yeah, because there were hundreds of women of color at private universities in the mid-seventies!"

"You're right," I agree. "*Not* a coincidence. Dear God—what now?"

"I was hoping you'd help me figure that out."

"How did she seem to feel about the whole thing? The fact that she told you seems to indicate that she needed to talk about it, even if it was under cover of that old chestnut, 'I have this friend who—'"

"I could repeat Elaine Shaw's account to her and see how she reacts."

"Hmm. What kind of a woman is she? Does she have friends to talk this over with? She may not, you know. She may have left Ardrossan and closed that chapter in her life. If she has come to terms with what happened and doesn't want to go probing old wounds in public, I could understand that. It would be her word against his, and who needs all that dirt flung around?"

I feel a pang of guilt for not telling Yvonne about the file. I ought to tell her, and Giles ought to hand over the file to the police.

I do not tell her.

Then the inevitable happens. I am having a coffee with Tim in the Eatery, going over the members of his tenure committee and his likely external reviewers, when Giles turns up at our table.

"Did you get the email?" Yes, definitely still furious with me, and definitely still the most beautiful man I have ever seen. So much for the theory that one night with the ogre would break the spell.

"What email?"

"Semester review. Yours, not mine. Elizabeth wants to see both of us on Friday."

"Oh, my giddy aunt…"

"No, don't worry." Tim waves away my concern as if it was a fruit fly. "That's all part of the care the college lavishes on its rookies."

"I don't think so. I had seven drops and withdrawals from the Comedy class, and this week I got three emails whining for my permission to withdraw late. What's the policy of late withdrawal?"

"You mean the official one or the actual one we practice?" Tim asks, rolling his eyes.

"I can't save your tush every day of the week!" Giles has not sat down.

"You leave my tush out of it!"

His eyes narrow, and my heart beats faster because we both remember. The skin of his stomach sliding along the skin of my buttocks; me arching my back to offer him access to the hidden parts of my body and my soul. Two pillows under my belly to tilt me at the angle he wants me, his hard shaft sliding playfully, a little menacingly, down the cleft between my ass cheeks till it finds its slippery way home. His hand burrowing down till his fingers find me.

I guess now I know why you are not supposed to have sex with people you work with.

"You told me to pamper them. Giles told me to be a bitch. Why do I listen to you at all?" I pretend to be more upset than I am, to justify my tomato-colored face.

"Why do you listen to *him?*" Tim corrects me. "My advice was good! However you conduct your classes later on, in your first year you have to be uber-submissive!"

"We didn't hire her to be submissive!" Giles fires up. He has flushed, too, with anger or with arousal, perhaps both.

"Of course she has to be submissive! If she values her skin? Yes, she does, and then some!"

Chapter 29

Since it seems inevitable that I will be shot down, my only consolation is that it is Ma Mayfield rather than Matthew Dancey who is wielding the gun. Giles and I are waiting in front of the Dean of Studies' office, and it's a toss-up whether I am more afraid of Giles or of Ma Mayfield.

"Giles, I'm sorry. Could we not—"

"Don't worry about me," he cuts in, his face like a stone. "I can be professional about this. You do the talking. Ignore me. After all…" He shrugs sardonically.

"Look, I'm truly sorry, but don't you—"

But we are called in, and he doesn't want to hear anyway.

"Now, Anna, I regret that your first semester at Ardossan has been somewhat fraught with…difficulties." Elizabeth seems calm and collected, as usual. "So I would not lay too much stress on this, but I have received written complaints from six students in your general education class." Elizabeth fans out half a dozen email print-outs on her desk, and I can see that none consists of fewer than two paragraphs of text. "Four of them suggest that your behavior in class could be regarded as sexual harassment."

At this, my jaw drops. Literally. I lose control over my facial muscles and my mouth falls open.

"Now, look here, Elizabeth." Three minutes into the meeting, Giles is already riding to the rescue. "You know perfectly well that these accusations are preposterous! I don't know why these students have it in for Anna, but it's not because she acknowledges the sexually charged language of Elizabethan sonnets!"

Elizabeth puts on her glasses and picks up one of the emails.

"'She intimidated me and others with expression like, "Baby, you make my pips squeak!" and "Get outta here!" (said with a broad New York accent that gave it a Mafia quality). When she wanted to interrupt students who were conferring with each other about points made in class, she would signal this by "slicing her throat" with her flat hand.' Here is another one. 'Professor Lieberman chose to focus on the sexual content of the plays under discussion. Her jokes often had a sexual coloring, too. This created an uncomfortable learning atmosphere for those of us who do not come from families that talk about such things at the dinner table.' One more? 'Professor Lieberman is obsessed with sex. Not a single class session went by without mentioning sex or things related to sex. She made me dread coming to classes.'"

Giles cuts in acidly. "These class sessions have filthy minds, mentioning sex all the time instead of studying grammar and syntax."

"Mockery of grammar is no rebuttal of content, Giles. Anna?"

"I—I don't know what to say." And that is about all there is to it. But it is expected of me that I go on. "I am truly sorry. But I would ask you to take the whole class's end-of-term evaluations into account before you declare me guilty of…sexual harassment."

"Or an obsession with sex," Giles adds. *Bastard!*

"Nick Hornberger has made sure that no one seems to be talking about anything but sexual harassment these days," Elizabeth says caustically. "Unfortunately there are other issues. Anna, I understand you failed students for handing in their work late?"

"Not…as such. It says in the syllabus that I will take off a certain number of points for tardiness—just as I do for mild instances of plagiarism. We are talking about Madeline Harrison, aren't we?"

"Amongst others." Elizabeth nods. "Carolyn Turner complains that you advised her strongly against going for Honors in her English Lit Major."

"Carolyn Turner is just about now realizing that off-the-cuff recall may have got her through high school, but it won't get her through college, at least not this one. I predict that she won't last out her third year. And with her grades, she shouldn't even go for a Major in English Lit, let alone an Honors Major."

Ma Mayfield leafs through the girls' files.

"They both seem to maintain their Bs; Madeline less solidly than Carolyn, but nonetheless. They aren't exactly failing, Anna."

"If students' grades even out as Bs," Giles says, once more throwing himself into the fray, "it just goes to show, first of all, that everyone knows who the generous graders are, and secondly that we have a grade inflation going on. And a solid B is no recommendation for an Honors Major! In two years' time she'll be trying to get into grad school!"

"*Ceterum censeo...*"

"Yes, I know I keep harping on it, but I wouldn't, if I saw a spark of acknowledgement in your eyes, Elizabeth!"

Giles is sitting on the edge of his seat, one hand flat on the surface of Elizabeth's desk, and he is using it to underline his points in a manner very different from the laid-back professor lolling in his office chair. It makes me uncomfortable that he is once again fighting my battle for me, but it seems to have been his war before it ever became my battle.

"I'm not disagreeing with you," Elizabeth says placidly. "All I'm saying is you cannot fight the system."

"I'm not interested in the system. I'm interested in maintaining a bit of common sense, that's all."

"*Your* common sense."

"Oh, please! How does it involve my class, race, or gender if I point out that allowing our students to tyrannize over us with their willful, rancorous evaluations will lead to the decay of our academic standards?"

"It doesn't. But it involves our budget." Elizabeth isn't cowed by Giles's intensity at all. My feeling that this is an old struggle between the two of them is confirmed when he throws himself back in his chair.

"Of course," he says sarcastically with a nod. "Frank Harrison is a wealthy alumnus who gave generously to the university when his son studied here a few years ago, as had his father before him and his father before him."

"Precisely."

Giles knuckles his eyes in defeat and runs his fingers through his hair, like a cat worsted in an encounter with the neighbor's dog.

"Apologize, Anna. Apologize and change Madeline Harrison's grade. Behave like the submissive young professor they expect you to be. A few words and ten seconds of paperwork may earn us thousands of dollars."

"I wouldn't want any of my actions to harm the department," I say cautiously. "And—"

"And you'd be a fool to harm yourself." His eyes glance past mine as he says this, and the sentence reverberates between us. "You can't afford to refuse this…request by your Dean."

"No, I can't." I look at Elizabeth to signal my acquiescence with the powers that be, and she shrugs, not unsympathetically.

"No, you can't."

"Right. Well, ladies, I'll leave you to it." Giles gets up, still angry, but he replaces the chair he had taken from the large table in Elizabeth's office, and he does so quietly, and quietly he shuts the door behind himself.

Elizabeth unfolds her hands and makes a few pencil notes in the student files.

"I value Giles greatly," she says finally, and I can tell that she, too, is upset; otherwise she would not speak to me about a tenured colleague. "But this puritan streak of his is a nuisance! Well. I'm sorry, Anna, that you had to bump up against the realities of private education so early in your term here. But don't worry, I have to make a note of it, of course, but nobody will care about it when you're up for your three-year review."

"Unless it happens more often." I feel defeated rather than obstinate.

"Well, I see no reason to start a debate about principles at this point, Anna. I share Giles's view that a teacher who is popular with everyone must be doing something wrong." She relaxes her manner a little. "How was Notre Dame?"

Oh, my God.

"Fine, thank you."

She smiles at my hollow tone. "Don't look so dismayed. Richard Prewitt is an old friend of mine. He wrote to me especially to congratulate me on our choice of junior faculty, and I can assure you his praise is not easily earned."

I recall the elderly professor who was extremely complimentary about my paper, both in the discussion and over coffee afterward.

"Oh! Yes, he was very kind."

"So, keep up the good work, Anna, but try to pull the New York brusqueness a little. Will you do that?"

"Yes, ma'am."

Friday afternoon, reading week. The place is deserted. I need to regroup. Get my act together. Think. *Sexual harassment.* Will I ever live that down?

This might still work out. A slap on the wrist, yes, but in the balance also a commendation by a valued friend of the Dean of Studies. It seems all is not lost yet.

I have not been upstairs in the dome since I took Irene there on Family Weekend. Why I have the strong urge to go now, I am not sure. Maybe because I feel unfairly treated and so, to even the scales, I will do something forbidden. I will use my secret key. The box of tissues has long gone; maybe Selena and her seducer have found a new *locus amoris.*

This is not a space in which one would ever want to switch on artificial light. Candles, perhaps, but electric light would hurt the eyes. I walk across to the long, partitioned windows and ease one of the crank handles out of its holder. Amazingly, it turns, and inch by groaning inch one of the roof segments lifts and slides above its neighbor, revealing a slice of gray December sky. The wind blows surprisingly hard into the room, and the dome starts singing; the door slips off the latch and creaks.

I understand why Selena and her young man sometimes stay the night up here. It must be wonderful to hide out among the stars. It is overcast today, but on a clear day, or during a clear night, this must be a wonderful place to make love. Cautiously I climb the wooden steps to the biggest telescope that is mounted on a high oak table. I peek through it, but the lens is so grimy I can't see a thing. My back will probably be covered in dust, but I stretch out on the table top, next to the thick round pedestal of the telescope. If the stars were out, I could see them all. Dizzy. Frightening, as if the firmament would fall and bury me. Me, tiny, tiny me; a speck, and yet, with the man inside me, his rod of life glowing, igniting me, we would be the center of the turning world.

I understand Selena.

Selene.

Σελήνη

Goddess of the moon.

The whole moon turned blood red, and the stars in the sky fell to earth, as figs drop from a fig tree when shaken by a strong wind.

"What are you doing?"

I shriek and snap upright like a switchblade.

But it's no rapist on the rampage. It's worse.

"Nothing," I say, in the same rough tone of voice. He pushes the door firmly into its frame. The noise seems deafening, as do his footsteps on the floor, because there is no other sound, except the singing of the wind in the hemisphere of the dome. And my hammering heart.

"Giles, it was Selena who did the graffiti! That must mean she's—"

"Not interested." He comes very close, till his flanks touch my knees where I'm sitting on the table top.

Incredibly, his fingers fasten on the top button of my blouse and undo it. There is no hesitation in his movement, although his male fingers are a little clumsy with the tiny plastic discs. Awkward, but not at all rough. Or hurried. I'm watching, going to pieces while I'm watching, as he undoes button after button, methodically and without haste or hesitation.

I stare down at his hands hovering over the open shirtfront, and although he has barely touched me, all the parts of my body capable of swelling are doing so. This is how the seamen on the Titanic must have felt, watching helplessly as bulkhead after bulkhead was inexorably flooded. Flooded, and going down fast.

But it's no iceberg bringing me down. A slight tremor in his fingers betrays him, and it may be a sudden flagging of courage or a calculated move to pluck at the sinews of my restraint, but instead of sliding beneath the cotton fabric to touch bare skin, his hands slowly cup my breasts still hidden inside the blouse and bra. Miraculously, I manage to stay silent as a bolt of lust sizzles along the nerve strands connecting my breasts and my womb, only my breathing becomes faster as I watch his hands, slow and warm and firm, and my whole body relaxes against them.

I hear him sigh, his mouth very close to my ear. He seems to have been waiting for my body's response, because now he parts the front halves of my blouse, pushes them apart with his fingertips almost negligently, and the tickling sensation is a delicious promise against my skin. I want to close my eyes and drift off in this wonderful erotic memory that I'm having, this memory of having sex with Giles Cleveland, but at the same time I'm mesmerized by the sight of his fingers gently squeezing my flesh. Up on my perch I am a little taller even than he; our foreheads are close enough to touch as we are looking down at his hands on my breasts, as if we were both spectators at an event that is happening without our volition.

Still I haven't reached out for him. I need my hands to steady myself on my less than secure seat, and when he hooks his thumbs under the flimsy fabric and pushes it over my shoulders, gathers it behind my back in one large fist, my elbows are pinned to my side not only by my blouse but also by my astonishment. For a moment he holds me like this, a pinioned bundle of assistant professorship, my breasts pushed against his chest, which is of course securely encased in cotton and tweed, and I can tell the sight pleases him. He has not looked me in the eye once since he has entered the room.

So infinitely gentle before, then suddenly this force, and I hope and trust that we are only playing, because for a few breathless moments I cannot move a limb. If he is lowering his head to my neck to sink his teeth into my flesh till they draw blood, there is nothing I can do. The atavistic fear of the male flares up in me, instinctive and fierce, then his mouth touches the tender skin below my ear, and the sensation is so intense that I gasp with the shock of it, oblivious to whether it's pain or pleasure he is giving me.

"That's right," he whispers, but I don't know whether he's enjoying my pleasure or my apprehension. With his mouth he explores the sensitive skin that covers the big artery in my throat, stops for a moment above the wildly pulsing area of flesh, and I tremble with sensation, I grope blindly for his hands, his wrists, to steady myself, my fingers inch into the sleeves of his jacket but I can't feel much of his skin, he's protected by his clothes, while every nerve end in my body overloads as my blood pounds against the soft pressure of his lips. Never have I felt so keenly the dangerous, voluptuous pleasure of surrender. I'm baring my throat to him like a bitch to the alpha wolf. And he knows.

"God, woman! You're like an animal in heat!"

I couldn't suppress the long, low moan if my life depended on it, and I arch myself toward his mouth for more. He grips me harder and leaves a trail of heat along my throat, to the top of my breast, the nipples as hard as marbles in anticipation of his mouth.

"Giles, please…"

He nestles his face against the side of mine, into my hair. Very still.

"Say that again."

I shrug my arms out of the blouse sleeves and wrap them around his neck.

"Giles," I whisper against his ear, because I know that he isn't demanding my submission, he's asking for my tenderness. "Giles, please…"

Without further ado he cups my left breast, fastens his hard, tender mouth on the tip and suckles it; his other hand is splayed across my right breast, its tip between its fingers, circling it with its thumb. His bright, silver-streaked head is in my arms, so close to my heart, and I know that I have never in my life been so comprehensively, so painfully aroused as by this man.

With one impatient movement he pulls me against himself, my thighs on either side of him. He is holding me by the waist and his fingers dig into the muscles running along my spine, but if I want more of him, I'll have to get it myself.

"Kiss me," I whisper.

"No."

For the first time since he has come in, he looks at me, and in the dim light of the sky above our heads, he is beautiful. But he is not enjoying this in the same way he enjoyed sleeping with me at Notre Dame. He isn't happy. He was so radiant with pleasure then, so frank and unguarded in his delight that I would open my legs for him and welcome his touch. What I see gleaming at the back of his deep-set eyes now is a tense wariness, coupled with a determination I can't identify.

"It's such a loving thing, isn't it? A kiss. I don't feel particularly loving toward you these days."

"Then let me go!"

"You don't want me to touch you?"

"No!"

To my surprise he appears to accept this. He bows his head in apparent resignation, only to reach behind me and clasp my wrists again, bend my elbows so that my lower arms are parallel with each other and he can pin them together with one hand, none too gently.

"I'll just test that, if I may," he murmurs, his voice hot in my ear. The fingers of his free hand find my breast, thumb pushes hard nipple into soft flesh, again none too gently. Then he bites into the side of my neck.

I shudder and cry out. But no amount of outrage can curb the blatant, voluptuous need that wells up in me like a spring tide. He is biting hard enough to startle me, his mouth slowly descends to my shoulder, leaving tingling seals of his possession, but not hard enough to frighten me. In my struggle to free my hands, I shrug my shoulders and bruise his mouth. He swallows a curse and rears up; we are both panting, both torn between lust and rage. The gray specks in his eyes glitter like polar ice, and I have to fight down an impulse to apologize, to shy away.

Well, fuck that!

A smile creeps into my eyes, I can feel it, and I know it looks like satisfaction.

"Serves you right." My voice is hoarse, but well audible.

He doesn't even reply. His fingers tighten around my wrists and his mouth seizes mine. Our tongues clash; he is kissing me. He said he wouldn't, but he's kissing me and I'm responding blindly, ravenously. His mouth, however angry he is with me, is a wonderfully sensuous mouth, demanding yet tender when he kisses me, surprisingly malicious when it returns to my shoulder. He has released my wrists, and after shrugging out of my bra, I sling my aching arms around his neck, leaving space enough between our bodies only for his hands on my breasts, and with them he is as rough as I need him to be now. He pulls me close; the wool of his jacket is rough against my hyper-sensitive skin, his stomach hard against my writhing crotch, and I try to stifle my moans in the warm, fragrant nook of his throat, in his hair, my burning face against his.

"Say that you want me!"

His voice rattles in my ear, and I can only whimper in response; my bones and my flesh are melting down into a heaving mass of sensation, melting against his fully dressed body, when I'm so naked.

I know what he wants. He wants me to bare my soul to him. He wants to see me naked and defenseless, while he is safe in his tweed armor. I lean away from him so that I can reach down between us. The fabric of his jeans is stretched so tight by his erection I have difficulties even opening the top button, but feeling it, just feeling it through his pants, makes me nosedive for disaster.

I jump down from the table to pull down my underwear, but my boots take forever to unlace. Giles laughs and curses with frustration as he watches, then — "Oh, damn it all!" — he lifts me up onto the table top, crouches down and pushes himself up between my legs, as if he were the thread and my legs, held together by the pantyhose, were the eyelet.

"Very sexy, these boots, but not very—" he brushes against me, misses me "— not very practical!"

We laugh, and then we moan, because there is nothing under the sun and the moon like this fusion and this friction. No wonder the Ancients thought that the universe was made by gods and goddesses fucking.

Held fast between my legs, he doesn't have a lot of room to maneuver, so he plunges deep into me, moves with deep, short thrusts, pulling me hard against his stomach.

"Look at me." His voice is like the low rumble of thunder at the end of a scorching summer day.

I peel my cheek from the damp tweed of his shoulder and try to focus on his eyes. They are flickering, like those of a man determined to maintain consciousness under the influence of an overpowering drug. Even now, with my arms and legs clutching him to my body, my pubic bone grinding into his stomach, and his cock wreaking havoc inside me, the sight of his face gives me a jolt. He's so beautiful, I want to die for him, and I'm going to die, here, right here on his cock, if he keeps on doing what he is doing.

He stops.

"Look at me!"

"I c-can't!"

I can hardly breathe, let alone speak, and as for looking at him while he is doing this to me — he must be joking. I try to ride him, to tear my pleasure from him on my own terms, but he holds me fast by the waist, neither pressing me down nor lifting me off, he just holds me still, and I want to howl with frustration.

"Anna."

It crunches my heart into a tight, frightened ball, he says the word so quietly, so tenderly.

"Please," I whine. "Just fuck me! Just fuck me, please…"

"Anna. I want you to look at me."

I do, like a girl awaiting a particularly insidious kind of punishment.

"I will fuck you. I am fucking you. But I want you to look at me while I'm doing it."

And he rocks against me, slowly, so deeply, and when I whimper, he leans forward and kisses me as slowly, as deeply and as thoroughly as he is fucking me. It's not enough for him to make me drown in my desire for him, the sheer, voluptuous pleasure of feeling him with every square inch of my body, inside as well as outside. He wants to make me drown in *him*.

"Come for me, Anna."

I'm close, so close, my feet are halfway over the ledge of the cliff, but I'm afraid to jump, frightened of the fall, frightened that he won't catch me.

I feel him hunch his shoulders, then he pushes his hand down the front of our bodies, the large palm of his hand lies flat against my hot, sweaty stomach, then his fingers reach my clitoris and press it, just press against it, his mouth is on my breast, and he sucks me into an orgasm as keen and hard-edged as a swig of whisky straight from the bottle—sharp, almost painful. My cry of release echoes in the firmament like a cry of pain, and I claw at his shoulders, at his back, to pull him still deeper into me. The still center of the turning world.

I clench my pelvic muscles around him, deliberately now, and we both catch our breaths.

"You're still h-hard!" I gasp, and if I weren't still so far gone, this statement of the obvious would make me laugh.

He leans back a little, in the circles of my arms and legs, to see my face. The angry light at the back of his eyes has gone, but he is still fierce with unspent sexual energy.

"Say that you want me!"

I pull myself against him and tilt my hips up against his stomach so that the tip of his cock slides firmly along the sheath of muscle that holds it.

"I want you," I whisper into his ear as if it were a secret.

He grabs my butt and lifts me off the tabletop—a welcome move, because the hardwood edge is beginning to bruise my flesh—and turns to look for a surface more conducive to physical pleasure. I look for the sofa and scream.

"*What?*" Giles cries, alarmed at my shocked reaction.

The dome is dusky now, and full of shades and half-light, but it is light enough to see that there is someone sitting on the sofa. A bulky figure, his legs crossed, watching.

Nick Hornberger is watching us as we stagger and yelp in our entanglement of limbs and clothes, a beast with two backs. Giles stumbles against the pedestal of one of the smaller telescopes, and in our career across the room he slips out of me. He can't free himself of me, caught as he is between my legs, and I guess I understand why Hornberger is laughing out loud. That doesn't make me less protective of my man, though.

"Listen, asshole!" I steady myself against Giles's body as he leans against one of the bookshelves, heaving. "You have been extremely voluble about your right to fuck who you want whenever you want and where you want! So why don't you grant the same privilege to other people, and fuck off out of here!"

"My word, this one has spunk!" Hornberger pretends to be impressed. "A feisty little bitch, but I see she's more game than that frigid wife of yours, Cleveland."

I look at Giles, and now I am really scared. His face is a sneer of humiliation, and I truly think that if he had his arms and legs free, he would fling himself on Hornberger and start a brawl. But we are not in a saloon in Ardrossan Gulch, and Giles has his arms full of naked woman. How am I going to restore the dignity of a man with his pants around his knees and pantyhose around his back?

"Giles?" I don't think he can hear me. He is heaving with emotion, and his seething panic makes me panic, too. If I let go of him now, he will fall into an abyss of shame and self-loathing, screaming, his arms and legs flapping ineffectually. With my arms and legs I draw him harder against me.

"Giles!"

He inhales, and his face relaxes. He even looks at me.

"He isn't important," I say with as much conviction as I can. "*I am.*"

He gazes into my eyes, and I see his pupils flicker, perhaps in recognition; he blinks. Slowly his eyes narrow in a smile, and he pulls me closer so as to cover my nakedness from view.

"You heard what the lady said, Hornberger. Fuck off, do."

Hornberger rises from the sofa, and I feel another lurch of fear. We *are* very naked, Giles and I.

"Do you think I will? Just like that? I hear things aren't going so well for you, Anna. I heard about the stench bomb on Family Weekend. And your students drop out like flies because your class discussions are too prurient? What will the Provost think when he hears about your trysts with a tenured colleague on college premises?"

"All right." Giles grabs me and walks back to the big table. "Hold on!" He ducks and slips out from between my legs, pulls up his pants and takes off his jacket. "Cover up."

I draw my knees up to my chest and huddle under the warm tweed without pushing my arms into the sleeves.

"Now. You will not drag Anna's name through the mud, nor mine. And I'll tell you why. It all hangs on a slim file that I have in my possession, and have had, for weeks."

"*You* have it!" Hornberger's shoulders stiffen, then he deflates like a brawny balloon. "How did you get it off him? And—when?"

"Found it in Anna's office when we cleared out Corvin's hoard. Call it chance. Call it fate. That was in the first week of the semester, actually, so you could have saved yourself the bother of prowling around in people's offices and just molested a few more of our students in the meantime."

Hornberger is making a good show of keeping his countenance, but he is completely bowled over. "Can we talk about this? Perhaps we can—"

"Oh, shut up, Nick!"

"What will you do with it? Hand it over to the papers so they can run another article about me?"

"You *are* paying rather dearly for free sex with young women." Giles hesitates. "Was it worth it?"

"Depends on the finale of this little farce," Hornberger jeers, showing his teeth. "Fucking a woman like you just fucked that one makes you feel like a god, doesn't it? That's got to be worth some risk."

Giles gazes at him.

"Yeah," he says after a long pause.

Hornberger returns to the subject closer to his heart than student totty. "What are you going to do with the file?"

"If you refrain from bandying a lady's name about the place, I will make sure it does not reach the hands of university admin, nor of the police. I would ask you for your word, if I thought it was worth anything."

Hornberger shifts his weight to one foot and seems to consider the deal offered to him. I am considering it, too.

Chapter 30

The moment Hornberger pulls the door shut behind him, I realize that Giles and I are no longer on the same side.

"You better get dressed," he says and throws me my bra and my blouse, turning his back to gaze out the dark window while I wriggle back into my crumpled clothes. I am so cold now, with shock and with the December air howling in through the roof, that my fingers are numb and useless.

And where do we go from here?

I don't even know where "here" is. The moment Giles traded in the truth about Hornberger's past for the preservation of my good name? The moment Giles managed to rise above his humiliation at the hands of another man to stay true to his woman? The moment he began to thrust into me again, after holding off so bravely for my pleasure? The moment he came into the observatory and, without so much as a by-your-leave, started to undress me? The moment I realized that Selena is our mysterious graffiti artist and vandal? The moment Ma Mayfield told me that my students have accused me of sexual harassment?

Where do I pick up the thread?

"Don't worry," Giles says. "He won't tell the Provost."

"No, I-I know. I'm not worried." I hand him back his jacket, and he casts me a glance full of ironic disbelief.

There is so much to talk about. I just want to be quiet.

Giles has himself perfectly in hand. Polite, suave. Avoids eye contact. As if he has lost interest in me already.

"I'm not going to apologize, if that's what you think."

"What about?" I stare at him, stupidly. My crotch is wet and cold. It's a good thing I came by car this morning.

He gives one of his sarcastic spurts of laughter.

"I swore to myself that I wouldn't touch you again, since you are obviously, upon reflection, not interested. And I know that you are wise to keep away from me. But the moment I catch you alone, unaware, I pounce on you, like a—" He breaks off in complete disgust. "Like a Hornberger!"

"Giles, please—" I reach for his hand, but he is too upset to be touched. "Don't shout at me! You've turned me inside out. I can't cover up so fast…not enough to fight."

"That! That's exactly the problem!" he explodes, and I flinch. "I *want* to turn you inside out! It's the most exciting thing I have done in my entire life! There—pathetic, isn't it? Whenever I touch you, you come all over me, and you're not even faking it, are you? Or have you been faking?"

He frowns at me as if this was a thought to horrible to contemplate. I shake my head.

"I understand scruples," he goes on, a little calmer. "I have them myself, and to spare! This thing, whatever it is, frightens the hell out of me! But I'm English, so I'm the hypocrite!"

"Giles—I didn't say that."

"I waited for your call all week, after that night at Notre Dame! I'm such a goddamn idiot!"

"I wanted to call you, I almost did! But—"

"You got cold feet. I gathered that."

"No! Well, yes, that too, but it's also a question of—well, of priorities! I can't just—just because we—this is all new to me!" Another ironic snort, and I blush but persevere. "No, I mean being here, the place, the work, and it's hard, well, you know that. But I love what I do, and I want…I have to make it work! So how can I start fucking a professor in my department? You *heard* what Hornberger said, and I'm sorry, but he's right! 'New hire accused of sexual harassment and caught having sex with a colleague on campus!' I'd be finished! You *said* I must have a clean slate or I won't get tenure!"

Saying the words confronts me with the enormity of my actions, and my voice becomes shrill with panic.

"Is it the danger that does it for you?" he suddenly wonders. "Do you get off on the risk that someone might walk in and catch us at it? Never time for tenderness. When we have time, a whole night, you hold me off and run away, but when I jump you, you hurl yourself toward me as if your life depended on it. I can't figure you out, Anna. Not at all."

"There's nothing to figure out! *I do not want this!*" I'm scared, and so I shout. I'm scared I'll be fired. I'm scared Giles is right about me. I am scared of tenderness.

"Right. Well, I'll remember that from now on."

And then he storms out. His footsteps echo down the stairs and then the corridor; he's walking fast, almost running.

A passionate man, this Englishman. What a lovely, wonderful, unbelievably sexy, passionate man he is, this man I've just rejected. Again. Sensitive, too. Touchy.

When I finally get home, I am shivering with cold and nerves so badly that I can hardly fit the key into the lock of the cottage door. The living room is strewn with the evidence of my preparation for the day, including shoe polish and brush. Would he have pounced on me if I had been wearing slacks and loafers, instead of a skirt and Mountie boots? A moot point, now. He did pounce, and I hurled myself at him as if my life depended on it.

Maybe it does.

I've never heard that love-sickness can be cured by hot water bottles, but I definitely need one. And a drink. While the water is heating up I rifle my extremely modest liquor cabinet, which offers me a choice of Bordeaux and a complimentary box of mini-bottles of liqueur that was left by the previous tenants: cherry, apricot, peach, and plum. I opt for the red wine and drink it straight from the bottle in large gulps. I thought the bottle was almost full; I opened it the other day to take a few spoonfuls to cook with. Maybe I have started tippling in my sleep, because now it is little more than half full. That'll do me, though.

Ten minutes later I am sitting in my bed, under the covers — still in my tweed skirt and blouse, though I have discarded the damp panties and the boots — with a bottle of hot water in my lap and a bottle of Bordeaux in my hand. The shivering appears to ease up a little. But the longing doesn't. I know in a corner of my head somewhere that what I said to Giles was just and reasonable. Heartrendingly painful, but reasonable and necessary. But my head stops at my throat, which is tight with tears, and below that there is only heartache and desire.

I fall asleep. It feels like three minutes, but it is really three hours; my watch on the nightstand says it is ten o'clock. The shivering has almost stopped, but I feel very peculiar. Woozy, yes, after half a bottle of red wine and some apricot cordial, and little nauseous, but that isn't it. When I get up to go to the bathroom, I feel very woozy, and when I pull on my pajama pants, my skin feels very odd. I run my hands along my naked stomach, and it clicks. My skin is burning because I have a fever.

I used to get fevers regularly when I was a kid. Whenever something was too exciting or upsetting, I was sure to start shaking and my temperature would climb very fast. "She's too thin-skinned," my father would tell my mother.

The weekend passes in a daze of memories, dreams, and nightmares. I still feel Giles's hands and mouth on my body so vividly that I wake up several times thinking he is in bed with me, and the illusion is always a sweet one. But I also dream of Logan Williams bringing a box of condoms to class and laying them out on the table in front of him. When I ask him what he thinks he is doing, he says Professor Hornberger told him to bring these, and was I crazy, fucking a strange man without using any protection? Then there's a faculty meeting. Elizabeth Mayfield takes my hand and leads me over to a small side table, and I realize that with her other hand she is pulling Nick Hornberger. He and I have to sit apart from the others, and at some point he reaches over, takes my arm and gives me a Chinese burn.

I drift into and out of sleep, drink gallons of water and all my fruit juice, and pretend that I'm not there. Once, the telephone rings. I rear up from a deep and druggy sleep, but by the time I've made it out of bed and picked up the receiver, all I hear is the bleeping noise of someone's impatience.

"Mom, it's me. Listen, did you just try to call me?"

"No, I didn't. Dad and I are about to leave the house. Mary and Phil have invited us to the movies, although your father would prefer to stay at home in front of the television, as usual."

In the background I hear my father protest that he loves going to the movies, but not with Mary and Phil, and not in the afternoon.

"Okay, you go and have fun. Oh, Mom—when I was a kid and I used to get those fevers, how long did they usually last?"

"Your fevers? Heavens, child, how should I remember that?"

"What about her fevers?" My father's voice is closer to the mouth-piece now.

"Here, Sam, you speak to her."

"Hi, Dad, it's only—you know I got those fevers when I was a kid—"

"You have a temperature? How high?"

"Um…I don't know, I was asleep. Last time I checked, around lunchtime, it was one hundred point eight. But yesterday it went up to one-oh-two point four."

"Measured rectally?"

"Yes." I hate these conversations with my father.

"Any other symptoms? Gastric? Respiratory?"

"No, Dad. I'm not ill! I'm pretty sure it's just…stress. I'm run down, that's all. It never went on longer than a couple of days, right?"

"Listen, at the clinic they were saying there's a professor at your school who molests female students? Is that so?"

"Looks that way, yes. It's an epic story. I'll tell you when I come home for the holidays."

Some of it, anyway.

"Keep out of harm's way, kid!"

"I'll see what I can do, Dad. It's…it is hard."

It is only the fever that makes me add this confession, and I wish I hadn't. But then my father floors me.

"Well, you're all alone down there," he says. "You have no one to look after you."

I rush back into sleep. Hide in unconsciousness. I will wait. I will not return to life until this craving for Giles has subsided. I will wait till my body has absorbed this drug, this illicit, damaging desire, and flushed it out of its system. I will wait till I feel nothing.

On Monday morning, a minor breakthrough: I am finally able to take a shower, the first since Giles and I—I close my eyes and lean back so that the beams of hot water massage my breasts.

Turning you inside out is the most exciting thing I have done in my entire life.

Chapter 31

I'm not done hiding. But on Tuesday morning I have to give an exam, so I crawl out of my quilted cave, breakfast on ice-cream, and switch on my PC. Plenty of emails, but none from the sender I hope-and-dread to see. What if it was him, on the phone? And what could he possibly want to say? Whatever it is, I don't want to hear it.

When I arrive on E-4 — weak-kneed and sweaty from the mild exertion of driving here and getting to the elevator — Andrew Corvin's office door is open. Like the door to a cage in the zoo.

Tessa, Martha Borlind, and a couple of grad assistants are hovering in front of my office, conferring in low voices. Now and then one of them advances a step or two so she can peek into the hoarder's den, carrying back information like a bee carries honey to the hive. I hear Corvin's voice before I hear theirs.

"…damned insolence! Fifty years I've worked here…kicked like a dog…I won't have it! I will not have it!"

"Good grief, what's with him?"

"Rage," says Tessa. "I was walking back from the Modern Languages restroom when I saw him trying to get into his office. Is there another lock on the door, or something? Because he couldn't get in, and he was really *crazy*. Not just annoyed. Panicking."

"He grabbed the fire extinguisher off the wall and started banging it against the door," Martha says. "That's when I called security. I don't know what's taking them so long!"

The door handle is now dangling uselessly on some splinters of wood. Corvin seems to be frantically moving around the piles of paper and junk, cussing like a trooper. I take a deep breath, brace myself, and step into the room.

"You! Get out of here!" He glances around, and with the strength and speed of rage, he picks up the fire extinguisher and hurls it at me. I step back out of sight and it crashes against the wall.

"Sir! Calm down! Listen to me!"

"It's all your fault, you—you *interloper!*"

"It is not my fault!" Cautiously I poke my head round the door. "My lock was changed, too, and no one told me about it! They did the same thing to me, Andrew!" This does stop him in his tracks for a second as he tries to process this information. "Think! What did you have that they wanted? The file! Hornberger needed to find the file, so he—he and Dancey, I suppose—had the locks changed so they could search your office. And mine!"

He is breathing hard, swaying, and now I'm worried he really is going to have a stroke.

"Come, sir, you are not well. Will you not sit down?" I hold out my hand as to a wild animal. He doesn't take it, but he doesn't resist as I reach around his elbow and lead him to the only chair in the room.

"Nothing was taken, I promise you that! Hornberger was only looking for the file!"

"I couldn't get in," he tells me, in the astonished voice of an old man. "I couldn't get into my office!"

"I know, sir, and I understand how very upsetting this is for you."

"Dr. Lieberman."

A bearded man I've never seen before appears in the doorway. With an abrupt movement of his head he tells me to come out into the hallway and moves in.

"Campus Security," Martha whispers to me, eyeing the hunky guard standing by. The bearded man coaxes Corvin out of his jacket and takes his pulse, making sure he's okay. All the while he keeps up a chatty, inconsequential conversation with him, in the course of which Corvin says that he has been staying with his daughter in Vermont for two months.

This information, and the fact that Corvin has evidently not tried to get into his office since before Yom Kippur, finally gel in my head. It can't have been Corvin. Hurling the junk in the Dumpster back into my office, probably. Complaining about my heels, possibly. But not the fish. If what he says is true and he was in Vermont for the past eight weeks, someone else must have attacked my door with rotten herring.

"Anna, what did you mean, Dancey and Hornberger had the lock on your door changed?" Martha seems to feel that this accusation is outrageous enough to justify her asking me about it, and it doesn't help that Tessa is also watching me with a mixture of compassion and alarm.

"All the locks on the fourth floor are due to be changed," I say blithely. "Ours were first, that's all."

Martha, perfectly aware of having been fobbed off, disappears back into her office in a huff, but Tessa waits till I have unlocked my office and follows me in.

"Is that the file I found? When we came to straighten up your office?"

"Yes. But Giles won't want you to know about it, so try, if you can, to erase the memory from your mind."

"Is it about Professor Hornberger's —"

"Ssshh! Ssshh." I silence her with my finger in front of my mouth.

Later that afternoon I receive an email from someone whose name I do not recognize, but the address ends in *qmul.ac.uk.* My skin heats up and my heart rate doubles.

What do I want?

"Deb, Queen Mary College has invited me for an interview."

"Oh, well done, Anna! You will come, won't you? I know they can't reimburse you for the full cost of—"

"I bought a ticket in October, as a pledge of good faith."

"God, this is exciting! You're in with a real chance there, Ewan Buchanan said."

"I am? No internal candidates? No political considerations, like having an ethnic minority on the shortlist?"

"Don't be silly. When is it?"

"January eighth."

"Do you want me to come up?"

"No, you needn't. But if I could come and see you for a few days beforehand?"

"We'd love to have you. Always. Any time." There is a short silence between Bristol, England, and Ardrossan, Virginia. "And how are you—otherwise?" she asks discreetly.

"Well, I'll say it like they say in the movies: 'I gotta get outta here!'"

"I'm sorry, Anna. Unrequited love is really the last thing you need during your first year on a new job. Or, at all, really."

Have I not spoken to Debbie since I overheard Giles and Amanda in her office?

"That's not quite the state of, um, affairs any more. Giles and his wife are divorced. He would have an affair with me, if I wanted to, or perhaps it would be more truthful to say that I—" My voice catches in my throat. "Anyway, I'll end it. I will, Debbie."

"On a scale of one to ten, how much do you like him? Anna?"

"Eleven. Twelve. A hundred." My laugh doesn't sound like a laugh at all.

"Then maybe you should risk it. If you love him, you should risk it."

"I won't."

"Anna, what if he is your *beshert?*"

My heart misses a beat, and I have to grab the edge of the desk for support.

"I don't believe in *beshert.*"

Giles Cleveland is not the man cut out for me by Fate to be my partner in life. That is what the Yiddish word *beshert* literally means. Cut out to be someone's soul mate. I just hope that Giles isn't cut out to be my Nemesis.

Chapter 32

My guilty conscience about Selena, dormant while I was grieving over the affair I cannot have with Giles, prods me into action when I come home from work on Tuesday and give way to the O'Neals' Toyota Land Cruiser driving through the gate, followed by Pop and Howie in the truck. I stand holding the gate and just catch sight of a brown and gold furry bundle on the truck bed. A bolt of anguished recognition courses through my body. I stare, and the truck's outline blurs as tears run down my face.

I was so proud of myself for not blubbing over Giles and the mess at college. But my feline acquaintance is a loss that pushes me over the edge.

"I saw they shot the bobcat."

With Karen alone at home, I make my move. She is preparing supper but assures me, as usual, that I am not in her way. She sits me down with a mug of tea and a cookie and goes on peeling potatoes.

"Hmm? Oh, yes! It's been around for a few weeks, and Pop finally got it."

Any further comment, any protest or question, would make me sound so much like a greenhorn from the city that I give it up.

"Do you know that you make me feel very young every time I come here?"

She laughs. "Would you care to explain that, please?"

"Well, you're so…motherly, I feel like a kid coming home from school. A drink, a cookie, and then I'll go up to my room and do my homework."

Her face darkens. "Maybe you'd like to give that daughter of mine a hint about how to appreciate what she's given."

But I'm not here to talk about Jules the Grouch.

"So the O'Neals were here?" Floating my balloon gently in the breeze.

"Yes, the men are on work detail at the church. They're overhauling the yard."

"How is Lorna holding up? There's talk of her losing her job for talking to the press."

"Do you know, I think she's satisfied." Karen rests her potato and knife on the table. "She is *the* most self-righteous woman I have ever met — no competition! And God forgive me, but I envy her. No self-doubts! No second-guessing!"

"How long have you known them?"

"Quite a while. Pop and Howie struck up a friendship at church with Lorna's husband, Bill. The girls are close enough in age to play together, so that's convenient. You can imagine that Lorna isn't really my type, nor Shirley's, but we make an effort. Keeping quiet is all it needs, really." Karen pulls a face at me, embarrassed at speaking ill of someone who evidently considers her a friend.

"And Selena is the eldest?"

"Yes, Selena, Sidney, Stephen, Stacy, and Susanna."

"Karen, will you tell me your honest opinion of Selena without asking me why I want to know?"

Karen looks up without betraying any sign of surprise.

"You mean apart from the fact that she is pregnant?"

All I can do is stare at her. When I try to speak, I produce nothing but an incoherent stutter, and it is not a show of amazement. I am truly stunned.

Karen shrugs. "I'm as sure as I can be, just going through the stages again myself."

"But, Karen, she — "

"And she stole two of my pregnancy tests."

"What?"

"I always kept some in the bathroom cupboard, to be able to check…how I'm doing. Well, one time, in summer, the four girls were playing family and came up to us to ask if 'this' was a thermometer. I was mortified! But Selena knew where I stored them afterward. When I went to get one this time, I noticed that two were missing."

"And it can't have been the twins again?"

"No, because I moved them into the top drawer of the bathroom cupboard. Even I can't reach without a footstool. I don't think I told anyone about it except Lorna and Selena that time, so I'm pretty certain she took them. And look at her! You see her more often than I do, did you not notice anything?"

"Of course I did. I saw things, but I didn't add them up, because I'm a stupid academic who has never been pregnant. Her friend told me she was vomiting a lot, but she—the friend—took it for bulimia!"

"Well…not too far off the mark."

"Bulimia and morning sickness? Hardly the same thing!"

"No, what I mean is that Selena was anorexic when she was a teenager."

"Oh, come on! Nobody can be *that* screwed up!"

"Lorna O'Neal's eldest daughter?" Karen throws me a speaking glance and goes on peeling. "I'm so used to seeing her all skin and bone that I couldn't even say since when she has been looking normal. Not all that long, two years, maybe?"

"In other words, she was ill when she started college?"

"Oh, yes. Lorna never talked about it to me, never even seemed to notice it, but I thought at the time Selena isn't stable enough for college, never mind her good grades. And she wasn't. She missed one semester, I think after her second or third year, to go on a rest cure. Since then she has recovered her weight a little."

"So that's why she looks so pasty. Her behavior at college—I can't really tell you, I'm sorry! But something must be done!"

Karen remains silent, while my mind is whirling.

"I guess I know what you mean," she finally says, "but I can't agree with you there."

"But she can't go on concealing all this! She may do herself a serious injury! In fact—"

"Oh, I thought you meant, terminate the pregnancy."

"Well, no. Selena would never agree to that."

For the first time Karen shows evidence of curiosity. "Do you know who the father is?"

"I'm afraid I do."

On Friday Tim turns up at my office door.

"I need minding," he says, a little reproachfully.

"What? I'm sorry — oh, gosh, Tim! Your tenure committee! How could I forget! When will they meet?"

"They *are* meeting. Have been, for twenty-one minutes and fifty-four seconds…twenty-two minutes. Can I sit down for a moment?" He does, like a poor sinner waiting for his verdict.

"Come on, let's walk."

"I can't leave the building!"

"Of course you can leave the building. You think they're going to call you in and ask you to explain note thirty-four in chapter three?"

"Why? What's wrong with it?" He stares at me, alarmed.

"Oh, Tim. Come on, walkies."

Tenure review makes defensive second-guessers of us all. And sots, if we are at all that way inclined. When I stand up to take my coat off the hook, I smell alcohol on Tim's breath, but I stifled every comment I was tempted to make in recent weeks, so I stifle this one, too. I steer him eastward on my cycle path and then left into the forest.

"You cycle along here, in the dark, alone? Are you mad?" For the moment he is distracted from his plight.

"Do you think it's too dangerous?"

"There are several frat houses along the edge of campus, and I wouldn't like to imagine you involved in the scenes of debauchery that take place here on drunken summer nights."

"Oh, you can't scandalize me with a frat party. I have Sodom directly behind my cottage." I tell him about the pickers' camp, and this cheers him up no end.

"You mean they've built a camp site, all amenities provided, so that these kids can pick fruit during the day and have weed-filled orgies during the night? That's not very God-fearing!"

"I know, but apparently they don't care what a bunch of kids get up to in the woods, as long as they are legal and, well, legal. The pickers have almost all gone for the winter, so there're only a few Poles left to help on the farm."

"Been presented with any more condoms lately?" he asks, coughing discreetly. "What was all that about, anyway?"

I tell him about Logan, and that amuses him even more than the pickers' camp.

"And Giles knew about this?"

"Yes, I…he advised me on how to deal with Logan."

Tim gazes straight ahead at the path. "See, I told you he's a nice guy."

"Yes, you did."

"Then why don't you kiss him already!"

I almost trip over my own feet. "*What?*"

Tim is embarrassed, but he is even more annoyed than he is embarrassed. "What about Giles?" he asks ruthlessly.

Panic. "What *about* Giles?"

"I want you to keep Giles here in Ardrossan! Don't you get it? Why do you think I've been throwing the two of you together?"

All I can do is shake my head in disbelief.

"I — I don't even — know where to — *throwing us together?*"

"Of course."

"What do you mean, *of course?*"

Tim digs his hands into his coat pockets.

"I'm worried that now he's divorced he'll go back to England!"

"Tim, are you — do you love Giles?"

"Of course I love Giles! But I'm not *in love* with him, if that's what you mean, you silly girl. But I don't want to work in this place without him!"

That makes two of us.

"It's a cunning plan, Tim, but like all such plans, completely bonkers. Apart from the tiny detail that I'd be risking my reputation and my chances of renewal if I started having affairs with tenured colleagues!"

"Don't be stupid." Tim kicks a stone out of his way. "Nobody would care. A bit of gossip, a few snide remarks — but aren't you getting those anyway? It's not like you're writing your dissertation with him or anything."

"It's. Not. That. Simple!" I am so bowled over by his nonchalance that I stop in the middle of the path to shout at him.

Tim frowns at my vehemence, then he grins.

"So you have thought about it."

"What? No! I'm just—look who's talking, anyway! *You're* hiding in a closet sealed off like a panic room, but you're telling *me* an affair with Giles wouldn't hurt my tenure prospects? Hypocrite!"

"That's different."

"I'll say! Will you come out when you have tenure?"

I expect a rebuff for this diversion, but he pushes his fists into his coat jackets and turns to walk back on the path.

"Maybe. C'mon, I'm getting cold. Martin…is holding a shotgun to my chest."

"Tired of playing hide-and-seek, is he?"

"He wants us to move in together officially, or he'll throw me out. Out of his apartment and out of his life."

"I don't blame him. Well, how much do you like Martin, on a scale from one to ten?"

Tim throws me a disgusted glance, then he sighs.

"It's not that. I hate all that labeling."

"Bullshit. Everyone is labeled everywhere all the time. You don't have the guts to try to be happy, that's all."

"Oh, yeah? Tell me, Dr. Freud, how happy are *you* on a scale from one to ten?"

I acknowledge this hit with a shrug and a nod, but I cannot answer him. Instead, I slip my arm into his and lean against him as we walk.

"A hot cup of tea would make me happy now."

We have just sat down in the Eatery when Sam Ruffin and Terry Nyman appear and indicate by surreptitious thumbs-up that the department committee has approved Tim's application for tenure. Now the chair, the Dean, and the Provost have to do the same.

"Mental note," I murmur into my mug. "Must mail order for his-and-his bath towels. When's the house-warming party, Timothy, darling?"

Chapter 33

The fall semester concludes with two parties, but I am not much looking forward to either of them. The first is Bernie's and Elvira's house-warming. I know, because she told me, that one item on Elvira's agenda for the evening is to introduce me to as many single men as she can manage. It's nice of her to do that, and I make an effort to play my part. The long-sleeved black dress that covers my knees and collarbones is what is known in some circles as "sexy *tznius*." *Tznius* is modest attire according to Jewish orthodox custom. The sexy part is that it is close-fitting and has tiny mother-of-pearl buttons all down the back. It works, in a severe sort of way, but I don't do it justice. I know I'm an ungrateful wretch, but I simply cannot muster the spirit to flirt, let alone be really interested, in any man who isn't Giles Cleveland, and I feel appropriately guilty when I make my excuses and flee without having encouraged anyone to even ask me for my phone number.

"You're choosy," Bernie remarks, a little reproachfully, when he sees me to my taxi.

"I'm in the wrong place. I'm sorry, Bernie."

The second party is the annual Ardrossan Christmas fête. The original tradition, which required guests to turn out in Victorian costume, has been relaxed to allow all sorts of period, vintage or fancy attire, but I am warned that Not Making an Effort is frowned upon. So once again I am sitting in the back of a cab, all dolled up, this time in a dark burgundy taffeta sheath dress with lace detailing, knee-length, a little Givenchy, something Audrey Hepburn might have worn in the early sixties. And yes, I have long, burgundy gloves to go with it, and tonight I will wear them. What nobody knows except me and the little devil sitting on my left shoulder is that the sheer black pantyhose I seem to be wearing are actually a pair of thigh-high stockings with very fancy lace tops. I have never worn them, and tonight they will keep the gloves company.

The façades of all buildings between Rossan House and the Observatory have been decorated with festive garlands of light bulbs; enormous Christmas trees are ablaze by the two main entrances, and an area has been fenced off in the yard for a huge log that will be lit on fire when the President, from his stage up on the portal of the Observatory, has welcomed us to the party. Incongruous but mouthwatering smells are wafted on the mild winter breeze, of gingerbread and mulled wine, hot baked goods and, less appetizing to a vegetarian, frying meat. It's a splendid sight; smiling people admire each other in their elaborate costumes, and in the firelight, the neo-gothic buildings look more like a fairy-tale film set than ever. It is a pity that I have no prince to guide me through the crowd.

I take my coat and a bag of books up to my office and on the way there have the dubious pleasure of receiving a wolf-whistle from one of the security guards posted on each floor. They are not taking any chances this time.

"Baby, you look ab-so-lute-ly fabulous!"

Being enveloped by Tim's enthusiasm in his cobalt blue suit and tie with a dark blue shirt underneath is like being hugged by the Cookie Monster; it's a great comfort, but one gets a little breathless after a while.

"Get yourself a drink," he urges me. "You're behind by two cups of punch!"

"Yes, I think I need some liquid fortification. This is overwhelming!"

"Yeah, you can say what you like about the old place, but it does look pretty. Pity there's no snow. Two years ago we had snow before Christmas, and a lot of it, so someone organized a sleigh drawn by four horses. What a sight! Enough to bring tears to the eyes of all the alumni. Unfortunately it all got out of hand when a couple of drunken undergrads dressed up the horses as reindeers and one of them bolted and knocked over half the madrigal choir. One of the horses, I mean, not one of the students. Come!"

"Tim. Tim!" I grab his arm and force him to look at me. "I'm not bein' 'orrible, darlin', but you reek of gin. And you can't. Not on campus, not even today. Especially not today. Consider who you might end up talking to."

I can see that his first impulse is to tear away from me, but he manages to control himself.

"Shit!" He inhales deeply and runs his hand through his short curls. "It's this confounded waiting! I can't bear it anymore!"

"Yes, you can. Almost done now."

"No, it's not almost done, damn it! Three more hoops, and I can't even—there's nothing I can do, except help cover up a case of sexual assault!"

"I know. Come on, we'll buy you a baked apple. That will take the smell away, and then you can have some horrible sausage."

When Tim has had his baked mouthwash and we have provided ourselves with a German sausage for Tim and punch and a big pretzel for me, I ask conversationally, "Where's Martin?"

"Don't start, Anna. I may meet him later on. There's no—"

"Hey, you two!" Erin and Yvonne slowly work their way toward us as if they were wading through a strong current. "Seen any graffiti?" Yvonne murmurs when she is close enough.

"Did you see the guards everywhere?" Tim exclaims. "Totally pointless! On a night like this, either no one will see you or everyone will see you!"

"You could have said that about Homecoming, too, and Family Weekend." Erin takes my cup and tries the punch. "Mmm, this is nice. Yvonne, do you want some?"

I have done my best to push Selena and her graffiti habit to the very back of my conscience, and except for five minutes on Thursday—when I considered writing her an email with a cryptic message like *Three strikes and you're out!*—I succeeded. That is my deal with myself: three strikes and I'll report her.

And then what?

The dome of the Observatory looms ominously above the glittering décor and the flames dancing in the yard. How *could* he? How could Hornberger seduce a girl who he knew was emotionally unstable? Worse, how could he get her pregnant? But then he may not know that Selena is pregnant. I could well believe that she has kept her condition secret from him. Her vandalism and the graffiti, not to mention her self-destructive behavior, are probably a kind of safety valve to let off steam. The problem is that as her pregnancy progresses and as the noose around Hornberger's neck tightens, the pressure on Selena rises. I can't imagine what she is going to do next. What *can* she do, really? I must talk to someone about her. I must talk to *her*; it is as simple and as uncomfortable as that.

And there is another reason for the weights pulling at the nerves in my stomach. It is two weeks since I saw Giles. Haven't even caught sight of him from afar, or heard his voice round a corner in the hallway. Maybe he is doing both of us a favor by avoiding me, but I long for him with an intensity that is made up in equal parts of hopelessness, desire and shame. I know I am doing the right thing by not giving in to this. I just wish that doing the right thing did not feel as if I had amputated a limb.

"Oh, there're Eugenia and Vern—and they look awesome!"

Eugenia and her husband have come as a fashionable couple from a twenties jazz club, and they do look absolutely gorgeous. After we have all complimented each other on our get-ups, Eugenia grabs Tim's wrist.

"But we should toast you for having survived the first round! Plain sailing, Tim, in case no one told you yet. Impressive work! Here's to three more slam dunks!"

And for once Tim keeps quiet and just smiles and blushes with pleasure.

The more crowded and festive the occasion becomes, the lonelier I feel. I want to ask Tim whether Giles isn't attending tonight, but I don't dare. I'm worried he would see the state I am in. How can one absence be so conspicuous? Among hundreds of faces and voices, the bells, the torches, the crackling fires, the music, the speeches, the sketches, the singing—

And then I see Selena. In a severe dark gown with a hooped skirt and lace at the throat, she looks more striking than I have ever seen her. Jane Eyre, pregnant with Rochester's child. Instead of fleeing the place when she found out that he was seducing her into sin, she stayed and became his whore. It occurs to me that the graffiti may not have been directed at Natalie at all, or maybe it meant both herself and Natalie. She is holding a mug of something, and she is there with a group of other graduate students, but like me, she seems to be isolated by her thoughts, and like me she is staring up at the dome.

"I don't believe that man!"

Erin's choked exclamation comes at precisely the same moment as Selena's face, rigid and expressionless before, registers emotion. I only have to follow her horror-struck gaze to detect Hornberger among the crowd. We are not the only ones to have seen him; a murmur of surprise, perhaps of disapproval or outrage, runs through the air.

"You gotta hand it to him," Tim says. "He's not floored by adversity."

Erin fumes. "How *dare* he?"

"Look, look at Demers!"

Graham Demers, our President, at one point in his life worked for a high-ranking management consulting group, so he is wise in the ways of the world and not easily fazed, but it doesn't need a reader of micro-expressions to see how dismayed he is at Hornberger's — evidently unscheduled — entrance. But the *pièce de résistance* is, no disrespect to her, the piece of ass accompanying him.

"Wow. Just wow," Vernon Russell mutters, only to choke a cry of pain when his wife elbows him in the ribs.

"At least she's more than half his age," Yvonne says caustically.

The ravishing brunette on Hornberger's arm is thirty-five, if she is a day. She looks as if she had been sown into the black gown that she is wearing, her shoulders and décolletage are immaculate, and her make-up and jewelry are just this side of expensively sluttish.

"She must be costing him a pretty penny," states an English voice behind me.

"Giles!" Erin exclaims. "There you are! Gosh, you look — Ginny, doesn't he look — "

"Wow," Eugenia says, still annoyed at her husband. "Just wow!"

The women's voluble response masks my own amazement. Giles Cleveland — who wore his college tie on Family Weekend, just to wave the flag — has come dressed up as a gentleman of the Old South. I am so stunned I can hardly look at him to take in the details, let alone look at his face. Buff-colored pantaloons, knee-high riding boots, and a dark green frock coat with brown-and-yellow-patterned vest, his hair brushed back from his forehead.

This is so unfair of him.

One hand disappears into the pocket of his pants; I can just see a strip of white shirt held together by golden cufflinks. It is a movement at the same time poignantly at odds with the formality of his suit and curiously expressive of what I perceive, after all, as a hint of self-consciousness.

"Where's your Scarlett?" Erin asks, a little acidly. She looks very stylish in her Bloomsbury Group outfit, but now she seems to regret the sexually neurotic touch that comes with looking like Virginia Woolf or Ottoline Morrell.

"Mm, you know, I've gone off Scarlett," Giles says. "I'm getting a bit old for those high-maintenance teenagers."

"Would that were true of all our professors," Eugenia mutters.

Partly to appear unimpressed, partly because I am suddenly anxious, I turn to check how Selena has reacted to Hornberger's latest stunt. But Selena has disappeared.

"A good evening to you all!" Elizabeth slowly edges her bulk through the crowd. She is one of the few women who can carry off the layered look, and that is what she sticks to, probably wisely. "Now may not be the best moment, but when the outcry has died down, I want to take you, Tim, and you, Yvonne and Anna, to see the President. You're here to mingle. Network, my dears, network. Let me have a drink first, then I'll introduce you."

"Do you think they'll let Hornberger stay?" Tim asks. "Or will he be marched off campus by a posse of security guards?"

"Innocent until proven guilty." Elizabeth shrugs. "It may well be his last Christmas at Ardrossan."

"Anna!" Yvonne whispers to me when Elizabeth turns to talk to Erin, Eugenia, and Vernon. "If *she* is as outspoken as this about the matter, it must mean Hornberger is finished!"

After curtseying and listening prettily to all the anecdotes and jokes of the college worthies Elizabeth introduces me to, I join the procession of light around the campus, with a speech and a song at each significant spot. Later, and frozen through, I am recovering by the fire of one of the gingerbread stands with Tim and Martin, a wiry, shaven-headed sociologist who is very clearly the calm anchor in this relationship.

"I'm so bad at that," I gripe. "Small talk with the VIPs! It's going to break my precious little assistant-professorial neck that I'm crap at networking!"

"You're not bad at it," Tim points out. "You just think you are, because you hate it."

"They weren't listening to what you said. I can guarantee that," Martin remarks, looking me up and down with an exaggerated leer. "Very sexy dress. Even on a woman."

"Stop that!" Tim protests. "We can't both flirt with Anna, and I saw her first!"

"Ah, but what neither of you boys has seen…" The punch must be working its dangerous effect on me, because I step behind a big trash can and quickly hitch up my skirt to display the lace top of my stocking.

"Oh, you brazen hussy." Tim grins. "Anyway, don't show us, show Giles."

The name rushes into my blood vessels like a triple gin and tonic. My face must have registered my reaction, because Martin, more sensitive to embarrassment than Tim, clicks his tongue and tries to change the subject.

"Well, I don't know about you, but I'm freezing my ass off out here. Will you come in and—"

"Hey, honey! Tim, hi! Lurking in the shadows?" Bernie emerges from the crowd, a glass in one hand and a woman's purse in the other. "Not for nothing, guys, but this girl is wasted on you this evening."

"Says the man who looks like Billy the Kid," Tim shoots back, a little pissy.

Bernie takes this jibe at his expensive-looking cowboy outfit in good humor, admitting that Elvira had expressed doubts, too.

"You should have listened to her."

"Why, you don't like the rugged look?" He grins. "Anyway, Anna-Banana, before Elvira comes back, for old times' sake—" He puts one arm around my taffeta shoulders and kisses me on the mouth before he struts off.

"You're kissing the wrong man." Tim glares at me through narrowed eyes.

"I didn't kiss him at all!" I snap, indignantly.

"Never mind," he relents. "Where *is* Giles? We need to get Elizabeth's card signed."

The spring semester starts on January fifteenth, Ma Mayfield's fifty-fifth birthday, and some strategic thinker realized that we would never get a present sorted out and a card signed if we left it till then. He also bought a pint-sized crystal-and-sterling bottle, which he produces from a dark leather box in his office.

"And this is genuinely eighteenth-century?" Erin examines the sparkling piece in its velvet case.

"No, I got it from Sears for nineteen ninety-nine," Giles says.

"Seriously, where did you get it? The Internet?" Eugenia straightens up from signing the card.

"London. I know a guy who sells that sort of thing. And no, it isn't fenced goods!"

"'Last week, mysteriously disappeared from the Duke of God-I'm-Posh's billiard room, antique crystal to the value of—argh!'"

Giles grabs Tim by the neck and shakes him.

"Listen, son, don't get fresh just because you've passed the first round of your tenure review!"

"My tutor in Cambridge collected this sort of stuff," I tell them. "He wasn't supposed to keep it in his office at all, because of insurance, but he did it anyway."

"Tristan Millard was your tutor?" Giles asks, mildly interested. With the air of one humoring a precocious child, he picks a yellowing, slightly tattered booklet out from beneath the velvet bed and hands it to me to read. Despite ourselves, nerds that we are, we get involved in the topic and I only realize that the others left the room when Erin sticks her head through the half-open door.

"Tim, c'mon — the taxi's here! Sorry, Giles, but I had to bribe the driver with the promise of an extra-large tip, so — Tim, now, please!"

"Yeah, yeah, yeah, I'm coming."

Tim grabs his coat and makes for the door before I can decently get up from that damned leather sofa. I was all right in Giles's office on that sofa in my burgundy taffeta dress as long we were a crowd of six. I'm definitely not staying for a company of two, and since he has also gotten up from his chair, I'm assuming that we see eye to eye on this one.

"Bye, Giles! Bye-bye, love!" And Tim is out the door.

And I'm suddenly so shy with this man I've hardly been able to look at all evening because I don't want to let him see the adoration glowing in my eyes.

"Yes, well, it's a good thing we've got that sorted out. One item off the holiday list, I guess." I glance round for my coat. "I think I'll try my luck with the cabs, too, now."

Then everything happens very fast. I'm reaching for the doorknob, and he is suddenly right behind me. One hand, left of me, slams against the door, the other, by my right shoulder, slams against the light switch and turns the key in the lock. Suddenly the pale glimmer from the electric bulbs in the garlands outside the windows is the only source of light, and it isn't much. I wince at his unexpected physical violence, but not for a nanosecond am I afraid. His hand is on my waist, his fingers dig into my flesh; he spins me round, my shoulders and the back of my head bump against the door.

And then he kisses me. Giles Cleveland bends down from his great height to kiss me, and it is a big, wet, angry kiss, full of pent-up emotion. The fingers of his other hand slip round my neck, and I couldn't avoid his mouth even if I wanted to.

"This is for letting that guy kiss you!" he growls above me in the dark.

"Bernie? But he isn't——"

"And this one is for wearing lace stockings in my office!"

"How do you——" I gasp for breath when he finally releases my mouth.

"Well, you didn't put them on for Tim and Martin." The gaze from those light eyes exposes my most unacknowledged motives. "Did you, Anna?"

"N-No, but I——" His first fury spent, his kisses become, if any-thing, even more thorough, but now they are less of an assault. His objective is to turn me on, not to punish me, and now he is allowing me——daring me——to respond. I realize only hazily that he has clasped my thigh, pulled it up to his hip and pushed back the hem of my dress till his fingers reach the lace top of my stocking. He draws me against himself, not roughly now, but in a way that leaves no doubt that resistance would be futile.

I don't resist him at all. With his fingers crooked around my knee he pulls me onto the smooth, hard slope of his thigh between my legs and rocks me gently back and forth, his other hand in the small of my back.

Although I could hate myself for it, it is the most deliciously sensual feeling, being in the hands of this angry, beautiful man who has set his mind on arousing me. His fingertips are on my naked flesh, high up on my thigh. He feels for me blindly, and my body is responding just as blindly to any touch, any movement of his. My good angel, a bedraggled little figure squatting on my right shoulder, warns me that we'll be copulating on the floor in a couple of minutes if his fingers inch any higher. His other hand glides down to my ass, one of my ass cheeks fits comfortably into his hand, and there is a worrying inevitability in the way he yanks me against his rock-hard thigh. Oh, God—does he really mean to fuck me now, here, in his office?

"Please, no, don't—"

He cuts me short huskily. "Hold still."

In delicious obedience I slip my arms round his neck as he hauls me up and against the length of his body. It's like an electric shock running through me when it becomes very clear that his thigh is not the only part of his nether regions that is as hard as a rock. One of my legs is still wrapped around his hip; his probing fingers reach the edge of my panties and then, through the thin lace of my panties, his fingertips feel my soft, swollen flesh. And I want to die with desire and shame, I'm so wet for him. Now he knows how wet I am for him. This is so embarrassing—oh, God, this feels so good! My arms tighten around his neck and I press my face against his shoulder. He smells of expensive cloth, a little of rum punch and shaving cream, but the predominant fragrance is that of Giles himself, which I can't define at all except that there is a hint of licorice in it and that it's the loveliest smell I can imagine.

Still there is nothing frantic in our movements. We are dancing on a tightrope, in more senses than one, a supreme rush of adrenaline balanced by a supreme effort at control.

Suddenly he stops.

"Don't do that…"

He lets go of my thigh and steps back from me. In a flash of shame and disappointment I take my hands off him. The anguish of finding myself rejected is so intense that tears shoot into my eyes. The moment seems to stretch out forever, but it can only have been a couple of seconds during which he looks down at me. Then he takes my hand and leads me over to the sofa.

"Giles—" I have no idea what to say. It's just that I feel that I ought to say something. "We cannot go on doing this! It's crazy!"

"It drives me crazy that I can't touch you. And you'll have to resist me harder if you really want me to stop."

He kisses me again, slowly and deeply. Already his mouth is familiar, the way the tip of his tongue runs along the sensitive corners of my mouth, the way his lips soften against mine. Oh, the delight of a man who knows how to kiss! Both his hands clasp my butt again and drag my hips against his, and I'm no longer kidding myself. If he wants to fuck me here, now, in his office, I won't stop him.

He pushes the low table to one side with his shin and sinks onto the sofa, pulling me with him. I try to sit demurely with my feet on the floor, but he hooks his arm underneath my knees and lifts me right onto his lap, my legs along the length of the seat. The dim light from the Christmas festoon shines onto him, and my heart skips a beat. He looks radiant. I smooth the silver hair back from his forehead and marvel at the look of happiness on his face. Incredible as it may sound, he is as delighted with me as I am with him. We kiss and kiss; his hand slides up from my waist to my breast. With his thumb he chafes the hardening tip until I gasp.

"I was hoping you'd say that," he whispers against my mouth. "But as you're wearing those stockings…"

Then his hand is on my silken knee, caressing my thighs with a mixture of delight and confidence that is absolutely irresistible. Again his fingers glide across the lacy border between silk and skin, only this time they're doing so on the inside of my leg, which is a dozen times more sensitive than the outside. For a while that's where they remain, traveling along the lace edge from thigh to thigh.

"You're not angry with me anymore?"

His fingers tighten on my flesh. "Don't ask me that."

"Giles, please…"

"I wish I could take you in the middle of Library Square," he says, and I can hear his hurt in the hoarseness of his voice. "At midday, on a hot day in summer. So I could see your face, and the whole world could see your face, when you come for me!"

The back of his index finger runs over my lower lip, and I catch it between my teeth, bite and release.

"I don't *come for you*, you arrogant male!"

"Yes, you do." His fingertip returns to the danger zone on my lower lip, and I nibble at the pad of flesh, but gently. "I know very well that I can't *make* you come." He is watching my mouth, his eyes glistening. "If you're willing, I can help. That's all."

His wry statement makes me laugh; I don't know whether he is being coy or candid. "Mommy's little helper."

His eyes shoot up to mine. For a second or two he looks almost shocked; then his features soften.

"Kiss me again," he whispers, and there is now a catch in his voice that tells me as much as the state of his cock that playtime is over. I kiss him without hesitation, and as our tongues meet, his fingers slip inside my panties and he finds me. My entire consciousness gathers in the pool of sensation between my legs; my whole self is at his fingertips as they inch across the fleshy mound and descend into the moist curls of hair. For perhaps a quarter of a minute he sits motionless, cupping me in his warm, large hand. Then one finger, the whole length of it, dips between the swollen, exquisitely sensitive lips. My hips pick up the rhythm and move against his hand.

"Like that?" he asks huskily.

"Y-Yes…" I cling to his body, lost in the waves of agonizing pleasure as his fingers stroke me with exactly the right pace and pressure.

"Lift your skirt."

With my free hand, the one not wrapped around his neck, I hitch my dress up. The white shirt cuff and the dark cloth of his jacket mirror the pale skin of my thighs gleaming above each stocking top. I've spread my legs as far as my panties allow to give the gentle, skillful hand as much scope as possible. His golden cufflink flashes in the light shining in from the windows, and when he rubs his knuckles against the sopping flesh, his fingers glisten with moisture.

"This is the most erotic thing I have done in my entire life." His voice is thick with passion, but also something else, something that sounds like awe. I look up to see whether I can have heard that right. My heart beats high in my throat, and it's not just arousal. He looks at me, and we're both so serious that I can hardly breathe.

"Keep moving," he whispers.

I look down to watch my hips buck slowly against his hand, and so I see him adjust the angle of his wrist. Before my brain can process the significance of that movement, my body has already registered it as the ignition of thousands of nerve ends. His middle finger pushes deeply and effortlessly into me. I arch myself against him and bite on the cry of pleasure that is choking me. I feel him slip out and instinctively reach down and grab his wrist to make him stay with me.

"Up!" His hand is on my ass and he lifts me up to pull the damp bit of lace over my buttocks and down my legs. I kick and struggle until I can free one foot, and at once he spreads my legs wide, adds another finger to the first, and fucks me with them—hard and deep. Even if I tried, I couldn't keep silent. All I can do is to stifle my moans against the side of his face. My face, my whole body, feels feverish; I'm breaking into a hot sweat, and the determined career girl that still lurks somewhere in my mind asserts herself one last time in feeble protest.

"I'm…I'm getting you all wet!" I gasp, thinking of the pantaloons I'm sitting on, and his hand, covered up to the knuckles with the liquid evidence of my desire. He doesn't even bother to answer that. His left arm, which had been clamping my shoulders to steady me in his onslaught, relaxes a little, but it's only to vary the pace of his right hand between my legs. His arm around me tightens, and I sag against his shoulder and say goodbye to that earnest girl who wants to control everything. I don't need her now, because Giles Cleveland is holding me, and he has everything under control…his mouth finds mine, and his tongue moves against mine with the same slow, languorous deliberation as his fingers, keeping me steady on a high plateau of arousal.

"Tell me what you want me to do."

I arch my hips against his hand—that's a rhetorical question if ever I heard one—but it's no good, I need him to…

"…fuck me again!"

And I mean it. I don't care that we're in his office, with a huge party going on around us, I need him to unbutton his pantaloons and come into me. But he smiles, slowly, a little mockingly, and drives his fingers into me, with a deep and upward thrust that reduces me to a shuddering heap. I sink completely into a trance-like state; there is nothing in the world now except his mouth and his hand.

"Ah! Oh, no!" I sit up, shocked to the core. "Oh, my God! What—what was that?"

What that was—when he slowed down, when his fingers almost slipped out of me—was that I ejaculated. I felt a hot, unfamiliar kind of release—not in my womb at all, just a brief, soft sense of suddenly melting, and although I didn't see anything, the soft, innocent sound of droplets of fluid sprinkling the leather upholstery between my legs echoes in my ears as loudly as so many gunshots.

"Oh, God, I'm-I'm so sorry! Did I just—this has never happened to me before, I swear!"

"I'll take that as a compliment then."

"No, I'm—oh, you're laughing at me? How can you laugh? I didn't know this was going to happen! Oh, look, you're—oh, this is all wet—oh, my God!"

"Hush!" His grip tightens; he draws me close. "Hush!" he commands. "Stop flapping!" Again I feel his body quiver with laughter. "Hush, now!"

He's leaving me no choice but to be still, but in his embrace I'm still heaving with shame, and probably with the sheer physiological shock of suspended…rapture.

"Breathe! Breathe out!"

I obey. I concentrate on exhaling, and I calm down. Suddenly I'm exhausted to the marrow of my bones and afraid that I really will fall asleep. If only I could stay like this for ever. Sleep, and forget that I've squirted all over Giles Cleveland's office. And his sofa. And his Ashley-Wilkes frock coat.

"All right?" he asks.

Dumbly, I shake my head.

"Look at me."

I shake my head again.

"Look at me!" He holds me away from himself, and I force myself to raise my eyes to his face. He looks so bright and young and happy that I have to swallow a sob rising in my throat. "You beautiful idiot!" he says lowly. "Do you really not know how incredibly sexy that was?"

"No! No, I do not!"

We are silent, and as my body cools off, inevitably, the implications of the situation become overpowering. We have done it again. Will we go on doing it till we are caught again? Why am I hell-bent on ruining my career and making myself notorious for lewd behavior on campus? It seems that this, as the Comte de Valmont puts it, is Beyond My Control.

"Would you like me to call you a cab now?" he asks, his voice completely neutral.

"Yes, please."

Giles has himself and the situation completely under control.

I pull my cold, wet panties back on and fix my stockings. I catch him watching me, still with a look of utter fascination.

"They work."

"Where's my…coat?"

He holds my coat for me and I step away from him the moment my arms are in the sleeves. And so I slink out of his office, along the dimly lit corridors out to the waiting taxis. Hardly anyone is around now. I have no idea what time it is. I ask the driver; it's half past eleven.

When the taxi turns into the dark lane that leads up to the farm, it starts snowing. Thick, white picture-book flakes float down from a black sky. They dot the windshield and melt, they settle on the black fields to my left and the naked trees to my right. The world blurs; I realize how close I am to tears. It's so beautiful and calm and still, and I'm such a complete mess. This is what I need, the still, cool simplicity of snow in the woods. Instead, I have to catch a plane to New York City in seven hours.

Chapter 34

I shut off my senses against the sight, the feel, the smell of my underwear and hastily stuff it into the washing machine. The gown will have to be dry-cleaned. That'll be a situation to rise above, the dry-cleaning lady's face when she looks over my sex-stained party dress.

A quick shower, and the hot water on my face, in my hair, is a luxurious pleasure that I relish till it runs tepid. Then I quickly soap my armpits and reach between my legs to wash away the evidence of my stupidity, my weakness—and suddenly tears are running down my face. I don't know how the tears can be even hotter than the water, but they are. Hot and bitter. I'm still so swollen, so sensitive; it feels like oil or syrup that doesn't dissolve in water. My hand glides easily between the slippery folds, like his hand did, just now, when he held me.

I cup my hand over it like he did and cringe with anguish. It's a gesture of such tenderness, such appreciation. His tenderness, my response, it's all so easy, so straightforward, so clear, like the snowflakes in the night sky. And I'm wasting it all, out of cowardice.

"Mom, it's Anna."

"Anna! Yes, on the…on the sideboard, Sam! When does your flight get in tomorrow? Do you want us to come and pick you up?"

"No, Mom, I'm…I'm calling to say that I won't be coming home tomorrow."

Now I have a hundred percent of her attention.

"Not coming home? What are you saying? Are you ill?"

"No, I'm not ill. I'm all right. It's just that I can't leave right now."

"Can't leave? Why not? It's the holidays, isn't it? You don't have to teach?"

She's getting annoyed, but long years of experience have taught me that this is how my mother expresses disappointment.

"Mom, I'm sorry. The truth is…I've met someone, and I can't leave…I can't leave right now."

Silence.

"You mean, you can't leave your new boyfriend for a few days to come and see your parents during the holidays?"

"He isn't my boyfriend."

"Well, what do you want me to call him? Your lover?"

I'm tempted to say that he isn't my lover, either. I've squirted all over his office, but he's not my lover, and if I don't do the right thing now, he never will be. But long years of experience have also taught me that there's no point in sharing my private life with my mother.

"I'm hoping he'll be my friend. This is important to me, Mom, so—"

"More important than your family?"

Now I'm getting annoyed, too.

"Oh, Mother! Must you be such a stereotype?"

"I have no idea what you're talking about."

"Look, Mom. I don't want to fight. But I have to do this, so please—"

"You've been crying!"

"Yes."

More silence. A mother's sigh.

"Well, I only hope this'll work out better than the last one… that Irishman!"

Her tone has mellowed, and I know perfectly well that she is sounding me out. I wish that I could tell her what she wants to hear.

"Yes, Mom, so do I. Listen, I have to go. Give my love to Dad and Nat, and to the kids!"

I sit and stare at the receiver that I've only just managed not to slam down on the hook. My heart pounds high in my throat. It is guilt, and a wild sense of liberation. I have defied my mother. I can do anything.

I quickly blow-dry my hair, forking my fingers through it. This makes me look as if I had stuck two fingers into a wall socket, but as I'm going pull my Patagonia hat over it, that doesn't matter. Wooly knee socks, corduroys, t-shirt, sweatshirt, woolen sweater, my Barbour coat, boots, scarf, mittens. Ready. No, I'll need my new Goretex rain slacks. Now, ready. I get the bike out of the shack and set off along the road, slowly, with no acknowledged destination. It's snowing harder now; the world is a dark, moonlit flurry around me, with a cone of light from my bike lamp always wobbling in front of me. Like a trekking version of Luke Skywalker, I slice into the whirling feathers with my battery-powered saber of light. There is no wind; the flakes are falling at a calm, unhurried but steady pace, and they look so much like feathers that I begin to feel quite cozy, pedaling through the darkness.

The main road is not a pretty sight. The few cars still out at this time have mushed the soft white blanket into a cold gray pulp; this is like snow in the city. I push my bike across as fast as I can, eager for the glistening quiet of the other side. When I turn off the lane toward the lake into the track that leads to the cottage, my heart beats faster, and not just because the absence of street-lighting and the snow-and-earth mix on the ground are making it hard to cycle. It has stopped snowing, except for a few forlorn flakes, but the only light is the egg-shaped moon, my bike lamp, and the expanse of white ground reflecting both. It has never occurred to me that winter could be lighter than summer. The cottage sits at the end of the track like part of the scenery of a stage production of *Hansel and Gretel*. Dim light glows from two of the windows. I'm only about thirty yards away from the cottage and its oblivious inhabitant, but it could be miles away. I don't think I have the courage to knock on his door. I did it once before, at Notre Dame, but this time I feel even more pathetic, like a supplicant begging for consolation because I can't come to terms with the life I have chosen for myself. If he had wanted to take me home, he would have suggested it.

I grab the bike and turn it round to push it back—and my movement sets off the barking and snarling of dogs in the darkness across the path. It's a frightening sound in the dark silence, and it's coming closer very fast.

"Andrew! Toby! *Stay! Now!*"

But they have reached me already. Immobile, I stand and let them sniff at my mittens and my legs; their tails are wagging, and I wonder whether they remember my smell and that I am a friend. And then he has caught up with them.

"I'm terribly sorry about this! Are you all ri—"

In the darkness, I only recognize him by his gait and his voice. I don't know how he knows it's me, motionless and dumb.

"What are you doing here?" This gruff question leaves no doubt that he has recognized me. My heart is beating so hard that I literally can't breathe enough to speak. I swallow, inhale, swallow again.

"I came by bike."

He doesn't reply to this, not even to ridicule its idiocy. The dogs are still very excited, wagging their tails like mad and sniffing around, in comic contrast to the two humans, who might as well be frozen into statues.

"Were you going to come in?" His voice hasn't softened. I decide not to attempt speech at all and only nod. In silence we trudge the short way up to the cottage. I'm still so breathless that I can hardly keep up with him. I don't know what to say to him; I'm frightened of seeing his face, and very reluctant to let him see mine.

I don't know what to do!

"Coat?"

Awkwardly I take off my jacket and stuff the hat, the scarf, and the mittens into the sleeves before I hand it to him. While he is feeding the dogs, I try to get my bearings. It's obviously a cultured individual's home, with shelves full of books, piles of books on tables and the floor, piles of paper, a large desk along a large window out back, presumably overlooking the lake, now an expanse of black glass. There are radiators, but the room seems to be heated by the fire in the grate behind a fine-mesh safety curtain; the air smells of burning wood and summer camp. There is a portable CD-player on the table, and some CDs, but no TV set. On the walls are more large-sized prints and more photographs of hills and water.

I'd love to take a closer look, but of course I can't; in fact, I remain exactly where he left me. A more determined woman would already have taken off another two or three layers of clothing and arranged herself in a seductive pose on the couch by the fireside. The thought is exciting, but I know perfectly well that I resemble that woman about as much as I resemble Priscilla, Queen of the Desert.

Giles returns, in thick woolen socks and a frayed-looking Norwegian sweater, and I can't help smiling at him. He looks so handsome and so sweet in his scruffy lakeside clothes. When he sees me smile, his features relax. God, is he nervous, too?

"This is lovely," I say, idiotically.

"Well, I think so. Mandy hated it. She kept the apartment in town, I burrowed down here. Easily parted."

Burrow down. The words, the feeling, echo in my mind.

"Will you take your pants off?" he asks.

"W-What?"

"You're still half covered in plastic. Perhaps that's unnecessary."

With some difficulty I scramble out of my rain pants, which for some reason I could pull on over my boots but don't seem to be able to pull off over them. I wriggle and struggle and eventually have to take off the boots. When I straighten up, Giles is leaning in a doorframe, watching me with unholy amusement.

"Cute. But stick to the stockings, on the whole. Oh, talking of which —"

He disappears into what I take to be the bedroom and returns with something long and shiny in his hands. "You forgot your gloves in my office."

I'm red in the face anyway, with cold and the effort of undressing, so this flush of embarrassment doesn't really matter. "You took them...into your bedroom?"

"Oh, yes," he says, with a silken yet faintly menacing tone in his voice. I'm a little weirded out by that, until I imagine what I would do if he had ever left any piece of clothing in my office.

"Drink? I can offer you beer, wine, but red only, tea, of course, with a shot of whisky, if you like, although it's a single malt I brought from Scotland, so it's spoiled if you dilute it. You could have a wee dram...do you want to?"

He is no longer avoiding my eyes. Animated, charming, self-confident, suddenly, but still Giles. Still with that aura of diffident reserve around him, still an Englishman. I find him absolutely irresistible. Of course we are going to have more sex tonight.

"Yes, I'd like that. But can I have a cup of tea, too, please?"

"Sit down. And shove the dogs away if they bother you."

Toby and Andrew have finished their supper and are very eager to check out the intruder who is usurping quality space.

"They're *not* allowed on the sofa—down, Andrew! The kettle's just heating up."

I watch him as he gets a bottle of whisky and puts it down onto the low table in front of me, a small pitcher of milk, ditto. He removes the grid from the fireplace and puts two more logs onto the fire. I could sit here forever and simply watch him move around his house, still in socks, so deft and capable. There is this feminine side to him, maternal almost. It's as if he were looking after me—well, he *is* looking after me, of course, as I'm his guest. And if I don't mess it up, these deft and capable hands will hold me, later, and I will be allowed to touch him. His hand, pouring whisky, his thighs and knees, so lean and hard in the jeans as he squats down to stoke the fire. His broad, strong back. The wayward little lock of gray hair that curls behind his left ear. *Oy!* I will break my heart over this man, and I'll have nobody to blame but myself.

To my profound relief, he sinks into the armchair at right angles to my sofa.

He lifts his whisky glass. "*Slawnchevuh.*"

"What was that?"

"*Slainte mhath.* It's Scottish and means good health."

"I see. Well, *l'chaim.*"

He smiles at me, and we drink. I couldn't say whether it's the drink or the smile that starts the glowing in my belly.

"Gosh, yes," I sigh. "That's much better."

He refills our glasses and sits back, absent-mindedly fondling Toby's massive head by his thigh.

"Have you been…unwell?" he asks. A cautious opening gambit.

"Well, yes, actually."

"Do you want to talk about it?" He is looking at me with a faint, and faintly sardonic, smile on his face, but I carry on.

"There's this man I…like. Worst possible situation. We work together. And you know the old saying. Never dip your nib into the office ink."

I nurse a mug of milky tea between my sleeve-covered hands and pretend that I have to concentrate on drinking from it.

"Does he like you?" He is looking at Toby, who is resting his head on his master's knee now, blissfully oblivious to everything but the fingers behind his ears.

"He likes touching me."

"Yes," he says quietly, "he does." He glances up at that, and I don't look away. "He likes it very much. But he's not a green boy any more, and he knows that it will end in tears. Whichever way it will end, it will end in tears."

"I know. It's a pig's breakfast."

What more is there to say?

"Do *you* like it?" he asks the back of Toby's head. "When he… touches you?"

Although the blood pounding in my chest and my throat is almost choking me, I set down my mug of tea and stand up. Both dogs raise their heads, alert but unwilling. "Sorry, Toby. May I cut in here?"

And I sit down on Giles's lap, my knees between his thighs, and snuggle into him. He doesn't push me away, even when I hug him with both arms around his neck and nestle my face into the fragrant warmth of his throat.

"I like it more than anything."

Chapter 35

"Feel this." He takes my hand, and I am taken aback by what I suspect he is going to do, but he presses my palm flat against his chest. Wool, cotton, skin, ribs, hard but warm, and the fast beating of his heart. Very fast.

"*Two* scaredy cats," I whisper. The skin of his neck is hot under my lips, and it smells all Giles-y and lovely. His right hand has begun to stroke my thigh, a bit like he fondled Toby's ears a minute ago. I like that; I'm not ready for sex yet.

"At least I'm only a senior colleague and not your chair."

"Hell, yes. I don't think I could ever have done this if you'd been chair, Giles."

"I knew that."

"Even my brazenness has limits, and—what?" I lift my head from his shoulder, only to see him grinning at me with a strange expression in his eyes. Expectancy.

"I knew you'd never consider an affair with me for one second if I'd accepted the chair."

All I can do is stare at him as the penny drops.

"I don't believe that! You—refused—"

"Yeah." He nods, still grinning. "I admit it was a gamble. Not that it was such a big sacrifice. I have no desire at all to be involved in any capacity whatsoever in Nick's crimes and misdemeanors. But I thought I had a very slim chance with you as a colleague, and no chance at all as chair." He wraps his arms around me and squeezes hard till I cry out. "I wanted this. Want."

Our eyes meet, and expectation sends a shiver over my skin. All the things we haven't done yet.

"What about your plane?" he asks. "Weren't you off to New York tomorrow morning? Or are you thinking of doing a runner again?"

"I told my mother I'd met someone and couldn't leave right now."

"Oh, the truth. Did you tell her it's me?"

"Good grief, no. She worries enough about me as it is, in her own way. No proper job, no husband, no children."

"Do you want children?"

This is one question I did not expect. I sit up and look at him.

"I don't know what your plans are," he goes on, blushing, "but maybe it'll help you to make up your mind about…all this, me, if I tell you straightaway that I can't have any children. I'm sorry, this is really presumptuous of me. I shouldn't even—"

"You just told me that we can't have an affair, and now you're talking about why we can't have a family?" Maybe I should pretend to be more surprised, but I am too glad to pretend.

"No! Look, I just want to be straight with you, that's all—"

"And I appreciate that." I cup his face in my hand and kiss him on the lips, very tenderly. "Thank you for telling me. Why can't you?"

He flushes with embarrassment; I can actually feel his body heating up.

"Lazy sperm. During my last year at school I had mumps, and that seems to have permanently damaged the—Christ. I can't believe I'm making you listen to this!"

"No, go on!"

"Well, it all counts against me, doesn't it? I should look for a woman my own age, past child-bearing, not one young enough to be my—"

"Don't say it!" I warn him. "And I'm not!"

"It's all so bloody wrong!"

"It doesn't feel wrong," I point out.

He looks at me, his face open and his eyes alert.

"No, that's the problem."

"I think I need another sip of that there firewater." I sit up on his lap and reach across for our glasses of whisky. "What am I drinking?"

"Talisker. It's made on the Isle of Skye. Do you like it?"

"I do. I can't think of anything I'd rather have right now. It's suitably overpowering."

We laugh together, and the laughter — and the alcohol — clears the air a little.

"I think you should take one of those layers off."

So much for his qualms. Relieved that I haven't lost him, I scramble out of my thick woolen pullover.

"Doctor Lieberman!"

"What?"

"You're wearing a Columbia sweater!"

"Oh. Ah. Yes."

"Now, for that show of disloyalty you forfeit that same sweater."

"Oh, okay." Meekly I lose the sweatshirt, too. When I reappear, I nudge him with my elbow. "Go on then."

"Doctor Lieberman! You're wearing a very cute t-shirt with a little…let me see, sunflower on it."

"No! I mean — I'm zero for two here."

"What, this?" He tugs at his Norwegian sweater. Hesitates.

"M-hm. Yes, this."

Reluctantly he pulls it over his head. He's wearing his white Ashley Wilkes shirt underneath, and I don't really see what the fuss was about.

"This is nice…why were you so — oh."

I am enjoying the feel of his lean chest underneath the shirt and had just wrapped my arms around him again when a certain female odor reaches my nostrils.

He smiles and raises his eyebrows in self-mockery. The rosy tinge in his cheeks is so adorable that I could *eat* him; at the same time I remember the crumpled underwear in my washing machine and feel ashamed.

"Giles, that is…"

"Pathetic?"

"…so sweet!"

He groans at my delight, and when I shift on his lap to be able to sit astride him, unbutton his shirt, and plant slow, lingering kisses on his throat and chest, he groans again, but differently. Undressing him is like undressing a girl. He watches me with that slight blush on his face, his eyes move from my face down to my hands on his shirt buttons, on the smooth skin of his chest, with just a small nest of gray curls in the hollow of his ribcage, around the dark pink nipples…then back up to my eyes. He's watching me like a girl who feels the touch of a man for the first time, and under the flat of my palm I feel his heart beat hard, and his breath quicken. Blood pulses in my lips, and I lean in to kiss him. I want to make him *beg* for it. I clasp his wrists and pin them to the back of the chair above his head; he crooks his elbows willingly and watches me, waiting, his eyes a dark, moist green.

"I wish I was strong enough to hold you like you held me," I whisper into his ear.

"You do? What would you do?"

I drive his wrists into the upholstery with both hands and swoop down to bite his neck. The odd thing is, I can't. My jaw seems to lock just before my teeth would begin to pinch his flesh; it's as if I lost control over my muscles. I can't bite him. I can't.

"I wouldn't hurt you…I couldn't."

"Did I? Hurt you?" He's serious, troubled, underneath his arousal. I don't want to make him feel bad, but I don't want to lie, either.

"No, but you almost frightened me."

He nods. Lowers his arms to draw me against himself. "I was so lonely. And you were so…lovely." His hands slide under my t-shirt and up my naked back. "Did I leave any marks?" His fingers inch upward to caress my shoulders.

"You'd like that, wouldn't you? Actually, I don't know."

"I think I should have a look." He clasps my waist and pushes up my t-shirt with the backs of his hands. Is there anything better in this world than slowly undressing with an appreciative partner? I wriggle out of his arms and slide onto my knees on the rug on the floor.

"You did notice, didn't you, that I'm not circumcised?" The corners of his mouth lift on half a grin when he says this, my hands on his zipper. "European *and* Gentile."

"Yes, I noticed that. Not to worry," I reply solemnly, but his stomach erupts in a spurt of laughter when I say this, because as I'm freeing his cock from the confines of his jeans and the shorts underneath, I have to swallow. Hard.

"Hard" being the operative word here.

He wraps his fingers, his beautiful, hard, strong fingers, around his beautiful, hard shaft and strokes it lightly.

"What you see is what you get…"

I inhale for a quip.

"…but it won't behave like the meat of the striplings you've been fucking."

That word, uttered calmly in clipped English accents by this silver-haired gentleman, sends another wave of blood into my belly.

"So far it has been behaving rather better," I murmur, leaning in. "Let's see if it stays that way."

I replace his hand with mine and shuffle closer until my knees touch the bottom of the chair; with my other hand I spread his thighs a little wider. Ignoring Giles's sharp intake of breath, I run the tips of my fingers along its hard, silky length and gently squeeze it between the balls of my hands. I smooth down the soft wiry hairs, some dark, some gray, and run my fingers deep along the clefts of skin between thigh and groin, teasing the tightening, fleshy sac with my knuckles, as if by the way.

"I wish I could dance around it." My voice is husky with anticipation. I run my thumbs up and down its curved belly, pull back the foreskin from the head and tenderly chafe the snake's throat and chin. "Like dancing around a sacred tree…or a maypole…"

Giles stares down at me as I kneel between his thighs and worship his cock, and he's so turned on by my words that he looks almost scared, with a deep crease between his brows. I smile up at him and run my hands across his white loins and flat belly. His penis arches up from its nest of hair, and without taking my eyes off his face I lean in and kiss the shiny dark pink head.

"Oh, *God*…"

I can't help grinning at his wide-eyed alarm, and the velvety shaft brushes my flaming cheek.

"'Like woman wailing for her demon-lover,'" I quote. Nibbling and licking my way down to the fuzzy base and up to the tender head again. "Her demon god…this phallic god…I totally see why people adored it. It's so beautiful."

And I raise myself up on my knees and slowly slide my mouth over the first four inches.

The sound that fills the air is surprisingly close to a wail, but it didn't come from my throat.

"L-Listen, I—" His fingers grope for my arms, my hands. "I should say that it's been a while since I've done this…had this done to me, rather, and…"

"It's been a while since I did this, too."

"It has?" His gaze is like a pool of green water with gray clouds chasing across it.

"Well, you wouldn't let me, remember?"

"Mm-hmm." But he tugs at my shoulders, urgently, and lifts me up so that I lie on his naked chest. "I have to kiss you. Come and kiss me."

Kissing Giles Cleveland is like going to the fun fair in the morning, knowing that in the afternoon your best friend is having a big birthday party and you'll be allowed to stay the night at her house. An endless series of pleasures, after which I get to make love to him. When I push his shirt over his shoulders, he leans forward willingly enough, but because he is still wearing the cufflinks, he can't pull the sleeves off over his hands. I watch his efforts for a couple of seconds, and a hot rush of inspiration runs through my body.

"Wait, I'll help…stand up."

Because now I shall be horribly revenged for what he did to me in the observatory. I step round him, ostensibly to undo his cuffs. There is a small scuffle; he's impatient to be rid of this encumbrance, but I grab his shirt tails and quickly tie them in as tight a knot as I can, and another on top, to make sure.

"Now, look here, young woman!" The look on his face is priceless.

He tugs at his manacles more violently, and then with as much force as he can. The muscles in his arms and shoulders ripple most beautifully, but the cotton shackles hold fast. I exhale slowly. Had the shirt torn under his struggles to free himself, I'm sure he would have given me the hiding of my life. I'm almost frightened of him for a moment, because for a moment he seems frightened of me.

The dogs, who lie curled up in front of the fire, lift their heads, and Toby warns me off with a deep, chesty growl.

"It's all right, Toby," I say confidently. "It's only a game." Another growl, but more quietly; the big head sinks back onto his paws. "That's a good boy, Toby. Only playing."

"Listen, my girl, this is not how we play this game!"

It is an effort to ignore his resentment, but I manage to bat my lashes at him, all limpid innocence.

"But it's you, professor, who taught me this game!"

He thinks, and then, on an unwilling crack of laughter, he relaxes. The tension eases up a little. Was he really worried that I might hurt him?

"You didn't mind that."

"No." I put my flat hand against his chest and push him down onto the sofa.

"Hey!"

"And I promise you, you won't mind this." He lies sprawled helplessly across the three-seater, one leg up, one down, his hips raised a little in the air because he's lying on his shackled hands.

"No, but, Anna—aah…"

"Hush, you'll frighten the dogs."

The strangled sound that came from his throat when I slowly sucked him into my mouth turns into a choked laugh.

"Toby…Andrew…help!" he wheezes, but quietly, so as not to alarm the animals snoring in front of the fire. With my fingers ringed around the base of his shaft, I hold him in my mouth, suck on the head in fast, short movements, and wiggle my tongue around its slithery smoothness. Giles's irregular gasps for breath are punctuated by the most gratifying moans of pleasure, and when I gently knead his tensing balls in my hand, he arches his hips in a convulsion of response that stabs his cock deep into my throat. He cries out, I gag, and the dogs woof their irritation.

"Giles, I fully intend to make you come loud and long, but I won't if it means I'll have the dogs at my throat because they think I'm killing you."

"You *are* killing me."

"My dear boy, I haven't even started. And I'd prefer it if you didn't stick your cock between my tonsils."

"Sorry, I didn't mean to." He raises his head from the sofa and looks his contrition past his naked chest and stomach down at my face between his legs. "Really, I didn't. I mean, I wouldn't."

The most incredible suspicion dawns on me. "Giles." Very tenderly I tug at his cock, upward, downward, sideways. "How many women have done this to you?"

He lies very still. Stares up at the beamed ceiling of his cottage.

"Several," he finally says. "But not the woman I was married to for eleven years."

This is fascinating—and very welcome—information, but I will leave its discussion till later. Mentioning his ex-wife has made him go a little limp, but in no time at all I lick and suck, nibble, and squeeze him back into a rod-like state.

His eyes flit up to mine a fraction too quickly. "Look, I wouldn't want to seem ungrateful, but…I'm really rather uncomfortable with this."

"What, with this?" I kiss the hollow of his throat while I'm running my hands along his shoulders and his arms down to the cotton shackles at the small of his back. "Or this?" He winces when I tweak the skin of his stomach with my teeth. "You're surely not uncomfortable with this?" I push his jeans and boxers over his knees and pull them off his long-muscled legs.

"Yes, actually, I feel extremely un—"

"Shhhh…" His embarrassment turns me on, and knowing that I will make him lose control in a very short while gives me a sense of power that is unfamiliar and extremely arousing. "I have not yet… seen you…"

"Seen me?" Again he glances up at me a little uncertainly.

"Yes, seen you. Touched you." I feel myself slowing down, relaxing. The higher faculties of my brain shut down, and primeval, atavistic impulses take over. Bodies moving against each other, skin against skin. Giles watches me with slow bright eyes as I put another log on the fire and as I turn round to pull the t-shirt over my head. The blazing fire caresses my naked back and puckers the skin around my nipples. Slowly I unbutton my corduroys.

"The stockings are left to your imagination, I'm afraid."

Going by the expression on his face and the response of his twitching cock, one would think this is a man watching a woman in black lace suspenders, a nipple-exposing corset, and six-inch heels.

"I really very urgently need to touch you," he says.

"Maybe…but it's my turn."

Naked but for my sensible cotton panties and my knee socks, I squat on my haunches and run my hand up the inside of his long, hard thigh, brush past his balls, and explore the strands of muscle, the bones and ribs rising from smooth surfaces of flesh and skin. His blush has deepened, and his chest looks as if he had been out too much in the sun. This may be the only time I'll get to touch him like this.

"I seem to end up naked all the time when we meet, while you hide inside that tweed armor of yours." Careful not to squash any sensitive parts, I climb onto the sofa, my knees between his, stretch out along his naked length, adjust my hips, and close my thighs tightly around his erection.

"Am I too heavy like this—?"

His half scathing, half desperate grunt is answer enough. He stares at me, helpless in his arousal, and then his head sinks back and he closes his eyes.

"This is torture."

Stretched out on top of Giles Cleveland I move my hips in slow, deliberate gyrations and clench the muscles in my thighs, using his rock-hard cock as an instrument of stimulation, which does nothing for my detachment but feels absolutely wonderful.

"Is that nice?"

"Nice! A nice Jewish girl shouldn't even know what to do with a foreskin…certainly not…not know how to—oh, yesss!"

"*Shmuck*," I whisper against his throat, keeping up my restrained but effective medium-dry humping.

"W-What?"

"That's what *shmuck* means. It's Yiddish for foreskin. Well, actually, what it means is jewelry."

He has to laugh. "Well, I can't tell you how ecstatically glad I am right now that I still have mine!"

"One can do strange and wonderful things with them. I'll show you."

I roll off him and with my fingertips deftly manipulate the creamy, silky skin around the hard shaft underneath. Now we are both looking down past his flat belly, and I adore the sight of his arched cock between my fingers. Giles catches his breath and releases it in a hiss.

"Sit on me…ride me. I need to feel you. There are some condoms in the bathroom cupboard. I think."

I am tempted to do as he asks—but no. I want to remain in control. I want to turn the tables on him and make him come while I'm watching him.

I push my hands underneath his buttocks and cup the smooth, firm globes, lift his hips a few inches higher to arch the middle of his body. His fingers grope for mine, and we hold hands while I do what I can to give him the blowjob of his life. I'm so caught up in what I'm doing, so aroused myself now by the noises he makes in response to my manipulations, that I almost miss my cue. With my wrists supporting his balls, I can feel him tightening, ready to explode. I let him slide out of my mouth with a plop and wrap both hands around the hot, moist shaft.

"Why wouldn't you let me touch you, earlier?"

"What? God!" he cries and rolls his hips to maintain some friction. "Don't stop! D-Don't stop now!"

"But I'm not stopping at all," I object sweetly. "I'm just pausing!"

"I'm going to get you for this!" He thrashes around on the sofa, trying to loosen his shackles.

"Yes, Professor Cleveland, sir, but not yet."

Very slowly I pump him inside the tube of my hand and fingers while I kiss and lick my way up from the tender, defenseless flesh above his hairline to his warm throat that smells more intensely of Giles than ever, and to his mouth.

"Tell me," I whisper between slow, deep kisses that he receives almost passively; he is too far gone. I hadn't been sure whether to expect that he would relax, after his initial discomfort at being tied up. But when he opens his eyes they are blank with sensation.

"Hmm?" His voice comes from somewhere deep in his throat, low and hoarse.

"Why you wouldn't let me touch your cock when we were making out in your office."

He closes his eyes again and swallows before he answers. My hand maintains a slow, steady rhythm of stimulation, and I can tell that he has about five percent of his consciousness available to answer my question.

"Because I thought I'd be able to keep my hands off you, if you… didn't want me. But I was frightened of…this. That if you touched me, like this, I would want you again and again. Ludicrous, really, because I do…anyway."

I gaze down at the flushed, defenseless face. I can't allow myself to hope that this might be a beginning.

When I take him into my mouth again, I stop thinking. I make love to him with my lips and tongue and teeth and fingers, respond instinctively to the tensing of tissue, to his sighs and gasps. I'm no longer focused on egging him on; I no longer try to control his arousal. All I'm doing is reveling in his smell, his skin, his hardness, his softness. I'm reveling in the fact that for a few minutes I have made him forget any other woman who has ever touched him.

"Pleasedon'tstopdon'tstopdon'tstoppleasssse…Oh, no, don't—"

I suck him deep into me until I feel a load of jizz hit the back of my throat. Mission accomplished. Milking him with both hands, firmly and slowly, I swallow and let him slide out of my mouth. This I want to see. He groans as if his entrails were on fire; his hips buck in spasms of release, and the next few milky white blobs land on my breasts and throat, run down my fingers onto his belly. I don't think he was looking at me when he came, because it's only when the spurts of cum subside to pearly drops that he raises his head and opens his eyes. I can't suppress a grin—half of pride, half of tenderness.

"Why, Professor Cleveland…I always knew you had it in you."

He is gasping for air, for the moment too weak even to laugh.

"You're only so cocky because…I have my hands tied and…my spirits drained!"

"Not at all. I'm your willing handmaiden, sir. Here, let me clean you up."

Very tenderly I take him between my lips and suck the wet, fragrant, softening shaft into my mouth again. He catches his breath as if I'd bitten into him.

"Not nice?"

"It blows all remaining fuses in my brain…but yeah, it's lovely. But you have to be gentle with me."

Satisfied, I settle my head against his thigh and very gently, with infinite tenderness, suckle his wilting cock. Inhale the smell of his sex in his hair, on his skin. Hold his drained balls in the hollow of my hand. Wait for the turn. Was this the climax that is followed by a falling action and imminent ending? Or is this a beginning? While I'm lying against his naked body, with his cock in my mouth, I almost don't care.

"Why did you come?" he asks after a long while.

"Hmm? I didn't."

"No, I meant, here. When I was wandering through the snow feeling sorry for myself."

I pull my knees underneath my body and squat between his legs.

"Will you thrash me if I untie you now?"

"I don't think I'd have the strength," he sighs. "You've shot yourself in the foot, my girl. Middle-aged men are completely incapacitated for hours by ejaculations like that."

"That's okay. Honor is satisfied."

Cautiously, I push my hands under his buttocks again and feel for the cufflinks.

"So—you came here to make me come?" he insists.

I sit up and angle for my t-shirt and sweater while Giles very gingerly frees himself from his shackles and moves his arms about. Flexes his hands. Groans as the blood tingles in his fingers.

I've pulled on my clothes without wiping his cum off my chest. I want him on me. This is no time for niceties. "I had this terrible sense of…waste. And I knew for a fact that it wouldn't get better at home, but worse. I just wanted to be outside, in the snow, and calm down. And then suddenly I was here. I don't know, Giles."

The beautiful naked man sitting next to me on the sofa smiles. It's a wistful smile, as if he, too, thinks that this will be our only evening together. Then his expression changes and he flings himself on me, wrestles me down onto my back and kisses me with a vehemence that startles me.

"G-Giles!"

"Mhmm." He raises his head and licks his lips. "I think the last time I tasted my spunk was when I lost a bet with Rupert Harding."

"You shock me. And who is Rupert Harding?"

"Oh, he was my best friend at school." He wriggles his torso between my thighs and slumps on top of me in all his naked glory.

"Ooofff…from what I heard about English boarding schools, I would have guessed that you tasted *his*."

"Haha. No, I lost a bet—I can't honestly say that I remember what it was all about. Something entirely puerile, no doubt. Something to do with the form master's hairpiece, I think. Anyway, I lost, and I had to wank into my hand and taste the blob of cum on my finger. It was very exciting. I wouldn't have had the courage to do that if I hadn't been…you know, honor-bound."

"What a fascinating life you have led!"

His eyebrows twitch in ironic acknowledgment, but his eyes and his mouth are serious.

"No, I haven't."

"Are you sad?" I ask, and even I can hear the anxious tone in my voice.

He smiles and scoots down the sofa so he can push his head underneath my t-shirt and sweater, like a small boy who hides from the world. His playfulness makes me laugh, but there is something strangely arousing in the childish — child-like — embrace of this broad-shouldered, gray-haired man.

Meanwhile his hands roam over my naked thighs and under my t-shirt in a way that is not in the least child-like. He reappears, cradling my hips in his hands, and trails an intoxicating line of kisses across my belly just above my panties and along the insides of my legs. His lips and nose caress my crotch through the hot, damp cotton. I feel him settling his lips over my clitoris, the tip of his tongue finds the tip of my clit, and for a crazy second I regret not having a cock that he could suck into his mouth.

"Will you stay until I've had a proper go at you?"

His tongue burns the hard little cotton-covered nub of flesh. Slowly he laps at it, teases it, and the sensation floods my pelvis like an epic deluge of lust and makes my heart pound almost painfully in my chest. His lips form an O over my clit, and he exhales slowly against it.

"Y-Yyy-aaah!"

"Is that a yes?"

"Giles!"

"Hmmm?"

"Giles, stop that. Or finish it, but don't—"

He raises his head and looks at me with a mixture of amusement and exasperation.

"Don't *tease?*"

"Yes…no."

His eyes narrow, and I brace myself for the imminent assault.

"Oh, all right." He shrugs his shoulders in a show of unconcern and clambers onto his feet. "The fire needs stoking anyway."

For the second time this evening I watch him busying himself around the room, this time stark naked, which to my delight doesn't seem to bother him at all. I curl up on the sofa in my socks and sweater and watch him. The long, well-defined strands of muscle in his legs and his back, his pale, tight buttocks gleaming in the dim light.

"I can't believe that none of the older boys at school had a crush on you." I lean on my elbow and smile at him. Giles looks up from the grate, clearly taken aback. "You have such a fine ass… 'arse,' as you'd say."

"Well, as for that, madam, your own little tush is very fine, too."

"Thanks…but I wasn't fishing."

"As indeed, why should you? You're used to men lusting after you."

There he stands, slimmer and more angular than Michelangelo's *David*, more boyish, but just as perfect in his nakedness, and suddenly there is an acid tone in his voice. I register the electric flash that runs along my nerves. Wait while it peaks and fades. A remark like that would have really hurt me, a few years ago. I am more resilient now. I have grown, I am a little harder, and generally much better at protecting myself.

"And I thought I was paying you a compliment," I muse aloud. "I'm sorry if I've trespassed into a no-go area, Giles."

And it works. His rigid posture relaxes. I hadn't even seen him tense up, but he relaxes and casts down his eyes.

"What, school-boy crushes?" He had already forgotten about that question. "Oh, I'm not bothered about that. The geography master fondled my bottom once or twice, but then he fondled pretty much every boy's bottom. Why do you ask?"

"I don't know. I guess I was thinking how young you look, and what you must have looked like when you—"

"Were." His voice is dry as winter leaves. "Young."

"No!"

He grins at me with that ironic incredulity that makes me want to hit him.

"Are you hungry?" he asks. "Have you eaten?"

"I'm not hungry!"

"Drink?"

"You're horrible! I'd like a glass of water, please."

He gives a curt nod and walks off into the kitchen, to reappear a few seconds later with two glasses, a jug of water and an open but full bottle of red wine.

"When did *you* open the wine? I didn't hear you."

With a grim expression around his mouth he pours water into my glass.

"Earlier. Before I took the dogs out. I was going to get well and truly plastered tonight."

"Oh, you had plans? I'm so sorry! You should have said! I wouldn't have stayed!"

I'm not going to let him get away with whatever mood he has dropped into, like into a vat of sadness. Maybe that's all it is: post-climactic *tristesse?* Don't think so. My taunts make him pause; he seems to be looking at the mouth of the bottle hovering over my glass.

"I'm glad you've come." He doesn't say it as if he were glad. "I'm glad you're here."

"But?"

He sighs and pours me my drink. Then, finally, he looks at me.

"But I wish you hadn't made me come…like that."

A ball of lead plummets into the pit of my stomach.

"You think that was sluttish of me."

"What? No! That's not at all—no!"

"You think a girl who gives head on the first…date—"

The rest of my protest is stifled against his naked shoulder when he pulls me roughly into his arms.

"You're crushing me!"

"I'm sorry…"

He releases me from his bear hug, and we laugh together, dazed by the intensity of feeling that is between us, and cowed by the misunderstandings that fly thick and fast.

"Let's not talk," he says dumbly. He lays a hand on my knee and runs it up my thigh, then both hands, on both legs, and he is so lovely and so sad, and I don't want to talk either. I don't want to fight. I don't want to spoil this. But.

"But what *did* you mean?"

"Nothing."

"Giles!"

"Look!" He isn't looking at me; he's looking at his hands on my knees. "It's just that Amanda, my ex-wife—"

"*Is* she your ex-wife?" I ask, a little pissy.

"What? Oh, yes." He grins. "All over now."

"Because she wouldn't give head."

"No! Well, I don't know. She said it was demeaning. Eighties' feminism and all that, but I think she simply didn't like it. She hated it, frankly, and I hated her turning it into a political issue. Because I don't think it is that! If she doesn't want to be so…intimate with me, she doesn't, but there's nothing inherently denigrating in a blowjob. Why should there be? Patting someone on the shoulder can be far more denigrating, in a certain context, than—oh, I'm raving again! I'm sorry. I can't explain."

"Yes, you can. Do. Please."

He rouses himself to greater effort, but he still doesn't look at me, not even when I clasp his hands in mine.

"Well, what I mean to say is that for me…it still feels…special, as if it *meant* something. I know it doesn't, so you needn't tell me how absurd that sounds, but—well, it makes me feel like one of John Donne's poet-lovers. You suck my life's spirit from me, from my body, and I'll be a hollow man who'll sicken and die unless you give me your spirit in return. I'm sorry, I can't really talk about it in less high-falutin' terms!"

"What you're saying is you're sorry that you let me have you." At this, he looks up, surprised at how poignantly I have summarized him. "But *you* already had *me*, remember?"

"At Notre Dame?"

"At Notre Dame, and in the observatory, and in your office! My life sounds like an X-rated movie."

"But that wasn't the same."

"How wasn't it? Of course it was!"

"I've never pleased you as you did me, just now!"

He looks like a boy who insists that he has been wronged. He knows it, too, and is ashamed of his insecurity. A few years ago I would have started arguing with him; now I am wiser. I wrap my arms around his neck and snuggle against him. He is warm and smells of arousal. I breathe softly into his ear, making him and myself giggle.

"Do you know, it's quite ridiculous how sexy you are…even when you're being silly."

"Anna—"

I cut him short with a slow, deep kiss.

"Let's go to bed, Giles, hmm? And bring a pen and paper. Maybe we can start a chart."

Chapter 36

I wake on a deep, indrawn breath. Ten inches away from my face is a naked male arm, crooked against a naked male chest. The shock of recognition seeps through my body like hot treacle, sluggishly.

I cannot move. If this is post-coital languor, it has merged fatally with my general state of exhaustion. My limbs, absurdly, feel like leaden sponges, my eyelids are swollen with passion, and I think also tears; my brain is a ball of soggy cotton wool.

"Hey," whispers the man who has done this. "Fancy seeing you here."

With a supreme effort I arch my back to peer up into his face, although I can hardly keep my eyes open enough to see. What I do see is a quiet, intent smile, and I know that my swollen eyes are smiling back.

"Hey." My voice breaks on a croak. Even my vocal cords are mush.

His cheek rests against the back of his hand, pushed between his face and the pillow. "Good morning."

I groan and burrow underneath the warm, fragrant cover. The night is over. My body doesn't want the night to be over.

"Can't get up…fucked me into a pulp."

His chuckle erupts against me; he seems to be much more awake than I am. Wondering where he gets his energy, I surrender myself to the heaviness that drags at my limbs. *Briar Rose.* That's what the

Brothers Grimm called the princess in the folk tale who pricked her finger on a spindle and slept for a hundred years until a prince came to kiss her back to life. I could sleep for a hundred years and then some, and a prince and a prick certainly have something to do with it.

"Stay where you are," he whispers against my ear. "I'll take the dogs out."

We spend the day getting to know each other, in bed and out of bed. And in between, we talk. I tell him everything I know about Selena, and he agrees that Hornberger most definitely knew about Selena's anorexia.

"I told you he enjoys their emotional torment. Go on, off you run!" We are out walking the dogs, and once away from the lakeside path, he takes them off their leashes and they charge into the snowy mush like children. "I found out that Amanda was having an affair one evening when I picked her up at her office. He'd been there, with her, and he knew I'd be there in a few minutes. She was…sucking him off, and he came all over her face, her hair, her blouse. When I turned up, she was in such a state of hysteria that I thought at first she'd been assaulted."

"But—you said she didn't give head!"

He shrugs. "Maybe he has a nicer cock than I."

I look up at him, and I can see that he is flippant rather than hurt.

"She did, eventually, try to explain. I think it's a combination of factors." That sounds too coolly analytical even to Giles, and he pulls a face at himself. "She felt bad because she knew that I was disappointed that she didn't like oral sex, or any kind of sex, really, for most of our marriage. I sound like an obsessive, don't I? It's not that. Really, it was more about the way this reflected our whole relationship. *Polite.* We were always so polite to each other. Friends, at first, but emotionally so cautious, and physically…so wrong for each other. Nick clocked from the start what her weaknesses were, and he liked her to give him quick blowjobs in her office. Just to humiliate her and intensify the disgust she felt for herself. So, to put it another way: a girl with issues about her body, about conforming to expectations, a girl brought up to be hard on herself, will find in Nick the perfect self-harming tool."

"Are you thinking of Selena or of Amanda?"

"Both."

I am watching his profile, wondering about the wisdom of getting involved with a man who is still so emotionally involved with his wife. Ex-wife. Perhaps it is a good thing, then, that I am not actually getting involved with Giles.

He glances down at me and smiles.

"You look worried. Don't be. I'm only trying to explain. I do need it to make some sort of sense, and I've never had to explain it to someone I care about."

That is the closest either of us comes to a declaration. We do not talk about our dead-end situation again. There is nothing more to say. We need to be together, we can't be together, and that is all.

"But what are we going to do about Selena?" I return to the topic later that day when I am chopping vegetables in Giles's kitchen. Neither of us was hungry enough for breakfast; I even declined the coffee he offered me because my heart was still racing with the excitement of it all. The excitement of being here.

"Some hot chocolate, then?"

"Oh, yes! Would you laugh at me?"

He came over to kiss me. "Only in a good way."

By teatime, after two hours outside in the woods, I am ready for some food. I am on chopping duty while Giles beats eggs and heats up the pan. Everything he does is delightful to me, and I want to savor every moment of this experience, but I must be careful not to slip into the melancholy of remembering it while it is still happening.

"Right—a few minutes under the grill, and grub's up!"

"Giles…"

"Hm?" He turns round, and I step between his woolly feet, push up his sweater, and duck my head under it.

"I'm sad!" My voice is muffled by cotton and skin, and I'm not sure he heard me, because he doesn't respond, only hugs me. Then he leads me over to a chair, sits down in it, and pulls me onto his lap. I wrap my arms around his neck and press my face into the fragrant nook below his ear.

"You'll feel better for some food," he says after a while. "Let's eat, and then I'll see what I can do to console you."

It takes us about fifteen minutes to have a slice of frittata each and a glass of water. Then I look up from my plate and see him looking at me.

"Done," I say softly. Underneath the table my foot is feeling for his; a quarter of an hour without touching is already too long.

"Not yet, you aren't." He grins and marches me over to the sofa in the living room.

His elbows on either side of my arms, he rests his chest against my crotch — the contact makes me gasp with a sudden flare of electricity — and covers my breasts with his hands.

"One of the reasons I thought you wouldn't like me is that I've got small tits," I say, a little meekly.

Giles, who was in the process of leaning in to suck one nipple peeping through the grid of his fingers, groans and drops his head so that his forehead rests in my mini-cleavage.

"Well, because Amanda's got these huge knockers!" I try to justify my neurosis.

"I don't even know any Amanda."

"Hers are — "

"When I married her, they weren't."

"What? But — so — they're fake?"

He lifts his head and looks down at me with a mixture of resignation and sarcastic humor. "No, they're real. Real silicone."

"So you don't like — "

"What I don't like — sorry to be brusque here, Anna, but it's a sensitive subject! What I don't like is women who obsess about their boobs! And what makes me incandescently angry is women who insist on having their perfectly fine and healthy boobs cut open to have a blob of insulating material stuffed in there!"

"No kidding. It does make you angry."

He laughs, unwillingly. "Yeah, it does."

"You're really very sweet, Giles." I arch myself against him, my legs spread wide. I lift them and wrap them around his back to pull him closer.

"No, I'm not," he contradicts me. "I had some of the worst fights of my life about this topic."

I wait to see whether he will say more. I have lost all interest in Amanda Saunders' knockers, but I am very curious about Giles's buttons.

"I suppose it was a clash of two neuroses," he says at last. "It was frustrating for me not to get through to her at all. She kept telling me that it was her body and she could do with it what she wanted, but what she didn't understand, or didn't want to understand, was that by hating her tits, she made me feel that she also hated what I did to them. That sounds terrible."

"No, I think I know what you mean. The wife's anxiety was about her appearance and the husband's was about his performance. Nothing surprising there, really."

Hell is being married to the wrong person. Or maybe Giles is simply too screwed up to be in a close intimate relationship with a woman without overpowering her with unrealistic expectations. On the other hand, after a couple of encounters with Amanda, I see that a man might have a tough time of it with her in his bed. And Giles took the plunge and is evidently making an effort to understand why he drowned, while I never had the guts to do more than dip my toe in.

"Well, I love what you do to my boobs," I announce sheepishly.

"Oh, you do, do you?" He wriggles out of his clothes and pulls my legs on either side of his ribcage. My arms are full of a strange, tall, naked man, and my legs, and my heart, and—

"Please. Giles, please…"

"Hmmmm?"

"Come into me—"

"Ah."

He raises his head, and we realize in the same second that the condoms are still in the bedroom cupboard.

I say what no woman should say in a situation like this.

"Well, of course *I* had a full medical before they let me sign my contract."

"I had one when I came back from England."

"Needed one, did you?" I ask, jealous, turn my head and bite into the inside of his arm. "And how many women have you had since then?"

"Only one."

Damn him! And damn her!

"And did you have unprotected sex with her?" I ask politely.

"Only once."

"*What?*"

"In the observatory, you silly girl! You know this! You were there!"

"Oh." I can feel my ears turning red. "That's true…how reckless."

"Can I trust you?" he asks me seriously.

"Yes!"

"Then let me come into you."

And suddenly I'm frightened. He straightens up, on his knees in front of the sofa, and my hands go to his wrists—to hold onto him, to steady myself, not to stop him, although I'm so frightened that I stop breathing. It is an eternity since I've been so close to a man—have I ever been so close to a man?—and now here it is, here *he* is. So lovely, with his hair falling across his forehead. So lovely, and so grave. He looks up from the few inches of space between us.

"Breathe…"

The sound that comes from my chest is something between a laugh and a sob; I grab his wrists more tightly, painfully, I think, but he is beyond feeling my fingers when we are both staring down at the engorged arch of his flesh; how smooth and soft and vulnerable it looks, especially the head, unhooded now, naked to my gaze, and naked to my own dark, secret flesh.

"You're tense." His voice is worried, reluctant.

My chest is rising and falling fast now, but my fingers let go of him.

"Yes…I'm frightened."

The corners of his gray-dappled eyes crease as a tiny light of amusement flickers in them. Self-irony. At the drop of a hat, at the erection of a penis, he is ready to distance himself from himself, look on, and sneer.

"I'm frightened, too." He doesn't say that ironically at all.

I wriggle higher up onto the sofa so that I can rest my head against the back and my heels on the edge of the seat.

"He isn't." I smile, nodding at the alert, eager animal that rises from its nest of grizzled hair. It twitches, and a few drops of transparent liquid run down the shaft. That makes me smile even more; I like that he likes being looked at.

"No, because he can't see beyond the tip of his…nose."

That makes me giggle, and him, too, but he doesn't want to be distracted now. He clasps my hands, our fingers interlock, and he cautiously nuzzles the tip of his cock into my hot, expectant flesh. Slowly. Cautiously. Just the tip. Moves his hips in slow, short, probing thrusts, and his *schlong* glances up from its aim, wetting its belly in my sopping folds. I grip his fingers harder and it dips down, dips its head deep, slides slow and deep into me. Deep, and slow, at first, but I'm gone already; I gulp air into the tiniest vessel of my lungs—and then the noise is deafening. The dogs, snoring to our quiet exchanges, are up and join in the chorus of human voices. I don't know that I screamed, but I must have done; my throat feels tight with need, and Giles is shouting at the dogs to be quiet, but of course that doesn't help at all.

"Oh, don't shout!" I gasp, between tears and laughter. "They're just preventing murder in their pack!"

Andrew, tail wagging, comes up to us and sniffs at the skin of my belly, which sends me into another fit of giggles.

"Back off, Andrew! This one's mine!"

Andrew sits on his hind legs but woofs with indignation.

"That's right! I'm top dog here, and this one—this one's my bitch, so—stop yapping! And you—" He glares down at me, very hot and bothered. "And you, stop laughing!"

"Yes, but—"

"Hold on. Hold on to me!"

One arm clamped around my waist, the other hand under my butt, he lifts me up and strides over to the open kitchen door. Giggling, I wrap every available limb around his body, although he's still so hard inside me that I could balance on his cock alone.

"In there! Go on, in!" The dogs bustle into the kitchen, and he slams the door behind them. "And now, Professor Lieberman…" I feel the warm wall of the chimney against my back. "Oh, God…I should have had you against my office door yesterday night!"

"Why didn't you?"

"You wanted to go home."

"I thought you wanted to get rid of me."

His hands clench underneath my ass. He closes his eyes and groans.

"Giles."

"Mmhm."

"Where's the file?"

"Termagant! Will you stop nagging me about the file? I have it safe."

"Here? Or at the department?"

"Safe."

"No, you have to listen to me!"

I climb onto his lap and look into his eyes. His face dissolves in front of me.

"Sweetheart, what's this?" He leans forward and kisses the tears off my cheeks.

"We have to hand it in, Giles. I feel awful, hiding it. Like an accomplice."

"You're not hiding it. I am."

"But why do you want to shield Hornberger from justice? I-don't-un-der-stand!" With my palms pressing down on his shoulders, I stress each syllable.

"I rather thought I was shielding you from gossip," Giles observes, not visibly impressed by my vehemence.

I sink back onto his thighs and rest my forehead against his chest. For a whole minute I stay like that, struggling to muster the courage to say what I want to say.

"If it just concerned me, I'd hand it in." My voice is muffled by the skin of his belly.

"You haven't thought that through."

"Look, Giles!" I sit up so he can see how serious I am. "You can think and think, but wrong will remain wrong and it's *wrong* to protect Hornberger!"

"It's more important to me to protect you than to turn him in."

"And to protect yourself." Because there is a subtext to this topic that we have so far carefully avoided.

"*That* does not weigh with me."

"Doesn't it?" Maybe the time has come to have this out. I climb off his lap and huddle up on the other side of the sofa. "My 'reputa-tion' can hardly be more important to you than it is to me."

"Can't it?" he echoes me flippantly, and I can tell he is going to be difficult about this. "But I'm a gentleman."

"There is nothing gentlemanly about not allowing me to make my own decisions!"

"You haven't got all the facts." Suddenly he is not flippant at all.

"Then *give* me the facts!" I explode. "Heavens, Giles! *Talk* to me!"

He looks away from me, into the fire, and for a few moments I really think he isn't going to answer.

"When Nick turned up in the observatory…that time," he finally says, still not looking at me, "he had his phone with him."

I wait for him to say more, and then it clicks. My hand, when I raise it to my forehead, is ice-cold. That, or I have a temperature again.

"There's a picture? He took a picture of us?"

Now Giles looks at me, and I understand how much of his ironic grin is about feeling helpless.

Chapter 37

I am no longer angry with Giles for withholding this little piece of information from me. However closely the sword of Damocles is hanging over the precious few days we have together, at least it was not accompanied by a pornographic photograph.

"And he isn't bluffing? Have you *seen* this picture?" I rally in a last-ditch defense later that evening when we're snuggled up in front of the fire.

"Good thinking, Sherlock, but I've seen it."

I'm tempted to ask for details, but Giles shakes his head.

"Why didn't he tell us there and then?"

"He said you're such a hothead, you'd have told him where to stick it. He thought I'd be more reasonable on my own."

"So the deal is, you hold onto the file and he'll hold onto the photo?"

"Mm-hmm."

"God, I hate that."

The scene has clouded over, and on the morning of my fourth day I decide that I must go home today, if only to get a change of clothes.

"You've had fresh undies each morning," Giles points out with the face of an Angel in the House, and it's true. Because we are going through so many bed sheets, he has been doing a load of laundry every day.

"Squidgy, slimy, oozy, gooey, sticky—oww!" he protests as I fling myself on him in the bed and wrestle him down. "I meant me! Did you think I was talking about you? Never!"

What with one thing and another, it is past four o'clock and getting dark again by the time we set off. I am grateful that Giles has offered to drive me and my bike back to the farm, because it's no longer white and clear but wet and windy-cold. But I am also grateful that he doesn't ask to come in or when he will see me again. I don't even know whether he *wants* to see me again.

"Thank you, Giles." More I cannot manage. I feel myself welling up, and I don't want to cry in front of him.

"It was my pleasure, Miss Lieberman." He bends down to give me a quick kiss on the lips, and then he's off.

I'm glad there's no Walsh about as I slowly push my bike up to the garage. I lock it in and trudge across to my porch.

I miss him already.

I'm also pretty certain that I didn't close my shutters before I set out in the small hours of Saturday morning. Maybe Pop Walsh went round the house to do that, thinking his Yankee greenhorn tenant had left for four weeks without battening down the hatches.

The moment I open the front door, I know that something is wrong. It's too warm, for one thing. I left the heat on low, assuming that I would be back in the morning; now even the little hall is warmer than I usually keep it. What I didn't leave on is the radio, and I certainly didn't leave it on in the bedroom, quietly playing country music.

Perhaps it is this detail that reassures me I won't be clobbered to death by housebreakers. It may still not be wise to venture any further, but fear is only one of my instinctive reactions. The bedroom door is open a crack, and when I cautiously push it open, I wonder what I expected to see. What I did not expect to see is three naked young people having sex on my bed. I recognize the blond girl, Logan's fuck buddy, and I can only assume that the two boys, one tall and lean, one darker and stockier, are Pop Walsh's farm helpers. They have the girl between them on all fours, one leisurely humping her from behind, one holding her bobbing head around his cock. It is a very peaceful, relaxed scene, and shocked as I am, I don't think I will start shouting quite yet.

I take a few steps further and peep into the living-room. They have candles burning in here, and there is a fragrance of orange in the air. On several blankets, draped over the sofa cushions that have been pushed together on the floor, Jules Walsh lies naked on her stomach, being massaged by Logan Williams. He is wearing boxers and a t-shirt, and as I watch, struggling to take in this invasion of my private space, I try to decide whether he is also masturbating her. Not yet, or not now, seems to be the answer to this one.

"Okay, people, end of party." I switch on the ceiling light, and Jules screams before bursting into tears.

"Get dressed, Jules, and stop blubbering!"

I walk back to the bedroom and throw out the Polish trio; the girl giggles, but the two boys seem to be stoned out of their heads. Without resistance or great hurry they pull on their clothes and disappear into the darkness.

"The first thing you'll do is strip my bed and put the sheets into the washing machine."

"Hey, man, don't—"

"Don't what, Logan?" I snap at him, showing him how very little amused I am. "Don't 'Hey, man' me, for a start! You call me 'Dr. Lieberman, ma'am,' or I'll call the police. Get on it!"

He shrugs and does as he is told. Meanwhile I lean in the doorframe and watch Jules, still sobbing, blow out the candles and rearrange the sofa cushions.

"Do you want me to put the red dress in with the sheets?" Logan calls from the bathroom. He sticks his head out through the door. "Only because there's also a lot of cunt juice on that. Dr. Lieberman, ma'am."

And this is where the absurdity of the situation reaches the critical degree and I can't keep my face straight any more.

"You really are a little shit, Logan Williams!"

At first he is not sure how he is to take this apparent change of atmosphere, then he steps out of the bathroom into the hall.

"Actually, no, ma'am, I'm not. If I was, I'd have allowed Pavel, Karol, and Elka to clean out the place long before now. I'd also have deflowered that young lady there—" He nods his head to indicate Jules in the living-room.

"You mean to tell me you haven't?" I ask with awful irony.

"Jules?" he calls. "Have I fucked you?"

"No!" She appears from the kitchen, too upset now for tears. "He hasn't!"

"Yeah, because you're saving yourself for Mr. Right. Anyway, I thought you told me you wanted out of this place. Juvenile delinquents don't go anywhere except jail."

"She's fifteen!" Logan says, disparagingly. "She's a black girl on a white man's farm! She has no idea who or what she is or wants to be!"

"I'm sixteen!"

"Well, I'll tell you what she is: no match for persuasive, personable scum like you!"

He gives a sardonic laugh and shakes his head about my ignorance.

"True. Had I *wanted* to fuck her. But guess what: I didn't! And you know why not? Two reasons! One, I have no mind to be sent down for statutory rape! She's fifteen! Sorry, sixteen—whatever. I can do sums! And two, my kid sister went down that road. She's eighteen now, and she's already chalked up one abortion, one gang rape, and one bout of STD. You may think I'm scum, but I'm scum with principles!"

I look around me. "Yeah, you make Mahatma Gandhi look like a pimp!"

He scratches his cheek, grins, and shrugs.

"Jules, is he telling the truth?" I demand of her.

"About what?" she asks cautiously.

"What do you *think?* Did you have sex with him?"

"No! Not…really."

I groan, more impatient with her cageyness than with his *chuzpah.*

Logan comes clean. "Somewhere between second and third base. Dr. Lieberman, ma'am."

"I'm still waiting to hear that from you, Jules."

She stares at me, in equal parts frightened and appalled.

"The thing is this, Jules, if I have any reason to suspect that Logan's—or any other boy's—penis or finger beyond the first knuckle has been inside you, I'm going to drag your sly, secretive little butt to the gynecologist before you can say contraception! Have I made myself clear?"

"Jesus, you *are* a ballbuster," Logan says, half grinning, half annoyed. "Leave the kid alone!"

Jules has started crying again, and I give up.

"So whose idea was it to break into my house? You did that before, a few times, didn't you?"

He shrugs again.

"Logan, how can I take you seriously if you behave like a fifteen-year-old, too?"

"I have a key! It was my idea!" Jules speaks up. "And I was sixteen last Sunday!"

"Well, at last you're standing by your man! Simple rule, Jules: you don't make out, let alone have sex, with a boy you don't really, really like! And if you really, really like someone, you help them when they're in trouble!"

This shames her, and I'm not sorry.

"Did you or the others take anything? Apart from my eggs and my wine?"

"We replaced the eggs! We were cold and hungry!"

I remember Giles in his kitchen, in t-shirt and jogging pants, making vegetable frittata for me.

"No, we didn't," Logan says earnestly. "Unless the others took something when I wasn't looking, but I don't think so. I told them I'd beat the shit out if them if they did. Are you missing any valuables?"

"I'll let you know. Now go away. Oh, and, Jules…" I hold out my hand, and she stares at it.

"Give her the key," Logan orders her, and she digs her hand into her coat pocket and extracts a single key on a length of brown string.

"What will you tell my mom?" She wells up again, and I can't decide whether I prefer her tearful or petulant.

"I don't know yet, Jules. You'll just have to wait and see. That goes for you, too, Logan. I guess I should be all pedagogical about this and make a deal with you, like, I won't tell anyone if you write me nothing but A essays for the rest of your time at Ardrossan. But I really don't know whether I want to be so magnanimous."

"And I don't know whether I'd take the deal."

"Then we both have something to think about, don't we?"

"It's me."

There is a short pause in the line. "So it is."

"Giles, do you think I could come back tonight, with my essays, a change of clothes, and my PJs?"

He gives one of his spurts of laughter. "You won't need PJs."

While I'm waiting for the washing to be done, I wander around the cottage, checking it for theft or damage. It is a relief, in a way, to know that I wasn't imagining the subtle changes I noticed around the house recently, and I lived in shared housing for too long to be very deeply upset about the idea of people using my stuff in the kitchen, or even sleeping in my bed. Still, all that is very different from a group of young people effectively breaking into my home to have sex parties there.

I am worried that I am foisting myself on Giles and he is too polite to say so, and when I knock on his door, a rucksack on my back and a sack of groceries in my hand, I fully expect a lukewarm welcome. His eyes are very bright and very alert, and he is very polite indeed, taking the groceries off me and assuring me that I shouldn't have.

"Are you all right?" he asks when I've peeled myself out of my coat and boots.

"Yes, I am, but you won't bel —"

The rest is stifled by a big, thorough kiss, after which he literally flings me over his shoulder and carries me off into the bedroom. I didn't think I would be in the mood for sex, after that little intermezzo at my cottage, but the moment I see his face and feel his body against mine, I decide I am not going to allow a anyone to spoil him for me.

"I missed you," he whispers into my hair.

"Oh, my sweet." I hug him more tightly and raise my hips against his. "Then you'd better take better aim, hadn't you?"

This makes him laugh so hard that he can't take aim at all for a few minutes. It is almost ten o'clock by the time the quiche is in the oven and Giles has drawn the cork of a bottle of Chardonnay.

"You seem very sporting about it," he remarks, eyebrows raised, when I have described my domestic situation. "Are you taking this too lightly?"

"I don't know. Maybe. But they're young, and after all…it's just sex."

"I have to say I have little sympathy left for Logan Williams," he says.

I sip my wine. "Hmm."

"You're going to let him off, aren't you?"

I gaze at him across his little kitchen table. "It's so lovely to touch someone you like. I guess I'll have to talk to Karen. She was odd when I tried to broach the subject before. Evasive. I imagine she's tired of hearing complaints about her daughter."

"If you shield the girl, she'll only get into more trouble."

"What would you do? Lock her up?"

"She'll be knocked up by next Christmas."

"Yeah, maybe. Talking of which, what are we going to do about Selena?"

He pulls a face at me over the rim of his wineglass.

"You mean, what are *you* going to do about Selena?"

"Oh, Giles! She needs help!"

"'If she's caught the Nicholas, it'll cost her a thousand pound ere she be cured,'" he quips.

"You don't like her because she has fallen for Hornberger! I don't much like her either, but I'm not just frightened for her but also of her. I think she's a liability, Giles. And she won't confide in anyone unless she is confronted."

"Are you worried she'll start leaving gunge on your office door, too?"

"Oh! I haven't told you!" I reach across the table to touch his hand, which makes him smile, catch it, and link his fingers with mine. "It wasn't Corvin! It can't have been, because he's back and almost had a heart attack when he tried to get into his office and couldn't because the lock had been changed. He says he spent the last two months with his daughter in Vermont."

Giles seems suitably impressed with this news and more interested than in Selena O'Neal's plight. "So Dancey was right? It was that spoiled little rich girl?"

"Madeline Harrison? I don't know. Yes, it must have been. That college of yours is full of psychologically unstable, violent young women — why is that, Giles?"

He grins. "Your guess is as good as mine. Well, that's a lot of words you're going to have with quite a lot of people, isn't it?"

I drop my head between my hands and groan. "I want the holidays to go on forever."

On his shelf I find a large picture book about British landscape and literature, and we spend a happy two hours leafing through it, comparing favorites and telling each other anecdotes about the places we visited.

"…and there's a pub in the village that sells the most fantastic homemade pasties, just heaven after a long hike. Remember that for when you're next there."

I look at his profile, so close to mine on the sofa.

"Giles."

"Hmm?"

"Tell me again why we wouldn't work."

"Because I'm twelve years older than you." He sighs, leans back and continues to enumerate his mental list. "Because I can't father any children. Because your situation in the department is vulnerable and will remain so for years to come. Because I'm sure that your parents would have fifty fits if you spent your fertile thirties with a goy—an infertile one at that! Shall I go on?"

"When did you last have your…baubles…tested?"

"My baubles?" He laughs, but it's partly to cover his embarrassment. "Never as such. I was told at the time that given the extent of the inflammation, it was very likely that my fertility had been, uh, adversely affected. At some point Mandy and I stopped using contraception to see whether she would get pregnant, but she didn't. So I have to assume that my…baubles…are empty."

"Well, that's a bit lame! You should get tested! I'd be willing to assist you with the necessary, um, preparations."

He stares at me, defensive and outraged at the same time.

"Listen, stop deluding yourself! All my little swimmers are dead! If there *are* any little swimmers; I've never really made it my business to enquire into the—"

"Oh, I'm not much bothered, myself," I say nonchalantly. "I'm just thinking of the next woman you have sex with. Unlike me, she may actually know that she does want children, so it would be useful to know the exact facts, wouldn't it?"

My ingenuous little monologue upsets him so much that he jumps up, stalks over into the kitchen, and starts sorting the dirty dishes into the washer.

"End of conversation," he mutters when I follow him. "You're doing neither me nor yourself a favor by pretending that you do not want children! You're in your first year on tenure track. You're thirty years old!"

"Fair point. The sense I have at the moment that I don't necessarily need a child to be happy may change. Or it may not."

He stares at me, a dirty plate in one hand, a chopping knife in the other.

"Don't start, Anna! It's no good! Even if you weren't on tenure track, it would be grossly selfish of me to—"

"You *married*, knowing yourself infertile!" I protest, by now seriously hurt. "I hear what you're saying, but don't pretend you're being all noble and unselfish!"

"Yes, and look at what a resounding success my marriage was!"

"What if a woman wants you more than she wants a child?" I shout, pushed over the edge.

"She may think that for a while, maybe, if the sex is good enough."

"Cleveland—you're a bastard!"

It hurts to be reminded of the limits of our little affair, but the hurt disperses the haze of vague hopes and fantasies in my mind. That evening we don't make love again, but there is no question of either of us sleeping on the sofa. I'm sad, but after all, I knew that this would make me sad, so I have no one to blame but myself. I wake in the middle of the night, in the pitch-black bedroom, and I miss him. I feel for his thigh, for the waistband of his pajama pants, for the warm, fragrant skin of his groin. His warm, half-erect cock. More tenderly than ever I cradle his soft, heavy balls in my hand and kiss them softly, so gently.

His fingers close around my naked arm.

"Anna…" His voice his faint and gravelly, but I don't know what he means, so I go on caressing his flesh because that is all I *can* do to show him what I feel for him.

"*You led them…in the night by a pillar of fire…to give them light in the way wherein they should go.*" I smile and clasp his pillar of fire in my hand.

His fingers are kneading my arm, and I can hear him breathe in ragged, uneven gasps. I hunch up my knees and pull off my panties, then his shirt that I've been wearing as a pajama top. My face fits snugly into the hollow of his throat as I stretch out on top of him.

"You multiplied their children as the stars of heaven," I whisper, *"and you brought them into the land that you had told their fathers to enter and possess."*

With my knees I spread his legs so that my thighs are cradled between his. When I slide him into me, he moans like a man in a dream. I clasp his hands in mine and crook his arms so that his palms face up, like a sleeping child's.

"So the children went in and—" I ride him slowly, my elbows on either side of him, keeping him immobile *"—and possessed the land, and…thou subduedst before them the inhabitants of the land and gavest them…into their hands…that they…"*

My mouth finds his throat, finds it stretched to a long, smooth column of skin and muscle as he arches himself against me, gasping for breath in long, deep gulps.

"…that they might do with them…as they would…"

He thrusts himself into me, shuddering, his lean, solid male body underneath me, and I feel his strength and my power over it.

"My sweet," I murmur against his throat, my cheek pressed against his heaving chest. "My poor, sweet, lovely boy."

In the morning, the noise of the shower wakes me. Without even going into the kitchen to switch on the kettle, I boot up the PC and search the online phone directory.

"Hey." He comes to look over my shoulder, toweling his head.

"Hey."

I glance up, check whether the night's interlude had any lasting effects. Giles still looks like a boy, young and disheveled, with a quiet, slightly bashful smile on his face. I hold out my hand for his and draw it to my lips.

"Sweetie, I'm afraid I'm going to pick a fight with you."

He laughs, then sees that I am in earnest. "What about?"

"About your reputation."

"So, where to?" he asks when he has steered the Volvo onto the main road.

"Southside, Oakland Park."

I am holding the file on my knees, but I am not tempted to look at it again.

Bartholomew Road is a residential area bordering on a business park; the houses are garishly decorated with lights and stars and reindeer, and there are several Santa Clauses scaling the rooftops.

"Number twelve sixty-seven. Here." I unclick my seat belt and open the door.

"Wait!" He grabs my elbow. "You will regret this!"

"I hope I will never regret having done the right thing. Will you regret it?"

He looks at me, looks me over. Sighs.

"Not for myself, no, but I may well regret not having stood up to you!"

For half a minute or so I think there is nobody home, or the people who are home won't open the door for us. Then there is the sound of a chain being latched, and the door opens a crack.

"Mrs. Randall? Louise Randall?"

She is a tall woman, quite big now, with a mass of silvery-dark hair done up into a loose chignon.

"What do you want? Are you collecting for something?"

"No, no, I'm…I'm Anna Lieberman, and this is Giles Cleveland. We are English professors at Ardrossan University."

This produces the reaction I had feared. The door is slammed shut, and her voice, though muffled, is angry.

"Go away! Are you reporters? I have nothing to say to you!"

"Mrs. Randall!" I put my mouth close to the door. "Louise! I promise you we are not reporters! I just want to give you something, and you can decide what to do with it!"

Silence.

"Listen, Louise, I'm not going to stand out here shouting for all your neighbors to hear. Am I right in assuming that when you were young you went by Mary-Lou? And that your maiden name is Tandy? Just tell me whether I'm right!"

Silence.

The door opens again, but the chain is still in place.

"Keep your voice down," she says, much calmer now. "I'm not going to ask you in. I have guests, and they're asleep. As for that fine *gentleman*, I don't want to talk about him. There's no point!"

"I don't know about that, but it isn't for me to decide, or for anyone, except you. This—" I hand her the file "—is yours. I—we—came by it by accident, and we feel that you should have it. Take it to the police, or burn it—it's up to you."

She stares at the plastic folder in her hand, dumb with emotion.

"This comes thirty years too late."

"I know. But if we keep it, we're protecting him, and if we hand it over to the police, we are interfering in your life in a way that I don't want to be responsible for."

She nods, mechanically, and undoes the chain.

"The past is never just that, is it?" she says.

"Past, you mean? No, I guess it isn't. Or just."

At this she smiles wanly.

"No, it isn't. Well, they do say that choice is a burden." She weighs the slim folder in her hand. "Not very heavy, is it?"

I smile back, relieved that she is recovering her sense of humor. Even if it is of the gallows variety.

"If you wanted to get in touch with us at all, don't hesitate, via email or the phone." Giles digs up his wallet out of his back pocket and pulls out his card. "Anna will shout at me for having said this, but I think you should go to the police and make sure that his ass ends up in jail."

"Giles!"

"That's all right," Louise assures me. "I won't rush into anything, and I sure won't be guided by another white male professor's opinion. No offense, sir."

Giles smiles at her, and I can see that even on Louise Randall in her present plight it has the usual effect.

"All the best, Louise. I don't know whether I can say Merry Christmas, but—Merry Christmas!"

A week after I should have flown home, Giles takes me to the airport and kisses me goodbye at the gate. We both know it is reckless to be seen like this in public, but as far as I'm concerned, the public can go boil its head.

"Be good," he murmurs into my ear, and I can only nod. "When will you be back?"

"On the twelfth." I did not tell him that I'll be flying in from Heathrow. I have not told him about London, neither the job nor the interview. I don't know why not, maybe because we didn't talk about the time after the holidays at all. Or maybe because I don't know what I think myself. Giles will be flying to London the day after tomorrow to spend Christmas with friends and be back two days before me. We might bump into each other on Trafalgar Square, theoretically. It will be very strange to know that he's in London when I am, but—no. I haven't told him.

<h1 style="text-align:center">Chapter 38</h1>

I had expected Giles and his cabin by the lake would dissolve into a sweet but hazy dream the moment my plane touched down at LaGuardia, but the very opposite happens. It is as if I had spent a week in the best place in the world and had been cast out into a chaos of people, noise, stench and loneliness.

I brace myself for the maternal onslaught, but Gloria remains *shtum* on the subject. It is as if I never planned to arrive seven days earlier. She feeds me and fills me in on all the depressing family details, but she doesn't ask a single question about the man for whom I risked a big family rumpus. I'm guessing I have Nathan to thank for that. He and Jessica have decided to file for a divorce.

"Mom hasn't asked me a single question about…about Giles," I inform Nat glumly.

"Couldn't very well," Nat tells the baseball glove he is he is trying to fix. "She didn't even know his name. Giles, huh?"

"Yes. So she took it really badly?"

"Could say that. On top of my little train wreck. Of course she has decided he is a married Catholic or a convicted criminal, or you would have told her about him."

"No, he's not. He's a divorced WASP."

"Jesus, Anna!" he breathes and looks up. We stare at each other for a second and then double up in convulsions of laughter.

My relatives make up for my mother's ostensible lack of interest in my love life. The first thing everyone asks me is whether I have met anyone "down there." Some of them know about Nick Hornberger, and for once I am happy to make him the topic of conversation. At least they'll know the worst of him *before* he ruins my career at Ardrossan.

It is my father who eventually takes the bull by the horns, while my mother has her back turned to us in the kitchen.

"So this is all a recent development, this man that you met?"

"Not all that recent, but—yes."

"Don't make her talk about him, Dad. She's found herself a WASP."

"Nat, you're not helping!"

"Well, statistically speaking, given the demographics in your part of the country, that wasn't unlikely," my father tells the egg whisk he is trying to fix. "I will admit, however, that I'm a little surprised. You're going out with a Republican? Most of these Came-Over-in-the-Mayflower families down there are Republican, aren't they?"

"Well, he isn't, and his family didn't."

"Didn't what?"

"Come over in the Mayflower. They were parliamentarians in the Civil War."

"Parliamentarians? What are you talking about?"

"Not *this* Civil War. The English one, in the seventeenth century. Giles is English."

Nat gives me a delighted slap on the shoulder.

"An Englishman! Just what you always wanted!"

"C'mon guys, gimme a break. Start *kvetching*, or I'll feel even more guilty about this than I already do."

"Why should we complain?" Mom shrugs sarcastically. "Our daughter is only going to live on another continent, thousands of miles and an ocean away from her family, among strangers. That's no reason to complain, is it?"

"No one said anything about another continent, Mom!"

"How much of this is because he's English?"

"I don't know. This could be about a dozen things! He's smart and funny and kind—I find that attractive! He's older than me—yes, I find that attractive, too! He's the most beautiful man I have ever known—and that—"

"Yes, yes, we get your point," Dad hurries to interrupt me, evidently afraid of where my enumeration will take me.

"—but none of that is why I love him!"

"*Love!* Almighty!" My mother groans and throws up her hands.

"I'm not going to justify this to you. I'm not." I couldn't, even if I wanted to, because I'm so upset that tears are clogging up my voice. If there is one thing guaranteed to fend off my mother's enquiries, it is tears.

"You're thirty years old, I'm sure you know best." End of discussion. When emotions boil over, my mother flees from the kitchen.

"No, I don't know best!" I fire up. "The whole thing is a complete mess, Mom, and I have no idea how this is going to end! I'm frightened what will happen if we go on, and I'm frightened what will happen if we end it! And I knew beforehand that talking to you about it wouldn't help me resolve anything—that's why I almost didn't come home! I knew I'd have to sit here for two weeks, pretending that I'm fine, when this is…*choking* me!"

That night I stay at Sheena's because the girl who rents my old room has flown home to Ohio to see her family over Christmas. I feel like a nomad, with my rucksack and my laptop. No, worse. I feel like a tourist. Irene and Jacques, like a lot of couples that are thinking about breaking up, have rented an apartment together, and I stay with them for another couple of nights. When Irene hears that I'll be flying to England for ten days, she is immediately suspicious.

"Are you going to see him there?"

"No."

"Then why are you going?"

"To see Debbie and Dave in Bristol, and Lisa and Gavin in London, and hopefully Kate Allard for tea one day. I haven't been for ages. Eighteen months."

Irene watches me play with my salad.

"But you have been seeing him, haven't you?"

"Yes."

"And?"

"And nothing. Nothing you didn't know before."

"I think you are going to see him," she decides. "Is that the plan from now on, to fly to England for dirty weekends with your colleague?"

"I am not going to see Giles over there! I'm going for a job interview."

Irene's reaction—a long sigh and a long pause—is worse than I had expected, though less vociferous.

"If you must, you must, Anna. There's obviously not enough here to keep you, and that place down there is a madhouse."

"You did hear that I said job *interview*, right? I may stay at Ardrossan a good while yet, provided they don't fire me. Which they might, given the fact that—" I hesitate. "Given the fact that some of my students have accused me of sexual harassment. Oh, and you know who Selena, the girl in the observatory, has sex with? And who got her pregnant?"

Predictably, this distracts her attention, and even Jacques gets involved in our debate about the various words I will have to have with various people when I get back to Ardrossan. It's the most enjoyable evening I spent with them in years.

But when my plane circles in a holding stack above Buckinghamshire and we approach Heathrow from the west, with the Thames glistening like a silver snake in the sun and the pilot alerting us to the fact that visibility is good enough to see Windsor Castle, tears are running down my cheeks. I don't even try to stop them.

"Sorry—are you all right?" my neighbor asks me. He has been sleeping or reading the whole time, while I have been sleeping and staring out the window the whole time. This is the first sentence he has addressed to me.

"Yes, I'm sorry." I brush away the tears with my sleeve. "I'm just realizing that I will have to come and live here."

"That is, indeed, a prospect to reduce anyone to tears," he says dryly and hands me a paper tissue.

Before I make my way to East London, I travel down to Bristol for a few days' coaching and counseling.

"Look, I'm gonna do what I do, okay? And either it's enough or not. I may not even want this job!"

"That's your strength," Dave says, punching the air. "You can go in confident and strong! But don't come across as too American — well, you know that, don't you? But don't try to be English, either. You're fine as you are!"

"So…what about your *beshert?*" Debbie asks me when we're alone. "Oh, dear — as bad as that?"

I dash away the water from my eyes.

"Yeah…really bad."

"Have you been, er, seeing him?"

"Mm-hmm."

She nods. Then she shrugs. "Well…"

"What?"

"Well, if you get the job at Queen Mary, you could —"

"Go on sleeping with him for six months and then leave him?"

She shrugs again.

"I don't think I *could* leave him," I say.

"But if you get the job?"

"I know. I don't know."

"If he didn't exist and you got the job?"

"Oh, in that case…" My chest expands with relief. "I don't know. I *feel* I would come back to England. I *feel* I would want to. But I feel so many crazy things at the moment, how can I trust my judgment? Giles will have to ditch me. I can't."

"Wait till he breaks up with you? That's miserable!"

"Yes, I know."

On Monday morning Debbie and I take the fast train to London. Under the grubby glass dome of Paddington Station, we part company.

"Right," she says resolutely. "Remember — it's all about choice. That's all. You want to have the choice, Ardrossan or London. That's all."

I make my way across London and amble along the busy Mile End Road toward a nondescript brown brick building. It looks like a cross between a big dental practice and a community center, and while the traffic is rushing past me, I wonder whether I am crazy to even consider leaving a place as beautiful as Ardrossan. But when Ewan Buchanan picks me up in the hall, I am strangely calm and, suddenly, wonderfully focused.

"And you would really move to the UK?" It is the oldest among my interviewers, a man with an almost-white beard and a red bowtie, who seems skeptical.

I was prepared for the question, but none of my prepared answers seem appropriate.

"Yes. Yes, I would."

"Anna has flown in from the States." Ewan Buchanan comes to my aid. "Surely that speaks for her motivation!"

"I'm sure her motives are most honorable," Professor Simpson agrees. "I would like to have them explained to me, that's all."

I have a job. I don't need to lie.

"Well, sir, I spent five of the past ten years in England, and by and large they were the better years, personally and professionally."

He waits for more.

"The truth is, I think I would be more productive living in England. And happier."

Back at Heathrow I have that bizarre feeling at the end of a holiday that I only just arrived two days ago. Bored with the trashy novels on the shelves of W. H. Smith, I select a volume about British country houses up for sale and in need of refurbishment. That will keep me dreaming on the flight.

"Anna?" a male voice addresses me. "Anna! What are the odds!"

So lost am I in thought that it takes me several seconds to recognize the burly, bouncy redhead. Paul French has been to see his children and his mother and is waiting for his flight back to Chicago. He suggests coffee, and I don't see how I can refuse.

"It's amazing how fast you can get from London to New York these days! You'll be making the trip more often in future, won't you?" he says significantly. "Maybe you should get yourself a job in the old country, too. Mind you, pay-wise, that's bad advice, and so I told Giles. I earn heaps more at Notre Dame than I did in the UK."

For a moment or two I'm too confused to answer.

"Have I put my foot in it?" he asks, pulling a face of contrition. "Forget that I —"

"What do you mean, Paul?"

"No, no, he obviously didn't…well, I assumed Giles would have mentioned it."

"Is Giles going back to England?" I sound calm, but Paul French is no fool.

"Look, I assumed —"

"Where?" As if that was the point. But I'm too frightened to ask *when*.

"They've offered him my old job at UCL. That's why he came to see me at Notre Dame, to discuss the offer. God, Anna, I'm so sorry, I assumed he told you! Don't tell him I —"

"I won't tell him you told me," I say slowly, thinking fast. "Don't worry. I won't say a word."

Chapter 39

The first thing I do when I get home—no, wait, let me rephrase that. The first thing I do when I return to the cottage on the farm is check each room for evidence of interference, but everything seems to be as I left it. The rocking chair sits in a corner of the study looking as if the previous tenants had forgotten it. Then I call the main house on the phone, but no one picks up. The moment I put the phone down, it rings. Caught out, I automatically pick up.

"You're back."

"Got in twenty minutes ago."

"Can I see you?"

I breathe and try to be mindful of the intense and ambivalent feelings raging in my stomach. He will have left this country by the summer. I can risk having an affair with someone who will only be here for another few months. *Can* I risk it?

Why didn't he tell me?

Why the hell does Giles never tell me things?

I could have sex with Giles Cleveland today. Do I want to, or not? Simple, really.

He turns up on my doorstep less than fifteen minutes later, more handsome than ever, and very cautious, careful not to overwhelm me, but raring to go. He dutifully enquires after my journey and my jetlag, and I could play hard to get, but I don't want to tease him. I want to pummel him and shout my disappointment at him, but I do not want to tease. My orgasms are powerful and effortless; vaguely I wonder why this is. Maybe because, for all his impatience, Giles is a very attentive lover, watching me, making sure of me, enjoying my pleasure even more than his own. Maybe it is because my body, remembering and anticipating its hopeless yearning for his, melts into the present moment without reserve or reservation. If I'm going to crash this plane, I'll do it full throttle, in free fall. During some desultory talk between two bouts of sex and the soup and homemade bread that Giles pulls out of a basket like a male Red Riding Hood, I casually mention that I bumped into Paul French at the airport.

"Which airport?" he asks, frowning.

"Heathrow." I pause for a reaction, but his face is blank again. "I was in England. To see friends."

"You didn't say."

"No, I didn't."

He was quick to suspect Paul of having tattled, but Giles is not a man quick to speak. So we eat, both of us withdrawn and a little wary of each other, and I wonder how we are ever going to sort ourselves out.

Afterward — showered, wined and fed — I zonk out on the sofa.

"I suppose you'd like me to leave you to it now." Giles is leaning in the open doorway.

"I'm sorry, Giles. It's more that I can't really ask you to stay. I have nothing more to offer today…"

"You're still on English time. It's the wee small hours for you."

"That's certainly what it feels like." I can hardly keep my eyes open, and being snuggled up under my quilt doesn't help. Exhaustion is a plausible reason to push him away. "Anyway, you have the dogs to look after!"

"They're sleeping at a friend's house." He is still leaning in the door, watching me.

"Are they having a pajama party?"

He comes over, sits down at the bottom of the sofa and slips his hands under the quilt to find my woolly feet. Edging closer, he pulls them onto his lap and starts kneading them. His fingers inch higher, pushing up the legs of my pajamas.

"Giles, really…I'm totally knackered." I try to pull my left foot out of his grip, but his fingers are surprisingly strong around my ankle.

"Not to worry. I'll get my money's worth."

"*Money's worth?*"

"Shhhh…"

I'm too tired to make a scene. If he won't take a hint, let him sit there and massage my calves; he won't get any more sex out of me tonight. I have a heartache.

"Horrible man," I murmur before I drop off.

I wake up confused and annoyed. Too groggy to recall my dream. It aroused me and I want to go on dreaming, but some commotion woke me. My quilt and my pajama pants tangled, legs naked. Butt naked.

"Giles! What are you—no! Don't *do* that!"

He raises his head from between my thighs. "Why not?"

I hadn't encouraged him to return the favors that I enjoy doing for him, and he hadn't insisted; I assumed that we both preferred it that way.

"I thought you didn't…well, you haven't…"

Without breaking eye contact in the dim light of the reading lamp, he runs the tip of his tongue around my clit, then gently pulls it into his mouth and suckles it.

"I'm just shy," he informs me.

I try to cover myself up, clutch, ineffectually, at my blanket, and try to push his head away, but if this is to be the first time I refuse sex to him, I must be more awake. And more determined. When I yank at the silky hair between my fingers—I can't remember whether it was to pull him closer or to pull him off—his fingers feel for mine, tenderly at first, but then they are like a vise around my wrist and secure my arm between my hip and the seat of the sofa so that I am trapped by my own weight. His other hand comes for my other wrist and clasps it in a way that allows no resistance.

"Relax," he murmurs.

His fingers slip over my eyes, light and warm…God, I'm so tired…then they are back on my hips, my thighs, pressing into my flesh, massaging the strands of muscle into uselessness. I rear up when the slow, soft caress of his lips and tongue becomes more insistent; I try to struggle, but he shoves his hands underneath me so that his fingers can clamp my elbows to my sides and my knees are forced apart by his shoulders. So wide open. Panic.

"Giles—I don't like this!"

"Yes, you do."

Unfolding me, unfurling me layer by twitching layer, Giles draws nearer to my core.

For what seems like hours I drift into and out of sleep, floating in a warm, slow stream that occasionally runs faster, more turbulently, and I tense up, subconsciously fighting against the undertow. Then I give in. Even when I'm sucked under, I do not drown. Finally I emerge, gasping for breath, climaxing against his mouth with long, soft, fluid contractions.

He waits till I am done; his lips are warm and slow on the damp skin of my belly. Never in my life have I been more deeply sated. Every fiber, every cell in my body is limp with the exhaustion that comes after long and intense stimulation.

"No! Oh, G-Giles, no, I c-can't!"

"Yes, you can."

He settles himself between my wet thighs and slides into me. I'm too weak even to scream, although his cock pierces me with a thrust of exquisite torture, as if my whole body were a sheath of nerve endings. I manage to clamp my arms and legs around him, to have something to hold onto, to stop my chest from exploding. He makes no attempts at finesse now; a few minutes, and he lies on top of me, heavy, surely uncomfortable on the sofa that is just long enough for me. With my arms around him and my fingers in his hair, damp at the nape, I think of newborn babies, squidgy with goo, resting on their mothers' sweat-drenched breasts.

Tears run out of the corners of my eyes, into my ears, onto the cushion.

He lifts his head.

"Is it something Paul French said?" he murmurs.

And now I'm sobbing helplessly, hopelessly, stunned with the loss of him who is still inside me.

Chapter 40

Giles must have carried me over into the bedroom. At least that is where I wake up, and I doubt I would have been able to walk there. My wrist watch on the bedside table says half past seven, but it takes me an age to figure out whether it is morning or evening and whether I'm on Greenwich Mean Time or Eastern Standard Time.

I am alone in my bed, but like a lover in a movie, he has left a note.

Gone to pick up the dogs. Thank you for last night G.

It takes me another six hours to get up, partly because I feel as if I had swum across the Atlantic instead of flown across, partly because I don't want to wake up and think about the biggest mess I have ever got myself into. So much do I not want to think about being Giles's farewell fling before he leaves for University College, London, that all other chores seem attractive.

Karen answers the phone, and I ask her to come over as soon as is convenient. My voice must have sounded ominous, because ten minutes later she knocks on the door.

"Sorry to make you trudge through the slush, Karen, but I suspect you may not want witnesses."

I prepared myself for a confrontation, but she denies nothing and grows very quiet.

"I'm sorry, Anna." She plays with the handle of her teacup, and I notice how tired she looks. Christmas is never a relaxing time for mothers.

"Is there more?" I say after a pause. "I had hoped you'd be sorry, but—is that all?"

"You took the key off her? That's good. Hold onto it, hide it somewhere in the shack, but hide it well."

"Karen!"

She sighs and hides her eyes behind her hand for a moment.

"Why do you think the previous tenants left?" She waits for me to catch on. "When they found out, they went straight to Howard. I don't blame them! You will, too, and I don't blame you, either! But I can't stop her. I have no control over her." Karen's lips tremble, but she won't cry in front of me. "You can't imagine the row we had over it. But she can't resist the pickers. They make her feel important and…grown up, I guess."

"But, Karen, at this rate she'll end up pregnant before she's finished school! You don't want her to end up—"

"Like me?" she says bitterly. "It seems inevitable. I'll get her on the pill, now that she's sixteen. I don't know what else to do."

Her defeatist attitude makes me angry, but I have no solution ready, and the longer I reflect on her situation, the more I see how complicated it is.

"There must be something you can do!" I finally say, lamely.

"Take her and move out?" Karen's smile is twisted with suppressed tears.

A day later and twelve weeks early, Howard Walsh III is delivered by emergency caesarean section. Grandma Shirley, whom I meet on my way to the car, is unable to give me any details beyond the fact that he is expected to live and that he weighed eight hundred sixty-five grams at birth. Karen is also being kept in for observation, and she—Shirley—feels it would probably be too much for Karen if they all went to visit her all the time.

"She'll want some peace and quiet now. We'll see her when she gets back home."

The only silver lining on all these black clouds is that my course evaluations were not as disastrous as I had feared. The graduate students were very sweet and generous, and the remaining undergraduates in my Comedy class also liked me. Ma Mayfield informs me in an email that the complaints about me have been shelved for the time being, but I should prepare myself for spot checks of my teaching next semester. Fair enough. English Lit doesn't get more hardcore than *Paradise Lost*, and whatever groans and grumbles it will provoke, they won't be about sex. Maybe I have had enough of sex for the time being.

On Saturday afternoon the phone rings, but I surprise myself by not answering. I'm busy. I'm prepping my semester, sorting out clothes, cleaning the cottage. Leave me be. I'm in a mood. Resentful. Irritable. Isn't it downright childish, this desire to give yourself up to another, to relinquish all agency and responsibility and just let your body take over? Honestly, I think that is what this whole sex thing is all about. Hormones. Like a computer with data overload, my body has shut down. Too much stimulation, too much sex. Silly. We all have jobs to do, don't we?

I only realize how angry I am when I arrive at the Observatory on the first Monday of the spring semester and the whole place is in an uproar because Nick Hornberger has been arrested for sexually assaulting a fellow student thirty years ago.

"Do you know what really pisses me off?" I snap at Steve Howell, whose morning seems to be spent loitering on the fourth-floor corridor to greet every new arrival with the news. "That this guy is absorbing so much of our time and attention! I'm here to teach literature, not to gossip about dirty old men!"

"Anna, I don't think—"

"For heaven's sake, Steve, would you scan the supermarket tabloids for stories like this? No, you wouldn't! I bet you feel superior to the housewives who buy them, don't you? Well, *be* superior, then!"

He stares at me, a twisted smile on his face, half incredulous that I said what he heard me say. Poor Steve. But I really can't stand him.

So Louise Randall, née Mary-Lou Tandy, decided after all that vengeance may be the Lord's, but justice can at least try to kick Nicholas Hornberger, née Eagleson, in the balls. My first instinct is to phone Giles to talk this development of events over with him, but—no. I'm here to work.

The noises coming from Andrew Corvin's office convince me, if there was any doubt, that he must have been away for most of the winter semester, because the walls are so thin that I hear him clomping around, pushing furniture from one corner of the cramped room to the other, and occasionally even talking to himself. The noise is less eerie than the silence that I interpreted as evidence of vigilante malignancy, but after a while it becomes very distracting. Might as well have the next word.

When I knock, all activity in the room comes to a halt.

"Sir? Professor Corvin? It's Anna Lieberman. Your next door neighbor? May I have a quick word with you, sir?"

There is more silence, and then a cough, which I decide to interpret as a permission to open the door and peek in.

"Get out! You have no right! No one has the right to—"

Quickly I beat my retreat, more stumped than ever by the choleric fossil ensconced next door. Literally. I couldn't see much, but he seems to have built himself a small fortress out of boxes and piles of books, with a corner of an air mattress and a sleeping bag visible behind it. A kettle, mugs and plate on a stack of old journals, and a row of instant soups.

"Hi, Tessa! All set for the next semester?" I stick my head into Tessa's office, where she and her colleague Mel are quietly chatting. "Listen, I just tried to speak to Corvin, but…nothin' doin'. Does he *sleep* in his office now?"

They look at each other and shrug. "Like, overnight, you mean?"

"Yes, he seems to have a sleeping bag in there and a kettle and cup noodles."

Mel whistles and makes a circling movement with her finger next to her temple. "Not that I haven't pulled the odd all-nighter in here," she admits. "But I'm not Methuselah."

"Hmm. And Selena? Have you seen her today?"

This is a far more loaded question, and I get a sense that this had been the subject of their conversation.

"Why?" Mel asks.

"Why? As in, 'Sooner or later I may or may not answer your question'?"

Tessa hastily jumps in. "No, we haven't. But we both enrolled in your class on *Paradise Lost*, so she should be there tomorrow, if you want to speak to her."

"I do want to speak to her. If you see her, please ask her to come and see me. It's urgent."

The little impromptu birthday celebration for Ma Mayfield is embedded in the semester opening finger-food-and-wine-with-classical-music, and I gather from Yvonne that the idea is simply to claim everyone's attention at some point, sing "Happy Birthday" and hand over our present. Dean Ortega was informed of this plan and indicated that she would also say a few words, but on the whole the occasion is to be kept low-key and informal.

"No one will want to make a song and dance about anything today, what with…the news," Yvonne says, a little piqued, on our way across to Rossan House.

"Did Louise speak to you?"

"She did."

"About the file?"

"She didn't catch your name, but she had Giles Cleveland's card, and—well, you're not all that difficult to describe, Anna."

"Giles found the file among the jumble in my office. He had heard of the incident, but he didn't know the file was in the folder till I told him that Nick was called Eagleson before he married. I couldn't tell you, Yvonne, I'm sorry."

"That's all right. All for the best, probably. You felt you had to be loyal to Giles."

"Of course, and I am, but why…what's your point, Yvonne?" I stutter.

Now I get a long, significant stare over the blue rim of her eyeglasses.

"Well, if there's no point to be gotten, maybe there's no point to be made," she says with a shrug. "After all, it's none of my business what you and he were doing driving round Shaftsboro together at Christmas, when you told you me you were flying home."

"Look, I can—" But I can't explain.

Yvonne, seeing my mortification, relents and quickly touches my arm.

"Don't worry about me. But take care, honey."

To begin my second semester at Ardrossan with a clean(ish) slate, I follow Elizabeth Mayfield to her office after the lunchtime gathering and ask her for ten minutes of her time. She was more touched by the crystal bottle than she cared to show, and I apologize for what I am about to tell her.

"It can't be worse than having a colleague arrested for rape, can it? Go on."

So once again I relate my version of Selena's story, omitting only the razor blade with pubic hair in it and the scene involving Giles, Hornberger, myself, and awkwardly placed pantyhose.

"There is a great deal of hearsay and surmise in all this, Anna."

"I know. That is why I didn't come to see you sooner. And I want to make clear that I am not *reporting* anyone. Technically, she has committed acts of vandalism, but—"

"Technically?"

"No, I know, but—well, honestly, I'm not in the least interested in a few walls and windows. She did worse damage to herself, and she almost succeeded in hiding it. I'm not surprised that her…misery, distress, whatever you want to call it, manifested itself as anorexia. Anorexia is not for wimps! She is headstrong and calculating, but that doesn't mean she isn't in need of help. Most particularly if it turns out that she really is pregnant with Hornberger's child and he is going to prison!"

Elizabeth sits behind her desk, her hands folded on the desktop, not visibly impressed by my vehemence.

"On days like these, I hate my job," she says.

This was a word I should have had earlier. As I hurry across Library Square in a cold, gray drizzle, I feel as if a huge burden had been lifted off my shoulders. Strange. I should be in a panic, shouldn't I? Nick Hornberger now definitely knows that Giles didn't stick to his part of the bargain, which was to conceal the file. But I don't believe for a minute that he is going to expose Giles and me.

Expose. For what? Fucking in the old observatory. Small fry.

When the phone rings that evening, I pick up. It's Tim.

"Hey, Professor Blundell. Have you come out of your closet yet? You've been tenured for over a week!"

Tim is not amused. "Look in your inbox."

"What? Tim, I—"

"Put the phone down and look at your emails. And don't panic. Call me, or better still, call him. I'm trying to get hold of Gill Miller."

"Who is Gill Miller?"

"The college's computing officer." He slams the phone down and I run upstairs, my heart beating high in my throat. What? *What?*

Damn dial-up! Who has dial-up Internet access these days?

An email from Nick Hornberger to the English department mailing list, subject: "An Englishman in New York." The picture loads painfully slowly, but I know what it is before I've seen more than half an inch.

You couldn't tell, really, who it is, if there was more than one female on the Observatory faculty who wears Mountie boots.

After staring at it for what seems like hours, I switch off the modem, go downstairs again, pull out the Shaftsboro phone book from under a pile of books on the living room table, and pick up the phone.

How can Hornberger send emails if he is in custody?

Funny, how your mind, when you stumble and fall, fastens on one tiny detail.

And what if I'm wrong? Doesn't matter, now.

"Mr. O'Neal? This is Anna Lieberman. I am one of Selena's professors, and I was—yes, that's right, I'm the one who lives in Howard Walsh's cabin. Mr. O'Neal, I was wondering whether Selena is at home. It's rather important."

But Selena is still at the college.

Ah, well. Nothing else to do, have I?

It is still raining in a thin, cold spray, cold enough to see one's breath. Several windows are lit on the fourth floor; one of them may be Selena's, or it could be Tessa's. The great hall is still well-lit, but there is hardly anyone around. I nod a greeting at the security guard playing with his phone.

Steve Howell's office door is closed, but dim light and soft jazz music are trickling into the hallway through the cracks where the door doesn't shut properly. Light, too, under Selena's door.

I don't even knock. She jumps in her chair and gives a little yelp, but I quickly close the door behind me. A hard-working graduate student at her desk past eight o'clock on the first day of the semester. Some library books on her desk. I pick one up.

"*The Devil in Renaissance Drama.* Do you know, I think if Satan was really an aging university professor who gets off on deflowering Christian virgins, the world wouldn't be in the state that it's in."

"I don't know what you mean. What do you want?" she manages to say, and the steely defensiveness is never far from her surface.

"No, Selena. What do *you* want?" I sit down in Natalie's chair.

The question throws her, and she falters.

"Hmm? What did you hope to achieve, for instance, by sending round that photo of Giles Cleveland and me? What do you hope to achieve," I say, raising my voice above her protest, "by making yourself the tool of such a man? He isn't even fascinatingly evil! He's just…middle-aged and panicking!"

"You and Cleveland dumped him in the shit!" she flings at me, goaded into a reaction. "Cleveland said he'd keep the file!"

"No, Selena, Nick dumped himself in the shit when he forced himself on that student! The only wrong in this case is the one that he committed! The only injustice is that he wasn't called to account for it at the time!"

"I don't want to talk to you." Her chin trembles, and I remind myself that this screwed-up young woman will be a mother in a few months' time.

"I can well believe that. I tried to help you, and you tried to shame me in front of all my colleagues." I lean forward on my elbows, chin in hand. "Luckily I am not ashamed of loving Giles Cleveland, and although I'd much rather make love to him in private, I am fair enough to admit that if I make love to him in public places, I risk public attention."

Now she is staring at me with a mixture of disbelief and fascination.

"I'm not ashamed of loving Nick, either!" she announces, like a creed.

"Selena, your bad luck was to be seduced by a man with a lot of experience and no scruples. He broke through your defenses, which was necessary and liberating, but it's still only sex. You want to love a better man, don't you?"

"I do love him!" She jumps up, and I sense that this is the one thing that makes her feel on firm ground.

"I know you do. Big feelings, big words. God's words."

Her rigid posture relaxes a little. "You—you know about the—" She bites her lip.

"The graffiti? Yes. I'm sorry, Selena."

"And will you tell?"

"That's hardly your most pressing problem!"

"What?"

"Your belly is beginning to show," I inform her matter-of-factly.

Now she is scared. She takes a step back and bumps against the wall, her arms crossed protectively in front of her.

"It isn't! How do you know about that? *How do you know that?*" Her cheeks are bright red.

"I talked to Karen Walsh about you. You stole her pregnancy tests."

"Did she tell my mother?"

"Don't you think that if she had, you'd know?"

"Anyway, it's too late for an abortion!"

"Selena, for heaven's sake!" I explode. "How old are you? If you want to have this child, have this child! Move out of your parents' house. Break up with them, if need be. Bring the child up on welfare. But stop kidding yourself that you love a man who has fucked and ditched more students than you or I have teeth in our mouths!"

Now she is just staring at me, apparently speechless with emotion, her hands still shielding her belly.

"Tell me, Selena, does Natalie know about you and Nick? Does she know about the baby? Is *that*—God, I'm so slow! Is *that* why she reported Nick? To get revenge?"

Selena nods, her cheeks flaming. I think she is going to burst into tears, and I almost hope she will, to release her pent-up feelings.

"But that means that Nick knows about the baby, too. What does he—"

"He doesn't!" she insists hotly. "At least…I don't know. I didn't tell him."

"You didn't—oh, Selena. Why do you torture yourself like this? Are you worried he'll ditch you if he finds out you're having his baby? Selena! How will you get out of this mess? You need help."

"I don't need help!"

"That's right. You're managing brilliantly on your own."

"I hate you! *I hate you!*"

For a crazy moment I think she is going to attack me, but she grabs the bunch of keys on her desk and runs out of the room, slamming the door. I run after her, and I can just see her disappear up the spiral staircase into the dome. Steve opens his door.

"What's all the—oh. Hey."

We look at each other, and I can tell by his twisted grin that he has seen the photo.

"Embarrassed?" I ask as I walk past him toward the staircase. "Join the club."

"*I'm* not the one with cum on my skirt," he mutters. "Or with pickled herring on my office door."

His provocation would be like water off a duck's back, but something in his manner makes me stop and turn back.

"What do you know about the herring, Steve?"

"What don't I know about the herring?"

"*You?* You did that?" I know I look stupid, but I am beyond caring about looking stupid.

"No, I didn't." He hesitates. "*I* didn't. But then you didn't tell *me* that I behave like a territorial tomcat."

Of course. How could I have been so slow? I always knew it wasn't Madeline Harrison.

"Well, you can tell Dolph that he is the least of my problems. And congratulations for showing so unambiguously that he didn't deserve the job he didn't get."

The security guard in the great hall is now on the phone. I indicate that I want to talk to him, and he covers the mouthpiece with his fingers and looks up.

"There's a student on the fourth floor, Selena O'Neal, who has locked herself into the dome. She has shown self-harming behavior before and," I add maliciously, although I don't believe this for a second, "she may be suicidal. If I were you, I'd hurry up and get her out of there."

He stares at me as I walk off. "Hey! Hey, you can't just—"

"You rather than me, baby!"

Outside in the dark parking lot, the cool drizzle on my face feels wonderful, and I stand with my eyes closed for a long minute before I get into my car.

Now what?

Talk to Giles, I guess.

Poor Giles.

I'm about to turn the ignition key when the passenger door opens and a man flops into the seat.

"For fuck's sake!" I yell at him.

"Yeah, I know."

My heart is pounding in my chest, but I am so ridiculously relieved to have him near me, and evidently in a state of wry composure, that I start giggling. And then I'm crying again.

"Sweetheart," he says, drawing me against himself across the barrier of the emergency brake. "You really have to stop this, or I'll begin to take it personally, this crying."

"It *is* personal!" I sniffle onto the waterproof shoulder of his Barbour. "I d-don't want him to humiliate you again! In f-front of everybody! I'm so sorry, Giles! I'm sorry I-I'm so s-sorry I didn't stop you!"

"Didn't stop me doing what?"

"F-Fucking m-me!" I cried so much during the past few weeks, but it was nowhere near enough.

"I didn't fuck you, Anna. I made love to you."

"Oh!" I wail. "Don't be sorry you did, Giles!"

He pulls me closer, laughing quietly.

"Why would I be sorry? And why would I be humiliated? Because now they all know that the sexiest, most beautiful woman in the whole college likes me to make love to her? That's not how humiliation works among men, Anna! It's you I'm worried about."

"You don't m-mean that!"

"Which bit?" He pushes me away a little and scans my face. "Well, Kay Chang is a very beautiful woman, too, perhaps I was too quick with the superlative. And there's an assistant professor over in the art history department, she's a right little stunner, and—"

"Don't be like that," I whisper and pull his head down for a kiss.

"Do you remember?" He cups my face in his hands and kisses the corner of my mouth.

"Oh, yes…so silly of you not to come in when I invited you. We lost weeks, because of that, Giles, and we have so little time anyway!"

He hears me well up again and draws me into a bear hug. "I know, love. But I'm not sorry that we started this, and I would hate to think that you are. Are you?"

I don't trust myself to speak, so I shake my head.

"Do you regret giving Louise Randall the file?"

"No! I hate you for leaving me!"

"Anna—"

"Shut up!" I don't know where this comes from, but now that I have blurted it out, I can't stop. "Why didn't you *tell* me? Why do you never *tell* me things?"

"Anna, I'm in love with you."

"That makes it worse!"

He grins, ruefully. "Probably."

"So why leave me?"

"Don't I have to?" he says, looking into my eyes. "How can I start an affair with a colleague on tenure track unless I know I'll be gone before any damage is done?"

"Oh, ha-bloody-ha!" I jeer. "Damage? Like what? A compromising photo? Like my broken heart?"

"It won't break your heart." He is sitting back in his seat, staring out the windshield.

"Not *it! You!* Of course you're breaking my heart! You've been breaking my heart ever since I first saw you, you arrogant English *git!*"

"Don't say that, Anna."

"So you want I should fuck you but not love you?"

He smiles at my syntax.

"I don't expect you to love me."

"You mean you don't *want* me to love you! Because that would be so inconvenient, wouldn't it? It would complicate our nice, easy, fluffy little affair!"

Giles shakes his head. "No. You're saying things you know are not true."

"And to think that I have been so ashamed of chickening out and hurting you. And all the while you were just having a farewell fuck. Wow, Giles. That's…pretty shitty behavior."

"What the hell did you expect? You knew this…we…have no future! You knew this would hurt in the end!"

"Yes, I knew it would hurt, but I didn't know how it would end, or when! But *you* did! Why didn't you *tell* me? 'By the way, Anna,

I'm quitting, I have a new job in London. If we're discreet, we can get away with a little affair.' What's so difficult about saying that?"

His jaw locks, but he has nothing to say for himself.

"You accused Amanda—sorry, but this seems relevant! You accuse Amanda of refusing to talk about how your marriage was going down the drain. Seems to me that it takes two to be in denial!"

He looks down at his knees and shrugs. There *is* an insecure sixteen-year-old in Giles Cleveland, and I know he will not stand up to me. A praying mantis would now go for his jugular.

"When were you going to tell me?" I ask, more calmly.

"When I could bear it."

"When you could bear it. Well, thanks, Giles. Thanks very much for your kind concern for my feelings!"

"I wasn't even sure whether I would go," he says, asserting himself. "You make it sound very straightforward, but it wasn't. They wanted me to sign the contract in October, but I said I needed to talk to Paul French first. But after that…after Notre Dame—" He glances over at me and shrugs again.

"So you've known for two months!"

"No, no. I held off. I couldn't believe you'd come to me…like that, and then pretend nothing had happened." An ironic snort is comment enough, and I'm glad he is leaving it at that. "I signed after Nick caught us together in the observatory."

I need a minute to digest this, and to control the tears pricking behind my eyelids.

"You thought about staying here?" There are tears in my voice, too.

"I was about to risk the withdrawal of the offer, yes. Caught between a rock and a hard place." He grins but thinks better of spelling out the innuendo.

"If you'd asked me to come home with you, after Nick caught us, I would have. You pushed me away, Giles."

"I know."

I look over at him in the half-dark of the car. "Why?"

"Because, Anna, implausible though it may seem to you, I am actually doing what I can to protect you."

"Don't protect me from what I want!"

He opens his mouth to counter this, but I interrupt him.

"The only other man I've ever—" I catch myself in mid-sentence and glance at him quickly, embarrassed. "When I was in my early twenties I loved someone very much, someone who just wanted to have sex with me. He was fond of me, fond enough to want my love, but he didn't want to…he didn't want to be with me, either. He came to London to spend a weekend in bed with me, and at the end he told me he was engaged to be married to someone else."

And it took me years to get over it.

Giles reaches over, clasps my hand and draws it to his lips.

"Anna, I don't just want to have sex with you. You know it's more…it's a lot more than that. But I can't ask you to be with me. It wouldn't be right. It wouldn't be…honorable."

And suddenly this discussion ends the same way it began.

"Oh, for fuck's sake, Giles!"

I yank the key out the ignition and jump out of the car, slamming the door as hard as I can. The Subaru is hardly perturbed by my little anger. The drops of rainwater on the roof twinkle in the light of the street lamps like the stars in a clear, cold night.

Halfway up the entrance portal, he catches up with me.

"Go away and be an immature, screwed-up English schoolboy somewhere else!" I am not shouting. But I am about to knee him in the groin, and he is well aware of it.

"Anna, don't. Don't fight with me. Please."

"But that's what happens, Giles! You lie to people to keep them sweet, they find out about it, they feel jerked around, they shout at you! Which part is it that's coming as a surprise to you?"

"You are very self-righteous for someone who has applied for a job across the pond herself."

This comes so completely out of left field that all I can do is stare at him, slack-jawed. "How do you—"

"People keep asking me whether I know you and what I think of you." He shrugs. "I always tell them the same thing, although I'm not sure any more that I'm doing you a—" A blood-curdling noise drowns out the rest of his words. "That's the fire alarm!"

Oh, my God.

"Giles, Selena ran up to the dome! What if—"

It is raining more heavily now, and we run toward the huge dark building and up the monumental entrance steps. The great hall is empty, except for the ear-splitting wail of the siren.

"It's probably just someone having a smoke in their office!" he shouts.

I shrug, too worried to reply.

"It could be anywhere," he tries again. "You don't know that it is on your floor!"

A few people trickle into the hall, some with their fingers in their ears, none of them particularly concerned, among them a security guard.

"Hey!" I tap his shoulder to get his attention. "Contact your colleague! He's up in the dome, the fire may be there!" He tries his walkie-talkie and shrugs; it's too loud. Giles taps my shoulder and points at Steve, Nancy Benning and a handful of other, vaguely familiar people, who come running down the stairs of the east wing.

"It's somewhere along the hallway on E-four!" Steve yells, but he hardly stops on his way out.

Even plugged by my fingers, my ears are beginning to hurt. I see Giles chewing on a piece of tissue, which he rolls into balls and pushes into his ears.

"Give me your keys!" he mouths, and before I can process the intention behind his request, I have handed them over.

"No! Giles! No!" But he's off, and much faster than I can follow him. The staircase is deserted, and I can't smell anything, until I reach the third floor. Someone comes down the stairs, but it is only the security guard, and he is coughing violently and shaking his head.

"The girl! Where's the girl?"

"Don't know! Locked in, doesn't answer—there's smoke up there! Come!"

"No, I must—"

"Are you all crazy?"

He clamps my upper arm and drags me downstairs, and struggle as I might, I have no chance against him. We reach the great hall just as the fire trucks arrive and the alarm is switched off. Like on the morning after a long night in a club, every sound is now muted, except the hammering of my own heart. I can't hear what the security guard tells the fire fighters, but they run up the staircase with their gas masks and huge rucksack-like contraptions on their backs.

A megaphone sounds across the hall. "Keep calm and vacate the premises now! Please vacate the premises *now!*"

A few more people are trickling into the hall from all directions, and it is only the sight of the firefighters and the flashing engine outside that jolts them out of their irritation at being interrupted at their work.

Now I know what it feels like to be on the brink of madness. I'm so scared, I can only manage one second at a time.

Don't panic.

Wait.

Wait.

Wait.

"Please, ma'am, you have to leave the building." The crew leader comes up to me, and I realize what a nuisance I am to him for skulking behind a pillar.

"I will, in a minute. Look, it's not dangerous down here. I have to—"

His face becomes even more impatient as something behind me catches his attention.

"No, sir, you can't get in here! No—stop!"

"What's going on?"

The voice stabs into me like a knife. Nick Hornberger, as big and broad-shouldered as any of the firefighters, stands in the middle of the entrance portal, staring. Without thinking twice, I rush up to him and slap him across the face, as hard as I can. My hand stings like hell, his cheek must feel worse, and he is not amused.

"Are you mad? What do you—will you restrain this woman?" He turns to the firefighter, who is staring at me, stunned.

"I had hoped you were stuck in a holding cell, being buggered by some Crips with *schlongs* like baseball bats!"

This makes him blench. "You fucking little do-gooder! Did you egg Giles on to hand the file to the police? I *told* him this would happen if he told you!"

"The police? No, we gave it to Louise Randall. Mary-Lou," I add. "*She* reported you. And good for her!"

"There's a fire in this building!" the crew leader asserts himself. "You can't stay here!"

As if to confirm this, a loud groan rises from the crowd outside. I run out onto the landing; everyone is staring up at the dome.

"The dome's on fire!" someone shouts.

Oh, God.

"Selena's up there. And Giles has gone to fetch her. Did you know you knocked her up?" I am beyond shouting, but Nick's eyes widen with sudden comprehension. It seems he didn't.

And then I hear them, the firefighters' heavy boots on the marble steps. The awful, intense nausea of fear rises in me again, and I tear away from the man holding me by the arm to run back inside to see Giles, wracked with coughs behind a gas mask, uncertain on his feet but upright, supported by one fireman, Selena carried by another. They are led straight past us into the cool, wet night air and down the steps to the medical response truck.

I don't want to be in the way, but I need to see him, so I lurk at a short distance, just making sure. His ribcage seems too tight, he stretches out one arm while the other rests against the gleaming white metal.

"Anna…" he wheezes. I wasn't even sure he had seen me, but he wants me to hold his hand. "I lost your keys upstairs."

"Forget about the keys." I clasp his hand between mine and press it against my cheek. He reeks of smoke, and his face is an odd shade of flushed pallor. "Are you all right?"

"Think so." He breathes deeply, and more calmly.

We watch as Selena, sobbing, is laid on a stretcher and pushed up into the back of the truck.

"Sir, you had better put this on." A young paramedic hands him an oxygen mask and adjusts the valve on the metal container. "Do you want to sit down? Do you feel dizzy, nauseous or confused?"

"I'm all right."

"Please, sir, do you feel dizzy, nauseous or confused?" the paramedic repeats impatiently.

"No! I don't need —"

"Giles, please! You've played the man enough!"

He groans, coughs, and slips the tube around his head and the openings into his nose.

"How is the girl? She's pregnant," he tells the paramedic. "Did she say that she's pregnant?"

"Yes, sir, and she's in hysterics. But as far as we could see, she's not—um—hurt in that way."

"Not bleeding?" Giles urges him.

"No, sir, she isn't. Sorry, I must—" He dashes off.

"What's Nick doing here? Why isn't he with her?" Breathing heavily, Giles nods at the girl inside the truck.

"Don't know. Returning to the scene of the crime, maybe. He didn't know she is pregnant, though. Stupid male chauvinist heroism!"

Giles frowns. "Heroism? Nick?"

"No, you!" I laugh and cry and the same time. "You could have—what if you had—"

"No, no, don't you see? I helped save his child. I'm free of him now. Of Nick and all that. Now I'm free of it."

I try to digest this, and I dimly understand what he means, But if I'm honest, I don't really care. He is safe. That's all I care about.

"Anna…"

"Breathe, don't speak!" I clasp his hand again, but he reaches underneath my coat and round my waist.

"Come close!"

I snuggle against him, push the plastic tube out of the way with my nose and gently kiss the soft, stubbly skin under his ear.

"That's nice. Anna, the fire didn't come from the dome."

"Not? But Selena—"

He shakes his head. Breathes. Then speaks.

"Her key was stuck in the bloody…door. It…she couldn't get out. I had to smash the door in…with the fire extinguisher." He grins wanly at the irony.

"But then—"

"Corvin…Corvin's office."

"Oh, my God! Was he—was he in there?"

"Don't know. It was all full of smoke. The firemen pulled me away before I could get to him."

Another groan comes from the crowd, and shards of glass are sprinkling onto the asphalt. We step out from behind the truck and look up; smoke and flames are now pouring out the windows as well as the roof of the dome.

"Stand back!" the megaphone sounds again. "Stand back from the building!"

"What a mess," I murmur, hiding against Giles's body. "What a God-awful bloody mess."

"Some of the mess is that you don't know what you want."

When I am angry, I flare up like a firecracker. Giles glimmers like a slow fuse. He doesn't usually shout back when I shout at him, but when I have cooled down again, he goes on smoldering.

"I'm glad you weren't burned to a crisp up there. That's gotta be a good sign, right?" I doubt that flippancy will throw him off the scent, but the last thing I want tonight is to go on arguing with him.

"Mm-hmm."

"I know that I want to come home with you tonight," I offer.

At last, a sort of smile. He pulls me closer, and his hand inches lower. "That's something to live for, isn't it?"

Now I'm riled, too. "Well, do *you* know what you want?" Oddly enough, I have the feeling that I have been manipulated into asking him the question he wanted me to ask him.

"How did your interview at Queen Mary go?" he asks, as if he was merely making polite conversation.

I stare up at him, uncertain about his train of thoughts. He shrugs, as if he was bored, but I recognize the tell-tale tightening of the muscle next to his mouth.

"It's just that if you didn't make a complete hash of your interview, and if at Queen Mary they know a good thing when they see one, you could…" He hesitates.

"I could…?" I ask, leaning in.

Giles looks down at me, into my eyes, and my heart runs hot with anticipation.

"You could '*come and live with me and be my love*,'" he quotes. "'*And we would all the pleasures prove…*'"

Epilogue

It is a year to the day that we all assembled in the large auditorium at the Observatory of Ardrossan University to pay our last respects to Professor Andrew Corvin. While the President spoke of duty and dedication, all I could think of was that frantic old man in his fortress of paper. Giles reached over and, with the back of his four fingers, brushed away the tears running down my face. I slipped my fingers into his, and we sat hand in hand for the whole ceremony.

I'm not saying the following few months were easy. But the advantage of being exposed is that you no longer have to hide. Giles accepted with wry good grace the fact that all his colleagues and an unknown number of students had now seen his naked butt, even if it was only on a grainy little photo. Tim declared in gleeful tones that the term "sneaky fuckers" had never been more apt. Yvonne came to my office and, without a word, gave me a hug; Erin stopped speaking to me. The gossip and the whispers hardly registered with me. I was too happy. If it wasn't such bad form to kick a man who was already down, I would have sent Nick Hornberger a thank-you note. I guess they allow them to receive mail at Dillwyn Correctional Center.

Giles and I are not sitting hand in hand now. A carriage on the London Underground's Central Line is no place for public displays of affection, at least not during the rush hour. But it is crowded enough for me to surreptitiously press my thigh against his under the cover of his briefcase and my *Guardian*. I sent him a text before I left my office on the Mile End Road, which allowed him time enough to walk from his office down to Holborn. Sometimes, like today, we catch sight of each other across the platform and he comes to find me in the car. Sometimes, like today, he pretends not to know me, a tall, silver-haired stranger who comes to stand or sit next to me. Catches my eye. Accidentally brushes against me. Holland Park is our stop, and from there it is just a couple of walking minutes into a quiet side street.

"I know it's not Buckinghamshire," Giles said apologetically when he first took me to see the white-washed, three-story Victorian town-house. "But Reggie lives there with his family, and I can't really chuck him out. He's older than me, you see. So he has Bucks House, and we can have Holl House."

"Dear old Holl House," I said in my best plummy voice, seeking refuge in satire because I was so amazed.

He grinned. "But you wanted a posh English boy, didn't you?"

"I can't afford to live in a place like *that!*"

"You can pay rent in kind. Anyway, Queen Mary College is such a hopelessly dreary place, you need something a little more attractive to come home to."

"As it happens, I have something extremely attractive to come home to!"

"You do? Come over here under this tree and explain that to me."

One of the changes he made to the house before we moved in was on the top floor.

"You're not to look," he told me very sternly. "I want this to be a surprise!"

The builders came in and drilled and hammered for two weeks. Then, one August evening, Giles appeared in the kitchen with a scarf in his hand.

"Sweetie, we have a postcard from Tim and Martin. They're in…" I turned over the card. "In Thailand. He says they found a cheap flight back via Heathrow, so they're coming to see us on the twenty-ninth: '*Threatening invasion of Holland Park love nest.*' Well, thanks for the warning, Tim!"

"Talking of love nests." Giles twisted the scarf into a blindfold and stepped behind me. "Do you trust me, Dr. Lieberman?"

"Um…"

When I had felt my way up the stairs, which involved a lot of hands-on help from Giles, he stopped me with his hands around my waist.

"You will pretend to like it, won't you?" he joked in that way that betrayed his apprehension. "It's a bit silly, really, but—"

"Dude! Let me see it already!"

He led me five or six steps away from the landing.

"Careful now. Watch your shin! Lie down."

I crawled onto a bed, feeling the smooth softness of silken bed sheets under my hands and knees.

"On your back."

"You're not going to tie me down, are you?"

"No. Not today, anyway." He loosened the scarf around my head.

"Oh! It's—oh, Giles! It's lovely!"

"Is it really?" He smiled, shy, a little flushed, kneeling on the bed next to me.

The two small bedrooms had been turned into one large one, with a huge black metal bed in the middle. Above our heads was a domed skylight in the neo-gothic style, with Art Deco ornamentation and mulled glass panes.

"It's beautiful," I whispered, gazing up and around.

"Could you imagine sleeping up here?"

"Sleeping—no." I smiled and slid against him on the silken sheets. "Sleeping would be time wasted, wouldn't it?"

It is a pleasure to see that to Giles it has a deep and peculiar significance to move back into the house his grandfather bought in nineteen eleven, and to make it his own. This is his home ground, but it took him almost twenty years abroad to want to root himself in it. He says that by leaving Ardrossan, I left far more behind than he did, but it doesn't feel that way.

I feel that I have come home.

About the Author

Nina Lewis wrote her first story when she was nine years old, a drama of love and jealousy set in a circus. Her best friend and she performed it to themselves over and over again, for ever changing the dialogue, conflicts and endings. It strikes her as ironically appropriate that her first published novel is set on a college campus — the habitat of many a strange, loveable or fierce creature. When she isn't busy training animals to jump through the hoops of college education, Nina is knee-deep in her second novel, which is set in England during the French Revolution — historical romance being her favourite genre of fiction. Check her Facebook page for news and updates:

https://www.facebook.com/NinaLewisNovelist

＊＊＊＊＊Young Adult＊＊＊＊＊

Shades of Atlantis and *The Ember Series: Ember* and *Iridescent* by Carol Oates
Breaking Point by Jess Bowen
Life, Liberty, and Pursuit by Susan Kaye Quinn
Embrace by Cherie Colyer
Destiny's Fire by Trisha Wolfe
Streamline by Jennifer Lane
Reaping Me Softly by Kate Evangelista

＊＊＊＊＊Historical Romance＊＊＊＊＊

Cat O' Nine Tails by Patricia Leever
Burning Embers by Hannah Fielding

＊＊＊＊＊Erotic Romance＊＊＊＊＊

Becoming sage by Kasi Alexander
Saving sunni by Kasi & Reggie Alexander
The Winemaker's Dinner: Appetizers & Entrée by Dr. Ivan Rusilko & Everly Drummond
The Winemaker's Dinner: Dessert by Dr. Ivan Rusilko

＊＊＊＊＊Anthologies and Singles＊＊＊＊＊

Valentine Anthology including short stories by Alice Clayton, Jennifer DeLucy, Nicki Elson, Jessica McQuinn, Victoria Michaels, and Alison Oburia

It's Only Kinky the First Time by Kasi Alexander
Learning the Ropes by Kasi & Reggie Alexander
The Winemaker's Dinner: RSVP by Dr. Ivan Rusilko
The Winemaker's Dinner: No Reservations by Everly Drummond
Big Guns by Jessica McQuinn
Concessions by Robin DeJarnett
Starstruck by Lisa Sanchez
New Flame by BJ Thornton
Shackled by Debra Anastasia
Swim Recruit by Jennifer Lane
Sway by Nicki Elson
Full Speed Ahead by Susan Kaye Quinn
The Second Sunrise by Hannah Downing
The Summer Prince by Carol Oates
Whatever it Takes by Sarah M. Glover
Clarity by Patricia Leever
A Christmas Wish by Autumn Markus